PRAISE I

Wife by Wednesday

"A fun and sizzling romance, great characters that trade verbal spars like fist punches, and the dream of your own royal wedding!"
—Sizzling Hot Book Reviews (5 stars)

"A good holiday, fireside or bedtime story."
—Manic Reviews (4½ stars)

"A great story that I hope is the start of a new series."
—The Romance Studio (4½ hearts)

Married by Monday

"If I hadn't already added Ms. Catherine Bybee to my list of favorite authors, after reading this book I would have been compelled to. This is a book *nobody* should miss, because the magic it contains is awesome."
—Booked Up Reviews (5 stars)

"Ms. Bybee writes authentic situations and expresses the good and the bad in such an equal way . . . Keeps the reader on the edge of her seat."
—Reading Between the Wines (5 stars)

"*Married by Monday* was a refreshing read and one I couldn't possibly put down."
—The Romance Studio (4½ hearts)

Fiancé by Friday

"Bybee knows exactly how to keep readers happy . . . A thrilling pursuit and enough passion to stuff in your back pocket to last for the next few lifetimes . . . The hero and heroine come to life with each flip of the page and will linger long after readers cross the finish line."
—*RT Book Reviews* (4½ stars, top pick [hot])

"A tale full of danger and sexual tension . . . the intriguing characters add emotional depth, ensuring readers will race to the perfectly fitting finish."
—*Publishers Weekly*

"Suspense, survival, and chemistry mix in this scintillating read."
—*Booklist*

"Hot romance, a mystery assassin, British royalty, and an alpha Marine . . . this story has it all!"
—*Harlequin Junkie*

Single by Saturday

"Captures readers' hearts and keeps them glued to the pages until the fascinating finish . . . romance lovers will feel the sparks fly . . . almost instantaneously."
—*RT Book Reviews* (4½ stars, top pick)

"[A] wonderfully exciting plot, lots of desire, and some sassy attitude thrown in for good measure!"
—*Harlequin Junkie*

Taken by Tuesday

"[Bybee] knows exactly how to get bookworms sucked into the perfect storyline; then she casts her spell upon them so they don't escape until they reach the 'Holy Cow!' ending."

—*RT Book Reviews* (4½ stars, top pick)

Seduced by Sunday

"You simply can't miss [this novel]. It contains everything a romance reader loves—clever dialogue, three-dimensional characters, and just the right amount of steam to go with that heartwarming love story."

—Brenda Novak, *New York Times* bestselling author

"Bybee hits the mark . . . providing readers with a smart, sophisticated romance between a spirited heroine and a prim hero . . . Passionate and intelligent characters [are] at the heart of this entertaining read."

—*Publishers Weekly*

Treasured by Thursday

"The Weekday Brides never disappoint and this final installment is by far Bybee's best work to date."

—*RT Book Reviews* (4½ stars, top pick)

"An exquisitely written and complex story brimming with pride, passion, and pulse-pounding danger . . . Readers will gladly make time to savor this winning finale to a wonderful series."

—*Publishers Weekly* (starred review)

"Bybee concludes her popular Weekday Brides series in a gratifying way with a passionate, troubled couple who may find a happy future if they can just survive and then learn to trust each other. A compelling and entertaining mix of sexy, complicated romance and menacing suspense."

—*Kirkus Reviews*

Not Quite Dating

"It's refreshing to read about a man who isn't afraid to fall in love . . . [Jack and Jessie] fit together as a couple and as a family."

—*RT Book Reviews* (3 stars [hot])

"*Not Quite Dating* offers a sweet and satisfying Cinderella fantasy that will keep you smiling long after you've finished reading."

—Kathy Altman, *USA Today*, *Happy Ever After* blog

"The perfect rags to riches romance . . . The dialogue is inventive and witty, the characters are well drawn out. The storyline is superb and really shines . . . I highly recommend this standout romance! Catherine Bybee is an automatic buy for me."

—*Harlequin Junkie* (4½ hearts)

Not Quite Enough

"Bybee's gift for creating unforgettable romances cannot be ignored. The third book in the Not Quite series will sweep readers away to a paradise, and they will be intrigued by the thrilling story that accompanies their literary vacation."

—*RT Book Reviews* (4½ stars, top pick)

Not Quite Forever

"Full of classic Bybee humor, steamy romance, and enough plot twists and turns to keep readers entertained all the way to the very last page."
—Tracy Brogan, bestselling author of the Bell Harbor series

"Magnetic . . . The love scenes are sizzling and the multi-dimensional characters make this a page-turner. Readers will look for earlier installments and eagerly anticipate new ones."
—*Publishers Weekly*

Not Quite Perfect

"This novel flows extremely well and readers will find themselves consuming the witty dialogue and strong imagery in one sitting."
—*RT Book Reviews*

"Don't let the title fool you. *Not Quite Perfect* [is] actually the perfect story to sweep you away and take you on a pleasant adventure. So sit back, relax, maybe pour a glass of wine, and let Catherine Bybee entertain you with Glen and Mary's playful East Coast–West Coast romance. You won't regret it for a moment."
—*Harlequin Junkie* (4½ stars)

Not Quite Crazy

"This fast-paced story features credible characters whose appealing relationship is built upon friendship, mutual respect, and sizzling chemistry."
—*Publishers Weekly*

"The plot is filled with twists and turns, but instead of feeling like a never-ending roller coaster, the story maintains a quiet flow. The slow buildup of a romance allows readers to get to know the main characters as individuals and makes the romantic element more organic."

—*RT Book Reviews*

Doing It Over

"The romance between fiercely independent Melanie and charming Wyatt heats up even as outsiders threaten to derail their newfound happiness. This novel will hook readers with its warm, inviting characters and the promise for similar future installments."

—*Publishers Weekly*

"This brand-new trilogy, Most Likely To, based on yearbook superlatives, kicks off with a novel that will encourage you to root for the incredibly likable Melanie. Her friends are hilarious and readers will swoon over Wyatt, who is charming and strong. Even Melanie's daughter, Hope, is a hoot! This romance is jam-packed with animated characters, and Bybee displays her creative writing talent wonderfully."

—*RT Book Reviews* (4 stars)

"With a dialogue full of energy and depth, and a twisting storyline that captured my attention, I would say that *Doing It Over* was a great way to start off a new series. (And look at that gorgeous book cover!) I can't wait to visit River Bend again and see who else gets to find their HEA."

—*Harlequin Junkie* (4½ stars)

Staying For Good

"Bybee's skillfully crafted second Most Likely To contemporary (after *Doing It Over*) brings together former sweethearts who have not forgotten each other in the eleven years since high school. A cast of multidimensional characters brings the story to life and promises enticing future installments."

—Publishers Weekly

"Romance fans will be sure to cheer on former high school sweethearts Zoe and Luke right away in *Staying For Good*. Just wait until you see what passion, laughter, reconciliations, and mischief (can you say Vegas?) awaits readers this time around. Highly recommended."

—Harlequin Junkie (4½ stars)

Making It Right

"Intense suspense heightens the scorching romance at the heart of Bybee's outstanding third Most Likely To contemporary (after *Staying For Good*). Sizzling sensual scenes are coupled with scary suspense in this winning novel."

—Publishers Weekly (starred review)

Fool Me Once

"A marvelous portrait of friendship among women who have been bonded by fire."

—Library Journal (best of the year 2017)

"Bybee still delivers a story that her die-hard readers will enjoy."

—Publishers Weekly

Half Empty

"Wade and Trina here in *Half Empty* just might be one of my favorite couples Catherine Bybee has gifted us fans with so far. Captivating, engaging, lively and dreamy, I simply could not get enough of this book."

—*Harlequin Junkie* (5 stars)

"Part rock star romance, part romantic thriller, I really enjoyed this book."

—*Romance Reader*

Faking Forever

"A charming contemporary with surprising depth . . . Bybee perfectly portrays a woman trying to hold out for Mr. Right despite the pressures of time. A pitch-perfect plot and a cast of sympathetic and lovable supporting characters make this book one to add to the keeper shelf."

—*Publishers Weekly*

"Catherine Bybee can do no wrong as far as I'm concerned . . . Passionate, sultry, and filled with genuine emotions that ran the gamut, *Faking Forever* was a journey of self-discovery and of a love that was truly meant to be. Highly recommended."

—*Harlequin Junkie*

Say It Again

"Steamy, fast-paced, and consistently surprising, with a large cast of feisty supporting characters, this suspenseful roller-coaster ride will keep both series fans and new readers on the edge of their seats."

—*Publishers Weekly*

My Way to You

"A fascinating novel that aptly balances disastrous circumstances."

—*Kirkus Reviews*

"*My Way to You* is an unforgettable book fueled by Catherine Bybee's own life, along with the dynamic cast she created that will capture your heart."

—*Harlequin Junkie*

Home to Me

"Bybee skillfully avoids both melodrama and melancholy by grounding her characters in genuine emotion . . . This is Bybee in top form."

—*Publishers Weekly* (starred review)

Everything Changes

"This sweet, sexy book is just the escapism many people are looking for right now."

—*Kirkus Reviews*

The Whole Time

"Adorable. Sweet. Sparky. Sexy. Full of good food and wine and family and friends and all the things! I so need to see this series on TV one day! *The Whole Time* was such an adorable + fun + sweet + sparky + just beautiful romance—I loved it! Run to your nearest book dealer for your own Ryan—this one is mine!"

—*BJ's Book Blog*

No More Yesterdays

OTHER TITLES BY CATHERINE BYBEE

Contemporary Romance

Weekday Brides Series

Wife by Wednesday

Married by Monday

Fiancé by Friday

Single by Saturday

Taken by Tuesday

Seduced by Sunday

Treasured by Thursday

Not Quite Series

Not Quite Dating

Not Quite Mine

Not Quite Enough

Not Quite Forever

Not Quite Perfect

Not Quite Crazy

Most Likely To Series

Doing It Over

Staying For Good

Making It Right

First Wives Series

Fool Me Once

Half Empty

Chasing Shadows

Faking Forever

Say It Again

Creek Canyon Series

My Way to You

Home to Me

Everything Changes

Richter Series

Changing the Rules

A Thin Disguise

An Unexpected Distraction

The D'Angelos Series

When It Falls Apart

Be Your Everything

Beginning of Forever

The Whole Time

The Heirs Series

All Our Tomorrows

The Forgotten One

Paranormal Romance

MacCoinnich Time Travels

Binding Vows

Silent Vows

Redeeming Vows

Highland Shifter

Highland Protector

The Ritter Werewolves Series

Before the Moon Rises

Embracing the Wolf

Novellas

Soul Mate

Possessive

Erotica

Kilt Worthy

Kilt-A-Licious

No More Yesterdays

CATHERINE BYBEE

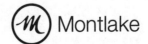 Montlake

This is a work of fiction. Names, characters, organizations, places, events, and incidents are either products of the author's imagination or are used fictitiously. Otherwise, any resemblance to actual persons, living or dead, is purely coincidental.

Text copyright © 2025 by Catherine Bybee
All rights reserved.

No part of this book may be reproduced, or stored in a retrieval system, or transmitted in any form or by any means, electronic, mechanical, photocopying, recording, or otherwise, without express written permission of the publisher.

Published by Montlake, Seattle

www.apub.com

Amazon, the Amazon logo, and Montlake are trademarks of Amazon.com, Inc., or its affiliates.

EU product safety contact:
Amazon Media EU S. à r.l.
38, avenue John F. Kennedy, L-1855 Luxembourg
amazonpublishing-gpsr@amazon.com

ISBN-13: 9781662517273 (paperback)
ISBN-13: 9781662517266 (digital)

Cover design by Caroline Teagle Johnson
Cover image: © Povareshka, © tainted / Getty; © Toria / Shutterstock

Printed in the United States of America

To my readers, who have made it possible to take my passion and make it my career

Chapter One

Nothing drove home one's single status better than Valentine's Day.

By noon, more than half of the female employees on the executive floor had flowers sitting on their desks. Cupid had wielded his arrow like an automatic weapon in the break room, which was where all the women trying to diet placed their gifted boxes of candy for anyone and everyone to dig into. Not to mention about a quarter of the staff members were expected to escape the office earlier than normal.

Alex saw hearts and roses, either physically or metaphorically, everywhere she looked.

And it was scratching on her last nerve.

She tapped down her jealousy like a child used a soft hammer while playing Whac-A-Mole. Then she'd turn the corner, see another floral display, and the damn mole would show its toothy grin once again.

Alex vacated her office and smiled at her painfully shy, overachieving assistant, Dee . . . past a dozen roses. "I need to see Chase. I'll be back before my ten o'clock."

"Yes, Ms. Stone."

Alex passed by the reception desk on the top floor on her way to the bank of elevators.

Kira, the receptionist, smiled at Alex through the stems of purple orchids as she walked by.

Alex attempted a smile, knew she sucked at it, and called the elevator.

Only after she entered the empty elevator did Alex release a woeful breath and allow her composure to fall.

She made a mental note to work from home next year on the Hallmark holiday.

Her brief reprieve from fake smiles didn't last long. The elevator stopped halfway down the building as two men in suits joined her.

She didn't recognize either of them.

But they most definitely knew who she was.

Their chatter halted the second they spotted her. The younger of them nodded, smiled, and turned away as fast as he could. The older man, probably in his forties, said a simple "Ms. Stone." And that was it.

"Hello," she offered back.

The doors closed.

No one talked.

The next floor pulled in two more employees, and the entire dance repeated.

That was the problem with being the CEO and co-owner of a billion-dollar hotel empire. A status that Alex hadn't had the previous Valentine's Day. No, last year Alex sat behind a desk in the Acquisitions and Mergers Department at Regent Hotels, where she was doing everything she could to help Regent dominate her father's company.

Then the man up and died, leaving her and her brothers to pick up the pieces of Stone Enterprises.

Bastard!

The elevator slid to a stop on the third floor.

Alex cleared her throat, and the people she employed separated like the Red Sea when Moses passed.

As the door began to close behind her, the collective sigh from the remaining occupants reached her ears.

Alex couldn't help but wonder if the employees' reaction to her presence would ever ease.

She moved past the much less formal entry to CMS, her brother's shipping company, and immediately felt lighter. On this floor,

Alexandrea Stone was not the boss. While everyone treated her with respect, none of them stopped talking when she passed by or quickly snapped back to their computers as if to prove they were working.

Most simply ignored her or greeted her with a genuine smile and hello. Here, she was only Chase's sister.

Alex liked that.

She rounded the corner to Chase's office and let him know she was there by a rap of her knuckles against his glass door. "Hey."

He was on the phone.

Chase waved her in and placed a single finger in the air.

"That all sounds good to me. I'll have Busa take this over from here. Yeah . . . I appreciate that," Chase said into the receiver to whomever it was he spoke to.

Alex closed his office door behind her and took a seat across from her brother.

"She's amazing."

Alex could tell by the soft smile that passed Chase's lips that he was talking about his two-and-a-half-month-old daughter, Hailey.

"Oh, trust me, she already rules the house . . . Thank you." Chase said his goodbye and disconnected the call.

"Rules the house, huh?"

Chase rubbed his eyes. "Day and night."

Alex made herself more comfortable, crossed one leg over the other. "Any sign of sleeping through the night yet?"

"If by *sleeping through the night* you mean five hours intermittently between ten and six, then sure."

Chase stretched out his back and opened his mouth wide with a full-blown yawn.

"I don't think I could do it," Alex said truthfully.

"Last night, Hailey decided to sleep three hours in a row."

"That's progress."

Chase shook his head. "Piper woke up in a panic and rushed to the nursery on the second hour. Scared me to death."

"What panic?"

"She dreamed that Hailey had stopped breathing." Chase ran a hand through his hair.

An ache settled in Alex's chest with the thought. "That's awful."

Chase agreed with a nod. "Mom said it's normal. She did the same thing."

"Still don't think I'm cut out for that kind of stress."

Chase pushed forward in his chair and placed his elbows on his desk. "So, what brings you down here?"

She blew out a breath and said what had to be said. "The holidays are over. The first quarter isn't looking any better than the last. We need to squeeze the trigger and make the cuts."

There wasn't a need to reference what she was talking about. Through no fault of their own, Stone Enterprises had expanded too fast under their father's reign, risking the health of the company. Alex had put off making the official decision to bring to the board until now.

"I'll back you in any decision you make," Chase told her, his eyes never leaving contact with hers.

"Thank you."

"Where exactly do we need to cut? And how?"

"I think the best approach is to unload the last acquisition Dad made. We sell . . . at a loss, and use the deficit as a tax deduction to offset the damage."

"How much are we talking?" Chase asked.

"That's hard to tell without knowing what the company will fetch. I know for a fact there were three other players in Dad's last acquisition. Regent's bid was solid. I was pissed when Dad got it." She laughed under her breath. "Now I have it and want nothing to do with it."

"Who on the board is going to scream the loudest?" Chase asked.

Alex shook her head. "I have Dee bringing up the minutes of the meetings leading up to the acquisition so I can figure that out. Schedule some lunches . . ."

"Golf?" Chase teased.

Golf was the one thing neither of them could bring themselves to do. It seemed, however, to be the spot where many corporate decisions took place outside of the boardroom. At least according to their soon-to-be stepfather, Gaylord Morrison.

The man had his own hotel empire and had rekindled an old friendship with their mother in the past year. His proposal took place at Christmas, and the wedding was set for April. Exactly one month after Chase and Piper's public nuptials.

Alex's brother and sister-in-law had tied the knot in between Piper's contractions while Hailey was being squeezed out into the world. A very spur-of-the-moment ceremony prompted by Piper freaking out about what would be written on Hailey's birth certificate. For Piper, the mother's and father's names needed to be the same.

"Lunch at the nineteenth hole is as close as I'll come," Alex told Chase.

"I could just ask Piper who the biggest obstacle is going to be?"

Piper worked as the executive assistant to their father before his death. The woman knew more about Stone Enterprises than the two of them put together.

"And if she doesn't remember off the top of her head, she'd be tempted to log in to the system and look it up herself. Then she'd see Dee's attempt at utilizing Piper's calendar and freak. Next thing you know, she's calling and trying to control what Dee is doing—"

He lifted his hands in surrender. "Understood."

"Dee is doing a much better job than I anticipated. Be sure and relay that to your wife." Alex uncrossed her legs and scooted to the edge of her chair.

Chase tilted his head to the side. "You know I'm going to be upstairs the rest of the week, right? You didn't have to come all the way down here to have this discussion."

Chase only spent one day, sometimes only half a day, in the office of his shipping company. The rest of his time was in the upstairs office beside hers.

"I needed the walk."

The sad smile on Chase's lips forced Alex to her feet.

They both knew she took on the majority of the weight of Stone Enterprises. With Chase's newfound fatherhood role, Alex didn't want him to feel pressured into picking up more.

Neither of them aspired to be the kind of man their father had been. An egotistical, narcissistic, womanizing asshole who put his family at the very bottom of his list of priorities.

"We can go over more details tomorrow," Alex said.

Chase nodded before she walked out the door.

With each step, her spine felt as if it were clicking into place, one vertebra at a time.

She slapped on a partial smile like one would lipstick and waited for the elevator.

The doors opened, and the occupants inside parted much like the ones she'd joined on her way down.

She stepped inside with a sigh.

༄

"I've seen you in the same blazer and skirt in three different magazines. We need to go shopping."

Alex sat in a foaming tub of hot water with her hair up in a bun and a glass of white wine in her hand. Candlelight flickered against the mirror of her bathroom, and the scent of the floral bath bomb she'd put in the tub filled the room with a mixture of jasmine and lavender.

The sliding-glass-enclosed bathtub and shower combo wasn't anything special. It was the kind of bathroom layout you'd expect in a condominium complex that said "average and affordable."

The complex that Alex could afford on her Regent salary.

She'd considered moving a dozen times since inheriting her father's fortune. But change didn't come easy for her, not to mention time was limited for exploring her options.

Her best friend Nick spoke from her cell phone that sat on the floor.

"Three magazines from the same walk down the street." The media loved taking meaningless pictures of whomever they deemed famous and plastering them all over their pages. She liked to play a little game when Nick made these calls. "What are the headlines saying now?"

Nick hummed. "Let's see. *Dr. Zee Weighs In on Alexandrea's Depression. Ms. Stone's Weight-Loss Goals Are Out of Control. Give This Woman a Sandwich.*"

"Let me guess. I was in the tan suit we bought last fall." She sipped her wine and waited for Nick's reply.

"Bingo."

She'd forgotten her sunglasses that day when she'd left the office for a long lunch. A lunch at which, ironically, she had eaten a sandwich.

"You are looking a little frail," Nick told her.

"It's Photoshop. I haven't changed."

"Still, we need to shop. And when's the last time you had a pedicure?"

Alex lifted a foot from the water, shrugged, and put it back in. "I'm good."

The sound that escaped Nick was a cross between a huff and a tsk. "No, no, no. Saturday. I'm picking you up at ten."

"I have to research—"

"Don't finish that sentence. I'm picking you up at ten, and we're not coming back until midnight. If you're going to look tired and starving in a tabloid, it's going to be because of a hangover. Bring your credit card *and* sunglasses."

"Nick, I—"

"Love you, bye."

And he was gone.

There was no use in fighting the man. He was more suited for her bank account than she was. Her gay bestie was addicted to shopping, spas, and glamming up for the camera. It was just the kind of man he was. Nick was the reason the closet in her condo overflowed with clothes. He was a stylist and a photographer who wielded his sexuality like a sword. It didn't matter what environment he was in, he always dominated. He was equal parts charm and funny. He was just as comfortable in a tuxedo for a gala event as he was dressing up as Dobby the house elf with a hint of drag for a Pride parade.

He was the best girlfriend she'd ever had.

His words, not hers.

He embodied the phrase "The good ones are either married or gay."

Nick was about as lucky in love as Alex was, however. Oh, the man didn't want for sex. No one Alex knew in the gay community did. With *GQ* features and a body sculpted by healthy food and exercise, Nick had all the sex he wanted.

Alex was jealous and told Nick as much every time he talked about another escapade.

There was no use complaining about her deficient sex life when she couldn't be bothered to even try and find someone to fill her bed. She worked a minimum of sixty hours a week and had to be told to take a day off by either Nick or her family. And looking for anyone more than a bed warmer was a pipe dream she'd given up the day her father died. A woman's appeal to the opposite sex was greatly reduced by the increased size of her bank account and intelligence. All the studies couldn't be wrong. And even if they were, Alex knew firsthand that men didn't approach her. At the risk of inflating her ego, it wasn't because she wasn't attractive. Most men simply didn't want to be upstaged by a wealthy, influential woman like herself.

So, the bubble bath and wine were a Valentine's gift to herself.

No one had to point out that she was lacking balance in her life.

A whole day off with Nick leading the charge sounded like heaven.

In her head, Alex shuffled the rest of her work week to squeeze it all in.

The tip of her big toe peeked out from the bubbles.

Yeah. She needed a mani-pedi in the worst way.

Chapter Two

The explosive sound of a gunshot ripped Hawk out of his sleep and had him rolling off his bed, his hand reaching for his 9 mm before he even opened an eye.

As he felt the cold metal of the weapon, he realized the vivid sound that woke him wasn't from an actual bullet leaving the chamber of a gun but a vibrational memory. A recurring dream that a therapist would have a field day unpacking if he was still mandated to see them.

Hawk rested his forehead on the side of his mattress and willed his rapid pulse to slow the fuck down.

He wasn't in the jungles of Guatemala, sweltering from the oppressive heat and humidity. The third-world electrical grid could barely keep up with the lights and fans, let alone air-conditioning. At least not in the accommodations Hawk found himself in most of the time.

The digital clock said it was four fifty in the morning.

There was no point in crawling back into bed to try and catch another hour of rest.

It wouldn't happen.

Reclaiming sleep wasn't possible if he woke from a memory. He refused to call his waking dreams nightmares. A nightmare was something real, happening . . . and inescapable. Dreams were nothing but emotion-stirring images in your head that shifted the second you opened your eyes.

After picking himself off the floor, he padded naked into his bathroom and straight to the toilet.

Twenty minutes later, his hair still wet from the shower, Hawk stood in his tiny apartment kitchen, waiting for the coffeepot to do its thing.

He scrolled through the morning headlines on his phone.

Starting with news out of DC, he skimmed the articles, his eyes catching the keywords he'd been trained to notice. Satisfied there wasn't anything worth his time or concern, he moved on to more global coverage. By then, the coffee had percolated enough to pour the robust burst of sunshine into a cup.

The first taste of java hit his throat with a sigh.

He dug past the infamous articles regarding the latest pop superstar and her football boyfriend before finding news with more meat.

Ukraine and Russia were still at war.

Ukraine was asking Washington for more funds.

The fight about the border was still a shit show, and Congress and the House were doing what they did best. Sitting on their asses doing nothing but pissing off the American people on both sides of the aisle.

But hey, at least the pop star was getting more kids to the voting polls.

In short, nothing had changed while Hawk was asleep.

Hawk tossed his phone onto the table, wondering if he'd ever break the habit of checking the news. Hearing about all the things he had absolutely no control over and could do nothing about. Reading the morning news had been an occupational hazard.

Literally.

Not anymore, he reminded himself. Which was probably why he hadn't done anything to break the habit.

Thirty minutes later, right as Hawk turned into the parking lot of his gym, his phone started to ring.

The name of the caller flashed on the information screen.

It was his boss.

Well, his boss *and* his friend.

"Yeah," Hawk said when he answered the call.

"Good, you're up."

"It's after six." Hawk couldn't remember when he'd slept past six in the morning.

Ed Vargas scoffed and dove right in. "I need you to run point tonight for the Bakshai reception."

"Am I supposed to know who that is?" This was the first time Hawk heard the name.

"Nasser Bakshai is receiving his father, Ashraf Bakshai, at John Wayne at three thirty this afternoon. They're first going to the son's estate in Brentwood, and then they're expected at a restaurant at eight."

Hawk pulled into a parking spot and sat with the engine idling. "That sounds like one driver, two clients." Running point meant three or more guards, with the point man calling the shots.

"I have five of you on this. Three visible, two on the sidelines. A point car and a decoy." Which translated into three in suits and two other bodyguards disguised as waiters or other patrons.

"Who is this guy?" Decoy cars were often saved for super-high-profile clients that had incurred literal threats.

"Big oil. The son's trying to make an impression on his father with overkill security. I'll email the details on the men and locations."

"How long is the assignment?"

"Dad leaves in forty-eight hours. After the reception, there will only be three of you. Two of you alert at all times."

Which meant one of them would try and catch some sleep in the back of one of the cars while the others tried to stay awake on an overnight assignment.

"Sounds good." They ended the call.

A forty-eight-hour assignment suggested that Hawk attempt to catch some sleep before it began.

He laughed at the thought as he stepped out of the SUV, his gym bag slung over his shoulder.

❧

The lovers' holiday only lingered in the break room. Picked-through boxes of chocolates and exactly three long-stem roses in a vase were all that was left.

A cup of coffee in hand, Alex made her way back to her office, saying good morning to anyone who looked her way. It was early, a good fifteen minutes before the official start of the workday, so there weren't that many faces to smile back at.

Dee was tucking her purse in a drawer when Alex approached.

"Good morning," Alex said.

The tiny, unassuming woman straightened her back, met Alex's gaze briefly, and looked away nearly as fast. "Good morning, Ms. Stone."

Alex had long since stopped suggesting that Dee address her as Alex. Dee resisted the familiarity almost as much as she resisted eye contact.

"Once you're settled, let's go over the calendar for the day."

"Of course." No eye contact, just a nod.

Alex had no sooner sat behind her desk than Dee was walking through the door.

"Please close it behind you." Alex didn't want any passersby to be privy to the board meeting agenda before Alex and Chase were ready to announce it.

The first twenty minutes of their morning meeting was a rundown of expected calls and meetings Alex had scheduled. Then there was Dee's priority list, which instantly shifted when Alex expressed her needs.

"I need you to uncover the board meeting minutes at the time of the Casa Noel acquisition. I need to know how the votes went on the board and who had the most to say about the chain. And I need you to be quiet about it."

"Quiet?" Dee asked.

"Don't tell anyone else in the office what you're doing. If anyone asks, direct them to me. The agenda at the next board meeting needs to start with the impending sale or liquidation of the Casa Noel Properties, with an immediate closing of ten percent of the hotels."

Dee looked up from her laptop, where she was typing her notes. Her fingers stopped moving. "Layoffs?"

Alex couldn't pretend that the layoffs were temporary. "We'll call them that. Schedule a meeting with Shelby in Mergers and Acquisitions for Tuesday. By then, I should have everything I need to tell him how to proceed after the board meeting."

Dee wasn't typing.

When Alex glanced up, she saw Dee blink twice. Her eyes lingered on Alex's before she gave her head a little shake and went back to typing. "Max will have an outline of Stone Holdings' shipping distribution center in Kansas to add to the agenda. I need a search on that leg as well."

"Mr. Smith?" Dee asked, clarifying.

"Yes."

"Will he be at the meeting?"

"Possibly. If he is, we won't announce it ahead of time. The media has finally calmed down, we'd like to keep it that way."

Max Smith was Alex and Chase's half brother. A man no one knew existed until after Aaron Stone, their father, died. An illegitimate son born from a torrid affair while Alex's father was still married to her mother wasn't someone Aaron boasted about.

Alex and Chase were informed of their brother's existence at the reading of their father's will. Because their father had left Max with his mother and didn't keep in contact with his lover, no one knew where Max was. At the age of two, Max's mother abandoned her son to the foster care system and completely disappeared. All the while, the woman collected the child support Aaron Stone provided through a matrix of mail forwarding and secret bank accounts. Still, in Aaron's death, the man did, in fact, acknowledge his son by way of an inheritance. One-third of everything.

It took half a year to find their brother. Once word was out that an orphan became an unknowing overnight billionaire, the media went wild.

Max was ill prepared for what followed and initially limped along with his new identity. He went from a completely blue-collar life to the executive floor of a multibillion-dollar company.

Now, he really was transitioning to his new life with surprising ease. He'd taken on traveling to and assessing the companies on the chopping block of Stone Enterprises.

The actual running of Stone Enterprises, and voting on the board, he left for Alex and Chase. Therefore, Max's presence at the board meetings wasn't expected. But the door was always open for him to attend.

"Everything about Casa Noel and Stone Holdings I need you to handle directly, do not farm it out to anyone, especially your temp. We don't need the rumor mill to reach the board members before we talk to them."

"Yes, ma'am."

Alex shivered. *"Ma'am."* Made her skin crawl. It made her sound as old as she felt. The need to correct Dee and force the woman to call her Alex, or at minimum, Ms. Stone, was like acid rising in her stomach.

Alex swallowed it down.

She was being petty and insecure. Two things Alex refused to be.

"I think that's it." Alex glanced at the time. She had eight minutes until her first call.

Dee closed her laptop and stood.

The fluorescent lights in the room flickered several times as if the power was attempting to go out.

Alex's computer started to beep, indicating the battery backup was about to click on, only the power didn't go completely out.

Alex hesitated and found herself looking up at the ceiling and then around the room.

Dee also stood in what looked like suspended animation.

Several thoughts ran through Alex's mind in rapid order. The first was *Is this an earthquake?* Only the building wasn't moving, and the massive sound that accompanied an earthquake didn't come.

Once she quickly ruled out an earthquake, she thought, *Is the power going out? Staying on? What is the building protocol when the power shuts off?* Alex knew the building had a backup generator that kicked on, making it possible to exit the building with a lighted path.

The emergency lighting in the office flickered on and then off just as rapidly.

Alex released a breath when the hum of the lights evened out.

"Good. I don't have time for a power outage today."

Dee opened the office door. "Did you want more coffee before I get into this?"

Alex almost never took Dee up on her offer to serve coffee. But the clock suggested she should if getting to the meeting on time was a priority.

And timeliness was always a priority. "That would be nice, thank you."

The coffee wore off by noon. While everyone else filtered out of the office for lunch, Alex ignored her jumpy pulse and started a fresh pot of coffee in the office kitchen before taking a cup back to her desk.

A small built-in bar refrigerator sat inside a cabinet that once housed an actual bar. When her father worked in the space, the man had a collection that could inebriate every employee on the top floor. Alex had since removed all the alcohol and replaced it with mineral water of several types and healthy juices that often substituted for lunch on days when she simply couldn't stop to eat.

Piper had hired a service to stock this personal space with fresh, quality, ready-to-eat options. It was a godsend on more days than Alex cared to admit. And the meals were so good, she was tempted to have the service stock her up at home.

The culinary arts and Alex had never made peace. If having a private chef wasn't so damn pretentious, she'd hire one. Not to mention, once she started using a chef to prepare her home meals, she was going to lose her grip on the realities of life.

So, like any busy executive that didn't have time to shop, prepare . . . and clean up after cooking anything worthwhile, Alex lived on easy-to-heat-up options.

Eventually her business life would slow down. At some point she'd feel like Stone Enterprises was on autopilot, or at least she'd trust the executive staff to do their jobs without worry that they were undermining her.

Just before four that afternoon, there was a rapid knock against her half-open office door.

She glanced up from her computer to see Floyd standing there.

Her fingers stalled over her keyboard, and she attempted a smile.

"Do you have a second?" he asked.

"Sure."

Floyd Gatlin was the VP of Stone Enterprises. A man who kissed up to her father when he was alive, praised the man in his death . . . and truly thought he would be appointed the CEO of the company with Aaron Stone's passing.

Neither Alex nor her brothers trusted Gatlin any further than she could pick the man up and throw him. But as scholars much better versed than her had said . . . keep your friends close and your enemies closer. And since she had only her gut telling her to regard the man with caution, she didn't have a legitimate reason to fire him.

That didn't stop her from looking.

"I wanted to make sure you had the correct address for tonight's reception." Floyd stepped into the office and stood a few paces from her desk as if he was truly just popping in for a "quick second."

Tonight?

Reception?

Had she forgotten a dinner?

Two clicks of her mouse brought up her schedule.

No. No evening engagements.

"There is nothing on my calendar."

The smile on Floyd's face fell. "I was afraid of this. I'm glad I stopped in."

When he didn't elaborate, she asked, "What reception?"

"Bakshai," he said as if that was supposed to mean something to her.

Her face must have given away her confusion.

"You don't know who that is?"

"Enlighten me, Floyd."

He took a couple of steps farther into the room. "The Bakshai family is part of a bigger company that owns a chunk of the oil in the Middle East."

"What does oil have to do with us?"

Floyd stepped around a chair in front of her desk and took a seat. "Your father kept an ongoing relationship with the Bakshais. A 'you scratch our back, we'll scratch yours,' if you will."

Alex searched her internal database to try and recall seeing the name on any of Stone Enterprises' documents.

"What kind of scratching have we done?"

"More introductions than anything. Your father felt it imperative to keep relations with families like the Bakshais. Especially with the increasing restrictions and red tape around conducting business in places like the Middle East. Likewise, Bakshai wants to know that companies and men like your father will be there for them when in need of a favor . . . or introduction."

This sounded like a golf date.

One she hadn't planned on.

"We're expected at a reception tonight?"

Floyd looked away. "Yes. I should have checked with you sooner. I saw the invitation come through, saw your father's email, and assumed it was forwarded to you."

All of her father's mail was forwarded to her.

"I can represent the company. It's not imperative that you go . . . or maybe Chase can—"

"No. I'll be there." Alex felt the tired behind her eyes already. She picked up a pen and poised the tip over a pad of paper. "Where and what time?"

Floyd rattled off the name of a restaurant and gave her a time before standing to leave. "If I see anything like this come through again, I'll be sure and forward the messages to you directly."

"Thank you," she told him. And meant it.

Floyd offered a nod and stepped out of her office.

Once he was gone, she buzzed Dee at her desk. At the same time, Alex typed in the name of the restaurant on her computer.

"Yes, Ms. Stone?"

"I need you to stop whatever you're doing and look up the name Bakshai. I need to know who they are, a snapshot of what they do, and who they do business with. And I need it before you leave today."

"Yes, ma'am."

Alex put the phone down and sifted through the restaurant's website. An entire page was dedicated to pictures of celebrity events that had taken place at the location. Swanky sophistication. The kind of place where you wore evening attire and not a business suit.

The kind of place where you hired a driver when you went unaccompanied.

Alex rang Dee again.

Chapter Three

To suggest that five security guards was overkill for the Bakshai reception would be an understatement.

First off, Ashraf Bakshai came with his own people.

Two of them.

One sat in the passenger seat of the SUV Hawk drove, the other in the car that followed.

Both men filled out their suits with an extra fifty pounds of pure muscle. Not that they needed to depend only on brawn to protect the man that paid them—they were both armed.

Hawk met the men with a handshake, but the conversation was nearly zero as they spoke Arabic and either didn't know or weren't interested in speaking English.

Nasser Bakshai, the son, stood at five ten tops, maybe a hundred and seventy pounds. He couldn't be more than thirty, but the man already had a wife and three children.

Hawk, Teach, and Charlie showed up at the Bakshai home an hour before having to drive Nasser to the airport to pick up his father.

When Hawk asked Nasser for details on any possible threats or hostility at the reception, he was told that the reception was to host businessmen he and his father worked with. But that Ashraf Bakshai was accustomed to layers of security wherever he went, hence the need to hire the five of them.

"My father is a very rich man. Wealth like his puts a target on his back."

But not the son? Hawk mused.

The reception was being held in an upscale restaurant on the outskirts of Beverly Hills.

Hawk jumped out of the dark SUV, along with the two unexpected bodyguards, while Teach and Charlie backed the cars into spaces reserved at the front of the establishment.

One of Ashraf's men peeled off at the door as Hawk flanked his assignment.

Hawk stayed a couple of paces back as attendees of the reception approached his client.

The radio in his ear kept Hawk in contact with his team.

"What's with the extra heat?"

The question was from Stevie. The only woman on this five-man team. She posed as one of the servers and circulated with a tray filled with wine. She eavesdropped on conversations and kept an eye on the kitchen staff.

"Dad brought his own security," Hawk announced into the earpiece that also served as a microphone to his team.

"Friendly," Charlie said sarcastically.

"You sure we're not expecting any trouble?" Teach asked.

Hawk looked over the heads of people surrounding the Bakshais and saw Teach standing at the far end of the room by an emergency exit.

"The Brentwood home only had an alarm system and two dogs."

So . . . nearly no security, mused Hawk. "If there's trouble, it will be aimed at the father."

The earpiece dangling out of Hawk's ear was somewhat of a magnet to those that turned their attention toward him. Some would open their mouths as if they wanted to introduce themselves, then they'd see the radio equipment and turn away.

"Does anyone else notice the distinct lack of women in this group?" Stevie asked.

Her question had Hawk skimming the crowd.

"Maybe it's a bachelor party?" Teach piped in.

Someone on the team laughed.

There were only two female guests in the room. The rest were staff members.

"From the looks coming my way, I wouldn't be surprised." Stevie was retired law enforcement. Retired by choice, not by age. In her midthirties, she decided, like many of Ed's employees, that working for a government paycheck simply wasn't worth the risk. Too many cuts, lack of support from the department, and the increasing discourse between the public and the force was a combination she didn't want to deal with for the next thirty years.

Hawk agreed.

Stevie was sharp. Her scores at the range were impressive, and she was crazy smart when it came to cybersecurity.

And she was a mother.

Hawk would bet money that it was her daughter that pushed Stevie to quit the department. Or maybe it was the soon-to-be ex-husband that forced that hand.

It didn't matter. Stevie was an asset, and Hawk enjoyed working with her.

Since Hawk was the closest in proximity to their clients, he kept silent as the team continued to banter.

From what he could see, the Bakshais knew a lot of rich and influential people. Big names in the American oil industry, politicians, businessmen that had people like Bezos and Musk on speed dial.

Not that Hawk knew any of these men by sight . . . or even name. But the rest of his team kept name-dropping like they were standing next to the red carpet on Oscar night.

Alcohol was flowing, but their hosts weren't partaking.

Which Hawk appreciated.

Playing bodyguard to drunks was not ideal.

Thirty minutes into the time at the reception, Charlie made an announcement.

"We have someone stirring up attention at the entrance."

"What kind of—" Hawk's words dropped off when he saw the room's distraction.

A woman who was most definitely not an employee had many heads turned. Dark hair pulled into a loose knot at the nape of her neck, slender, and wearing an evening gown that hugged her body and stopped just past her knees. She was taller than some of the men in the room, and while Hawk couldn't see if she wore heels, he guessed that she did. Her chin was high, her back stiff . . . and the smile on her face seemed forced.

And she was stunning.

～⑨

Attempting to look unaffected, Alex skimmed the room, searching out a familiar face.

The images of the hosts were drilled into her head from the pictures Dee had conjured off the internet. Father and son were at the far end of the reception in deep conversation with the men at their sides.

Two men, close to her deceased father's age, appraised her with a glance before turning away without so much as a hello.

When she'd introduced herself to an attendant at the door, she was met with the question *"Is Aaron Stone with you?"*

She'd been momentarily startled.

Did the Bakshais not know of her father's death?

"Only in spirit," Alex had replied to the door attendant.

Alex hadn't elaborated before handing her coat to the person collecting them and slipping a coat tag into her clutch.

A low murmur hummed around her.

A woman with a tray filled with wine and, strangely, highball glasses with what appeared to be whiskey stopped at her side. "Would you care for a drink?"

Alex eyed the wine. "No, thank you."

"You sure? I can have the bartender make you whatever you'd like."

Tempting. "I'm good."

The waitress nodded and moved on.

Alex kept a smile on her face as she glanced around.

Floyd wasn't in sight. Not that she ever wanted him as an anchor for any social or business situation. Still . . . it would have been nice to have at least one person she recognized to help break into a conversation.

Since there wasn't anyone in sight, she started across the room to the hosts.

Less than three yards from her intended target, she heard her name. "Alexandrea Stone."

She swiveled in the direction of a male voice.

The man smiling her way sat somewhere between fifty and sixty, his slightly salty hair was thin on the top. What he lacked on his head he made up for in a trimmed mustache and beard that complemented his profile. Like every other man in the room, he wore a cross between a business suit and something more casual. A lack of a tie here, a sport coat with slacks there. The man looked perfectly comfortable with the top button of his dress shirt undone and his tie left at home or shoved into the pocket of his suit jacket. It dawned on Alex then that the sophisticated evening attire the venue's website suggested wasn't carried through with this crowd. And while Alex preferred to be overdressed than under, she felt a prickle of unease begin to seep in.

She pushed the fashion statements aside and focused on the man who'd just called out her name. He stood with two other men, both holding glasses with presumed whiskey. Not one of them was familiar to Alex.

She stepped into their small circle and extended a hand. "Hello."

The man hesitated, then shook her hand.

"You don't remember me," he said without censure.

Alex offered a grimace that she hoped came off as something akin to apologetic. "Guilty, I'm afraid to say."

"Decker. Roy Decker. We met at the National Heart Association Gala that honored your late father." Roy's hand slipped from hers.

"There were a lot of people there that night." And she had been doing her level best to avoid anyone who praised her late father ad nauseam. Everyone had gone out of their way to add a condolence or a story about her father. And Alex couldn't escape that gala fast enough.

Roy introduced her to the men he was with, both of which were holding their drinks in a way that would made shaking their hands feel awkward. In fact, as she took a step in and started to extend her right hand, both men turned their shoulders slightly and either didn't see her attempt at the gesture or were avoiding it.

Roy looked beyond her, asking, "Is your brother with you?"

Alex stiffened. Seemed every time she went to one of these things, the question was always . . . "Where is your brother?" She'd wager that Chase didn't suffer the same question. "Chase or Max?"

"Ahh . . . that's right. You have two of them now, don't you?"

Roy's words grabbed the attention of the man on his right. The man whose name Alex had already forgotten.

"Apparently, I've always had two brothers since Chase and Max are older than me. Sadly, our father didn't share the news of our half brother until after his death."

Roy offered a strangled smile.

The man on his right . . . Elis, that was his name. Elis muttered out of the corner of his mouth, "You can't exactly blame Aaron for that."

It took everything in Alex to avoid snapping at Elis's comment.

Roy shuffled from one foot to the other.

Alex pulled back on her already fake smile and took note of Elis's wedding ring.

Asshole.

"Neither of my brothers are here this evening."

A long pause followed by nothing more than a nod.

Cheating her frame away from Elis and the other man, Alex focused on Roy. He, too, wore a plain gold band on his left-hand ring finger. "Is your wife with you tonight, Roy?"

The question made the other men stiffen.

"No," Roy said swiftly. "She, ah . . . she doesn't care to attend this particular event."

Alex wanted to ask why but didn't.

"Perhaps your wife and I can get acquainted the next time," Alex suggested. Knowing in her circle, there was always a next time.

"She would like that," Roy said.

"I promise to remember your name when we see each other again, Roy. If you'll excuse me."

Alex made brief eye contact with Elis and stepped away from the trio.

". . . *she doesn't care to attend this particular event.*"

What was so special about *this event?*

These mixers were a staple in Alex's new world. The one with multimillion-dollar portfolios and businesses that spanned several countries. Husbands and wives both attended, often offering an early out for the other should the event prove to be a waste of time and energy.

Alex fumbled with the strap on her clutch to wrap it around her wrist before she relieved the passing waiter of a glass of wine from his tray.

If the evening and this event were filled with men like Elis, she'd need a little something to get through the night.

She took a sip and once again skimmed the attendees.

Men.

The place was absolutely overfilled with suits and not evening gowns.

There was a woman on her right, young . . . a bit too bubbly and almost hanging on the arm of the man she was with. There had to be at least a twenty-year age difference between the two of them.

With the distinct lack of women in the room, the ones that were there stuck out like children running around wheelchairs in an old folks' home.

A blonde wearing a low-cut red mermaid dress stood beside a man who could be her grandfather.

Alex's gaze moved back to the couple closer to her.

The man wore a wedding ring.

His companion did not.

"*. . . this particular event.*"

The light in Alex's head turned on.

This was the cocktail party that men took their mistresses to.

No wonder no one was going out of their way to make eye contact with her.

Another sip of wine, and Alex placed the still-filled glass on a tray of a passing server and made a straight line to the hosts.

She needed to make an introduction and get out of there. There was no way in hell she'd be able to look a man's wife in the eye if she knew he was stepping out.

And since a few faces were starting to look familiar . . . faces that avoided her . . . Alex knew the men were thinking the same thing.

Alex was not welcome. And she'd bet ten grand that Floyd knew exactly what kind of party this was. And she'd up that bet by another ten that there wasn't an invitation in her inbox . . . buried or not. And Floyd knew that.

She'd have Dee do a dive into Chase's inbox first thing Monday.

With Alex simply moving close to the circle of men surrounding the Bakshais, their conversations faded.

Ashraf Bakshai met her eyes directly. His eyes started to travel down her body, in a way a man would at a nightclub.

Alex quickly extended her hand and made a hasty introduction. "Mr. Bakshai. I'm Alexandrea Stone. I believe you and your son were acquainted with my late father, Aaron."

That kept the man's gaze north of her chest.

Ashraf clasped his hand in hers and doubled it with his other hand. His grasp was a little too warm and held on way too long. "Yes . . . Aaron. I was sorry to hear of his passing. I wasn't able to attend his funeral, I'm afraid."

"It was rather unavoidable for me."

Ashraf released her hand with a final squeeze and lifted a corner of his mouth. "My condolences."

"Thank you," she told him. She was somewhat thankful he didn't wax on about what a good man her father had been.

A young woman started to move close to Ashraf's side.

The younger Bakshai made a gesture with his hand, halting the woman, while a larger man stepped forward and escorted her away.

At that point, Alex looked around and noticed at least one man watching them with an earpiece connected to a wire that disappeared into his suit.

They have bodyguards?

"Would you like a drink, Miss Stone?" A snap of his fingers, and a waiter turned toward them.

"No, thank you. I can't stay long, I'm afraid. I have another event I committed to before I received your invitation," she lied without pause. "Although I wanted to, at the very minimum, make an introduction."

"I'm glad that you did," Ashraf said in a tone that she actually believed.

"I admit that I did a little research and couldn't find any business relationship between Stone Enterprises and the Bakshai name. Were you and my father strictly friends?" Alex played dumb, ignoring what Floyd had told her about their relationship.

"I believe Aaron and I were always open to doing business with each other, should the occasion present itself." While Ashraf spoke, his son stood with silent, rapt attention.

"Good to know. I'd hate to be kept unaware of a venture between both our companies."

"No. You are correct. We have signed no contracts." Which didn't necessarily mean they didn't do business with each other.

The son stepped forward. "We were informed that your brother and you were taking over for your father. Is your brother here?"

Alex made a point to glance at the others standing around, listening to their conversation. "Chase is with his lovely new wife and their first child. I'm sure you remember those early days. I've taken on the evening events for now . . . at least until Chase manages a full night's sleep."

Ashraf smiled.

Alex hoped that her words sent the message that Chase wouldn't be attending the mistress event.

Not now.

Not ever.

"He is available at the office. I hope you'll feel just as welcome to reach out to him as well as me if that business occasion ever arises."

Nasser opened his mouth to speak.

His father cut him off.

"Are you sure we can't convince you to stay longer?" Ashraf asked.

Alex couldn't tell if that was her cue to leave or if the man was sincere.

It didn't matter. She wanted—no, needed—to get out of there.

The bodybuilder in a suit that had escorted the other woman away was back, his eyes kept flickering to hers.

Then it happened.

A familiar face caught her attention.

The CFO of Regent Hotels stood beside a woman who was not his wife.

Their eyes met.

Chester Sherman took a step away from the woman at his side, his smile fell.

Dammit. Alex liked Chester's wife.

"I really should go," Alex said slowly, turning her attention back to her host.

Chapter Four

"Who is she?" Hawk asked in his mic from the far side of the room closest to the entry.

Teach stood near their clients and was the only one that could possibly hear the conversation.

Whoever the stunning mystery woman was, her presence was causing many men to look and then avoid her.

In the time since the mystery woman had walked through the door, a smattering of other women followed. All of them did a beeline toward a man in the room.

It was only when Nasser Bakshai's arm slid around the waist of a woman who wasn't his wife that Hawk and his crew concluded the reason for so few female guests.

"They're all side pieces," Stevie had said. "Wives are not that attentive."

Sure enough, Hawk focused his attention on the behavior of the younger women and the men who openly pawed at them. Some more obvious than others.

When the mystery woman passed through the room, briefly stopping to speak with someone, Hawk felt a quick snag in his gut. This woman was much too put-together and held herself too high to be someone's extra.

It was then that Hawk peeled away from their client, switching places with Teach.

Meanwhile, his team kept chatting.

"Are they afraid of a scorned woman coming in and causing a scene?"

"Is that what she's doing?" Hawk asked.

"I don't think so," Teach said.

"There's a couple making an exit through the kitchen," Stevie told them.

Hawk's gaze shot to the door leading into the server entry.

"On it," said Carl, the fifth member of the team, who was dressed as a concierge of the restaurant and had access to the kitchen.

"She has to be someone's wife. There are some serious cold shoulders blasting her way," Charlie pointed out.

"Except Dad."

The team had come to call the older Bakshai "Dad" and the younger Bakshai "Son." It simply made communication easier.

"He looks like he wants her to curl up in his lap," Teach continued.

"Can you get close enough to hear them?" Hawk asked.

"Not without being obvious. I did hear something about a funeral."

"A threat of one?"

Teach chuckled. "They're way too polite to be threatening each other."

Yeah, even from his distance, Hawk could see the body language that didn't suggest conflict. Although the woman seemed to become more and more uneasy the longer she stood there.

"Looks like she's about to go," Teach announced.

Hawk's gaze zeroed in on her face.

Flawless.

Then she looked up, and those flawless features turned white.

Hawk followed her gaze.

The man she stared at looked green.

She turned back to the dad, pivoted, and headed straight toward the door.

She stalked through the crowd, which parted as if she were the oil in a bowl full of water.

Hawk took in the senior Bakshai, whose eyes looked her up and down now that her back was turned. His gaze less than polite.

He then motioned to his private security, said something, and nodded toward the fleeing woman.

The less-than-friendly muscle followed her out.

"I don't like this," Stevie said.

"Neither do I. I'm on her. Stevie, see if you can find out from the other staff members who she is. Carl, check the guest list."

"On it," Stevie announced.

"On it," Carl repeated.

The mystery woman zeroed in on the door, her smile barely there as she all but ran toward it.

Hawk averted his gaze and started to walk ahead of her.

She was close enough that he could almost feel the heat of her body.

She stopped suddenly . . . he thought he heard her cuss under her breath before pivoting toward the coat check.

Hawk hesitated.

When she turned around again, the smile was gone and replaced with tightly controlled anger.

Hawk doubled his steps to the front of the restaurant while Ashraf's personal bodyguard hung back.

The woman was completely oblivious to the fact that not one but two men were following her.

A woman as beautiful as her really needed to understand the basics of situational awareness.

She didn't bother putting on her coat as she stepped outside.

Her eyes darted around the darkened valet parking lot.

Hawk pulled his cell phone from his pocket and put it to his ear while standing less than three yards from her.

The valet approached. "Do you have a ticket?"

"No, I have a—" She stopped talking and pointed toward the SUVs backed up to the restaurant. "I think that's my driver."

She stepped from the curb and toward a darker part of the lot. As she walked, she started to open her purse.

Hawk watched at a discreet distance.

Until he saw Bakshai's man come up behind her.

Hawk knew the second she realized he was there.

She let out a shriek and jumped back, and her purse hit the ground.

The guard grasped her arm.

The fear on her face was palpable.

Hawk moved.

"Mr. Bakshai would like to offer you a ride home," Hawk heard the other man say in a very thick accent.

The woman tugged at her arm. "Let go."

"His car is—"

"I have a ride. Now let go of me."

"I'm afraid he insists."

Her back stiffened, and she twisted her arm, which the bodyguard still didn't release.

"What's going on here?" Hawk made himself known.

Her eyes darted to him.

She tugged her arm again.

Bakshai's guard let her loose.

"This does not concern you."

Hawk offered a noncommittal sound. "Actually, it does."

The woman took several steps until her back met the door of an SUV.

Hawk focused solely on the guard and took up the space between the two of them.

"Bakshai wants to see her safely home."

"Tell your boss that I'm very capable of taking care of myself," she spat. Her voice shaky.

Hawk's eyes never left the other man.

Knowing the man was armed, Hawk made a quick assessment of their distance from each other and the speed it would take to disarm him.

He could do it, but there was always a chance a round could go off.

The woman behind him, whose rapid breath gave away how truly scared she'd been, was in range.

He needed to de-escalate the situation without violence.

"I don't know how they do it where you come from, but scaring a woman in a dark parking lot and offering her a ride is considered threatening here. I'm sure Mr. Bakshai would want to avoid any unnecessary police activity."

Tension bunched under the muscles in Hawk's shoulders.

For the space of two breaths, Hawk actually thought this guy was going to challenge him.

"Do you need backup?" Hawk heard Charlie in his earpiece.

The bodyguard shifted his eyes to the woman before he stepped back.

Nose flaring, he turned and headed inside.

"Keep an eye on the extra heat," Hawk responded to Charlie.

"On it."

Hawk didn't turn away from the guard until he neared the restaurant door where Charlie stood.

Hawk twisted toward the mystery woman, stepped out of her personal space, and pulled the earpiece from his ear to talk.

The absolute physical relief he saw in her stance was instant.

Her hand went to her chest.

She was shaking. "Thank you."

"Do you need me to call the authorities?"

She shook her head. "No." Her gaze darted to the retreating man. "That was weird, right?"

It was. But why? Why would Bakshai send his goon after her? Who was she?

"It didn't look right from where I stood," he told her.

She knelt down to pick up her purse and the cell phone that had tumbled out of it.

"Dammit." She glanced at the cracked screen and shoved it in her purse.

"I'm sure Bakshai will pay for the repair."

"I don't need him to pay for anything."

"Do you know him?" Hawk asked.

"No. He's a . . . *was* a friend to my father. I thought I was walking into a business cocktail party . . ." Her words trailed off.

It seemed the spike of fear-fueled adrenaline gave way to the anger.

"It's definitely a cocktail party. I'm not sure about the business part."

"Yeah," she sighed. Her eyes caught his and then dropped to the earpiece slung on his shoulder. "Are you the restaurant security?"

"Not exactly." He didn't think it was wise to say that he was technically on Bakshai's payroll. "You really should pay more attention when you're walking into dark parking lots," he suggested, changing the subject.

"I know." She glanced around then. Her body shook. "Damn. I'm usually more . . . alert."

He was fairly certain that she was realizing just how quickly things could have gone south.

"Does that phone work? Or do you need me to call for a ride?"

She shook her head. "I have a driver. He's in one of these." She motioned to the black SUV behind her. One of the cars he and his team had arrived in.

She pulled her phone out of her purse again and tapped her fingers on a text message. "He probably had to park in the lot." Her screen lit up with a message. "He's coming."

Hawk moved out from the cars they were sandwiched between and offered her a wide berth to move around him.

"My name is Hawk."

She looked at him then, and for the first time since he'd spoken one word to her, she smiled.

Good God, the woman was gorgeous. And that smile . . .

"Alex," she told him.

He had a first name.

"Nice to meet you, Alex."

A nearly identical SUV pulled up to the curb, and the driver jumped out.

"The pleasure is truly all mine." She rubbed her arm where Bakshai's muscle had grabbed her. Hawk didn't see a mark in the dimly lit lot, but that didn't mean there wasn't one there.

Yeah, he needed to have a little discussion with the extra "help."

The driver opened the door to the back seat, and Alex climbed in. Seeing Hawk there, the driver moved around to the driver's seat.

"You sure you have everything? Your house keys didn't slide out of your purse?" Hawk asked.

Alex immediately looked in said purse and smiled again. "Got 'em."

"Good. Be more careful, Alex."

She nodded, her smile contagious.

And then Hawk closed her door and patted the car as if telling the driver he could move on.

Hawk watched as they drove away.

The bright white letters identifying the hired car were plastered on the bumper.

He had a name . . . and a number.

Sort of.

⌒

"Her name is Alexandrea Stone," Stevie informed him once Hawk returned the earpiece to where it belonged and rejoined the party. "The name on the guest registry was Aaron Stone."

"A husband?" Hawk asked.

He kept a distance from the Bakshais and noticed the moment the oversize bodyguard leaned in to talk to his boss.

Ashraf's gaze flicked around the room before landing on Hawk. The man furrowed his brow.

"Not sure," Stevie said.

Charlie chuckled into the mic. "You clearly don't keep up on the local news. Aaron Stone was the father."

"How do you know that?" Hawk asked.

"Stone Hotels?" Charlie asked as if expecting the name to ring bells in everyone's heads. "The dad died last year, left his billions to his kids. They were all over the news."

Sounded like the gossip columns to Hawk.

"Then she wasn't looking for a cheating husband," Teach chimed in.

Maybe not, but she'd seen someone who turned her complexion pale.

"From what I can tell, that's the only reason we're needed here— the suits at the party can't hold their liquor. But other than slurring their words, they don't appear to be the fighting drunk crowd," Stevie announced. "My grandmother has a better tolerance than these guys."

Hawk followed Stevie as she circulated around the room, offering glasses of whiskey. He had no doubt a grandmother to Stevie would know how to drink.

"What happened in the parking lot?" Charlie asked.

"Ashraf's man confronted her. Grabbed her, *offered* her a ride," Hawk whispered into his mic as his gaze met the senior Bakshai's and held.

"What the fuck?" Teach swore.

"We're here to protect them, not be a party to kidnapping," Charlie said.

Exactly Hawk's thoughts.

"Ed isn't going to like this."

If Ashraf was attempting to hold Alexandrea Stone against her will while Hawk and the team were on the payroll, they could easily be accused of being accessories to a crime.

Their services were provided to protect their clients from people wishing to do them harm, not be a part of harming others.

Hawk instantly recalled a moment in time when he stood in the sweltering heat of the jungle, the boss standing in a circle of men holding automatic rifles. Hawk being one of them . . . protecting the bad guy.

His gut told him that this cocktail party was a first-world equivalent.

"Eyes open," Hawk told his team.

"On the guests or the hosts?" Charlie asked.

"Both."

Hours later, when most of the guests had left, Nasser waved Hawk aside to talk with him.

The younger man's smile stood out like a Halloween mask. Stern and cold. "I'm told there was an incident earlier," he started.

Hawk had been waiting for this. And since the rest of the evening had been completely uneventful, there could be only one incident Nasser could be speaking about.

Hawk considered his words carefully. Decided on as few of them as possible. "There was."

"Care to elaborate?"

Instead of answering the man's question, Hawk asked, "Why were we here tonight? Why have extra security?"

"I told you, my father is an exceptionally wealthy man—"

"As were most of the people in this room, none of which brought bodyguards. Bodyguards that threatened guests in dark parking lots."

"That's not what happened," Nasser countered.

"You were there?" Hawk raised a brow in question.

Nasser narrowed his gaze. "You were hired by *me*. Your job is to protect *us*."

Hawk met the man's eyes. "True. Since this event appeared to involve men entertaining women that certain wives might not be fond of . . . I thought it best to follow the only unattached female as she left the venue. Make sure she wasn't a threat." Which was partially true but mostly bullshit.

That made Nasser laugh. "Women are not a threat."

The man was wrong about that, but Hawk kept that to himself.

"If you're unhappy with me or my team's performance, you're free to contact my superior." His politically correct words burned as they left Hawk's lips. "When you do, be sure and look over the contract you signed. You'll see that our service doesn't involve us engaging in or being witness to unlawful activities, such as assaulting women."

"No one assaulted—"

"He had a vise grip on Ms. Stone's arm," Hawk interrupted. "A grip she had to dislodge with force. Touching someone without consent is battery. Doing so at the request of someone else puts the blame on two people instead of one. If no ill will was intended, then my intervention may just have saved your father from criminal charges. And since I was hired by you, I could have easily been named as an accomplice. *That* is not in my job description." Hawk stared down at Nasser, an easy task since Hawk was half a foot taller.

Nasser shifted from one foot to another. Anything he wanted to say died on his lips.

"The services of you and your team won't be needed for the rest of the evening."

Hawk felt relief drop from his shoulders. "Very well."

He pivoted on his heel and spoke into the mic. "You heard the man, wrap it up. We leave in five."

Chapter Five

Hair drenched in a conditioning mask and swept up in a towel, wearing a bathrobe while leaning back in a massage chair, Alex sipped a glass of champagne as a technician painted her toes.

"God, I needed this," Alex admitted.

Nick looked exactly like her in the chair on her right. "Girl, same."

"Why don't we do this more often?" she asked.

Nick fixed her with a stare. "Let's see . . . Daddy died, left you all the money and all the responsibility, and you've hardly taken a day off since."

"It's been a big learning—"

"*Learning curve*," Nick finished for her. "You've been saying that for nearly a year."

"Maybe in five, I'll feel like I know what I'm doing." In five years, Alex would likely feel as if she'd aged twenty.

"You know you don't have to do this. You, Chase, and Max can appoint a competent CEO, step back, and collect a check."

"And do what?" She lifted the glass holding the champagne. "Work my way into the Betty Ford Clinic?"

"I wouldn't let that happen."

More times than she could count, Alex had considered exactly what Nick was suggesting. Yes, Chase and now Max were right there with her, making the big decisions about how to steer Stone Enterprises, but she was the one guiding all three of them.

Max had a lot more on his plate to learn than either she or Chase. Her half brother stepped out of his steel-toe shoes and blue-collar work when he learned of his vast inheritance.

He now resided in their father's estate in Beverly Hills with his girlfriend, Sarah. His story had been first-page news for months. Once thought to be an orphan, Max basically found and lost both of his parents in a matter of a few months. While he was now officially an orphan, he had Chase and Alex. Something Alex wouldn't change for the world.

"It's getting easier," Alex deflected.

"I'll believe that when we have more of these dates," Nick said. "And when are we going to buy you a house? I can't believe you're still in that oversize apartment."

"It's a condo."

"It's an apartment. You're a billionaire." Nick pointed his wineglass her way.

The technician looked up at Alex with a raised brow.

"Nick . . ."

"Billionaires don't live in condos or apartments. They live in lavish penthouses in Manhattan or sprawling estates behind gates with someone doing their laundry and cooking their meals. Even Max has figured that out."

"Dad's estate is perfect for him." Chase and Alex were only recently able to walk into the Beverly Hills estate and not cringe at the memories of their father within the walls.

"Speaking of real estate, when are Chase and Piper moving?"

"Escrow will close next month. But they have some remodeling they want done before they move in," Alex said.

The modest home Chase had owned before their father's windfall could have worked for him longer, except for the lack of privacy. Now that her brother had a family to consider, Chase was moving them behind gates and away from prying eyes and cameras.

Nick's face filled with a smile. "Now that's how you spend money. You need to take lessons."

"I spend plenty." She didn't. Not really. You had to have time outside of work to actually spend anything.

Nick rolled his eyes. "I'd bet my Swifty tickets that the last time you spent anything outside of a lunch or dinner, it was with me during the holidays."

He'd be right. "How much did those tickets cost?"

"Too much," he told her. "C'mon, Alex, let's at least narrow down where you want to buy."

Where was a huge question. "Someplace close to the office is best."

"Why? So you can work late and rattle home at ungodly hours?"

"Precisely."

"You always talked about a place with the ocean as your closest neighbor."

"Santa Monica is just as congested as where I am now." That's where Alex and Chase had been raised by their mother. They may not have had an ocean view, but that didn't stop Alex from spending plenty of time on the beach, watching the water. It brought her stress level down with each crash of the waves.

"Go north. Malibu."

"Too far." Her thoughts drifted to the event the night before. "Just yesterday, Floyd told me, last minute, about a meet and greet with an oil family that was in town. I wouldn't have had time to go home, change, and make it to the event if I owned in Malibu."

Nick furrowed his brow. "And what was gained by attending this last-minute shindig?"

Alex set her glass down and stared into nothing. "I discovered that Floyd is a world-class asshole, and the majority of men suck." She took a few minutes to explain what had happened. How the cocktail meet and greet was an excuse for men to party with their mistresses. "I couldn't get out of there fast enough."

"Sounds like a setup. One Floyd orchestrated to make you feel that way."

"Which is exactly why I'm not going to say a single word to him on Monday. I won't give him the satisfaction of knowing how the night went. And believe me, it was a shit show. When I left, Bakshai's oversize bodyguard followed me into the parking lot."

Nick's glass halted halfway to his lips. "Followed you?"

Alex glanced at her arm, still felt the man's meaty grip. "Told me that his boss wanted to make sure I got home safely."

Nick hesitated. "That doesn't sound bad, but I can tell from your expression it wasn't good."

She shook her head. "Scared the crap out of me. It was almost like he was insisting I let him drive me."

"The bodyguard?"

"I'm guessing that's what he was. The kind of guy you expect to stand next to a mob boss on TV. Big and bulky with an expression set on 'pissed off at the world.' I dropped my purse and busted the screen on my phone."

"What did you say to the guy?"

Her thoughts made room for Hawk. "I didn't have to say anything. Another man intervened. Thankfully." The flash of Hawk moving between her and the big guy and the relief she'd felt in that moment had her shivering.

"With a fist, I hope."

"It wasn't like that," she said. Though there had been a moment when she thought it might come to that.

"Was the parking lot dark?" the woman painting Alex's toes asked.

"Yeah."

"Was anyone else around?"

Alex diverted her attention to the woman. "No. Not that I saw."

The technician pressed her lips together and didn't make eye contact.

"Sounds like you're lucky," she said simply.

"And I need to escort you the next time," Nick added.

"Lucky, yes. As for an escort . . . next time I'll stay with the valet until my driver comes around."

"You should call out this Bakshai guy," Nick said.

"And what? Show him weakness?" Alex asked. "That's not how this game works. The minute you open yourself up, someone is going to be there to exploit you. Bakshai knew exactly what he was doing. A fake smile, a kind greeting, and a promise to get in touch should there be a need. I didn't think for a second he was sincere. The parking lot proved that."

She could certainly have perceived the incident as her overreacting. If not for Hawk.

He wouldn't have been overreacting. There was nothing about a dark parking lot that would scare a tall, broad-shouldered, confident man like that.

"You need to be more careful."

"You're right. I will."

Dee sat across from Alex first thing Monday morning with a laptop open. "Your meeting with Shelby is at nine tomorrow morning," Dee informed Alex. "Everything I could find on Casa Noel Properties is in your inbox, including the meeting minutes leading up to and including the vote."

"And Stone Holdings?"

"I'm still working on that."

Understandable, considering Alex had given Dee plenty of last-minute work to jump on the previous Friday.

"Once you've given that to me, call Max and see when he can come in for a meeting. Then rearrange my schedule to see that it works for both Chase and I." Alex would make the call herself, but Dee had a much better grasp of Alex's schedule than she did. "But before the board meeting on Friday."

"Yes, ma'am."

Alex clenched her jaw.

"How does my afternoon look?" Alex asked.

"You're clear after two, except for a scheduled meeting with Mr. Tanaka."

Alex scratched her memory to unearth the name. "Tokyo, right?"

"Yes."

That's right. Tanaka was in charge of the Stone Hotels in Japan.

"His employee file is in your inbox. You spoke with him briefly after Mr. Stone . . . your father's death. I've added last quarter's P&L statement."

Alex smiled, impressed with Dee's efficiency. "Perfect. Thank you. I believe we both have enough to keep us busy today."

Dee smirked, closed her laptop, and stood. "Oh, I almost forgot. Mr. Gatlin wanted a meeting with you this morning."

I bet he does.

"Do I have room?"

"Ten thirty or eleven fifteen," Dee said from memory.

Alex considered her options. "Eleven fifteen. And if anything comes up, bump him until tomorrow."

Dee offered a flat line of a smile. "Okay."

Alex opened the Casa Noel file Dee had pieced together the moment she was alone. Dee had summarized the board meeting minutes preceding the purchase of Casa Noel and color-coded the board members as to who was for or against the acquisition during that meeting.

Alex was thick into the pages of the report when Dee called from her desk.

"Yes?"

"There is an Ashraf Bakshai downstairs that is asking to see you. I told him your schedule was busy, but—"

A chill ran all the way up Alex's spine and snapped her head up. "Is Chase in?"

"No. We're not expecting him until ten."

What the hell could Ashraf want?

To apologize for his *help*?

Whatever it was, Alex wouldn't run from it.

"Tell security to escort him up. Only him. If there is someone with him, they need to stay in the lobby. Meet them at the elevator and bring Bakshai to my office. Don't close my office door. Give us ten minutes and then interrupt to tell me about my conference call I'm supposed to be on."

"You don't have a conference call."

Alex looked to the ceiling. "I don't wish to speak with Mr. Bakshai for more than ten minutes."

"Oh, okay."

"When he leaves, escort him to the elevators."

"Do you want security to wait for him?"

That would seem too obvious. "That won't be necessary."

Alex disconnected the call and closed the file in front of her.

Three minutes later, a soft rap of knuckles against her office door said they'd arrived.

Shoulders back, Alex stood. "Come in."

Dee entered first, quickly followed by Bakshai.

The man smiled as he crossed the room.

Alex rounded her desk and extended her hand. "Mr. Bakshai. I wasn't expecting to see you so soon."

He wore a tailor-made suit that Armani himself likely crafted. The man screamed money from head to foot. From the way he held himself to the shine on his shoes, which likely were never put away with so much as a speck of dust.

Bakshai's handshake was like the first. Firm-ish and lingering. "I was on my way to the airport and thought it was best to make this call in person."

Alex pulled free of the handshake and indicated the couch.

"Was there something that came up over the weekend where I can be of assistance?"

Bakshai's gaze skirted over the open door before he moved to the sofa.

He didn't speak right away, and when he did, he didn't answer her question. "You appeared to be in a rush when you left. I thought perhaps something had happened to prompt your hasty departure."

Alex took a seat opposite the man and tucked her legs to the side, crossing them at the ankles.

She considered keeping the narrative centered around her needing to attend a different event, then changed her mind. "I think we both know that the invitation was meant for businessmen like my late father. And that *my* presence was a surprise to you and your guests."

His eyes stayed locked on hers. The slight smile on his lips didn't waver. "That made you no less welcome."

His lack of denial wasn't expected.

"I doubt some of your guests would agree. However, I don't have time for gossip and have zero desire to interfere in the affairs of others. I'm much too busy for that."

"That doesn't make the knowledge any less valuable, Ms. Stone. Something your father and I knew very well."

She narrowed her gaze. "Is that why you host your event . . . annually? To gain knowledge?"

He sat back and considered her with a lift of his chin. "People in our position depend on every whisper to move forward."

"And here I thought it was hard work."

Bakshai let out a little chuckle. "That, too."

"Is this the reason you stopped by? To educate me on knowledge-gathering events?"

He shook his head. "No. That was an excuse. My associate was instructed to hand you my personal card as you were leaving. He told me he was unable to do so."

Alex didn't flinch. Which surprised even her. Was Bakshai testing her? To see if she'd mention the altercation or determine if she'd been scared? Was he weighing what it took to drive fear into her?

Or was the man simply covering his ass?

"Your *personal* card?" Alex wasn't happy with the unwelcome flutter in her gut. The one that told her this man was hell-bent on getting her alone.

Maybe allowing him into her office had been a bad idea.

Even with the door open.

Bakshai reached into the breast pocket of his suit and removed said card before extending it to her. "I'm having a gathering in Dubai next month and would love it if you could attend. There will be plenty of people there that would welcome your acquaintance. And before you ask . . . this event is much more gender equal."

"Your wife will be there?"

"There will be many wives there."

"You have more than one?" Alex asked with a lift of an eyebrow.

"The one I have costs me enough, I assure you."

Dee's voice stopped the conversation from continuing. "Excuse my interruption, Ms. Stone. Your conference call is on hold, waiting for you."

"Thank you, Dee."

Bakshai took the hint and stood. "I've taken up enough of your time."

Alex moved in step behind him.

He stopped at the door and turned. "My invitation is sincere, Ms. Stone. My guest list is very extensive, very . . . international. Much like your corporation."

Alex extended her hand again. "I'll consider it."

His handshake was much quicker this time. "Bring your brother . . . or brothers. Whatever you prefer."

How about a bodyguard? she instantly thought.

"Have your office call Dee. We'll see what we can do."

He placed a hand on her shoulder, smiled, and then turned to leave.

Alex closed the door and leaned on it. Fiddling with the card in her hand, she read his name and the international phone number.

No business logo, no corporate address.

Just his name and phone number.

Chapter Six

The gold backlit letters spelling out *Stone Enterprises* greeted Hawk as he stood in front of the reception desk in the lobby.

He'd debated making a phone call instead of a personal appearance most of the morning, then decided on the latter after reading one of the many articles about the new owners of Stone Enterprises.

Hawk found a motherlode of news articles about Alex and her brothers. Many of them indicating the fierce protectiveness of the siblings for each other.

Max was captured at a press conference challenging anyone who might think about threatening his sister. The man practically wore a T-shirt with the logo *fuck around and find out* printed on it.

Then there was Chase. The older brother who'd stood shoulder to shoulder with Alex in front of the cameras and then sheltered her when they exited into the chaos of cameras and microphones. Even the reporters wrote about the closeness of the Stone siblings and how rare and admirable it was in such a wealthy family.

Which was why Hawk stood in front of the receptionist now, requesting to see either Alex or Chase . . . maybe even both.

The debriefing Hawk and his team had combed over with Ed came to the same conclusion. Bakshai had to be hiding something, or the team wouldn't have been dismissed within twelve hours of showing up for the job.

If, at any time over the weekend, Alex Stone's name had ended up on the front page as a missing person, or worse, Hawk would have felt partially responsible for not following through.

This was his attempt at averting that future guilt should something happen.

"Can I help you?" the male receptionist asked.

"I'd like to speak with Alex Stone." Hawk took notice of the name on the receptionist's breast pocket. *Malcom.*

"Do you have an appointment?" the man asked, reaching to press numbers on his phone.

"I don't."

Malcom's hand fell away.

"Ms. Stone doesn't see—"

"I'll speak with Chase if she's not available."

Malcom furrowed his brow. "Do they know you?"

Hawk hesitated.

"You can make an appointment."

Hawk leaned forward. "Tell Ms. Stone Hawk Bronson is here. We spoke on Friday. She'll know what this is about."

When the man didn't move, Hawk looked directly at the dial pad and then back to him.

Resolved, Malcom tapped a few numbers and started talking.

"Hello, Dee. There is a Hawk Bronson in the lobby requesting to speak with Ms. Stone."

There was a pause.

"I told him that. If Mr. Stone is available . . . Okay."

A long pause ensued while Hawk looked around the lobby.

Unable to help himself, he took notice of the not-so-hidden cameras and the sensors that likely captured motion by alarms after hours. There were electronic passageways that required a badge to get through before reaching the elevators. More for a body count than security.

No metal detectors, no obvious security presence.

No real threat.

"Yes . . . okay."

Hawk turned back to Malcom. The man reached for something and then lifted a digital tablet. "Please put your full name and phone number in here."

Hawk did as requested.

Malcom scanned a visitor's badge and handed it to Hawk.

Then he tapped a few numbers on his phone. "I have another guest that needs an escort to Ms. Stone's office."

From a back room, a middle-aged man walked out wearing a jacket that had *Security* written on it. He wore a badge much like the one Hawk had been given. It was twisted in a way that Hawk couldn't see the man's name.

"This way," the security guard said.

Hawk walked behind the man and scanned his badge as they walked into the main building.

The elevator ride was quiet. Hawk purposely didn't try to chitchat with the man. Instead, he just observed and made several mental notes.

After a few stops on the way up, they were let out on the top floor, where Hawk was met by yet another receptionist.

This was a runway-ready blonde who smiled as Hawk stepped toward her.

"Mr. Bronson?" the blonde asked.

"Yes."

She stepped around her desk and thanked the guard, who caught the elevator before the door had a chance to close.

Hawk shook his head.

"Right this way."

The executive floor was impressive. Plenty of closed office spaces, tall ceilings, and what Hawk assumed were executive secretaries stationed outside of said closed office spaces. Lots of natural light, with live plants framing the windows.

"Is this your first time here, Mr. Bronson?" the woman walking him through the maze of the floor asked.

"It is."

"Welcome."

"Thank you."

A petite woman nearly jumped when Hawk approached what he assumed was Alex's office.

"Here we are," the blonde said.

Hawk thanked her with a smile.

The smaller, mousier woman knocked on the massive wooden doors before letting them both in.

Hawk stepped beyond the door, his gaze instantly settling on Alex.

The lush hair that had been pinned at her neck the Friday before was slicked back in a ponytail now. She wore a light cream-colored skirt with a matching blazer and heels with at least three inches.

The woman was just as beautiful as she'd been in an evening dress and moonlight.

"Hawk," she said his name with surprise. "Bronson, is it?"

"It is." He stepped fully into the office and noticed a man standing beyond the door.

"It's good to see you again. This is my brother Chase."

Chase approached and reached out a hand. "Apparently, I need to thank you. Alex was just catching me up on what happened on Friday."

"She *just* told you?" Hawk quizzed while shaking the man's hand.

"I've had a busy day and an even busier weekend," Alex said defensively. "And you just got here."

"How much did she tell you?" Hawk asked.

Chase opened his mouth.

Alex interrupted. "Wait. Before we get into that. How did you find me? I don't believe I gave you my last name."

"You were on the guest list."

She shook her head. "My father's name was on the guest list. Not mine."

True. "There were whispers around the room," Hawk conceded. "Your identity wasn't difficult to uncover."

Alex blew out a breath with what appeared to be resolve.

"Now . . . what exactly happened?" Chase directed his question to his sister.

Alex crossed the room. "Can I get you something to drink, Mr. Bronson?"

"Hawk. Mr. Bronson is my father. And I'm fine, thank you."

Alex pulled out what looked to be a sparkling water from a hidden office-size refrigerator. "Chase?"

"Stop stalling, Alex. What happened?"

She twisted off the cap and poured it into a crystal glass.

She walked to the sofa. "Sit, please."

Hawk took one of the chairs facing the door.

Alex cleared her throat. "As I was leaving the event, someone approached me in the parking lot. It scared me. Hawk was there and told the guy to leave."

Hawk saw the twitch in Chase's jaw.

"Someone?" Chase quizzed. His eyes moved to Hawk.

He stayed quiet.

"I think he was with Bakshai. He said something about making sure I got home."

Interesting. Alex wasn't telling the whole truth, and Chase knew it.

Alex met Hawk's gaze and let out a long-suffering sigh.

Chase pinched his brows together and kept moving his eyes between his sister and Hawk.

Alex growled. "Fine. It was Bakshai's guy. A bodyguard, I think? I don't know. He stood behind Ashraf the whole time I was talking to him."

"What did you and Bakshai discuss?"

"Nothing. The usual. *Thank you for inviting me. What was your relationship with our father?* He isn't a part of Stone Enterprises. We've never done business with him. Floyd told me at the last possible minute about the event. He said Dad went every year. That it was just a meet-and-greet cocktail party."

Hawk let out a small laugh.

"It wasn't that kind of event?" Chase asked.

"It was the kind of party Dad would have taken a mistress to. Pretty sure no one was there with their spouses. Everyone looked at me like I was a pariah."

"She's right about that," Hawk finally spoke.

Her eyes shot to him. "You noticed?"

He answered with a nod.

"I recognized a couple of faces and couldn't get out of there fast enough. Instead of calling my driver from the door, I walked into the lot, and that's when the guy approached."

Chase leaned forward. "Did he threaten you?"

Alex hesitated.

"God damn it, Alex. You should have called me."

"I *felt* threatened, but I can't exactly say he threatened me. It could have been a giant misunderstanding."

Chase turned to look at Hawk. "You were there. What do you think?"

"I wouldn't be here if I thought it was a misunderstanding."

"Why are you here?" Alex lowered her hands to her lap.

"Friday didn't sit well with me and my colleagues after you left. I wanted to follow up and make sure you were okay."

"Colleagues?"

"I work for a private security company. Bakshai's son hired me and my team to patrol the man's home and the event while his father was in town."

"You *work* for him?" Alex exclaimed.

"I never saw the man before Friday. When I asked if there was any threat, a true need for security, I was told *no*. That Ashraf Bakshai was a wealthy man that warranted extra security. Within an hour of the event starting, my team and I realized exactly what you did. The men wore wedding rings, the women they were with did not. When you stormed out, I followed. For all I knew, you were someone's disgruntled wife going into the parking lot to retrieve an Uzi."

"I'd be more worried about a machete," Chase said with a short laugh.

"I realized you were being followed by Bakshai's man and held back. Again, I wasn't sure if *you* were a threat."

"Do I look like a threat?"

Hawk swallowed, took a breath. "Beautiful women are often the most lethal threat."

The smile on Alex's face fell.

"Then I heard Bakshai's man talking, saw the fear in your eyes, and . . . I wasn't being paid to be a party to anyone being threatened or assaulted."

Chase sucked in a breath. "Did he hit you?"

She shook her head.

"He grabbed ahold of her arm," Hawk told Chase. "From my vantage point, it took a couple tugs to get loose. Later, Bakshai's son tried to deny anything wrong had taken place and then told us we could go home. Thirty-six hours early. Which is why I'm here," Hawk told them. "I don't know what this man's intentions truly were, but I didn't feel right not telling you to be careful. My boss and the team felt the same way."

Alex's expression went blank. Her fingers were tapping the side of the glass she held with uncontrollable nerves.

Alex stood and moved back to the bar. This time, she pulled out a bottle of wine and stared at it.

Then promptly put it back.

"Alex?"

She walked over to the door of the office and opened it. "Dee. Cancel my call to Tokyo. Make time later in the week with whatever Mr. Tanaka is able to do. Fix my schedule to accommodate him."

"Yes, ma'am."

The door closed again. Alex stared into nothing, the wheels clearly spinning in her head.

"Alex? Are you okay?" Chase asked.

She sucked in a breath. "Ashraf Bakshai was sitting right there at nine this morning." She pointed to where Chase sat.

"What?" Chase nearly yelled.

Hawk grappled with the information. "You let him in here?"

"I confronted him about what kind of party he threw but said nothing about the parking lot altercation. Nothing about Hawk. He told me that his *associate*—the bodyguard—was instructed to give me Bakshai's personal number but didn't get the chance. And then he invited me to Dubai next month for an influential gathering."

"The hell with that." Chase stood.

Hawk's mind spiraled. "Smart. Plausible deniability," he said aloud.

"What?"

"He gave you a reason for his associate to approach you in the parking lot. So, what his associate did from that point isn't on him. Then he casually extends an invitation. But not without first observing your inner workspace and how things operate here should he need to know."

"What does that mean?" Chase asked.

Hawk stood and moved to the large picture windows and looked at the street below. "Has Bakshai ever been in this office before?"

"Not that I know of," Alex answered.

"Do you have access to the cameras at the reception desk? Did you confirm his identity before he came up?"

Alex shook her head. "There are cameras but none that are linked in a way that we can view who is in the lobby. The reception desk is supposed to check IDs before letting people up."

"No one checked mine," Hawk informed her.

Alex and Chase exchanged glances.

"I gave them a name. They gave me a badge, and a 'security guard' escorted me. Unarmed security, I assume. And then, before I was even out of view of the elevators, your security was already on his way downstairs." He paused. "It could have been anyone walking up here."

To drive home his point, Hawk reached into the hidden holster on his waist and removed the 9 mm strapped there. He took out the magazine and emptied the chamber of the bullet sitting inside. He set the now-unarmed weapon on Alex's desk and reached for the knife he had strapped to his ankle. When he looked up, Alex and Chase were staring in silence.

Hawk approached Alex slowly, stood directly in front of her. "You have zero situational awareness, lady. Two men followed you out into a dark parking lot while you were looking in your purse. You knew damn well that the man who grabbed you and 'suggested he give you a ride' was employed by Bakshai, and yet you still let Bakshai into your office . . . alone. I assume. It's also worth mentioning, Bakshai was only supposed to be here for forty-eight hours. Which suggests he stayed in town to purposely confront you."

Alex's wide eyes stared into his, her nose flared with each breath she dragged into her lungs.

"Bakshai might be a wealthy man, but from the looks of this place and those thousand-dollar shoes you have on your feet, you could be just as big of a target. You might want to wake up."

Hawk noticed her tremble and stepped back.

He'd made his point. Hope he scared her enough to take some kind of action to keep herself safe.

He returned to the desk and went through the motions of loading his weapon and shoving it back where it belonged.

When he looked up, he saw Chase standing beside his sister, an arm on her shoulder.

Alex stared blankly out the window.

"I'll see you out," Chase offered.

Hawk hesitated in front of Alex. He wanted to apologize for putting that fear in her eyes but knew it wouldn't be sincere.

Their eyes met briefly; he saw a hint of moisture staring back at him.

"Thank you," she said in words so low he could barely hear her.

Her words broke a tear free.

Unable to stop himself, Hawk lifted the back of his finger to her cheek and brushed it away.

Her eyes flared and locked to his.

Hawk dropped his arm and followed Chase out the door.

They stopped at the secretary's desk. "Clear Alex's calendar for the rest of the day. Any future calls from Bakshai are funneled through me."

"Yes, Mr. Stone."

Hawk waited until they were alone in the elevator before speaking with Chase. "I was harsh."

"She needed to hear it." Chase sighed. "Alex is independent to a fault. Taking on this company has made it worse."

Hawk sensed that. "People feel safe in their workplace. More people around and all that. It's not always the case. At home we have locks, alarms, big dogs . . . or a baseball bat behind the door. Maybe a shotgun in the closet. Something tells me she doesn't have any of those things."

Chase huffed. "Alex lives in a glorified apartment. And not the kind with a doorman."

Hawk looked at Chase, horrified.

"Don't say it. I hear you. That needs to change. She's been dragging her feet to make a move, but this might just put a fire under her ass."

They stepped off the elevator and worked their way out the door.

Hawk handed Chase the Stone Enterprises access card and shook Chase's hand.

"I didn't want to say this in front of your sister, but I saw the way Bakshai looked at her. I've seen men in strip clubs be more discreet. I don't take Alex as someone that would reciprocate that with a married man his age."

Chase shook his head, whispered *fuck* under his breath.

Hawk reached into his back pocket and retrieved his wallet. He handed Chase one of his business cards. "If you need to get ahold of me."

"Thank you."

"Let's be clear, I'm not soliciting work here. I don't have to go around scaring people into believing they need paid security. Clients fall in our lap every day. Most of the time, after something shitty has happened."

"I appreciate that."

Hawk offered a nod, turned around, and left.

Chapter Seven

They say that the five stages of grief usually happen in order but that there is no real set amount of time that you spend in each stage.

While no one had actually died, Alex was keenly aware that something inside of her had. Alex was also fairly certain that she'd hijacked the anger phase at the beginning of the cycle and tagged it on at the end.

The denial phase was easy to see and had morphed into the bargaining phase with her brief thoughts of *Perhaps it was a misunderstanding* or *Maybe I was overreacting.* Anger was probably squeezed in there, but Alex couldn't see it. Or maybe the anger manifested by her gritting-her-teeth stage, where she refused to show any weakness and had let Bakshai walk into her office, knowing exactly what Hawk had said to her was true. Bakshai's thug had grabbed her arm. If you looked close enough, there were distinct marks on her arm to prove it. And he'd scared the ever-living shit out of her, as evidenced by the dropped phone and broken screen.

Then Hawk tossed her utter lack of self-preservation in her face, and her resolve pooled at her feet in a state of depression.

Depression she knew the half a bottle of wine . . . okay, three-quarters of a bottle of wine, didn't help later that night.

Her wine-soaked evening had her tossing over into acceptance before she fell asleep.

Something had to change.

Alex woke to a dry mouth that was spitting mad.

Hence the return of anger.

Anger was a much easier emotion to deal with than depression or hopelessness.

Alex was not hopeless, and she'd be damned if she let men like Bakshai make her feel that way.

The man thought he'd gotten away with whatever stunt he had tried to pull, but he was wrong.

Alex showed up at the office nearly an hour early. Long before any other employees on the executive floor arrived.

The security guard at the desk greeted her by name. Alex looked around the lobby of the building and tried to see it through Hawk's eyes. How difficult would it be to set up cameras that took pictures of everyone coming and going through the front door? And what would it take to be able to verify a person's identity with those images?

Stone Enterprises was not a high-risk building. They were not in the business of creating anything that needed safeguarding. They ran hotels and businesses around commerce and hospitality. They weren't inventing new technology that would revolutionize the world that someone would kill to patent first.

This building housed people, employees that didn't need to be walked through a metal detector on the daily. Hawk's demonstration was meant to show her that it could just as well have been Bakshai that yielded a weapon. Or more likely, his "associate."

Up on the executive floor, Alex directed her energy to the kitchen, where she started a pot of coffee. The lingering clouds from the wine the night before were still sticking and needed to shake free.

After waking up her computer, Alex opened all the blinds in her office, letting the entire wall of windows fill every corner of her office with light.

This had been her father's office. A place she'd never visited as a child.

It looked nothing like it had when she'd first taken over the space after his death. In the beginning, she and Chase shared the space but eventually settled on Chase taking over Floyd's office and converting a meeting room into Floyd's new space.

The artwork, office furniture, and paint on the walls had changed almost immediately. But as Alex saw now, it still wasn't enough. Her desk sat in the same space where her father's had been, and the sofa and chairs hadn't moved either. The office bar that she'd almost started drinking out of the day before had been repurposed, but it was basically the same.

It still felt masculine to her. And for reasons she couldn't put a finger on, she wanted . . . no, needed, that to change.

By seven thirty, she was on her second cup of coffee with her schedule for the next three months in front of her.

Her personal life wasn't reflected on her work calendar at all. Not that she had much of one, but her family did.

An auction event in the following month was the only personal day she was planning. Chances were, Chase would have a day or two that he'd be out of the office when escrow closed on their new house. Meetings with the construction team for his remodel, not to mention life with a newborn. Then there was the weekend of their ceremonial wedding celebration.

After their wedding, Chase was whisking Piper off to Paris and then Vienna.

Alex highlighted those weeks as an idea started to form.

After that, there was their mother and Gaylord's wedding in Texas. A Friday through Monday event that would likely make Chase and Piper's day look like a roadside carnival versus Disneyland and Epcot combined.

Chase and Piper would be back from their honeymoon with a couple of weeks in between all the marital bliss happening for her family.

Alex stared down at her color-coded mess of a schedule and tried to fit in time for things she had to get done.

A whispering of voices alerted Alex to the office coming to life.

Alex opened her office door to retrieve a third cup of coffee and came face to face with Dee, who jumped back with a squeal.

"You're here," Dee exclaimed.

"You okay?"

With a hand to her chest, Dee sucked air. "I didn't see you come in."

"I've been here for a while."

Alex locked in a stoic expression and glanced toward Chase's office. "Is Chase open for lunch today?"

Dee scurried behind her desk and clicked keys on her computer. "He's free after eleven thirty."

"Perfect."

In the staff kitchen, Alex used her personal cell phone and sent a group text to both her brothers.

I have something I want to run by the both of you. Can we meet for lunch today?

Chase responded first.

Sure.

Max took a minute. Where and what time?

Alex smiled at her phone.

∽

They'd hardly stepped out of line at the deli when Max started in. "Who the hell is this Bakshai guy?"

Alex glared at Chase. "You told him."

Chase just smiled. "You have two brothers now. I like sharing the burden."

"I am not a burden."

"Debatable," Chase teased.

Alex looked at Max. "My guess is Chase told you everything."

"It's a good thing Mr. Oil Man is out of the country," Max said.

The protective streak in Max was unmatched. He had no problem resorting to violence when it came to protecting his own. And since Max had grown up without a family, parents, or siblings, he defended his small circle at every turn.

"I don't think he'll be back anytime soon. And certainly not in our offices."

Their number was called at the deli counter. They retrieved their sandwiches and found a quiet corner table to talk.

"This whole thing with Bakshai had me thinking about our office setup."

"You mean *your* office setup," Max corrected before taking a large bite out of his pastrami on rye.

"You come in once in a while, and my guess is you'd be around more if you had your own space," Alex said.

Max gave a noncommittal shrug.

"I still feel like I'm a placeholder in Dad's life."

"Because you're in his office?" Chase asked.

"That and . . . events like Bakshai's. I've gone to every possible fundraiser, cocktail party, and black-tie event that's been thrown at me since stepping through those doors. I can't say that they were a complete waste of my time, our time," she corrected, glancing at Chase.

"Don't look at me, you took on most of that."

"My point . . . I've learned nearly nothing. Yeah, I can place faces to names of the people Dad knew, but to what end? This weekend I learned that Chester is shagging a girl that could be his daughter. What good is that knowledge going to do me?"

"Who is Chester?" Chase asked.

"The CFO at Regent. The ass. His wife is lovely. That might be something Bakshai would use to get something he wants, but that's not how any of us are going to run this company."

"Agreed," Max said.

"I'm tired of being discounted because I'm a woman. Do you know what I'm asked at every event I attend?" Alex asked both of them.

Chase shrugged.

Max shook his head.

"Where *you* are." She pointed a finger between them. " *'Where is your brother Chase?' 'Is Max here?'* I'm trying to fit into this patriarchal world where I feel the need to overcompensate for my sex. And why? We own the damn company."

"You're just figuring that out?" Max asked.

Alex smirked. "No. But I have had a serious case of imposter syndrome more times than I care to admit."

"You wouldn't know that to look at you, Alex," Max said.

"Thanks."

Chase lifted his sandwich to his mouth. "What does this have to do with the office setup?" he asked before taking a bite.

"I want to reclaim some space. Take a page out of the design Piper used for your office space downstairs. Stone Enterprises is us. The three of us. And before you say you don't want or need space," she said to Max, "keep in mind that your philanthropic work will require a team to pull off."

Max was in the process of starting a nonprofit organization to give troubled teens in the foster system a chance. Something he had personal experience with as a kid.

"Not to mention the outreach to our sister companies that you've been handling."

He nodded in agreement. "I'm still not wearing a tie."

Chase and Alex both smiled.

"By the way, are you coming to the board meeting on Friday?" Chase asked.

Max nodded. "I'll be there."

Alex refocused the two of them. "Chase, your office and mine are too cumbersome. Piper and Dee's space is too small, and in reality, we need more help. And a new role for Piper when she wants to come back."

Both Chase and Max were looking at her while they chewed.

"And . . . and Hawk was right. I should have met Bakshai where we were visible to everyone, not in a closed office. Although in my defense, I did leave the door open."

"A door you need to look around to see into," Chase pointed out.

She nodded. "I want to bust out the entire west end of the executive floor. We gut my office, your office, the space Dee is in now. We take out the conference room on that end, and we make the space ours. We wall off our section with doors that remain open during business hours but that can lock our space down after hours. Each of us will have equal space for our offices, with room for an executive assistant for each of us in the center of our wing. We take a large section and make a meeting space to mimic what is currently only in my office and add a small conference table for just us. A kitchen that only we can access. Everything is glass. The kind we can black out if we need privacy. Except for the living space. That stays visible." Alex visualized the space in her head with a smile.

"All this because of Bakshai?" Chase asked.

"It's more than that. I don't feel like myself at the office. When I walk out my doors and into the halls, I have this guard up." Alex reached for her neck and made a strangling motion. "People avoid me. They stop talking when I walk by or get in an elevator."

"They're afraid of you," Chase said, deadpan.

"I know. I want their respect. Not their fear." She paused. "Except for Floyd. He can fear me."

Max and Chase both laughed.

Alex leaned forward. "We've been at this for almost a year. A year where we didn't even know if we wanted this company and all it shoulders. But since none of us has so much as whispered to sell, I say we make it ours. We make this a family space within the walls of Stone Enterprises. A space where Kit can hang out and live his best dog life and Hailey can nap in times when she has to be close. And when she's older, she can do her homework in the conference room when she's grounded for sneaking out of the house to meet her boyfriend."

Chase dropped his hand to the table. "You just ruined my appetite."

Alex looked at her still unopened lunch. "What do you think? I'm sure Piper can help with the details. She loves design."

"You don't have to ask me," Max said. "It's your—"

"*Our.* It's *our* company and *our* space. We're going to be picking up Dad's pieces for a long time, so we might as well do it in a space that suits us."

"I think it sounds great."

"Anything to make your life easier," Max added.

Alex knew she could depend on the support of her brothers.

She opened her lunch and finally took a bite.

For the remainder of their meal, they talked about the board meeting agenda and what their collective stance was on everything that needed to be discussed.

஧

Chase stood with Max outside of the deli while Alex used the restroom.

"What was all that really about?" Max asked.

"You're picking up on Alex's quirks rather quickly."

"This is more than an office remodel."

Chase glanced around at the people walking by. "This Bakshai thing spooked her. And if you haven't noticed, our sister is a control freak. If there is one thing she hates more than being out of control, it's when a man is trying to control her."

"Like Bakshai."

"And our father from the grave. If Alex wanted to sell this building and buy another to clear our father's energy from the space, I'd support her. I'm surprised she hasn't altered her office more than she already has," Chase said.

Max glanced toward the door. "Has she lost weight? She hardly touched her lunch."

Chase nodded. "She's working too hard. We need to figure out a way to get her to delegate, or she's going to get sick."

"It needs to be her idea," Max pointed out.

Chase smiled. "Exactly."

Max sighed. "Me and my neck that is allergic to ties will come around more. I'm not sure how I can help outside of what I'm doing, but I can be there."

"I'd appreciate that. Especially when Piper and I are in Europe."

"You know what Alex really needs?" Max asked.

"A life beyond work?"

"I was going to say 'to get laid.'"

Chase winced. "Yeah, probably."

"Who is this Hawk guy?"

Chase blinked a couple of times. "Are you asking if he was interested in Alex?"

"I don't know. You met him. Was he a middle-aged, balding ex-cop or something?"

Huh . . . "No. He was our age." Now that Chase thought about it, Hawk had mentioned more than once that Alex was beautiful. And the way he looked at her before he walked away. "I don't know if Alex looked twice, though."

"Maybe because she was too distracted by the fact she could have been abducted and then preoccupied when learning she invited that threat into her space. If control is her thing, that would rattle her."

Chase placed a hand on Max's shoulder. "I think my wife needs to give Alex a call."

Alex smiled as she walked out of the deli while setting a pair of sunglasses on her nose. "That line was long."

Both Max and Chase turned to look at her.

"What? Do I have something on my face?" Alex swiped at her lips.

"Not at all."

They started toward the office.

"Max, I scheduled a meeting with our head of security, maybe you can help out with that," Chase said.

"I can—" Alex started.

"No," Chase interrupted. "You have enough to deal with. Max and I can correct some of the security issues Hawk mentioned."

"Do you think he'd be interested in giving the building a full assessment?" Max asked. "Seems like it's needed."

Damn, it was nice to have a partner in crime.

"Good idea," Chase said.

"Do you have his number?" Max asked.

"He gave his phone number to the reception desk downstairs," Alex told them.

"Really?" Maybe Alex had noticed the man.

"Yeah, I checked and then reminded Malcom that confirming identification isn't optional. I'm pretty sure Malcom thought I was going to fire him."

They slowed their pace as they approached the office building.

Alex turned and hugged Max. "Thanks for coming, and your support."

"Anytime."

Chase shook his brother's hand. "I'll let you know when this security meeting happens."

"The only day this week that isn't good is Thursday. Next week I'm completely open."

Chase's and Max's eyes caught, both of them had smirks on their faces.

Alex had zero clue.

Chapter Eight

"It could be a big contract."

Hawk sat in what was essentially a briefing room in Ed's office. PSS, or Private Security Specialists, ran out of an industrial unit in Sherman Oaks. The actual offices themselves weren't all that glamorous, nor did they need to be. There were times when a team assembled there for a briefing on an assignment, but most often, they were dispatched with a phone call. Ed had a small fleet of blacked-out Cadillac Escalades, Chevy Tahoes, and a few sedans. Most of which went home with whoever needed them. There was, however, room for half of Ed's vehicles in the industrial gated lot if they needed to be parked there.

Everyone licensed for armed escort used their own weapons. Though there were a half a dozen standbys of different calibers should the need arise.

The storage room held enough tech to make James Bond jealous. Everything imaginable for communications, spying devices for both visual and audible needs. Infrared night-vision equipment and, of course, bulletproof jackets that were high-tech enough to hide in plain sight.

Ed had built quite the business that thrived in the greater Los Angeles area.

"Do we know who runs their security now? Is it an outside service?" Ed asked.

Hawk had received a call from Chase Stone after business hours Tuesday night. He'd asked if Hawk could assess the security system in place at Stone Enterprises and consult on what needed to be updated or changed. *"I know you weren't there to drum up business, but finding people in this world that do the right thing even when they're not expecting a payoff is rare,"* he'd said.

Hawk agreed to bring it up with his boss and see what he could do.

"I'll get that information when I go in. *If* I go in."

"When did they say they wanted us?"

"Sometime next week is fine. A building as large as theirs will take some time, that is, if they want us to implement whatever it is we find."

A giant whiteboard took up one wall of the room. On it were the liquid schedules of employees like Hawk, Stevie, Charlie, Teach, and Carl. Whenever someone on payroll took up a permanent placement, they were taken off the board, and only when needed, one of the fluid team would fill in.

"Stone Enterprises is huge. If they like us at the office, it may spill out into their hotels and resorts," Ed mused.

Hawk hadn't even thought of that. "If that happens, I want a finder's fee."

"If that happens, I'll bring you in as a partner and you can run the entire Stone leg. And it will be a leg."

Hawk gave a fake shiver. "Management . . ."

"Don't pretend you don't like being in charge."

"Small teams, solo assignments, and only short durations. You know that's how I roll." And for good reason. Detachment, detachment, detachment.

Ed looked at the whiteboard and moved a few names around before adding a line item for Stone Enterprises on the bottom. "Start Wednesday. Take Stevie with you. See how much she can hack from the street. Let's see how weak their security really is. If you need more people, just yell."

∽

At the head of the table in the conference room, Alex addressed the board, with Chase on her right and Max on her left.

Directly behind her, Dee sat typing, jotting down the notes of the meeting in real time.

A little over half of the faces on the board were friendly, another quarter tipped toward the dislike side. Uncomfortable with Alex at the helm, and the Stone children in general. The remaining were downright hostile.

Melissa, their father's gold-digging disgruntled widow, only had a seat at the table because she'd bought out another hostile board member by the name of Paul Yarros. A man Chase, Max, and Alex were not unhappy to see go. But to be replaced with Melissa was a shock all of them had yet to get over.

The woman knew how to shop, spend time at the spa, and spread gossip. Running a business or weighing in on any of the executive decisions involving Stone Enterprises was not in her wheelhouse.

But the woman had been scorned after their father's death. She thought she deserved . . . and likely counted on, an inheritance that went above and beyond what she'd signed in a prenuptial agreement.

She'd been wrong.

The millions she did receive would have sufficed for any other person on the planet, but not a woman accustomed to luxury cars, estates all over the world, and a private jet to get you there.

The moment the reading of the will had been made public, Melissa had been seen talking with members of the board and executives across their industry.

Alex was still trying to figure out how she obtained the capital to have a place on the board, but so far, she had yet to learn anything.

So, Alex did what she had to do when looking at the young woman. She ignored her at all possible costs. Why pretend they liked each other? There wasn't a person at the table that would fall for that.

And then there was Floyd Gatlin. The second double face at the table. He might still have the title of vice president of Stone Enterprises, but the reality was, something would have to happen to Alex, Chase, and Max before the role of CEO was passed on to him.

And he hated that.

The fabricated late invite to the Bakshai reception was only one example of the antics the man used to unnerve Alex. He raised alarms before press conferences, did what he could to shake Alex's resolve during board meetings, and tried hard to bring doubt of her ability to run the company. While everyone knew the company was technically run by her and Chase, with Max as more of a silent partner who diverted his vote to his siblings, everyone knew where most of the responsibility lay.

On Alex.

"We have a lot to go over and would like to get you out of here before happy hour," Alex began. Considering it was ten in the morning, there were a few smiles at her attempt at humor. "Arthur, you have the floor."

Arthur Ripley, the CFO, presented the end-of-year statements that sat in a binder in front of each member.

Alex watched as Melissa opened the binder and turned the pages. The information on those pages wasn't for the public, and Alex couldn't help but wonder if Melissa would keep the data to herself.

A lot of numbers and noise were discussed and summarized before Arthur concluded, "Early numbers have proven that avoiding the acquisition of Starfield hotels was the right decision. There would have been a sharp decline in our overall growth had we taken that on, as Alex and Chase pointed out late last year."

"There's an awful lot of red in this report," Mrs. Monroe said from the far end of the table.

"Too much," Mr. Fergese added.

"Last year yielded more negative press affecting our market stability than it ever had in the past," Floyd stated.

"Press that couldn't be avoided," Chase said.

"We lost our CEO last year. This could have been worse," Mrs. Monroe stated.

Melissa made a breathy noise as if mentioning Aaron Stone's passing actually hurt her.

Alex glanced at Chase. Neither of them said a thing.

They'd been in the room when their father's will had been read. Like a scene from a soap opera, Melissa played the devastated widow until she realized it wasn't going to award her with more money. Then all that "grief" turned to anger.

"If we can just stay out of the negative side of the press, maybe we can see some growth this year," Floyd stated.

Alex looked past their vice president. "Unless you have more, Arthur, I'd like to address what will be needed for growth."

"I'm done."

Alex smiled. "As you all know, before coming here, my area of expertise lay in acquisitions and mergers. Four years ago, when the world was all but shut down and businesses were folding everywhere, fire sales of lucrative companies, or what was thought to be lucrative companies, happened everywhere. Which brings me to the Casa Noel hotel chain that we acquired during that time. At the time of that sale, I was on the team at Regent that Stone Enterprises bid against. I personally wasn't happy that Stone acquired it. Admittedly, when we took over as CEOs, Casa Noel was one of the first files I digested."

She paused and picked up the binder with Casa Noel's stats.

"Regent was in a much stronger position to turn Casa Noel around at that time, but this company kept driving the number higher, and Stone took it on. Even on sale, this was a bad decision."

"Fire sales, as you call it, is how a lot of growth has accumulated," Floyd said.

"Accumulating more just to have more acquires nothing but debt. And that is what Casa Noel is for us. There hasn't been one year where the company at large came into the black. They've been operating at a loss, and the only good that does is allow us the tax cut."

"Your father believed there was great potential with Casa Noel," another board member voiced from the end of the table.

"If we were flush with capital to turn them around, that could maybe happen. But we don't have it. Keeping the property and pumping profits into it from other areas isn't the answer."

"Are you suggesting we sell?" Mrs. Monroe asked.

Alex glanced at Chase. "Ultimately, yes."

"These properties sit on some of the best real estate in South America," Mr. Fergese pointed out.

"I remember Aaron talking about this. He believed it would turn a profit eventually and, if nothing else, could be sold later at a huge profit," Melissa said.

Alex's jaw actually dropped. If there was one thing Aaron Stone never did, it was discuss his company and business with the women in his life. Least of all Melissa.

"I remember that," Floyd said.

"Only it isn't turning a profit. And the only growth is property value over time. And depending on the month, that shifts," Alex said. "In order to recover what we spent on this, we're going to have to make Casa Noel look like it's growing to attract a buyer. And that will take some time. We send a team in and figure out how to cut ten percent of the operating expenses. That happens immediately. If we have to close down one of the hotels, or separate it as a single property and unload that, then that's what we do."

"That could put us in the black?" Arthur asked.

"Not long term, not with the value of the dollar in the countries where these hotels live."

"It feels like we're going backwards," Fergese said as he slumped against the back of his conference chair.

"You'll still get your distribution checks," Chase reminded him.

"I hate putting people out of work. And sadly, Max's report on Stone Holdings is going to show another weak link in Stone Enterprises . . ." Alex said with a sigh.

The door to the conference room opened, and Kira poked her head inside. "Uhm . . ."

Chase took to his feet and started to the door so that Alex could continue.

"We're closing down more?" Floyd asked.

"We expanded too fast," Alex pointed out. "It didn't go unnoticed. And the numbers don't lie."

Fergese, the man on his right, and Floyd all started debating at the same time.

Chase came back into the room and first whispered in Max's ear.

Max, who had looked rather bored, sat taller and gripped the edge of the table.

When Chase leaned close to Alex, she sensed something was wrong.

"Security is outside. There's a bomb threat for the building," Chase whispered.

Alex flinched.

"The authorities have been called. Security is setting off the fire alarm to evacuate the building to avoid panic."

Her heart started to pound.

Alex looked at Max and then Chase. "Is this real?"

Chase shrugged his shoulders and turned to the room. "I need everyone to stop talking."

Floyd was deep in a conversation with Arthur.

"We have a situation," Chase said again, right before the lights in the room flickered and the alarm in the building blasted.

Chapter Nine

Hawk heard his phone ringing over the sound of the shower spray.

He'd had a later-than-normal morning and a long session at the gym, resulting in a shower at 10:00 a.m.

He ignored the ringing and rinsed the soap from his hair. Whoever it was, he could call back.

Only the phone started up again as soon as the ringing had stopped.

He cut the water and grabbed a towel before reaching for his cell phone with his wet hand. "Yeah?"

"Are you watching the news?"

It was Ed.

"Midmorning? No. What's up."

"Seems our potential new clients are having a difficult day," Ed said.

"Stone?"

"Yeah."

Hawk held his phone between his ear and his shoulder as he tied the towel around his hips.

As soon as his hands were free, he put the call on speaker and walked to his living room.

"What's going on?" he asked. He turned his television on and flipped through the local channels.

"The bomb squad is surrounding the building."

Hawk zeroed in on the breaking news and turned up the volume.

A news reporter stood in front of the police line, talking into a camera. "Details have not yet been relayed to the press, but you can see by the police presence that the authorities are taking this threat very seriously."

The camera panned beyond the reporter and to the scene.

The bomb squad was out in full force, plenty of black-and-whites controlling the public, and what looked like hundreds of employees standing around staring.

The camera snagged on Alex and Chase Stone and the man the reporter was calling the *new brother*.

"How soon can you get there?" Ed asked.

"I'm on my way now."

"I'll meet you."

Hawk disconnected the call and stared at his television at the woman he couldn't quite keep away from.

∽

Sandwiched between her brothers, Alex stood by and watched as armored trucks, squad cars, the fire department, and at least one ambulance were all parked haphazardly in front of Stone Enterprises.

Once the alarm started to scream in the building, Alex's heart had lodged in her throat.

Much of the board didn't react at all to the flashing lights and noise. It wasn't until Chase yelled over the noise that it wasn't a drill that people started to move.

Seeing how so many employees didn't immediately find the nearest stairwell and start descending, Chase and Max ran through the executive floor, telling everyone to evacuate.

Alex couldn't believe how many people—women, mostly—were returning to their desks to retrieve their purses and jackets instead of leaving. Equally disturbing were those standing by the elevators.

Everyone who noticed Alex or her brothers gave them the same surprised look.

"It's not a drill," they said continually.

By the time their feet stepped outside of the building, there were already police cars skidding in and the sound of sirens coming to join the party. Only then did the employees truly figure out that something was happening.

"That isn't a fire truck," Mrs. Monroe said when an armored truck arrived with the words *Bomb Squad* printed on the side.

"There was a bomb threat," Alex told the older woman.

"Oh, my."

Floyd and Arthur stood close, watching along with Alex and her brothers.

The police started setting up a line and pushing everyone back.

"We need to see someone in charge," Max said to the first police officer that approached them.

"Do you work here?"

"We own the place," Max replied.

"As soon as we know more, we'll have someone talk to you."

Alex scanned the crowd in search of the in-house daytime security guard and couldn't see him.

Someone on a loudspeaker yelled up at the building and those still trickling out, "Please move beyond the police line as quickly as possible."

Busa, Chase's right hand in his company, slid in beside them. "What's going on?"

"All we know is there's a bomb threat."

Another fire truck rolled into the fray.

"Damn," Arthur exclaimed.

Almost as quickly as the sirens stopped, the media showed up.

Alex stared in silence as authorities ran around and employees huddled in clusters.

Within thirty minutes, Sarah had arrived and stood beside Max.

Chase had already called Piper to tell her they were all safe and asked that she call Vivian, Chase and Alex's mother, so she wouldn't worry.

Alex reached for her cell phone several times while they stood there waiting for answers. Only to remember that her cell was in her office with her purse.

"We should encourage everyone to go home," Alex concluded. "If there is a bomb in there . . . and it goes off . . ." She glanced around the huddled employees who stood by staring.

"Our cars are in the parking lot," Floyd stated.

Alex saw a motorized drone roll out from the back of the bomb squad truck.

"Call your wife or an Uber," Alex suggested.

Chase turned to the executive staff. "Spread out, tell everyone to leave. With any luck, this is all a false alarm and they can get their cars in the morning. If not, we have bigger problems."

For once, Floyd didn't argue.

Their senior staff moved through the mass of people, encouraging them to go home.

All the while, Alex stared at the unfolding scene. The thought of the building actually blowing up wasn't something she could picture. Was everyone out of the building?

Her heart rate and her breath were competing for who could race the fastest.

Dee approached from behind her. "Ms. Stone? Is there really a bomb?"

The poor woman looked like a panicked teen being pulled over for speeding as she stood there clutching her purse.

Alex attempted a reassuring smile. "We don't know yet."

"Oh, God."

Alex placed a hand on Dee's shoulder. "You should go home."

"My car is . . ."

"Someone will call you when it's safe to return to pick it up," Alex assured her.

Dee nodded several times. "Okay . . . yeah, okay. Be safe."

"It's probably nothing," Alex told her.

More nodding. "Right. Nothing."

Alex watched as Dee walked away.

From Dee's direction, two men approached behind dark sunglasses. *Hawk.*

He passed through the crowd with a confidence no one around them had. Tall, broad shoulders . . . a jacket that she knew likely hid a firearm. The sunglasses may have hidden his eyes, but she felt his stare directly on her.

Alex blew out a breath as an unexpected wave of relief washed over her.

Hawk removed his sunglasses.

"Hi," she said on a breath.

Their eyes met. "Are you okay?" he asked.

She nodded, shook her head, then nodded again.

Chase turned around at that moment and realized Hawk was there.

"I saw the news," he told them.

Chase immediately reached to shake Hawk's hand. "Hawk. Good to see you."

"Chase, Alex, this is Ed Vargas. He runs the company I work for."

Chase moved to shake Ed's hand.

"This is Max, our brother, and Sarah."

More handshakes.

"A pleasure to meet you. Sorry it's under these circumstances," Ed said.

"Do we know what's going on?" Hawk asked.

"No," Chase told him. "Nothing more than there is a bomb threat. No one has talked to us yet."

Ed and Hawk looked at each other.

Ed hooked his sunglasses on an inside pocket of his jacket. "I'll get some answers." And then, just like that, he ducked under the police tape and walked straight toward the uniformed police officers.

"Are they going to let him . . ." Alex's words trailed off when Ed moved from the police officers to those who looked to be in charge of the people operating the drone that was rolling toward the building.

"You only have to act like you belong and people won't question you," Hawk said.

Sarah moved to Alex's side and laced her arm through Alex's. "It's going to be okay."

Alex looked toward the building. "I know." At least she was trying to convince herself that it would be.

"Do you have any idea who could be behind this?" Hawk asked.

Alex shook her head.

"No," Chase said.

"Anyone fired lately, someone with a grudge?"

No sooner did Hawk voice the question than Floyd walked back into their circle. "Any answers yet?"

"We're working on it," Max told him.

Floyd looked up at Hawk.

Chase made the introductions. "Floyd is our vice president. Hawk Bronson is being brought in to assess our security measures. The plan was to meet with him next Wednesday."

"I wouldn't think we needed that a few hours ago," Floyd said.

"Alex and I had a few concerns."

"Where is the building security guard?" Hawk asked.

"No idea. We haven't seen him."

Was that an eye roll?

"Floyd, how long has Rodney worked security in the building?" Chase asked.

Floyd shrugged. "I don't know. Couple years, maybe. I never really see the man."

Hawk looked over the heads of those still standing around. "Who here would know?"

"Piper's not here, but she would," Alex said.

"Who is Piper?"

"My wife," Chase told him. "She was our late father's executive assistant before he died. I'll give her a call."

Chase pulled his phone from his pocket and stepped away.

Max slid into Chase's space. "Do you have any experience with this type of incident?" he asked Hawk.

"Yes."

"Is this response normal?" Alex asked. "All these resources?"

"When the threat is viable, yes."

"Viable?"

"Good reason to believe the threat is real," Hawk clarified.

Alex shivered.

Sarah put her hand on Alex's arm. "It'll be okay."

"I just hope everyone got out of the building."

Chase walked up from behind them. "Rodney has worked here for five or six years. Piper said that the building security only consisted of an alarm system and cameras before then."

"Did something happen to prompt a change?" Hawk asked.

Alex looked to Floyd, the only person standing there who had worked in the building at that time.

"I don't recall anything. Certainly not this. I would have remembered a bomb threat," Floyd said.

"Piper said the same thing. There wasn't any discussion about the change, but our dad requested the security be increased and authorized the hiring of guards."

Hawk narrowed his eyes.

Alex wanted to ask what he was thinking but saw Ed walking toward them.

"Well?" Hawk asked.

"They said 911 got the call. It came from inside the building."

Alex grasped Sarah's arm.

"Woman. But there is reason to believe it was AI generated."

"What did they say?" Max asked.

Ed looked at Hawk.

They both stayed silent.

"It's something bad, right?" Alex asked.

"We'll be able to hear the recording later. Suffice to say there was enough said to bring out the whole circus," Ed said.

Sarah straightened her spine. "Shit. Here they come."

Hawk, Ed, Chase, and Max all turned around.

Two reporters with cameramen headed straight toward them.

"Mr. Stone, Ms. Stone, what can you tell us—"

Alex shook her head.

Hawk turned and faced the media.

Chase lifted a hand. "We don't have anything at this time."

Floyd pointed to the north end of the building. "Is that Rodney?"

Alex peered closer. "Yes."

Rodney was walking away from the building, pushing a wheelchair with a woman in it.

The reporters swung their cameras in Rodney's direction.

"Who is that with him?"

Floyd spoke up. "I don't know her name. I think she's in Marketing."

"He must have stayed back to get her out," Max said.

Alex seemed to remember seeing an employee in a wheelchair but hadn't taken the opportunity to know who she was. "She must be scared half to death."

The media started toward the guard.

Max pushed in front of them. "Give them a minute."

Sarah dislodged herself from Alex's side and joined Max. "If they want to talk, we'll wave you over," she told the reporters. Considering Sarah was once a tabloid reporter, she knew what to say to hold back the media.

Hawk lowered his voice and said, "I wasn't impressed with Rodney when I was here last week. This makes up for it."

The movement of police vehicles and fire trucks brought Alex's attention back to the building.

"What's going on?"

Hawk moved close to her side. "They must have found something?"

Alex's gaze darted to where Hawk was staring.

A person in a bomb protection suit stood outside the armored vehicle.

Hawk placed a hand on her shoulder. "We need to move farther back."

Chapter Ten

Hawk stood with the Stone family across the street from the building that housed their business headquarters; they'd been there for hours.

The media, lookie-loos, and a scattering of employees gawked from the sidelines. But the majority of people had left the immediate area once the police line had been expanded.

As the scene in front of them unfolded, Hawk kept a close eye on Alex.

Once the initial shock began to fade, and perhaps the adrenaline with it, Alex became painfully silent.

When the anticipated explosion didn't occur and the movement and vacating of authorized vehicles started to happen, Hawk felt his own shoulders relax.

The incident commander pulled the Stone family aside and away from the numerous reporters waiting for a statement.

"This is Commander Owens," Ed introduced the man.

After a few handshakes, the commander launched into what they'd found.

"Did you find a bomb?" Alex asked straightaway.

"We found what someone wanted us to believe was a bomb," Owens said.

Hawk saw Alex's chin lift and stiffen.

"As I told Mr. Vargas, a 911 operator received a call approximately five minutes before we called for the evacuation of your building."

"The caller must have been very convincing," Hawk said.

"Why do you say that?" Chase asked.

"Because evacuating the building isn't the first thing done."

"He's right," Owens stated. "Evacuations come with their own risks. If there is a bomb, it could be anywhere. Scared and running civilians could accidentally set the thing off if it was, say, in a stairwell or behind a door. The caller informed the operator that the security cameras in the garage were tampered with before the building opened for business. But that in-house security wouldn't have detected the problem."

"How?"

"We're not sure yet. But your security guard was able to confirm that the cameras appeared to be live, but the time stamp didn't match up. We knew then the caller wasn't playing."

"But the bomb wasn't real," Max said.

"The threat was. There was enough reason to believe there was an explosive inside the backpack we found. A timer, wires . . . a clay substance."

"C-4?" Hawk asked.

Owens shook his head. "Play-Doh. None of it was hooked up."

Chase blew out a breath. "A sick joke?"

"Sick, yes. Joke, no. There was a typed note inside the bag. It said, 'Next time I won't call.'"

Alex leaned forward. "They're just trying to scare us? Why?"

"Good question. Answering that will bring us closer to finding out who was behind it. We have a lot of questions." Owens looked directly at Alex. "Most of which will start with you."

Alex drew back. "Me? Why?"

Hawk looked between Owens and Alex and back again.

"The backpack was found under your car."

"Mine?" Alex's eyes grew wide.

"That could be random," Sarah said.

Hawk immediately rejected the thought.

"These things are seldom random," Owens voiced Hawk's exact thoughts. "The threat was for the building, but it was under your car."

"I'd like to get a statement, ask some questions, and have you listen to the 911 tape. Maybe you can shed some light on the caller," Owens told them.

"That's fine. We'll cooperate in any way we can. Would it be possible to answer these questions at our family home?" Chase asked before looking over his shoulders at the swarming media. "We might be able to avoid some of this chaos there."

"Good idea," Max said.

"Give me about an hour, I'll meet you there," Owens agreed before writing down the address of the Beverly Hills home and walking away.

Hawk turned to Chase. "If it's okay with you, I'd like to hear the recordings."

"Of course." Chase turned to his sister. "Alex, why don't you ride with Hawk. Show him how to get there."

Alex blinked several times and shook her head as if she were displacing cobwebs. "That's fine."

As the six of them started to move in different directions, Hawk motioned for Alex to follow. "I'm over here."

For a second, Alex looked around her like she was forgetting something.

"What is it?"

"It's weird. I don't have my purse, or laptop, phone . . ." She glanced up at the building.

"You'll be able to get back in by morning."

She nodded and moved alongside him to his car. Avoiding the media that swung their cameras toward her.

Inside, Hawk dialed Ed to fill him in.

"Yeah?" Ed answered.

"I'm going with the family."

"Good idea. I'll stay here. Find out if they want me to bring in a team after the police are done."

"Plan on it," Hawk suggested.

"Keep me informed," Ed said and disconnected the call.

Hawk glanced at Alex, who leaned her head back and closed her eyes.

"You okay?"

She rolled her head to the side, those dark eyes looked at him, and a faint smile found her lips. "The shock is starting to wear off. As soon as I start getting pissed, you'll know I'm fine."

He huffed a laugh. "I like that."

Hawk put the car in drive and inched out of the traffic and crowd that still looked on.

"Owens is going to quiz everyone on who they think could have done this. You might want to give the question some thought before he comes."

"I'm not sure. There were plenty of people that didn't care for the fact that our father left us the company. Floyd . . ."

"Your vice president?"

Alex nodded. "He wanted the CEO chair. We've been collecting reasons for letting him go. But . . ." She paused. "He wouldn't have set off a bomb. He was in the building, so that doesn't pan out."

"If he is involved, he knew the bomb wasn't real."

"I guess. There's Melissa. We were in the middle of a board meeting, and she was there, too."

"Who is she?" Hawk asked.

"My father's widow. She and I are basically the same age. Dad didn't leave her any more money than what their prenuptial stated."

"Then why was she there?"

Alex shifted in her seat. "She bought out shares from another unhappy board member, Paul Yarros. Only none of us know where or how she came up with the capital for that. Paul is no longer on the board, so I somehow doubt he is on the list of suspects."

"Was there anyone from the board missing today?"

"No. Everyone was there."

"What about enemies of your father?"

"Who knows. One of the reasons I've gone out of my way to attend parties like Bakshai's is to learn who liked and didn't like our father. I'm sure he made enemies. The man was an asshole."

Hawk did a double take.

Alex laughed. "Trust me. You might be walking into what was once his estate, but those of us in it hold no love for the man that built his empire."

Hawk was quiet for a moment. "Mind if I ask why?"

"The short version . . . he wasn't a father. We were furniture when he and our mother were still married. Something to be seen once in a while, but never really appreciated. When my parents split, Mom received what was written in their prenuptial, which also had a cap on what she could ask for child support. It wasn't a lot."

"Define *a lot*?"

"We weren't poor. But it was nothing like we have now. Chase and I grew up in a typical neighborhood. Had the family road-trip vacations. We were both afforded college by our father. Somehow, not paying for our education shed a dark light on him." Alex offered a sarcastic laugh. "For a short time after the divorce, Chase and I were expected to visit him on weekends, time in the summer. Only we'd go to the estate, and Dad would be in Europe, or the Maldives . . . wherever he wanted to go. He'd hire nannies to care for us. Mom put a stop to that right away and took full custody. Dad never challenged her."

"Wow."

"That's only my and Chase's story. He abandoned Max altogether."

Hawk turned off the freeway and started up into Beverly Hills. "I looked up Max's story after we met. Sounds like your father was an ass."

"We truly never imagined he'd leave the estate to us. Neither one of us wanted it."

"Really?" Hawk asked.

Alex smirked and shook her head. "It is a lot of money, though."

That made Hawk laugh. "Understatement."

"Yeah, well . . . if it wasn't for our desire to find Max, we might have actually walked away from it all. But then we started taking on the company. People there were scared they were losing their jobs. The company CEO dies, business and stock are all over the place. We ended up roped in. We could have sold it all, but then what? I'm too young to not have an occupation, and as Max once said, it was too early to become an alcoholic, sitting around doing nothing all day. And none of us golf."

"Golf?"

She grinned. "It's an inside joke."

Hawk was caught up in her smile when the car behind him hit their horn.

"Past the stop sign, then veer right," she told him once Hawk turned his attention back to the road.

The estates of Beverly Hills were mostly hidden by huge gates and tall fences made of stone and often laced with shrubs. The farther up in the hills he drove, the less the houses could be seen from the street. "We're the next gate on the right."

Hawk slowed his car and pulled into the short drive before the iron gates.

Alex told him the key code to open them, and Hawk drove into a different world.

The tree-lined drive opened into a sprawling entry, complete with a fountain and ornamental statues that only the rich spent money on.

The house, if you could call it a house, was something only a millionaire could own. Rounded stairway entering the home, with columns, massive windows, and two stories of who only knew how many square feet. To the right of the home was a freestanding garage, where one of the many doors was open, and an SUV had been parked in front of it.

Hawk blew out a whistle.

"Like I said, it's a lot of money."

"Who lives here?"

"Max and Sarah. Chase and I didn't want it. Technically, it belongs to all of us. There have been times we've crashed for a weekend. Mainly when the press was hounding us."

Hawk put the car in park and cut the engine.

"Too many memories of your father?" Hawk couldn't help but wonder how deep Alex's daddy issues were.

"At first. It's easier now. He always had more staff than family here. After his death, the opposite is true. The home has its advantages. Gates, cameras, space that's hard to find in the city."

Hawk put his hand on the door handle. "You had me at gates and cameras."

Alex laughed again and then paused before exiting the car. "Thank you," she said.

"For what?"

"Taking my mind off of today. For coming. You didn't have to do that."

"Well—"

"You didn't," she interrupted. "Security threats and bombs are way out of our wheelhouse. Seeing you there . . . it was a relief."

Hawk tilted his head to the side and stared. "I'm glad I can help."

Her eyes narrowed ever so slightly before she pushed her way out of the car.

Chapter Eleven

Never in a million years had Alex ever imagined she'd feel at ease descending the grand staircase in what was once her father's estate.

But that was exactly what she felt now.

Soon after arriving at the estate, Alex made her way to the guest room she claimed as hers when she stayed in the home. It was in the opposite direction of the primary bedrooms and likely had never even seen her father's feet in it. At least that was her reasoning for choosing the room the first time she had to stay the night.

The spacious guest room had its own bathroom and a small sitting area on one side. The balcony faced the front of the house, unlike the rooms that Max and Sarah used, which faced the backyard, pool, and gardens.

Alex had a handful of clothing items to get her through, including two bathing suits that she only ever used there.

Alex took a few minutes of solitude and rinsed off in the shower. That alone helped shed some of the day's weight.

Wearing a comfortable pair of jeans, a sweatshirt, and tennis shoes, she pulled her now-loose hair over one shoulder before joining her family in the large living room in the very center of the estate.

In the time it had taken Alex to shower and change, Piper had arrived and brought Alex's niece, Hailey, and the ever-protective rottweiler named Kitty.

"You look more relaxed," Sarah said to Alex.

"I'll get there faster if someone can pour me a glass of that wine," she hinted to Chase, who was holding a bottle and filling a glass.

"No problem."

Alex crossed to her brother first, accepted the wine, and then turned toward her niece in Piper's arms.

"Where is Max?"

"Showing Hawk around. Giving him a rundown of the security system."

Alex took her first taste of the wine and let it roll over her tongue. "From Dad's private collection?"

"Of course," Chase said with a grin.

Their father had collected more wine than he consumed. Bottles worth thousands, sometimes tens of thousands of dollars. All sitting in a wine cellar, rotting, instead of being enjoyed.

"And I can finally have some," Piper said when Chase handed her a glass as well.

Alex sat beside her sister-in-law, took a second sip, and then put her glass aside. "I get to hold her."

"Be my guest," Piper offered.

"I can't believe how big she's getting." Alex lifted Hailey from Piper's lap and smiled down at her expressive, wide eyes. "Hi, sweetie," she said in a high-pitched voice. "Did you miss your auntie Alex?"

Hailey cooed and stuck her fist in her mouth.

"I spoke with Mom," Chase said. "They saw the news. Gaylord wanted to fly them in tonight—"

"That's not necessary."

"I told her that. But you know Mom."

Alex did. Vivian was the most dedicated mother on the planet. She'd always put Alex and Chase first and now, by extension, Piper, Hailey, Max, and Sarah. Considering that Max was a product of an affair Aaron had been involved in during his marriage to their mother, that was saying something. Not once did Vivian hold any ill will or thoughts toward Max. And in fact, she had embraced him as one of the family.

"They're coming in the morning," Chase told her. "She only agreed to that when I told her we'd likely all stay here tonight."

Alex looked up from her niece and considered what Chase was suggesting. Alex had no real desire to deny the need. The thought of returning to her place and wondering who was walking down the hall of the condominium complex made her shiver.

"Probably a good idea," Alex said.

The phone in the house rang in the way that indicated someone was at the gate of the mansion.

Sarah moved to answer it.

"Owens?" Alex looked at Chase.

He shrugged.

"Come in," Sarah said into the receiver. "It's Nick."

"Do you hear that? It's your crazy Uncle Nick." Alex lifted Hailey a little higher in her lap.

Soon after, Nick bounced into the house, past the foyer, and right into the grand living room. "I'm glad to see no one is blown to pieces," he said to the crowded room.

"Subtle, Nick," Chase told him.

Nick leaned in and kissed Sarah's cheek, then did the same to Piper, who had moved from the couch to greet him. "How is everyone?"

"We're doing okay."

Nick took a seat next to Alex and put his arm around her. "I came as soon as I could. Well, not when you were all standing around the building that wanted to go boom. Why on earth were you even there?"

"It didn't feel right to leave," Chase told him.

Alex agreed.

"How did you know that we came here?" Sarah asked.

Nick looked at Sarah with a tiny roll of his eyes. "I have this one on GPS. Someone needs to keep an eye on her when she's out on a date."

It was Alex's turn to roll an eye. "Because *that's* a thing."

"The news said they didn't find a bomb." Nick looked around as if he wanted someone to confirm or deny.

"Not a bomb. But they did find a bag."

Nick put a hand on his chest. "A warning? A joke?"

"We don't know," Alex said.

Voices from the back of the house moved closer.

Max and Hawk came into view.

Hawk found her eyes first, then he looked at Nick.

"Who is that?" Nick whispered with a little growl in the back of his throat.

Alex nudged her friend's knee to snap him out of the flirty phase.

Kit lifted his head off his paws, sniffed the air, and put his head back down.

"Apparently, we have a state-of-the-art system," Max told Chase as they moved deeper into the room.

"Except there isn't live monitoring of the cameras," Hawk said.

"Is that really necessary?" Sarah asked.

Nick leaned closer to Alex. "Hawk? The guy from the parking lot?" he whispered.

Alex nodded.

"Yum."

"Stop it," she barked in a sharp whisper.

Although hearing Nick's assessment had her taking another look at the man.

Hawk was a bit yummy. Taller by at least two more inches when she was in heels, which was every time she'd seen him. The man was not afraid of working out, his broad shoulders filled out his shirt and casual jacket. A jacket that hid a gun.

Were guns sexy?

She shook her head and refocused on the conversation.

". . . should at least be an option," Hawk was saying.

His jaw was strong, but not so etched it looked like a cartoon character. And stern. Had she seen the man smile? Alex pulled her thoughts inward and attempted to recall Hawk's smile.

"What do you think, Alex?"

Her eyes snapped to Chase. *Think about what?* "I'm sorry. My mind was . . ."

Nick chuckled.

Hailey decided that was a great moment to let out a cry. Not an "I need something" one but a "No one is looking at me" cry.

"Hailey agrees," Piper said.

Then Alex saw it. Hawk's smile. Well, not so much a smile as a hint of amusement. A lift of one corner of his lips, a dance of light in his eyes. It was . . . unnerving.

Sarah and Piper got up and walked out of the room. For what, Alex hadn't been paying attention to know.

Chase was saying something to Max.

And Hawk was staring directly at her.

His amusement waned, and the light in his gaze turned smoky and thick.

A shiver inched up the back of Alex's neck, her mouth was suddenly dry.

The phone rang, breaking the spell.

Alex pulled her eyes away and looked to Hailey.

At the same time, Hawk physically turned to face Chase.

Nick made a humming noise in the back of his throat.

"Stop," Alex muttered.

"Not on your life, darlin'." Pure entertainment filled Nick's face.

Alex lifted Hailey off her lap and placed her on Nick's. As she did, Alex took Nick's wine from his hand and set it aside. "Focus on the baby."

Nick made kissy lips to Hailey. "I can multitask . . . can't I, Hailey?"

"It's Owens," Max announced.

For a moment, Alex had completely forgotten why they were all assembled at the estate in the first place.

It all came back to her in a rush.

She reached for her wine and lifted herself off the sofa.

By the time Owens made it inside, Alex stood by the wall of windows that looked out at the back garden and the fading sun.

Owens had another man with him and quickly made the introductions.

"This is Detective Fitzpatrick. You'll likely see more of him than me moving forward. Unless our perpetrator decides to try this again," Owens announced.

The detective made the rounds, shaking hands.

"Thank you for doing this here," Chase said.

"Not a problem. Looks like a few of the news vans made it to the gate."

Max shook his head. "Nothing new about that."

Owens glanced around. "Your family has attracted a lot of media in the past year."

"I blame Dad," Alex said.

"The man is dead," Nick countered.

"Still on him." She lifted one finger in the air. "He dies." Another finger up. "He leaves everything to us." A third finger. "He kept Max a secret, and God knew that was going to be front-page news once the story broke. And now this."

"You blame him for dying?" Nick said.

"I blame him for everything." And she did. "All the bad press anyway." And everything else, but it felt childish to say out loud.

Piper and Sarah returned.

More introductions were made.

"Please, have a seat," Max encouraged.

Alex stayed by her perch at the window. Everyone else in the room took a seat except Hawk, who mirrored her stance as he leaned against one of the sofas.

"This is quite the place," Fitzpatrick said as he glanced around the room.

Chase, Max, and Alex all looked at each other.

Finally, Alex said, "It was inherited. Saying *thank you* feels strange. None of us were responsible for picking it out, decorating it . . . even the wine wasn't our choice." She tilted the glass to them before taking another drink.

The detective removed a pad of paper and a pen from the inside of his jacket.

"Who would be angry about that?" Fitzpatrick asked.

Chase, Piper, and Alex all said, "Melissa." At the same time.

"Melissa . . . ?"

"Stone. Our father's wife. Widow, that is," Chase said.

"Enough to put a fake bomb under your car, Miss Stone?"

She let the *Miss* go and focused on what was really important. "Angry enough? Yes. Smart enough? No."

Everyone in the room that knew Melissa murmured their agreement.

Sarah disagreed. "I wouldn't dismiss her. The woman figured out a way to get a seat on the board."

Nick looked at Alex. "She has a point."

"Melissa was at the office today and in the board meeting when we got the call."

"And our caller knew the bomb wasn't real. We can't eliminate anyone at Stone Enterprises today. In fact, an employee . . . or board member had direct access to the garage. And likely wouldn't have been questioned if they'd been seen," Fitzpatrick said.

"But the cameras were tampered with, right?" Max asked.

"Right."

Max shook his head. "According to the housekeeper here, Melissa didn't have the technical skills to turn on Netflix, let alone manipulate video footage on a security tape."

Alex pointed at Max. "Exactly."

"Did anyone see Melissa after the building was evacuated?" Owens asked.

Alex shook her head.

"It was chaos. I only remember seeing one person from the board right outside the building, but they didn't stick around."

Owens sat forward in his seat. "You mentioned Floyd Gatlin."

"He doesn't like us . . . and we don't like him," Alex said point-blank.

"Why does he still work for you, then?" Owens asked.

Alex noticed Hawk's attention intensify.

"He does his job," Chase said. "But that's not the only reason."

"I'd say there are two reasons why he is still there. Chase and I have been trying to keep the upset at Stone Enterprises to a minimum this year. And dismissing the vice president without solid grounds opens us up for a suit."

"Then there is the desire to keep your enemies close to see what they're doing," Piper added.

"You do feel he's an enemy?" Fitzpatrick asked.

Chase nodded. "But he did stick around today. In fact, he appeared more humble than I've ever seen him, and concerned. Maybe even a little scared."

"I have to agree," Alex added.

"Who else?"

"Paul Yarros was our most vocal member on the board. The man didn't agree with any of our decisions," Alex said.

"He is the one that sold his shares to Melissa. At the same time, he bought a hotel chain that we were passing on."

"Is this hotel competition?" Owens asked.

Alex scoffed.

"Not to sound pompous, but no," Chase told him.

"Anyone else?"

Alex couldn't think of anyone.

The others shook their heads.

Owens removed a cell phone from his pocket. "Maybe the caller will spark something."

He set the phone on the table.

Alex moved closer.

Owens pressed play.

"911, what's your emergency?"

"There's a bomb in the Stone Enterprises headquarters. Don't bother with security footage. I've taken care of that."

Alex shook her head and placed the glass of wine on the table.

"There's a bomb?" the operator asked.

"More than one Stone belongs in the family plot."

"Where is the b—"

"Tick, tock. Tick, tock."

That voice . . . it was . . .

"Where—"

Alex's hands started to shake.

"Tick, tock. Tick, tock. Any death is on her hands. Evacuate the building. Let her know I'm watching."

The call disconnected.

Alex's hand moved to her throat.

Everyone's eyes were on her.

Kit lifted his head, and a low growl escaped his gut.

"The caller sounded like you," Piper whispered.

"Exactly like you," Chase said.

Kit let out a bark.

Alex looked over at Hawk. "How is that possible?"

"AI," Hawk said slowly.

"But my voice."

Owens put his phone away. "You said yourself that you've had your share of the media recording you. Artificial Intelligence has quickly become a scammer's wet dream. If a computer has enough recordings of a person, they can type in what they want to hear, and someone else's voice speaks it."

Hawk broke his eye contact with her. "The caller never answered a question."

"Right," Fitzpatrick said.

"What does that mean?" Alex asked.

"It means the caller may not have been on the line. They could have recorded that, anticipating what the 911 operator was going to do and say. Leaving a brief pause that makes you think someone is there, but they aren't."

"And the call came from inside the building?" Chase asked.

"Or a recording from inside. That's going to take time to figure out," Owens told Alex. "We're focusing on the bag under your car."

"We'd like to talk with your Human Resources Department on Monday. Learn if there are any newly let-go employees. Talk to your Maintenance Department, learn who was on-site that normally wouldn't be. Electric company, repairmen," Fitzpatrick informed them.

"Of course. We'll cooperate in any way we can," Chase told them.

Alex walked back over to the wall of windows.

The backyard was illuminated by the lit pathways and sconces on the walls. Her eyes caught on a tree where the trunk was bright and the branches had an orange glow. Her eyes saw the landscape, but her head was still in the conversation. "When will we be able to get back into the building? Our employees will want to retrieve their cars . . . their things. I'm sure I'm not the only one that left their purse behind."

"By morning."

"We'll need to coordinate this," Piper said. "We don't need someone going around stealing purses."

"We have security cameras," Chase said.

"Lot of good those did," Alex scoffed.

Fitzpatrick and Owens both stood.

The others followed.

Piper took a sleeping Hailey from Nick's arms. "I'll put her down."

Alex stood rooted in place while the authorities said their goodbyes and left.

Nick moved to Alex's side and slid an arm over her shoulders. "Are you okay?"

Their eyes met briefly. "Yeah."

"Alex . . ."

"I'm fine."

Chapter Twelve

Hawk stood with Chase outside the estate as the authorities drove away.

"Do you have security in the building overnight?"

"Not between nine and five. Housekeeping roams around. I have no idea how long they're in there."

"Who has access after those hours?"

Chase shook his head. "I don't really know. Piper might."

"Tonight's normal close isn't going to happen. And in light of today's events . . . we have people that can come in."

"Thank you." Chase turned and looked at the estate. "But it's not the building I'm really worried about."

Hawk saw concern on Chase's face. "Alex?"

"In two weeks, Piper and I are getting married."

Hawk blinked. "Oh, I thought you were already—"

"Officially, we're married. The day Hailey was born." Chase waved a hand in the air. "Anyway, my point. In two weeks, we're going on our honeymoon. Which we can postpone, but I know how that will go over with my sister."

"Not well, I take it."

"No." Chase met Hawk's gaze. "She needs protection."

Hawk released a sigh. "I couldn't agree more."

"If I suggest a bodyguard, she's going to kick and scream."

Hawk narrowed his eyes, glanced toward the home. "Can her job be done remotely?"

"Some of it, yeah. According to Piper, our father had a lot of work-days right here."

"Max and Sarah . . . are they going anywhere while you're out of town?"

"Not that I know of," Chase answered.

Hawk nodded as an idea formulated. "I got this," he said.

Chase extended an arm to the front door. "After you."

Inside, the family had moved from the living room and now stood around the kitchen island. More wine had been poured, and food had been removed from the fridge and was now being prepped.

Alex sat at the island, toying with the stem of her wineglass.

Chase slid beside his wife and placed a kiss on her forehead. "I'm going to have to go down to the office and lock it up once the police are done."

"I'll go with you," Max said.

"Nick, can you stick around?" Chase asked.

"I always have an overnight bag," Nick said with a laugh.

Hawk cleared his throat. "Is it safe to assume that as a family, you're close enough to sleep in the same place without strangling each other?"

"I know I'll sleep better," Piper said.

"Me too," Sarah agreed.

Both of the women looked at Alex.

Hawk could practically see steam coming from her ears as the wheels in her head turned silently.

Alex said nothing.

"I have some suggestions and concerns while the police track down the person behind today's threat," Hawk started. "This house is secure . . . for the most part. With your permission, I'll have a team in here tomorrow to take the necessary measures to upload the video surveillance to live eyes. When sensors are tripped, the cameras go on and are fed to us. We can program zones for privacy purposes when the system is set at night when you're all here."

"Sounds reasonable," Max said.

"Now, the system at your office is obviously flawed, or we'd have footage of this person from the garage. Our team has to get in there, fix the weak links, and add what you don't have. And we won't know the extent of that right away."

Alex still wasn't looking at him.

"Our team can't keep anyone safe until this is all in place."

"How long will that take?" Alex asked.

So, she was paying attention.

Hawk settled his gaze on her. Those dark, smoky eyes found his. "A week . . . two. Maybe longer. Hopefully in that time, the police will be closer to finding this person, if not have them in custody." He paused. "In the meantime, it would be in the best interest of everyone for you to work remotely."

Alex's fingers stilled on her glass. "Remotely?"

"Here. Where security is—"

"No." Her jaw was set, those eyes hardened.

"The caller threatened you," Hawk said.

"He's right," Max added.

"Monday morning, every employee is going to have to walk back into that building, knowing that Friday, someone had threatened to blow the place up. How can I ask them to get to work while I hide out here?" Alex rested both forearms on the counter, an index finger tapped on the stone.

"Maybe we tell them the threat was against you," Sarah suggested.

"Making everyone even more paranoid if they see me in the office. No. That isn't the answer."

Hawk could confidently say he saw the moment Alex transitioned into her pissed-off state. Unfortunately, her logic wasn't flawed.

"Do you work out?" Hawk asked.

Her eyes swung back to his. "W-what?"

"Exercise? Daily runs? Walks in the park?"

"What does that have to do with this?" Alex shook her head.

"Humor me."

She sighed. "No. Not really."

"You used to run after work," Nick said.

"That was before this position sucked the life out of me."

That's all Hawk needed. "When you went for your runs, did you always go at the same time of day? The same route?"

"No. My work schedule wasn't always that cut-and-dry. My route varied."

"Why? Why did your route vary?"

She shrugged. "I'm a woman. Don't Get Mugged 101, vary your route so anyone watching can't predict . . ." Her words trailed off as the light bulb in her head turned on.

Hawk let the corner of his lip turn up.

He pointed two fingers in her direction. "And that's what you need to do now." He moved closer as if they were the only two people in the room. "If you go into the office—"

"When," she interrupted.

"On the *occasion* that you go into the office, your pattern is never the same as it was the day before. You work from here as much as possible, and when you're at the office, I'm with you."

"You? What, like a babysitter?" she challenged.

"You don't look like a baby to me." He stepped even closer and kept his voice steady and strong. "You look like an incredibly intelligent woman who understands that the very *real* threat today was targeted at her. You seem like the kind of woman who would never forgive herself if anyone in the building was injured or worse because you wanted to ignore the situation as we know it. If this person is watching you, and we know they are, they won't know where to place the bomb, or when. And since your job is to run a company when you're in the office, you can let me watch those around you when you do have to go in, so nobody gets hurt."

Her eyes moved back and forth from his several times before she forcefully turned away in defeat. "Fuck."

◦

The gunshot deafened Hawk's ears as screaming, hot pain tore into his gut.

The cool metal of his gun pressed into his palm, the muzzle centered on the bedroom door.

He sucked in short breaths as reality floated down around him.

He lowered the hand holding his weapon to the floor and closed his eyes.

Picking himself up, he glanced at the time. Four thirty in the morning stared back.

Five hours of sleep would have to do.

He'd joined Chase and Max when they returned to Stone Enterprises the night before.

Piper had gotten ahold of the property management service that the Stones used to take care of the building. Neither Alex nor Chase knew the faces behind the service.

Nelson Perry, head of property management, had arrived shortly after them the night before.

Nelson had been watching the news and apparently trying to get in contact with someone in charge but didn't have anyone's private numbers. Something that needed to change.

Ed had two security guards on the scene, one would have their eyes on the cameras at all times while the other patrolled the building and the perimeter of the property. The likelihood of the person behind this coming back so soon after this attempt wasn't very high, but they weren't taking any chances.

Between Nelson, the patrolling security guard, and the three of them, they locked down all of the exits.

Nelson had notified the housekeeping services and postponed their arrival until morning.

Up on the executive floor, Hawk had walked around quietly while Max removed the board meeting agenda pamphlets and put them away.

Hawk found Chase in Alex's office, standing in the center of the room, absently staring at her desk.

"Does something look out of place?" Hawk asked.

He quietly shook his head. "I keep asking myself why we're doing this. Why we're running *his* company."

Hawk took a long breath. "According to Alex, it's because none of you play golf."

Chase barked out a laugh and then continued to chuckle.

Hawk didn't think it was that funny, but he found himself laughing along with him anyway.

"True."

Max joined them. "No one on the board left so much as a personal pen behind. Laptops, purses, briefcases . . . they must have left with them."

Chase walked over to a closet and retrieved Alex's purse, then located her cell phone on her desk and tucked it inside. "Thank you for helping Alex see the need to have a bodyguard."

"She would have come to the conclusion herself . . . in time."

"Time we may not have," Max said. "Who knows when this person will try this again."

"You think they will?" Chase asked.

It was Hawk that answered. "Depends on what their goal was . . . or is. If they needed everyone out of the building so they could steal something, then maybe this is a one-time thing that put a target on Alex to distract everyone. If the goal is to scare Alex . . ."

"She's more pissed than scared," Max pointed out.

"Which might not work in her favor. It could escalate the situation. If the perpetrator can see her reaction. More reason to keep her out of the office as much as possible until we find this guy."

"We?" Chase asked.

Hawk shook his head. "Listen, I work with a lot of retired detectives, street cops, investigators . . . military. And if there is one thing they all have in common, it's wanting out of whatever branch they were in because of the frustration when their hands were tied and they couldn't dig deeper into open cases. If Owens and Fitzpatrick don't have a lead, and everything falls at a dead end, they will be moving on to the next case within a week. Unless our guy keeps poking the bear. And even then, they only have so many resources."

"A week?" Chase asked in disgust.

"They'll tell you the investigation is open. And it will be, but . . ."

"What do you think the likelihood is that this person will try something again?" Chase asked.

Hawk looked over at Max, who stood there shaking his head.

"There wasn't a guy I met in juvie that didn't have a score to settle with someone on the outside. They were vocal until they were physical. And those guys rotated in and out like a damn Ferris wheel," Max told them.

"Juvie?" Hawk asked.

Max shrugged unapologetically. "Misspent youth."

Hawk could appreciate that. "Max is right. You have to take the threat seriously. They went through some major effort to pull this off."

"*They* threatened our sister. We do everything we can to protect her," Max said.

"We will," Chase assured him.

They all left the building, Max driving Alex's car, Chase taking his truck . . . with the understanding that they'd be back in the morning to facilitate the employees coming in to retrieve their belongings and cars.

After a cup of coffee and a shower, Hawk skipped the gym and headed straight for Stone Enterprises.

Ed arrived with two replacement security guards at seven in the morning.

Hawk had already been there for an hour.

"Did you leave last night?" Ed teased.

"I slept." *Barely.*

They stood in front of the parking garage.

Remnants of the police tape flapped along a pole.

"I sent the contracts you requested last night. They were signed before I had my cup of coffee."

"They're not messing around."

"Nor should they be. Charlie worked with Owens a few times in the past. He's going to reach out and see what he can learn from them aside from what we already know."

"That will be helpful. When is Stevie coming in?"

"I told her nine."

They walked deeper into the garage, still packed with cars.

The main floor of the covered garage was ground level and then went subterranean. It sprawled under the Stone Enterprises building and went down four levels.

The main level, however, was where the executives of the company parked. Alex, Chase, and Max all had names on their parking spaces. Surprisingly, the three of them drove unassuming vehicles. Alex had an older-model Lexus, and both Chase and Max drove dual-cab trucks. The other vehicles on the executive floor were much more in tune with high-value positions. BMW, Porsche, Range Rover . . . Audi.

"Do we know if the security cameras record the license plates of the cars in this garage?" Hawk asked.

"Yes, as they're coming in," Ed said.

"Front plates are hit-and-miss."

Ed nodded. "One of the first changes we need to implement."

"We need a portable camera to record everyone coming in and out today."

"I'm already on it." Ed was all smiles. "You sure you won't take point on this entire job?"

"Can't. I'm the one that convinced Alex she needed a personal bodyguard when she's in public. I need to be available to fill that role."

Ed tilted his head to the side. "Since when do you like long-term one-on-one assignments?"

"This is different."

"How?"

Good fucking question.

"I'll take the load off you when I can. The family home is big, but secure. We can rotate security there—"

"How is this different, Hawk? Is it her?"

Hawk met Ed's gaze, his jaw tightened. "For people with money, they don't act like it. I don't think they realize what kind of target all those zeros in the bank put on them. Have you read their press?"

"I have. It's like a daytime soap opera. Dead father, missing brother, gold-digging widow. Sounds messy."

"It is messy. We both know I'm good with finding out who is tossing the dirt onto the mess. It's easier to do that when I'm around the target. Alex is the target."

Ed conceded. "I'll manage the crews. You manage the case."

Another reason why Hawk liked working with Ed. They were a security service, but they also focused on decreasing the threat.

"I can do that."

Ed looked at the concrete ceiling of the garage. "First things first. Better lighting and more cameras."

"Keyed entry," Hawk added.

"Twenty-four-hour off-site surveillance."

"And inside presence until whoever pulled this stunt is behind bars."

Hawk and Ed walked out of the garage when Chase's familiar truck pulled up in front of the building. He didn't bother with the garage.

Chase and Alex both exited the vehicle.

Hawk's gaze narrowed on her. "I wasn't expecting you."

"I'm not sure why not. Since I'm being forced out of my office, I'll need to transfer work onto my laptop without the office staff realizing I'm preparing to be out more than in."

Chase lifted both hands in the air. "I couldn't convince her to let me do it for her."

"You have your own crap to deal with." Alex headed toward the main entry of the building. "Are we the only ones here?"

"Security is inside."

"Good." She stepped in front of the automatic doors and waltzed through.

She bypassed the entry system that used a badge to calculate who was in the building and headed toward the elevators.

Hawk stood by Chase and Ed, watching her march away.

"Did she wake up pissed?" Hawk asked Chase.

"I'm not sure she slept."

Knowing the building was vacant, Hawk waited until people started showing up before taking the elevators to the top floor.

He found Alex at her desk with her head in her hands.

Hawk cleared his throat.

She looked up.

"It's getting busy down there."

She moaned and slowly lowered her head. "This is unbelievable."

He heard her frustration. "It won't be forever, Alex."

"Fine." She lifted her head, yanked open a drawer, started pulling papers out and shoving them into a briefcase. Once that was done, she typed a few things into the desk computer, then moved to her laptop, and then closed them both down.

Hawk stood out of her way when she walked out of her office and stopped at her assistant's desk.

"I need a few minutes."

"Take the time you need," Hawk told her.

She offered a placating smile. "Come back in two hours, then."

The sound of someone walking down the hall had both their eyes shifting in that direction.

Alex reached for the phone, paused, and then started talking. "Okay, Piper. What do I need to do?"

Hawk watched on as Piper led Alex through something on the computer. Within ten minutes, Alex was finished, and they were headed to the elevator.

"I need to be here on Monday. At least for a few hours."

Hawk expected as much.

"I'll pick you up at eight."

"Chase can drive me in."

Hawk shook his head. "He'll need his own car. I'll pick you up."

She looked like she wanted to argue.

She didn't.

The lobby was empty, with the exception of a security guard.

Hawk greeted him but kept his pace with Alex.

Outside wasn't the same situation. Cars were driving in, unloading passengers who all headed toward the garage.

Which was exactly where Alex was headed.

"My car is right here," he said, stopping her.

"I'm driving Max's truck back."

"That's not a good idea."

"I didn't ask your permission." She moved around him.

Two long strides, and he was in front of her, blocking her way. "I thought we agreed that when you are here, I'm with you."

She pointed the hand holding her briefcase toward the garage. "I'm getting into a car and will no longer be *here*. So, you're good."

Hawk reached for her briefcase and relieved it from her fingers. "Maybe I wasn't clear."

Instead of going further, Hawk turned toward his car and started walking.

"What are you doing?"

He opened the door to the back seat, tossed the briefcase inside, slammed the door, and then moved to the passenger door and opened it. "Get in, Alex."

She strode up to him, determination in each step. "Who do you think you are?"

"The man you hired to keep you safe. I can't do that if you're driving in the car in front of me."

"No one is going to—"

"Drive you off the road? Pull in behind you and in front of me? Cause an accident by swerving into traffic? No one is going to do any of those things. You're right . . . maybe, or maybe not. They may just drive up alongside you and pull out a gun."

She winced.

"Someone threatened to put another Stone in a grave yesterday, and they used your voice to make that threat. Don't be an idiot," he barked.

She took a giant step, putting her chest just inches from his. "I am *not* an idiot!"

"Prove it."

Her nose flared; her chest heaved.

There was something hot and magnetic in the anger behind her eyes. Hawk would be lying to himself if he said it wasn't a turn on.

Alex placed a hand on his chest, nudged him back, and then climbed into his car.

She sat in complete silence as Hawk drove.

He wasn't about to apologize for how he spoke to her. His tone seemed to be the only thing that motivated her to do the right thing.

"Have you ever had physical therapy?" he asked.

"W-what?"

Clearly, Alex wasn't expecting the question.

"Physical therapy. You know, to recover from an injury or surgery?"

"I know what physical therapy is. Yes, why?"

"Did it hurt? Did the therapy bring you to tears and make you hate life for the thirty minutes the therapist was working on you?"

She sighed. "Yes."

He glanced over, didn't see her expression through the dark sunglasses covering her eyes. "I'm your therapist, Alex. You can cuss, yell, scream, and plead, but I'm still going to do what I need to in order to keep you safe. And when it's all said and done, you'll thank me for it."

She stared straight forward. "You're arrogant."

"You're stubborn."

When her lips lifted, he knew he'd broken through her armor.

They arrived at the estate to find two black SUVs in the circular drive. One, Hawk recognized as part of Ed's fleet. The other appeared to be a car from a professional driver. "Are you expecting someone?" Hawk asked.

"My mom . . . and Gaylord."

"The boyfriend?"

"Fiancé," she corrected.

"Seems to be a lot of that going on around here."

Alex reached for the door as soon as the engine was turned off. "Yeah, well . . . someone has to keep the marriage industry in business."

That's an interesting comment, Hawk mused.

He followed Alex up the steps and directly into a beautiful, older version of her.

The mother.

Alex's mother didn't let Alex put her purse down before forcing a hug. "Oh, thank God. What are you doing? I thought you'd be here."

"I had to—"

"There she is," the booming voice of a man came from around the corner.

Wearing a cowboy hat and boots, jeans, and a button-up pearl-snap shirt, the man Hawk assumed was the fiancé strode into the foyer. "Where have you been, young filly? You scared your mama half to death."

"I went to the office."

Hawk stood back and tried not to grin as the parents lit into Alex for leaving the manor.

It was rewarding to witness.

"Your life was threatened yesterday, and you went to the office." The mother turned to look at Gaylord. "Went to the office!"

The mom was mad.

"Security is everywhere." Alex glanced over her shoulder at Hawk.

"That doesn't mean you need to be there."

The mom pulled away, as did some of her anger. "I'm just worried, honey."

"Chase is there . . . are you worried about him?" Alex asked.

"That's different," Gaylord chided.

"That's sexist."

Hawk crossed his arms over his chest and tried not to smile.

"Don't care if it is," Gaylord replied.

It was then that Gaylord looked directly at Hawk.

Hawk didn't wait for an introduction. He stepped forward and extended a hand. "Hawk Bronson, sir. Alex's—"

"Babysitter," Alex interrupted. "And he's just as bad as the two of you."

"I prefer *bodyguard, personal security* . . . I've never been one for diapers and binkies."

Gaylord teased a smile. His handshake firm and deliberate.

"Well, at least you had the good sense for that," the mother said, turning to Hawk. "I'm Vivian."

"A pleasure," Hawk said. "You're just as beautiful as your . . ."

Oh, fuck . . . he had not meant to say that. "Daughter," he finished, unable to pull the words back in.

"Thank you," Vivian said, smiling. "Hopefully I'm not as stubborn."

Hawk felt Alex's stare.

As much as he'd have liked to ignore it, he wasn't built like that.

He met her stare and added his own.

It was Vivian that pulled her away. "Max was telling us what the authorities are doing. Do you have any idea who could have done this?"

Alex kept her eyes on him as she walked with her mother, then snapped out of his orbit and left him in the foyer.

"Gaylord Morrison, by the way. Thank you for taking care of her."

Hawk shook his head. "I have a feeling it's going to be like watching high schoolers at prom sneaking drinks."

Gaylord patted him on the back and walked them both out of the entryway to the house. "Take it from a man who raised his kids without their mama . . . best thing you can do is anticipate her moves and beat her to them."

"That's good advice."

Chapter Thirteen

Vivian and Gaylord distracted Alex from the fact that she was practically an ex-con on house arrest.

And the house wasn't even her own.

When Monday morning arrived and Alex watched Chase prepare to leave for the office, a good hour before she would, reality set in.

"Don't look at me like that," Chase said over the kitchen island as he filled his travel coffee mug.

"Like what?"

He pointed at her face. "Like that. Like I'm the one that got to pick the biggest piece of cake for myself and you got what was left."

That made her smile. "I don't even like cake."

"Liar. You don't *want* to like cake. There's a difference."

Alex rolled her eyes.

"I'll be there by nine."

"I know."

"Remember . . . as many department heads as we can gather for the eleven o'clock briefing," she ordered.

They'd formulated a plan over the weekend.

Piper had constructed an email that was sent out to every manager on every floor, from the mail room to Accounting. The message was to clear their schedules and be able to jump to management meetings throughout the day.

Alex would arrive at nine, and at nine thirty the executive management would meet with the company lawyers and the heads of Human Resources. By eleven, they'd break into two groups, where she could preside over a briefing while Chase did the same with the other half. Then they would make a point to walk every floor, split into two groups . . . and assure the staff that it was business as usual. When that was completed, she'd make her departure. The only people that would know of her exact schedule would be the members of the Stone family and Hawk. And to a certain extent, Dee.

"And the woman in Marketing. I want to talk with her directly."

Chase tilted his head to the side. "Anything else?"

"Sarcasm isn't sexy."

"Good thing I'm your brother." Chase smiled. "I gotta go." He walked up, put both hands on her shoulders. "It's temporary, Alex."

She snarled, and Chase walked away.

With coffee in hand, Alex walked out into the outdoor room that overlooked the back gardens.

The fresh February morning air hinted at rain. But the cool felt good and helped Alex clear her head. Much as she hated to admit it, she liked the quiet and privacy that her late father's estate afforded. Even with her entire family residing in the home over the weekend, there was still plenty of room for everyone to find their own space.

Halfway through her first cup of coffee, Sarah joined her. "Am I interrupting?"

"Not at all."

Sarah took a seat on an adjacent chair and curled her legs under her. "Is it weird not rushing off to the office?"

"*Weird* isn't the word I'd use. *Frustrating, irritating* . . ."

"At least my old colleagues haven't been hounding us." Sarah's journalistic skills were lost as a tabloid writer.

"Only because it's an election year."

"Tabloids could care less about elections. They like sex, drugs, and leaked videos," Sarah teased.

"That sounds like politics to me," Alex said with a grin.

Sarah pushed her eyeglasses a little farther up on her nose. "How long do you think it will take before the office realizes that you're avoiding the place?"

"Less than a week. Considering I've practically lived there since we took over."

"That's what I concluded. And as a recovering tabloid reporter, I know that someone will inevitably find out that this whole thing was targeted at you, making your time in the office even less appealing . . . until they find our Play-Doh bomber."

"Play-Doh bomber?" Alex asked with a laugh.

"Sorry. Occupational hazard." Sarah stretched her arm out as if she was painting on the air. "Headline. *The Play-Doh Bomber Strikes Again.*"

"That's funny. Sad, but funny."

Sarah dropped her hand to her lap. "I asked Piper what your dad did in that CEO chair and how it compares to what you do."

"He was on autopilot. I'm not."

Sarah nodded. "I get that. However, it might be least conspicuous if you started to do some of the things your father did, business-wise, that would keep you out of the office."

"The issue with that is I'd have to schedule meetings, which become public knowledge. And as much as I hate how annoyingly right Hawk is about this, a random schedule is safer."

"Maybe . . ." Sarah sipped her coffee.

They sat in silence for the space of two breaths. "What do you think about Hawk?" Sarah asked.

"Arrogant." Alex tilted her cup back. "Smart, but arrogant. And bossy. He makes me look like a kitten."

"But good-looking," Sarah said over her cup.

"Hence the arrogance. He's probably used to women taking his commands without question. Broad shoulders and strong jawlines have a way of decreasing women's ability to think for themselves." And Alex could think for herself.

"Those shoulders, though . . ."

Alex looked up to find Sarah grinning.

"I thought you loved my brother," Alex teased.

"Oh, I do. I'm just saying . . . if you have to have a personal body-guard, you could do worse."

"You've been talking to Nick."

Sarah's eyes widened. "Did Nick say something?"

Alex laughed and shook her head. "Oh, please. Don't even pretend. Nick could care less what team a man plays on—he will ogle at the way they fill out a pair of jeans regardless."

Sarah sat back. "You did notice the jeans, then."

"Of course I did. I'm not blind."

"Good."

"Good? What good?"

"I'm just happy that there's a woman in there somewhere."

Alex set her cold coffee down. "There's a woman in here. She's simply dormant. I gave up on finding what you and Max have when I accepted Daddy's bank account."

"Why?"

Alex lifted her hands to the outside room of the mansion that was one-third hers. "This emasculates men. This encourages disingenuous men to sniff around. The more successful a woman is, the less desirable she is to the opposite sex. Unless the man is thirty years older, and lord knows I have daddy issues . . . but no. Just no."

"Hmmm."

"Hmmm, what?"

"I'm searching for the flaw in your logic."

Alex unfolded from the outdoor couch and stood. "When you find it, let me know."

"I will. Don't worry."

She turned toward the house and made it to the door before Sarah called out. "Those jeans, though . . ."

Alex laughed as she walked away.

⁂

Walking into Stone Enterprises with Hawk at her side couldn't have been much different than walking in with a German Shepherd. A trained one that wore a vest saying *I bite* on it.

Alex stopped at the front desk. "Good morning, Malcom."

"Good morning, Ms. Stone."

"You remember Mr. Bronson?"

Malcom cleared his throat. "I do. Good morning."

"Mr. Bronson and his team are now in charge of our security. If he instructs you to give access to anyone, please see to it."

"Of course, Ms. Stone."

"And be sure and get him a permanent ID card without any access restrictions for the building."

"Will do."

Alex placed a hand on the counter and smiled. "I wanted to thank you. I was told that our security and those of you at this desk were the first in the building to be told what was happening on Friday. It would have been easy to reduce yourself to panic, but instead, the evacuation of the building went as smoothly as it possibly could."

Malcom looked between her and Hawk. "Y-you don't have to thank me. I have friends in this building."

Alex pushed away from the counter. "Still. I'll personally make sure our thanks is represented in your paycheck. And those that were here on Friday."

Surprise lit his face. "Thank you."

Alex glanced at Hawk and then turned.

"Mr. Bronson," Malcom said, stopping them.

He put a temporary badge on the counter. "I'll have a permanent one sent up within the hour."

Hawk took the badge with a nod.

Because the workday had begun a good hour before her arrival, the lobby was empty, as was the elevator when they entered.

"That was a decent thing for you to do," Hawk said once the door closed.

"I'm happy to be in a position where I can."

"The perks of a stressful job."

"There aren't many," Alex confessed. "Most of the time it's—"

The elevator stopped, the doors opened, and a young man, somewhere in his late twenties, stepped in. One look at her, and his shoulders pulled back and a polite smile washed over his face. "Good morning, Ms. Stone."

"Morning."

When the elevator started moving again, Hawk said, "Most of the time it's what?"

Alex looked at the back of the man in front of her and shook her head.

Another floor, and another person stepped in.

A stressful smile, a curt nod . . . and tension followed them to the top floor.

Alex's shoulders pulled back with every step she took through the executive floor.

Floyd Gatlin's executive assistant and close friend to Piper, Julia, was the only one to offer a genuine smile. "Good morning, Julia."

"Hello, Ms. Stone."

"Julia." Of all the people in the office, Julia was one of the few she wanted to use her first name.

"Nobody else calls you Alex," she said under her breath. All the while sneaking peeks at Hawk, who hovered.

Alex glanced at him. "Julia, this is Hawk Bronson. He's with the new security team. You'll see him around quite a bit."

Julia nodded several times. "That's good. It feels weird coming to work today."

"I'm sure." Alex didn't add her own unease to the conversation.

"Dee called in. I was going to get a temp, but Chase said not to bother. I cleared your schedule and his. And cleared the conference rooms for your meetings today."

"Thank you." Alex glanced over her shoulder. "Is Floyd here?"

"He is. But he's downstairs with Human Resources. A lot of people called in today."

Alex glanced at Hawk. "I suppose that's to be expected. The authorities wouldn't have encouraged us to resume today if they believed there was a threat."

"Piper told me."

"Good. The more people that understand that, the better."

Julia smiled. "I'll do what I can to spread the word."

Alex tapped Julia's desk and started down the hall.

She detoured into Chase's office and closed the door behind her and Hawk.

Chase looked up from the phone in his hand and lifted a finger in the air. "Yes, we'll conduct those meetings after lunch. Good . . . All right."

Alex took a seat and dropped her bag on the floor.

Hawk moved to the windows and looked out.

Chase ended the call.

He wasn't smiling.

"What?" she asked.

"There isn't one department in this building where at least one-eighth of the staff didn't call in sick."

"PTSD," Hawk said from across the room. "It isn't reserved for combat."

"What can we do?" Alex asked.

"Floyd is figuring out which departments were hit hardest so we know where to focus our efforts to ensure safety."

"Then what?"

"Depends on how long it lasts. A quick brainstorm tossed out giving mental health days, bringing in a crisis team for counseling."

"It was a false alarm," Alex said with a sigh.

"A false alarm with a bag under a car isn't the same as the bomb squad finding nothing. Not to mention the direct threat of striking again," Hawk told them.

Hawk was annoyingly right . . . again.

"I can't blame them," Chase said. "If Piper worked here and I was somewhere else, I'd insist she stay home. At least until they have someone in custody."

As much as it sucked, Alex agreed. "We need Legal's take on this. People worked remotely for nearly a year. There has to be a work-around to keep operations from grinding to a halt."

"We'll get through this," Chase agreed.

"What about CMS . . . how is it on the third floor?"

"Busa is taking care of my company. We didn't have that many sick calls. Nothing compared to this."

"There's something to learn there. Unhappy and overworked employees are the first to call out."

"Those with shitty bosses," Hawk added.

Alex flashed him a cold look.

"Not you. Their direct boss. Number one reason people quit their jobs isn't the job . . . it's the boss," Hawk defended.

Chase huffed. "Dee called off."

"Dee is afraid of her own shadow. She doesn't hate us," Alex argued. "Besides, Piper would know if Dee hated her job."

Chase pushed his chair back from his desk. "We knew today would be a crap show."

"Have you seen the market? Are we okay?" she asked. The stock market was the true barometer of public perception.

"We're good there."

Alex stood. "That's half the battle."

"Did Mom and Gaylord get off this morning?"

Alex nodded. "They were leaving right as Hawk showed up."

"Owens or Fitzpatrick?"

Alex shook her head.

Chase glanced at Hawk, who also shook his head.

Concern was written on Chase's face. "We go on . . . business as usual," Alex said. One glance at Hawk, and the "usual" became slanted. "Somewhat," she amended.

Alex stood. "Do you think I should call Dee?"

"I'll ask Piper to reach out. She's not as intimidating as you."

"I am not . . ." One look at her brother, and Alex closed her mouth. "Whatever."

"Let's coordinate our schedules for the week before the day gets ahead of us," Chase suggested.

Alex pushed out of the chair. "Give me five minutes."

Hawk was at the door before she was, opening it.

She walked through the doorway and uttered, "If I thank you for every door you open, I'm going to sound like a parrot. If I don't thank you, I look like a bitch. Where is the middle?" she asked.

A few yards away, and he had his hand on the handle of the door to her office. "I'm never going to tell a woman to smile, but a nod works."

Alex stopped and looked him in the eye.

The corner of her lips turned up without provocation.

She added the nod for good measure.

Hawk opened the door, and she took a step toward it.

His hand coming between her and the room stopped her. "I go in first."

"It's my office."

He leaned in. "It was your car, too."

She wanted to argue . . . oh, how she longed to disagree with him.

Instead, she stepped back and let him go into her office first.

He deemed it safe after a look around the room and opened the door wider for her to step in.

"Thank you," she said.

Hawk crossed the room to look in the private bathroom at the opposite end.

She left him to his job and woke up her computer to pull up her schedule.

A few clicks later, and her printer started to buzz. "I don't know how I'm going to do all this without being here."

If Hawk heard her, he didn't comment.

Chase walked in right as her printer spit out the last paper. She took the stack and moved over to the sofa.

"Since everything from today has been pushed, I have to be here tomorrow," she started.

Hawk took a seat across from them and made a noise. "Huh."

"What?"

"Everyone expects that," he said. "So, you won't."

Arguing would be childish.

"What can be eliminated at the last minute?" Hawk asked.

Alex peered at the paper in her hands. She picked up a pen and started slicing apart her world. She then circled the calls. Those could be done from the estate. She put stars next to things that couldn't be missed or shouldn't.

Alex handed her Tuesday schedule to Hawk and moved on to Wednesday.

"Chase, can you take any of these on?"

He nodded and started slicing his schedule. "This can wait until we're back from the honeymoon. So can this . . ."

Then Wednesday was passed around.

Chase highlighted the meeting with Legal regarding the sale of the Noel properties. "This is all you," he said, handing the schedule back to Alex.

The days were passed back and forth several times. "If I come in the afternoon on Wednesday through the end of the day, I can squeeze together the in-house meetings."

Hawk nodded. "Thursday morning, you come in as usual, but you'll get a call that takes you out of the office by eleven. By two, you can pick up the calls at home."

Alex saw how it could work.

"Why is Friday empty after three?"

"The Hawthorn event," Alex told him. "I RSVP'd. I have to go."

"Is anyone else from the office going to be there?" Hawk asked.

"No."

"And you can't go instead?" Hawk asked Chase.

He shook his head. "Piper's parents are flying in and will be here through the wedding. I can't abandon her with them."

Alex glanced at Hawk. "Her parents can be . . . difficult."

"Okay. I need you both to leave your schedules looking like they did before we did any of this. Anyone hacking into a computer will see this. Can Piper piece this all together, the revised one that only the four of us know?" Hawk asked.

"Yes," both Alex and Chase said at the same time.

"Good." Hawk gathered the papers and, one by one, took a photograph of each. "I'll forward these to her now."

"I can—"

"My phone is secure." Hawk continued to snap photos.

Alex considered her cell phone with a frown. Could it be hacked in some way?

Chase glanced at his watch. "We've got to get moving."

Hawk took his last photograph and stood. "Shredder?"

"The cabinet behind the desk," Alex directed.

"I'll meet you in the conference room," Chase said as he walked out of her office.

Alex's gaze traveled down Hawk's back while he shredded their schedules. He wasn't wearing jeans but . . .

He turned, and Alex quickly looked away.

Damn Sarah for putting thoughts in her head.

"Ready?" Hawk asked.

"Yes."

Alex felt Hawk's presence at her side even more than she saw him. "It's weird having a shadow."

"I can blend," he told her.

She glanced at him, did a quick sweep of her eyes up and down his frame. "I doubt that."

Hawk's chuckle followed them to the conference room.

Chapter Fourteen

The entire building was scared to death of her.

That was Hawk's impression when he opened the door to his car and Alex slid in.

"That was painful," she said while pulling the seat belt across her lap.

Hawk took his place behind the wheel and donned his sunglasses before pulling away from the building. "I couldn't agree more. But I think we may be talking about two different things."

"What are you talking about?"

He glanced over his shoulder and pulled away from the front of the building.

"No, no. Ladies first."

"Okay, I'll bite. All the stares and sideway glances with you as my shadow," she said.

"You thought they were looking at me?" he asked.

"They were."

Hawk eased onto the street.

"No, Alex, they weren't. A few, maybe . . . but those stares were directed at you."

From the upper management to the cleaning staff, there wasn't one warm bone in the building when it came to Alexandrea Stone.

"I know when people are looking at me."

"You feel it, but you're not aware who is doing the looking. It's a bad habit that could stand breaking."

"I'm the boss, I command attention by my name alone," she defended.

"Isn't Chase the boss, too?"

"Yes."

"Yet he wasn't the one with daggers being tossed at him. It's my job to identify the people in that building that see you as a threat, and lady . . . I lost count by the fourth floor."

She shifted in her seat. "It was your presence."

"If that's what you want to believe." She'd demanded the same attention at the Bakshai event. Open stares, quick change in focus when she turned in someone's direction. Tense smiles and even more stressful laughs and attempts at conversation. It was painful for Hawk to witness. In the short time he'd known Alex, he'd seen her in control, out of control and scared, angry, and vulnerable. Then there was what he'd just traveled through over the last seven hours.

The mask she wore in the building was wholly different than what she was around her family. It was as if she were stepping onstage when the office doors opened and off when she exited.

"I need to stop by my place and pick up some of my things."

Hawk detoured past the freeway that would take them back to the estate and headed in the opposite direction.

He opened up the navigation on his phone and pressed her address, which was already preprogrammed.

"You know where I live." It wasn't a question.

"Yup."

"Why doesn't that surprise me?"

He didn't answer. "Did you and Chase make any changes when you took over the company?"

"Not changes. We stopped the excessive spending, the acquisition of the Starfield properties."

"No layoffs?"

"No."

During the meeting with Human Resources, they both learned that Fitzpatrick had requested and obtained a list of the internal employees that had been let go in the past six months. There weren't that many, and those that were in the unemployment line hadn't been with the company for long.

"Why the animosity, then? Who fed them that fear?"

"A CEO of a company dies, and everyone worries about their jobs. That's natural."

"But the fear doesn't apply to Chase," he mused.

"I think it's because I was the face they saw for several months in the beginning. He and Piper spent quite a bit of time searching for Max. Then Chase brought his entire operation of CMS to the third floor, where his staff is much closer and comfortable with him. And he married Piper. Someone who was the buffer to our father and likely much more approachable."

That made sense. "More human."

She shot him a look over her shoulder. "I'm not human?"

"I didn't say that."

She sighed. "You didn't. Truth is, I don't know exactly why I'm such an enigma. I had friends at Regent."

"Are they still your friends?"

Alex blinked a few times.

He took that as a no.

"Everyone on my team at Regent signed nondisclosures. My guess is people would worry for their jobs if they continued happy hour with me."

Hawk couldn't see her knocking back drinks at happy hour, not after what he'd just witnessed in her office building.

He pulled into the parking lot of a home improvement store.

"What are we doing here?"

"I need a few things for your condo."

Dressed in suits, and Alex in her three-inch heels, they turned several heads as they walked a store filled with construction workers and do-it-yourselfers.

From Hawk's vantage point, Alex noticed none of the stares.

Hawk loaded up a cart with everything he needed from the home security section. "Do you have screwdrivers, a basic tool kit at home?"

"Very basic, but yes. I made Chase step up when I needed stuff done."

They started for the register. "You two are close."

"We are. We both had an overwhelming desire to make our mom happy after the divorce. I know that sounds strange. Most kids only worry about themselves, but we felt how unhappy she was. We weren't about to make that harder."

"She loved your father?"

"I assume so, in the beginning. Then she felt guilty for walking away. We still catch her apologizing for the actions of our father. The man is dead, and she still says 'I'm sorry' for him. Such a screwed-up thing women do."

"Gaylord doesn't seem to pull that personality from her," Hawk said.

Alex's smile really did light up her face. "No, he's good. I'm glad they found each other. She deserves to be happy."

They stepped up to the self-serve register and scanned in the items.

Hawk reached for his wallet.

Alex stopped him. "It's for my place."

He opened his lips to argue, then stepped back. It was her home, and she was a client, not a woman . . . not a woman he was seeing, in any event.

Those thoughts rolled around in his head while they walked out of the store.

The complex Alex lived in was three stories. She lived on the top one.

The two-bedroom condo shared a hallway with several other units. As Chase had told Hawk, the security wasn't existent, and neither was the privacy.

They reached her door. Hawk lifted his palm.

It took her a second, but she sighed and handed him her keys.

"This will get easier," he said.

The door across the hall opened, and Hawk immediately tensed, stopped with the lock, and stepped in front of Alex. His hand moved to the firearm under his jacket.

A white-haired lady, all of four foot eleven and likely north of her eightieth birthday, poked her head into the hall.

Alex placed a hand on his arm. "Easy, tiger. She isn't packing."

"Alexandrea?" the woman asked, squinting her eyes and fumbling with a pair of glasses. "Is that you?"

Alex stepped around Hawk. "Yes, Mrs. Steiner."

The woman managed to place the glasses on her nose and smiled up at Alex. "I was starting to worry. I saw you on the news again. Did someone blow up your office?"

"No. Nothing that dramatic. It was all a false alarm." Alex smiled at the older woman and reached for her frail hands.

Mrs. Steiner made a ticking sound and kept shaking her head. Or maybe the ticking and the shaking were from some kind of medical condition.

"When you didn't come home—"

"I was with my niece. My brother and his wife needed some time away."

Hawk was surprised to hear the lie roll off her tongue with ease.

"Ahh, that's nice of you."

It was then Mrs. Steiner took notice of Hawk.

The older woman released her hands from Alex's and smoothed her bed-brushed hair with one. Her smile stretched from ear to ear. "Who is this young man?"

Alex looked up.

Their eyes met. And the unspoken communication was clear. Go along with whatever she said next.

"A *friend*." She tilted her head, her eyes wide.

"Like your friend Nicholas?"

Hawk cleared his throat.

Alex's eyes narrowed, and a sly smile took form.

"No," Hawk quickly said, not giving her the opportunity to change his sexuality in a white lie to save the old woman from knowing he was a bodyguard.

Mrs. Steiner leaned back a little then and did a full body scan behind her thick glasses. Her smile was slower.

"I'm Hawk," he introduced himself.

"Nice to meet you, Hawk." Again, her eyes moved up and down him. "I was starting to think she was a lesbian," Mrs. Steiner said in a hoarse whisper.

Alex sucked in a breath. Her cheeks flushed.

Hawk laughed.

"Mrs. Steiner. Are you trying to embarrass me?"

The old woman patted Alex's shoulder. "No, honey. I just . . . well, I don't see much company for you. Pretty girl like you should have more company."

She glanced at Hawk.

He nodded behind a smile he was poorly attempting to stifle.

"I'm glad you're all right. You usually tell me when you're going away," Mrs. Steiner said, changing the subject.

Alex cleared her throat. "I won't be home much the next few weeks. Can you keep an eye out for me?"

"Don't I always?" Mrs. Steiner looked up at Hawk again. "I'll leave you kids to . . . whatever."

Alex leaned over and kissed the woman's cheek. "Call me if you need anything. Do you have all your medicine?"

"Yes."

"Did you take your saltshaker off the table like the doctor said?" Alex asked.

"My blood pressure is fine. Don't worry about me." She shooed them away. "Go. It was nice meeting you, young man."

"Likewise," Hawk told her.

A few moments later, they stood behind the closed door of Alex's place.

Hawk started to laugh.

"Don't," Alex said, lifting a hand in the air. "She's old and very imaginative."

"I didn't say anything." But Mrs. Steiner's lesbian comment said everything.

"Good."

Alex moved into the modest living room and around the corner to a kitchen. When she emerged again, she held a toolbox.

A lime-green toolbox.

"That's very . . . bright."

"You can thank Nick."

He took the box, and Alex walked to a hall.

"Wait." He stopped her.

She hesitated.

After setting the box down, he walked in front of her and checked the remaining rooms.

No one lurked.

"All clear?" she teased.

Amusement bubbled under his chest when she walked out of the room. "Lesbian," he whispered.

"I heard that!"

Hawk laughed louder.

He opened the toolbox to see what he had to work with and then started to remove the packaging on the cameras and sensors. "How long have you known Mrs. Steiner?"

"Since I moved in. About six years," Alex called out from her bedroom.

"Is she always aware of who is coming and going around here?"

"She's old and has nothing better to do to occupy her time. What do you think?"

Two thoughts came to mind, first . . . Mrs. Steiner was probably a better camera than the one he was holding. And two . . . had Alex never brought home a man?

Naw . . . that couldn't be.

Hawk scanned the code on the camera into his phone, then looked up at the ceiling. "Do you have a step stool?"

"In the kitchen between the fridge and the wall."

In the kitchen, he found what he was searching for and then paused.

The white cabinets and stainless-steel appliances looked a lot like his. The simple décor was clean, fresh, with white and fawn green tones.

Back in the main room, which had a dining table at one end, he saw much of the same. There wasn't anything fancy or overstated in the home.

A sofa with an occasional chair across from a television that sat on a cabinet, not mounted on a wall. There was a picture of Hailey and another one of Alex with her brothers. A third of her and Nick with a white sand beach and turquoise blue water in the background. In the beach photograph, she was in a bikini top and shorts, her skin kissed with sun, large-rimmed sunglasses covering her eyes.

Of course, the woman had a killer body.

That was obvious even in a business suit. But the bikini?

Hawk's mouth went dry.

The sound of Alex's footsteps had him turning away from the pictures and placing the step stool next to where he wanted to mount a camera.

Alex returned to the room wearing a slim pair of jeans that hugged low on her hips. The belt she wore was more fashion than function, and the button up silk shirt was tucked in just enough to look casual and show off the curves of her body.

Hawk removed the mount kit for the camera, grabbed the tool he needed, and stepped up the small stool. "I find it hard to believe that a woman of your wealth doesn't have a security system in her home."

Alex moved to a closet and removed a suitcase. "You've seen my security. She has a name."

He smiled at that. "I think Mrs. Steiner's crime-fighting days are behind her."

"That camera isn't going to stop a criminal."

"True, but it won't require glasses to get a good description if someone did break in."

Hawk stretched his arms over his head and twisted the screwdriver. "You don't happen to have a drill?"

"Sure."

Hawk stopped what he was doing and glanced at her.

"It's right next to my welding kit I use on the weekends."

She rolled her eyes and went back to the bedroom with the suitcase.

Hawk kept making slow progress with the manual tool.

"I'm more surprised by the fact that you're still living here," Hawk said.

"I like *here*," she told him. "It's the only part of my old life that I still have." Alex paused. "That and my car."

"The 2015 Lexus?" That shocked him, too. Especially considering the cars that filled the massive garage at the Stone Estate. Ferrari, Porsche, Aston Martin . . . a dead man's cars, Hawk had been told, but much more in tune with what a billionaire would drive. Not a car old enough to require a smog check annually in the state of California.

"I bought it used from the dealership. It was a loaner. I got a great deal."

Hawk shook his head. "Have you spent any of the money you inherited from your father's estate?"

"Sure." Alex walked back into the room, rolling the suitcase with one hand and holding two large garment bags with the other. "On clothes," she said as she draped the bags on the sofa. "And shoes." She tapped the suitcase.

"That's filled with shoes?" Hawk asked, his hands overhead, his eyes focused on the rolling bag.

She nodded. "I'm fairly certain there is more money in shoes in this bag than I spent on my car."

"Seriously?"

"When your best friend is a gay fashionista, you can't get away with shopping at Target anymore."

Hawk chuckled at the image of Nick at Target.

Alex left the living room and moved into the kitchen. "I was happy with my life before my dad up and died."

It was strange to hear someone talk so flippantly about a parent dying. It was truly a testimony to how unloved Aaron Stone was by his children.

"I had my job with a competitor and was doing everything in my power to succeed as a *fuck you* to my father. There were people I hung out with after work. I'd come home to find another plant dead from neglect or overwatering. I was fine."

Fine . . . that was never a word that meant "fine" when said by a woman.

"And before you say it, I know the 'fuck you, Daddy' thing is all about childhood trauma."

At least Alex was self-aware.

Hawk finished with the first camera and moved to the second one. He glanced into the kitchen to find Alex tossing food from the refrigerator into a garbage can.

"Did anyone like your father?"

She peeked from behind the door, then moved back to what she was doing. "If he had any true friends, the kind that were there for him and not his money, I never met them. There were plenty of people at the funeral, all very *sorry for our loss*. But none came around after the reading of the will."

"After they realized they weren't named," Hawk surmised.

He moved back into the living room and angled the second camera in place, then started the whole process all over again.

"Yeah. Then those phony smiles and insincere words of wanting to be friends and the desire to know me on a personal level started reminding me of the things people would say to Aaron."

Hawk paused and digested her words. "You kept the car and the apartment to downplay your wealth."

Alex was quiet in the other room.

Were his words a surprise to her?

"Huh. Maybe."

The second camera went in a little faster. "I hate to break it to you, Alex. But you carry yourself like a wealthy woman. Anyone would have to be blind to not see it. And this place is a liability to your safety."

"That's the bodyguard in you talking," she said.

He thought about another time, and another woman. "That's experience talking," he corrected. "How many times have the media knocked on your door?"

"Too many to count."

"And those cameras with those reporters, do they show this building? The street?"

Alex walked in from the kitchen with two bags of garbage in her hands. "I'm not here when the media is chasing a story."

He sneered at her as he pushed in the last screw. "You're too intelligent to not recognize where I'm going with this."

She dropped one bag by the front door and reached for the doorknob. "I know. But leaving this condo is the last piece of the puzzle that will then cement my new life in place."

He stepped off the stool and stopped her from opening the front door.

Her dark, piercing eyes found his and held.

Hawk stood close enough to feel the heat of her frame and smell the scent of some exotic oil, or maybe it was her shampoo.

"Your personal bodyguard is stopping you from taking your trash out and tightening up . . . no . . . placing security measures in your home. Your old life is a ship that sailed a while ago, Alexandrea. You are dog-paddling to try and catch it while caught in the riptide. You can't go back. The sooner you come to terms with that, the longer you'll live."

They were silent then.

Either because she was processing his words or trying to find a weakness in them.

"No one calls me Alexandrea."

"Did your father call you that?" he asked softly.

"No."

His gaze drifted to her lips.

The image of kissing her, lowering his mouth to hers, was as intoxicating as a flame was to a moth.

Bad idea.

Those soulful eyes found his again. Damn if he didn't see a flame flicker behind those lids.

Alex cleared her throat and stepped from the door. Away from him. "I'm going to grab a few more things. How much longer to finish this?"

Hawk turned away. "Twenty minutes."

"Good."

Chapter Fifteen

Alex woke with a sharp breath.

She'd been dreaming. Something warm and exciting.

She squeezed her eyes closed and tried to remember what the dream had been about.

Then it came to her.

Hawk.

He'd been smiling down at her. Even though Alex couldn't remember what was said right before his smile, she did know that grin. The one that said he'd won. He'd said something, and she had no choice but to bend to his will. And he'd done so without any true demand.

The smile was arrogant and yet not.

The words in her dream floated in her head.

"I want you safe," he'd whispered.

The way his lips moved when he uttered those four simple words, and the depth of his eyes . . . that was the warmth and excitement she'd taken with her when morning crashed in.

Alex looked at the clock on her bedside, closed her eyes, shook her head, and looked again.

Eight. It was eight in the morning, on a Tuesday.

This was going to be her first full workday at the estate, but her day did start at eight.

Alex swung her feet off the bed and rushed around her room.

Cell phone in hand, she called Dee while pulling the T-shirt she wore to bed over her head.

"Ms. Alex Stone's office. How can I help you?"

"Dee, it's Alex."

"Good morning, Ms. Stone."

Alex paused to steady her breath. The bra she was about to put on was poised in one hand. "I won't be in the office today. Redirect my nine o'clock to next week . . ." Shit, there was something else that needed to be moved to work with the timeline she, Chase, and Hawk figured out.

Half-naked, Alex moved back into the bedroom from the walk-in closet and quickly opened her laptop. "And make my three o'clock a Zoom call, then send me the link." Alex set her phone down and pushed into her bra.

"I can do that."

"I'll conference call you in twenty minutes to go over the rest of today's schedule."

"Yes, ma'am."

Alex ended the call, tossed her phone to the side, and finished getting dressed.

Twenty minutes later, Alex sat behind the desk in her father's home office.

Dee stared at her through the screen of a computer and discussed the modified schedule for the day.

Piper poked her head past the door and lifted a cup of coffee in the air.

Alex placed a hand on her chest and said, "Yes, please."

Piper disappeared as Dee continued with the schedule.

By the time she was off the call, Piper had returned with a cup of coffee and two pieces of toast.

"You didn't have to—"

"Shut up and eat."

Alex busted out in a laugh as she picked up a piece of bread. "We've come a long way."

Piper took a seat across from her.

"Hawk suggested more security at the wedding."

"Sadly, he's probably right. But who knows, maybe the police will have a lead by then."

"I hope so." Piper sipped her coffee. "We can postpone our honeym—"

"Stop right there. You and my brother deserve time away. It's been a hard year for both of you."

"It's been a difficult year for everybody," Piper corrected. "When are you going to take some time off?"

"When I turn fifty?"

"Alex," Piper chided.

"Let's get everybody married. Get our Play-Doh bomber caught . . . then maybe." Alex took another bite of her toast.

"If you're going to work remotely, you don't have to do it from here."

"This is where the security cameras are, and where the opportunity for someone to place a bomb under my car is least likely to happen."

"Your father had homes in other countries. Why not work from there?"

Alex leaned forward, put the remainder of her toast on the plate. "Listen, I appreciate what you're trying to do. If I went to Italy, the time zone alone would make work even more difficult."

"Then go to Colorado. You have a lodge there. Do some night skiing, work four hours a day, and then try and remember what life was about before all this."

Alex placed her arms on the desk and thought about what it might be like to sip hot chocolate in front of a fire with snow falling outside.

And then, without wanting to, her thoughts drifted to how many employees across all platforms were at risk of losing their jobs. How she needed to minimize those numbers so people could keep food on the table. How would they feel if she was out playing in the snow while their worlds fell apart?

"And if the power goes out and I can't log in to get that work done?"

"Then don't work." Piper leaned forward. "I guarantee you, this company is not going to crumble if you step away for a week."

Alex sighed. She wanted to believe that.

"Besides, if there is still a threat—"

"If there is still a threat, then what? I still have security surrounding me? Hawk won't let me walk in a room before he scopes it out first. How does that work flying down a hill on a snowboard?"

"You don't tell anyone where you're going." Piper scooted forward. "Consider it, okay? Everyone in this house is worried about you. You've lost weight."

"I haven't."

"You have. I know the sale and closing of some of the Noel properties has you stressed."

"Nobody likes putting people out of work."

"It's business," Piper said. "And you didn't cause the problem. Just think about how many people would eventually be without a job if these properties continue to siphon profits from the larger company? Folding any arm of Stone Enterprises is gonna hurt. That has been weighing on you."

There was no arguing that. "I know."

"The wedding is less than two weeks away. Chase and I will be back a week after that."

"I thought you were going for ten days," Alex said.

"Do you think I can really be away from Hailey for that long? Take the week off before your mom and Gaylord show us how weddings are supposed to look. We all have four days in Texas with that. We come back refreshed."

Alex couldn't see her schedule breaking up enough to pull it off.

"If you don't do it for you . . . do it for Chase."

Alex narrowed her brow. "Chase?"

"We've gotten married, had Hailey . . . we're getting into our new house. All of which you've covered him for. He's feeling guilty, Alex. Max has even asked how he can take something off your plate. You'd be taking time away for everybody. Not just you."

When Piper put it like that, it was hard to flat out say no.

"I'll . . . I'll think about it."

"Thank you." Piper stood and walked out of the office.

Alex stared at the bookshelves and the dark walls that didn't do a great job of brightening up the place, even with the many windows letting the sunshine in.

Once again, Alex felt the weight of her father's dead soul in her space.

His space.

She pushed those thoughts aside and logged in for a conference call.

By noon, Alex walked through the estate, searching for Max.

She found him in the garage putting floodlights on his new truck.

"Modifying it already?" Alex asked.

Max smiled as he tightened a bolt of some sort. "The sooner, the better. If someone steals this one, at least it won't blend as much as the first one."

Max's home in the high desert had been broken into shortly after the world learned who he was. The new truck she and Chase had purchased for him was their way of convincing Max that they weren't lying to him about being the heir to a multibillion-dollar estate. What took him a bit to figure out didn't take any time for the thieves that trashed his rental home and stole his truck.

Alex briefly wondered what would have happened had Max been home when the thieves broke in.

Her thoughts flashed to her apartment and the cameras Hawk had installed.

No one had broken into her place, but she was arguably just as large of a target.

Max wiped his hands on a towel. "What's up?"

"Are you good with tech stuff?"

"What do you mean?"

"I want to turn the guest house into a temporary office. I won't last long in Dad's space without going crazy. It's hard enough at the office. I need to move the computer, printer. And if I unplug any of that stuff, it will never get plugged back in the right way."

Max stepped away from his truck and crossed to her. "I can do that."

"Thanks."

"You'll need a desk in there."

"No. The dining table is fine. It's temporary."

"Do you want that now or tonight?"

"By morning would be great."

"You got it."

෴

Hawk had the day off from being glued to Alex's side. Which was probably a good thing, considering how often he found himself staring at her lips.

With the estate covered by an on-site security guard watching cameras and readily available should something happen, Hawk continued the oversight of equipping Stone Enterprises with the updated technology to avoid a repeat of the bomb scare.

The building was much busier than it had been the day before. It seemed more people were comfortable with coming to work after the threat . . . or maybe they didn't think it was wise to push the PTSD card.

Word of his team increasing the safety of the building spread. No matter where Hawk went, he was greeted with smiles and thanks for being there.

Over the weekend, a construction team had been brought in, and the lighting in the garage was no longer an issue.

Contracts for the keyed garage entry system were signed, and that would go in the following weekend.

The small and inadequate security office behind the walls of the main lobby was moved temporarily while space for a much larger area started construction.

Hawk went over the plans for the new space with the owner of the construction company and the foreman who would be used on the job. A digital wall for monitoring the cameras, a steel impenetrable door with keyed entry. Automatic battery backup for the new system. And he wanted it all yesterday.

Chase and Alex had given him a virtual blank check. Doing so ensured that crews would be working around the clock to get everything in place.

Hawk's last demand on the companies doing all the work was the most important. No outside labor. Only seasoned, trusted employees were allowed on-site. Hawk used the bomb threat as a reason for his demand. Their company didn't need to be caught in the crosshairs of an active investigation with the authorities digging into the bomb threat. And should this person strike again, every new person on the scene would be suspected.

No one raised an argument.

It was after four when Hawk made his way to the executive floor, seeking out Chase.

Dee informed him that Chase was busy on a call.

"I'll wait in Alex's office."

Dee didn't seem to know what to do with that information other than stare before Hawk walked away from her desk.

Inside Alex's office, Hawk moved around and considered where he should place the truly hidden cameras he would have the following day. The kind that didn't come from a home improvement store or Amazon delivery.

The door to the office opened, and Chase walked in.

"I'm told you had a productive day," Chase said.

"Your spies are everywhere, huh?" Hawk smiled.

"Busa has his ear to the ground at CMS, and our employees mingle with others in the building. My employees aren't fearful of losing their jobs if they venture an unpopular opinion. They talk to Busa, Busa talks to me . . . It's a win-win."

"Which means your employees at CMS are your spies."

Chase nodded. "Yeah. Essentially. That and Julia. She's at the top of the corporate chain of gossip and texts Piper constantly."

"Your spies are right. There are a dozen things in process. By next Monday, you'll have a monitored garage. The key cards your employees use to enter the building will be used for the garage. If someone parks their car but never comes inside, we'll know it."

"And the guests coming into the building will have to utilize the outdoor lot," Chase said.

"As it should be," Hawk mused.

Chase moved to Alex's desk and stared at the empty chair behind it. "She hasn't taken a break," he said. "I can count on one hand how many days she hasn't been in that chair since our father died." Chase lifted one finger up in the air. "The day we found Max and confronted him. And that was only a half a day." A second finger went up. "The day we attended Max's mother's funeral . . ." Chase studied the ceiling for a moment, then lowered his hand. "That's it. Wait . . . and an hour or maybe two at the end of the day, and only because she has an evening event that requires her to go home and get ready."

"I'm surprised she hasn't gotten sick," Hawk said.

"True. But . . . my point is, her absence is going to be noticed."

Hawk shook his head. "I still don't think she should have a predictable schedule."

"I agree. We all do. Truth is, we're worried about her. Piper is trying to convince her to take some time off. Get out of town."

"She'd still need protection."

"Of course," Chase said. "That goes without saying. If we can convince her to go off the grid for a while, can I count on you to see that she's safe?"

Hawk found the question strange. "That's what you're paying me for."

Chase raised a brow. "True. Although I'm not sure how it would work if she went to Europe or played in the snow for a week in Colorado. Would you have a tag team watching over her?"

"Depends. If she's in a high-profile location, then yes. If she's truly off the grid and no one knows where she's at, then no."

Chase smiled then. "Okay. There's no way we're going to convince her to take off until after Piper and I are back. She'll never go along with us postponing our honeymoon."

"I feel for anyone trying to get your sister to do something she doesn't have her heart in doing."

"We have a little over two weeks to work on her."

A knock sounded on the office door.

"Come in," Chase called out.

Dee walked in with her hands filled with a bouquet of yellow roses in a glass vase.

"These came for Ms. Stone."

Chase stared at the flowers like he didn't know what they were. "From who?"

Hawk stepped forward. "Who brought them up?"

"A delivery—"

Hawk cussed under his breath, cutting her off. "No more direct deliveries to this floor. Pizza, flowers . . . anything."

Dee blinked several times, turned to look at Chase, then back to Hawk.

She held out the blooms. "What do you want me to do with these?"

Hawk took them from her.

"Thank you, Dee. We'll make sure the new rules are expressed to everyone."

"Is there a problem? Did someone threaten Ms. Stone?" Dee asked.

"It's a precaution," Chase said quickly.

Hawk moved to the desk and set the flowers down.

Dee left the room in silence, closing the door behind her.

Hawk stared at the small envelope with *Alexandrea Stone* written on it.

"Any idea who these could be from?" Hawk asked.

Chase shook his head. "If there was a man in her life, we'd know it."

Hawk reached for the card. "The last time someone sent her a package, it was under a car and disguised as a bomb."

Chase and Hawk locked eyes.

Hawk held up the card and looked for a hint of permission to open it. Not that he needed it, but if this were personal . . .

That thought left a strange taste in Hawk's mouth.

Yeah, he didn't need permission.

He pulled the small note from the tiny envelope and read.

I've heard of your troubles. I'm here to help if you need me.

    Ashraf

Hawk handed the note to Chase.

What the hell was Ashraf Bakshai doing sending Alex flowers?

"The oil guy?" Chase asked.

Hawk nodded.

"You don't think he could be behind last Friday?"

"That wouldn't have been my first guess."

But Hawk wasn't about to rule the man out.

Chapter Sixteen

Alex stared at the yellow roses as if she'd never seen a rose before in her life. "What the hell is Bakshai sending me flowers for?"

Hawk, Chase, and Piper stood beside her, all of them looking at the yellow buds.

"Yellow roses mean friendship," Piper pointed out.

"Three dozen is a serious friendship," Chase said.

"I'm not his friend. I don't know the man. Nor do I want to," Alex huffed.

"Men send flowers to open doors," Piper said.

"Do they?" Alex asked.

"Your father did. All the time."

Alex shivered. "That's gross."

"In fact, I'm pretty sure I sent yellow roses to women on your father's behalf several times."

"Women in a professional role?" Chase asked.

"Not routinely. But your father didn't like working with professional women. Patriarchy and all that." Piper picked out a bloom and held it to her nose.

"Bakshai and your father used the same playbook," Hawk said.

Alex caught Hawk's gaze. "You think he's hitting on me?"

The look on Hawk's face said he considered it.

"Yuck."

"Or maybe he constructed the Play-Doh bomb so he could do this?" Chase suggested.

Alex stared at Hawk. "What do you think?"

"I think I want to know more about what your father and Bakshai had in common. Why he was eager to get you alone, why he came to your office . . . and how that ties into this."

She paused. "You sound less like a bodyguard and more like an investigator every time I see you."

Hawk looked away. "I haven't always worked for Ed."

What does that mean?

"Should we bring Fitzpatrick in on this?"

"Do you think Bakshai is responsible?" Hawk asked instead of answering the question.

Alex couldn't see it. "What motive? To scare me into asking for his help? He has to know I have more resources than that. He hasn't made himself endearing to me. Like I'd turn to crying on the shoulder of a man I just met."

"You don't cry on the shoulders of the men you know," Chase said.

"Exactly! I have you and Max . . . Nick, and even Gaylord and everyone that comes with that whole Texas branch of our new family. Bakshai isn't on the list."

Hawk picked up the card next to the flowers. "Maybe there is a hidden message in this?"

"Seems cut-and-dry to me," Alex said.

"Maybe your father called on him with some *troubles* . . . or vice versa."

The three of them looked at Piper.

She shook her head. "I already did a search through past calendars, and outside of the event you just crashed, Bakshai's name doesn't come up."

Alex took the card from Hawk's hand, looked at it again, then tossed it on the table. "What do I do with this?" She threw both hands in the air. "Have my assistant thank him and move on? Call him and ask him what he means? Ignore the gesture?"

"You're playing chess here. Move the pawn. Have Dee thank him on your behalf. If he is playing a game, he'll make the next move. If he's looking at you as some kind of conquest, he won't give up so easily," Hawk told her.

Alex rested both hands on the table and let her head hang. "I half expected pity flowers from you or Max," she said looking at Chase through the corner of her eyes. "Not this."

Chase shook his head. "I know better, and Max is . . . where is Max?"

"He's in the guest house setting up an office space for Alex," Piper said.

"What's wrong with Dad's office?" Chase asked.

Alex lifted her head to glare at her brother. "*Dad's* office!"

"Oh," Chase said when he realized what she meant.

"I know, it's dumb. I don't care. The rest of the house has lost the feel of the man, his office . . . not so much." Alex hated that it bothered her so much. That the memory of him grated on her nerves, even after nearly a year.

"If you're going to be in the guest house, we will need another camera or two," Hawk said. "I'll see what we need and have someone on it in the morning."

"I didn't think of that," Alex said.

Hawk placed a hand on her arm. "That's not your job."

She felt his fingers squeeze briefly before letting go.

When he left the room, her gaze followed him out. Hawk's soft smile and gentle touch while making sure she was safe felt a little too good to be true.

❦

Hawk tightened his tie around his neck and then pulled down on the edges of his suit.

He didn't need to look like a guest but needed to blend in for the Hawthorn event Alex had to attend. Hawk had quizzed Alex on the event and didn't feel extra eyes were necessary. This wasn't Stone Enterprises as much as a personal endeavor.

"It's a dinner and an auction. My father attended every year."

"How many guests?"

"I don't know . . . a hundred," Alex had told him. "I've actually been looking forward to it."

The drive to the estate was starting to feel like the norm. Alternative routes had been figured out, and the best timing to avoid the worst of the traffic sometimes meant Hawk was early.

In the driveway, a hired black SUV waited with the driver standing outside the vehicle.

The service the Stone family used had been vetted and approved, which freed up staff from Hawk and Ed's team.

Hawk parked his car on the far side of the driveway and then walked over and greeted the driver.

Elliot, the middle-aged driver, had arrived early because he'd picked up Piper's parents at the airport and drove them in.

Hawk obtained Elliot's phone number since the man was on call for their return trip.

He checked his watch and started toward the house.

Alex was punctual for work events. The question was, Did she take her time for private ones?

Hawk rapped his knuckles on the door and paused. When no one answered, he went ahead and let himself in.

Voices in the back of the house told him where everyone gathered. He followed the noise and was met with everyone but Alex and two new family members.

Sarah turned and smiled at him first. "Hi, Hawk."

"Good evening."

Max stepped up and shook his hand. "How is everything at the office?"

"Construction teams are ready to invade and should be out by Sunday night."

Max smiled. "Glad to hear it."

Chase spoke a little louder than who Hawk had to assume were Piper's parents, who were doting over their granddaughter. "Hawk, these are Piper's parents, Margaret and Darryl."

Darryl reached across the island. "A pleasure."

"Likewise," Hawk said.

The Midwestern parents went back to talking with Piper and cooing over Hailey.

"Is Alex getting ready?"

"She'll be down any minute," Sarah told him.

Piper walked past him, her greeting a simple hand to his arm and a smile. "I don't know why we're all standing in the kitchen. Mom, Dad . . ." Piper walked back the way Hawk had entered and toward the massive front room of the house that had enough seating for twenty.

The family followed.

Hawk trailed behind.

Chase walked beside him. "Be thankful you're leaving."

"You don't like your in-laws?" Hawk asked.

"Piper gets stressed around them. I conned Max and Sarah into sticking around as a buffer."

Hawk chuckled. "I'll take an auction with strangers over family drama."

"You definitely pulled the long straw."

As the family funneled into the living room, the sound of a woman's heels clicked on the stone of the staircase.

Hawk slowly looked up and found Alex floating down.

Holy shit.

Hair that was almost always pulled back in a tight ponytail was fashioned in a loose bun, or updo, whatever women called it. Tendrils framed her face and wisped down her bare shoulders. Spaghetti-string straps on a burgundy gown that draped across her chest, went in to hug her slim waist and her hips before falling to the floor. A slit to the side showed her long leg and black stilettos with each step.

Hawk stared while the others in the room continued with their conversations.

Alex stopped at the bottom of the stairs and placed the long coat she'd carried on the banister before looking up and meeting his eyes.

She'd used a heavier hand with her makeup. Smoky eye shadow and black eyeliner. Her lips were the perfect complement of color for the dress . . . and her.

Hawk didn't think he'd ever paid attention to a woman's makeup before. Most of the time, he thought it was a waste. Alex was certainly beautiful enough without it, but like this, there wouldn't be a heterosexual man in the room that didn't look twice and have their wives hitting them to gain back their attention.

Hawk couldn't help but stare.

Was that a blush on her cheeks?

The smile that hinted on her lips said it was.

Wow, he mouthed, knowing she could read his lips.

Someone in the room whistled and broke the silence that stretched between them.

"Damn, sis. It's a good thing you have a bodyguard," Max called from across the room.

Bodyguard.

Hawk needed to remember that.

Alex was not his date. She was his assignment.

He stepped aside when she walked past.

Alex waved a hand in front of her face as if she were warm. "What was that? I didn't quite hear you," she teased.

Max laughed.

"That dress is Oscar-worthy," Piper said.

"I'll be sure and wear it there if I ever get a chance to go." Alex crossed to Margaret and Darryl. "Nice to see you again."

She kissed Margaret on the cheek and smiled at Darryl.

"Where are you off to?" Margaret asked.

"A fancy dinner that I won't be able to eat and still fit in this dress."

Sarah pointed at Hawk. "Make sure she eats."

Alex looked over her shoulder at him, a challenge written in her eyes.

"I'll see what I can do."

She turned back toward their guests. "We have all week to catch up."

"You look fantastic, Alex. Try and have fun," Chase suggested.

Hawk took the liberty of draping her coat over his arm before opening the front door.

They stepped out of the house and into the cooler air. "Do you want this on?"

She shook her head. "Not in the car."

Hawk placed his free hand on the small of her back as she descended the stairs to the car. He used the excuse that women in tight dresses and high heels had a tendency to lose their footing. But in truth, he simply needed to touch her.

She felt like porcelain under his hand.

Small and breakable.

Even though he knew Alexandrea was anything but.

Elliot opened the door of the car when they approached, and Hawk took the driver's place until Alex was seated.

He closed the door, then rounded the car and pulled in a deep breath.

This was going to be a long night.

Once Elliot was on the road, Hawk glanced over. "You're going to make me work for my money tonight."

She kept her eyes forward. "I never said I'd make your life easy."

Hawk chuckled and then took a deep breath. "You're stunning, Alexandrea."

She looked at him then, a flush to her cheeks. "Thank you."

They arrived at the airport thirty minutes later.

Elliot drove right up to the airplane on the tarmac, where a pilot stood at the bottom of the stairs to greet them.

Another reason Hawk didn't see a need for more security was because of the location of the Hawthorn dinner and auction.

It was in Napa Valley.

They'd be landing on a private airstrip close to the vineyard where the event was taking place.

"Hello, Carson," Alex greeted the pilot. "This is Hawk Bronson."

They shook hands. "Welcome aboard."

Inside the jet, Alex took her jacket from Hawk and hung it in a closet.

Carson told them their flight path, altitude, and approximate time in the air before closing the door of the plane and taking his seat next to the copilot.

Hawk took in the space. Plush deluxe seats framed the windows. A couch took up one wall, a large television was affixed to a half wall.

"Bathroom, galley, and bedroom," Alex pointed out to him.

As private aircraft went, this was one of the nicer ones that Hawk had seen.

"I've found where you spend your money," Hawk said.

"This was all Dad." As she took a seat and crossed one long leg over the other, the slit of her dress parted, and Hawk had to look away or risk drooling. "Can you believe Chase and I never stepped foot in here until after he was dead?"

That surprised him. "Really?"

"He wasn't much for sharing."

Hawk took the seat opposite her. "I suppose that's why you and your brother seem so well adjusted and down-to-earth."

She reached for the seat belt. "I can't help but wonder how long that will last."

"How so?"

"Between my dress, shoes, and handbag, I'm wearing five grand. We're on a private jet that's going to cost . . ." She closed her eyes and shook her head. "I don't even want to know how much . . . to go to an auction at a vineyard where I have every intention of dropping some of Dad's money on wine I don't need, but arguably want, with a body-guard at my side. How long will it take for me to start complaining about turbulence? Or the quality of the food at an event?"

Her humility was refreshing.

"So long as there are people in your life to bring you down here with the rest of us, you'll be fine. Besides, what's the point of making money if you're not going to spend it?"

"That's something Gaylord would say."

"Wise man."

The sound of the engines firing up filled the air.

"I've met some extremely rich people, Alex. It's the ones that treat others like garbage that you have to watch out for. You and your broth-ers don't have that in you."

The seat belt sign went on with a chime.

Carson's voice came over a speaker. "Ms. Stone, Mr. Bronson . . . we're about to take off. Please fasten your seat belts."

Hawk buckled in.

"Who?"

"Who what?" he asked.

"Who were the people you're talking about? The rich ones?"

He thought of the faces he'd just as soon forget. "No one you'd know."

She didn't press. At least not directly. "What did you do before you worked with Ed?"

How much should I tell her?

"I had a federal job."

"FBI?"

"No."

She looked at him silently.

The aircraft picked up speed as it raced down the tarmac before lifting into the air.

Hawk took a glance at his watch, noted the time.

All the while, Alex stayed silent with her unwavering gaze.

He sighed. "There are immigration and border authorities that check people and cargo on entry. And then there is another federal branch that stops drugs, human trafficking, firearms . . . you name it, from ever getting to the border. That's what I did."

Alex's mouth opened in surprise. "Undercover?"

"Sometimes."

Any smile on her face had fled. "That sounds dangerous."

"The people involved in that life don't like being intercepted." And already, he'd said too much.

"What made you stop?" she asked.

The sound of a gunshot, the flash of heat in his gut. The tear in his soul. "I had my reasons," he said, hoping she'd understand that he didn't want to talk anymore about the life he'd left behind.

The intensity of her stare wavered. "I guess that makes you over-qualified for babysitting me."

He wanted to thank her for not pressing.

Instead he paid her a compliment. "Dressed like that, I'm going to have my hands full."

Chapter Seventeen

Before they landed, Hawk showed her a couple of hand signals she could use if she needed him to intervene. She really wasn't sure why he bothered until they walked into the event.

Hawk helped her with her jacket, gave it to the attendant collecting them, and then stopped at the perimeter of the room.

"What are you doing?" she asked.

"I'm not a guest," he reminded her.

"But you're—"

"Going to be close by at all times, but not someone you need to introduce or explain why I'm here."

It never occurred to her that Hawk wouldn't be directly at her side the whole night.

Though she realized that she and her family had security several times over the past year, and none acted like they were a guest.

"Oh."

"I'll let the event security know who I am."

She looked around the room. "They have security here?"

Hawk smiled and dipped his head closer to hers. "Over there," he said, looking across the room at a woman wearing a suit and standing with her hands behind her back. "There," he said again. This time, it was a man, looking much the same, who stood by a back exit. "And the two we walked past at the door."

Alex looked over her shoulder, even though she couldn't see the two Hawk spoke of. "Oh."

He chuckled and stood tall. "Situational awareness, Alexandrea."

She shrugged. "That's why I have you, Mr. Bronson."

Hawk nudged her shoulder with his. "Have fun."

Waiters walked the room with trays of wine. Mainly reds, but a few whites were mixed in.

Alex skipped those and approached a tasting area and lifted a glass with a splash already poured.

A woman stood to her right and started a conversation right away. "This one is lovely. A perfect start to the evening."

Alex brought the wine to her nose.

She smelled berries.

"Have you been to this event before?" Alex asked.

"We never miss it."

Alex sipped the wine, and her taste buds sang. She and her family made a habit out of pulling wine from her father's cellar without looking at what the bottle cost. As Nick had said, *"The old man collected but didn't drink it. Now he's dead and can't."*

Now it was part of every family gathering.

Alex was certain the people at this event would be shocked to know that she'd paired a thousand-dollar bottle of wine with Triscuits. And poured out a wine just as expensive because she didn't like the taste.

"Is this your first time?" the woman asked.

"It is. I'm Alex."

The woman smiled. "I'm Kim. My husband is around here somewhere."

Kim walked with Alex to a couple more tastings before Alex moved back to the first one and asked for a full glass.

"Tell me, Kim. How does this work?"

Alex listened while Kim explained the process of the auction.

When Alex looked up, she'd find Hawk on the fringe of the room, his body angled toward her, his eyes either on her or on those by her side.

Alex found a pamphlet with the wine that was being put up. The estimated value and starting bids were written down. All the details of the wine, which Alex really didn't know much about, age, grape, region . . . and the points that apparently made up the price.

The very expensive price.

There had been a dozen or so bottles, or wineries, that stuck out as favorites that she'd sampled from her father's cellar. Wineries with bottles on auction now.

Alex excused herself from Kim's side and made her way to the auction table, gave them her information, and took a number so she could bid.

When she turned back to the room, a man slid in beside her.

"Good evening," he said.

Somewhere around forty, balding slightly, but that didn't take away from his kind eyes and easy smile.

"Good evening," she replied.

"I couldn't let the most beautiful woman in the room walk by without taking a chance and saying hello."

"You flatter me."

"As often as you'll let me," he said. "My name is Lawrence."

Alex shifted her glass of wine to the one holding her clutch. Then extended her hand. "Alex."

He took her hand and squeezed her palm in a way that said he wanted more than her name.

"I would have remembered if you'd been here before."

"It's my first time."

Alex glanced up and noticed that Hawk had moved a little closer, his eyes honed in.

Lawrence lowered his voice. "Are you the type to drink the free wine and watch or lift your number and make everyone else cry for their loss?"

"I'm not sure yet," she told him. "What about you?"

"A little of both." He raised an eyebrow.

Movement caught Alex's eye.

Hawk had shifted positions again.

Did he think she was in danger?

Lawrence asked what wine she was drinking. When she told him, he shook his head and took the glass from her hand.

"Trust me, if you like that, you'll love this."

He gently took her elbow and guided her to the far end of the tasting stations after setting her glass on a passing waiter's tray.

Normally, Alex wouldn't let a stranger tell her what she'd like and not like. But this was an event designed to have you try new things, and Lawrence appeared to know what he was doing.

And he was openly flirting with her.

The man wasn't overly handsome, but not unattractive either. They stood eye to eye, which was shallow of her to consider, but Alex liked what she liked.

Although Hawk was still three inches taller than she was in heels.

Lawrence reached around a guest and snatched a tasting pour for her to sample.

He watched as she brought the glass to her nose and then her lips.

Oh, yes. Richer, fuller body.

Alex smiled.

"See?" Lawrence asked, proud of himself.

"You were right."

He took the glass from her a second time and asked the server to fill it up, then took a glass for himself.

When they turned away from the people at the stations, Lawrence placed a hand on her back to guide her.

She felt herself stiffen on autopilot.

Flirting was one thing . . .

Alex shifted away from his hand.

If he noticed, he didn't flinch. He simply let it drop.

Hawk, on the other hand, scowled from across the room.

Alex caught his eye briefly. He looked like he wanted to pounce.

She shook her head, and he took a step back.

Was he protecting her, or jealous?

Alex didn't have an opportunity to figure out which before an announcement was made that dinner was about to be served.

"Would it be too bold of me to ask to join you?"

She smiled. "I don't see why not."

Although it might be a hazard to his health, from the look Hawk was throwing their way.

They took a seat at a table close to the auctioneer's podium.

The table slowly filled with people, and the conversation flowed.

A local couple who owned a winery in the area kept them entertained with stories of auctions of the past. Another couple, younger, were from South Carolina and were in the early stages of buying a winery on the East Coast.

It was refreshing to hear about someone else's business that wasn't remotely like hers.

When they asked about what Alex did, she told them that her business was the kind that made her want to drink the wine and left it at that.

Several times during the meal Alex found herself searching out Hawk.

While she cut into the steak that made her mouth water, she wondered what, if anything, he had eaten since they arrived.

Lawrence pulled her attention away from her thoughts of Hawk's stomach to ask how long she was staying in Napa.

She started to answer when someone stood up at the podium and caught the attention of the room.

"Welcome to the Eleventh Annual Hawthorn Dinner and Wine Auction. I see plenty of familiar faces and some new ones here tonight. Those of you who are joining us for the first time . . . you're right, we have purposely let the wine flow in hopes of loosening your wallets."

The woman leaned over and whispered in Alex's ear. "He says the same thing every year."

"However, we do promise that whatever you bid on tonight will be worth it."

The waiters moved around the room, removing plates and setting new, uncorked bottles of wine on the tables.

For the next ten minutes, the auctioneer gave a brief synopsis of some of the wine that was being auctioned.

Alex flipped through the pamphlet and smiled.

Oh, how her life had changed.

A year ago, she sat in her condo, drinking wine that never exceeded fifty bucks a bottle, and those were a splurge and certainly not the norm. Now she was here. Auction number in hand.

The room quieted as the first wine was brought up to the front, talked about, and the opening bid was set.

Alex watched the first round to see who was playing.

The second bout was much the same, a little livelier, and therefore ended at a higher price than the first.

The third was a label Alex had circled. A wine she and Nick had cooed over just weeks after her father's funeral.

The thought made her feel like an ass, but the feeling didn't last long.

The opening bid for the lot she wanted was three thousand dollars for six bottles.

Alex was the second bidder to raise her paddle.

The increments went up by a hundred, and a rapid fire of people shot the bid over five thousand in just minutes.

"Five thousand two hundred?" the auctioneer said to Alex.

Only when the auctioneer focused on Alex and one other bidder did she turn to see who was just as anxious to have the wine as she was.

The other person leaned forward, and Alex caught her breath.

Melissa.

"Five thousand two hundred?" the auctioneer asked again.

Alex nodded.

"Do we have five thousand three hundred?"

Melissa stared directly at Alex and raised her paddle.

What the hell was she doing there?

They went back and forth until the wine hit six grand.

Alex hesitated and eventually shook her head, letting the wine go to Melissa.

Melissa lifted her chin as if saying *I win*, then turned her attention back to those at her table.

Hawk moved along the side wall of the venue and caught Alex's eye. *Melissa?* he mouthed her name.

Alex offered a short nod and then turned around.

The entire dance repeated two lots later. But this time the lot was a case of wine, the bid ended at over eight thousand, and the wine was going home with Alex.

It became very apparent that anything Alex bid on, Melissa was right there with her. To the point where the room anticipated their volley and sat back to watch.

More times than not, Alex played Melissa, letting the wine go to her at a much higher price than the auction anticipated.

The last auction before the break between the less expensive and the ultra-exclusive lot was for two bottles Piper had shown interest in.

Alex waited until the wine in question was between two bidders, neither of which was Melissa, before she raised her number.

Melissa, as expected, joined in.

Alex never looked her way and kept bidding. Only when Alex hesitated, and the wine had reached a stupid number . . . did Melissa succeed.

When the auctioneer announced the break, Lawrence leaned forward and asked, "Do you know her?"

Alex barely looked at him as she reached for her purse. "She was my stepmother. If you'll excuse me."

Alex left the stunned table and walked to the back of the room where Hawk stood.

"Did you know she was coming?" he asked.

"If I did, you would have been told."

Hawk looked over the heads of the people moving around the room. "Do you know who she is seated with?"

"No."

Before they could talk more, a woman approached and grabbed Alex's attention. "Alexandrea Stone?"

"Yes, I'm sorry . . . you are?"

"Renee Clairemont. My husband played golf with your father. I'm so sorry to hear of his passing. We were at the funeral—"

"There were a lot of people at the funeral," Alex said. Her words were automatic since she hadn't made any effort to learn the names of the people who had shown up.

"Of course. I wouldn't expect you to remember us."

Alex felt Hawk's fingers graze her arm. "I'll be over here," he said as he snuck away.

When Hawk left her orbit, several other people approached. All of them knew her name, and she knew none of them.

So much for remaining anonymous.

There were those who knew her father and those who knew Alex's soon-to-be stepfather.

While everyone seemed pleasant enough, Alex's joy for the event had waned.

Before the auction continued, Mrs. Clairemont whispered in her ear, "I see Lawrence has found you."

Alex glanced to her table, and the man in question smiling over at her.

"We just met."

Mrs. Clairemont kept a smile on her face but defiance in her chin. "He and your stepmother have much in common. There is a reason he's here and unable to bid on the wine, my dear."

Alex swallowed. Of course. Too much charm painted on way too quickly.

"Thank you," Alex told her.

"Anytime. I do hope Melissa and Lawrence don't scare you off from this event. You're much more pleasant than your father was."

"So is a pit bull."

Mrs. Clairemont laughed as she walked away.

Alex slipped on a smile and returned to her seat.

Lawrence pulled out her chair and continued to say the right things and laugh at the right times.

Alex kept her newfound knowledge of the man's motivations to herself.

The auction resumed. And even though Alex hadn't planned on raising her bidding paddle again . . . she did. Twice, she spent too much money on wine she didn't need.

She waited for the guilt that didn't come.

When the auction ended, Alex said her goodbyes to the people at her table and was left with Lawrence.

"You've made this otherwise boring event much more memorable," he told her.

"It was very memorable for me." Alex smoothed her palm over her dress and looked him in the eye.

He took that as an invitation and reached out to touch her arm.

Alex turned to the side at the last second.

His eyes narrowed.

"Can I see you again?" he asked.

"A date?" she clarified.

He smiled.

"No."

That smile fell.

Instead of calling him out on his search for a sugar mama, Alex said, "I don't feel that . . . spark. The kind one should if they were going to date."

"I have a way of growing on people," he told her.

"Like a fungus?" she asked.

He scowled.

Alex pointed to the back of the room. "I need to go settle with the auction. Thank you for your company, Lawrence. Perhaps I'll see you next year."

"But . . ."

On the way to the tables set up to settle her bill, she noticed Hawk standing by with her coat draped across his arm.

Alex removed her cell phone from her purse and sent a quick message to her pilot.

When she was finished pressing send, a person stopped in front of her.

Alex met Melissa's smile.

"Hello, Melissa. I wasn't expecting to see you here."

"Your father and I attended every year."

"Were you even old enough to drink when you first attended?"

Melissa scowled.

"Are you here looking for the next Mr. Stone?" Alex couldn't help the dig.

"I'm doing everything I can to not need another one," Melissa admitted.

"Admirable of you."

Melissa dropped her smile. "The police came to me. Asking questions about buildings and bombs."

Alex noticed Hawk moving closer as patrons weaved in, out, and around the two of them.

"The police questioned a lot of people."

"That's not the impression I got." Melissa gripped her purse with both hands. "What I can't wrap my mind around is why you or your brother would think that I would want to blow up a building and a business that I am now part owner of."

Alex wasn't sure of that either, but disgruntled widows screwed out of millions because of a prenuptial had a way of making the list of suspects. "How *did* you come to be on the board? There is no possible way you had the funds to buy Yarros out."

Melissa smirked, not giving away even one card. "Some of us have to work to make the money in our accounts and buy our shares. We didn't have it given to us."

Hawk stepped close at that point, his eyes on Melissa.

She looked at him, then back to Alex.

Melissa's brows knitted. "You brought a bodyguard," she said flat out.

"We should go," Hawk said, reaching for Alex's arm.

Melissa leaned back. "Someone threatened you."

Alex wasn't sure what bothered her more, the fact that Melissa genuinely sounded concerned or that she'd made the conclusion at all. "See you at the next board meeting."

Alex turned.

Melissa stepped in front of her.

Hawk put his arm out, keeping Melissa out of reach.

She held up a hand and backed away. "Much as I'd love to take some of Stone Enterprises out from under you, and the occasional bottle of wine, I'd never stoop to violence."

Chapter Eighteen

"The guilty always say they're innocent," Hawk told Alex in the car en route to the private airstrip where the jet was waiting for them.

Watching one woman all night shouldn't have left him feeling spent.

But he was.

Primarily because there were so many people watching her.

Especially the man who whispered in her ear all night long.

"Melissa gains nothing by taking me away from the equation. Her kicks come from humiliating me, causing hell in my personal life. Leaking information to the tabloids is her speed. Bombs and AI-generated threats using my voice?" Alex shook her head. "She isn't capable."

Hawk couldn't disagree more. "I learned a long time ago to never underestimate the ones that look innocent, shy, or appear to be unintelligent. Women pretending to be something they're not isn't anything new."

"Same goes for men."

"In my experience, the egos of men make them much more vocal about their abilities compared to a woman."

Alex twisted in the seat and looked at him. "Women hide their capabilities from men, not other women. Especially women like Melissa. If she had presented herself as a strong, capable woman to my father, he never would have sought after her."

"That doesn't mean she isn't," Hawk pointed out.

"Maybe."

The driver pulled them onto the tarmac, and Hawk jumped out to lend Alex a hand.

She thanked the driver before taking the steps onto the plane.

Inside, Hawk was hit with the smell of something savory.

The pilot stepped out of the cockpit and greeted them.

"Thank you, Carson," Alex said.

A plate sat on a table in front of one of the chairs. The kind that was covered, like a dish from room service. Hawk assumed that was where the flavorful scent was coming from.

"I asked Carson to pick up something for you to eat," Alex told Hawk.

"I hope you like your steak medium rare," the pilot told him. "I figured you could nuke it in the microwave if it wasn't done enough."

Hawk's stomach rumbled at the promise of food. The finger food that was passed around at the event before the meal was served had been his dinner.

And Alex had noticed.

"I appreciate it," Hawk told Carson. But Hawk's gaze was on Alex.

"No problem at all. We were still at the restaurant when Alex sent the message."

Alex placed her purse and the bottle of wine she was holding on a chair and started to remove her coat.

Hawk stepped behind her and drew it from her shoulders while Carson closed the door to the aircraft.

Hawk lowered his voice. "That was very thoughtful of you."

She paused and turned her head slightly to look at him over her shoulder. "Mini quiches aren't enough for a meal."

He hung her coat in the closet. When he turned back around, Alex handed him the bottle of wine. "Can you open this?"

Taking the bottle from her, he moved to the galley in search of a corkscrew. "How much did this one cost?"

"Nothing." Alex sat and reached down to remove one shoe. "All the wine I bought is being sent. That was a parting gift."

"This is a long way from free," he said.

Alex set her shoes to the side and leaned back. "I still feel like I'm spending *his* money."

"It's your money now."

"Yeah, but he gave it to me."

Hawk pulled the cork free and found the wineglasses. "You work every day, Alex. You're earning it. You don't have to keep giving the dead guy credit."

He handed her the glass and met her smile with one of his own. "Is that what I'm doing?" she asked.

"I'm just a casual observer, but yes." He turned to put the wine in the galley.

"Do you like wine?" she asked.

"On occasion," he told her.

"Red wine and red meat go together," she said.

"I'm working."

Alex rolled her eyes, stood, and put her full glass of wine on the table next to his meal and then moved beside him in the galley and reached for another wineglass. "For the next hour and twenty minutes, you're a guest. Besides . . ." She placed a hand on his chest and patted what was under her fingers. "It would take more than one glass to affect *this* enough that you couldn't do your job."

His pulse skipped when those dark eyes looked up into his.

"One," he said quietly.

She placed the empty wineglass in his hand and stepped out of the galley.

The engines of the plane started up, and they both took their seats.

Ten minutes later, they were leveled off, and Hawk took his first bite. The food had cooled, but it was still hitting the spot.

"Did you enjoy your first wine auction?" he asked between bites.

"Aside from seeing Melissa, yes."

Hawk thought of the man who had glued himself to her side the entire night.

"And your companion?" Hawk fished for information.

"My what?"

"Larry." Hawk had asked around enough to know that Alex's dinner buddy had never come to that event with the same woman twice.

Alex chuckled a little. "He looked more like a Larry than a Lawrence." She sipped her wine. "He wasn't my *companion*."

Her voice held a hint of annoyance.

And that made Hawk grin. "He looked . . . cozy."

"Did he?"

Hawk hummed a yes to avoid talking with a full mouth.

"He wanted to be."

That was obvious.

Hawk swallowed his food. "Not your type?" he asked.

"If I wanted dependents, I'd adopt children. Not date them."

"So, he did ask you out." And why was Hawk even talking about this?

As soon as the question hit his head, he dismissed it.

Because Alexandrea intrigued the hell out of him. And she deserved someone better than . . . *Larry.*

Hawk took the last bite and looked up to find Alex staring at him.

"Was it good?" she asked.

"Delicious."

"Do you think I should have told Larry yes?" she asked.

Hawk coughed on the steak that suddenly wasn't going down easily.

He sipped the wine to ease the cough while Alex stared.

"What could a man like him possibly offer you?"

When she hesitated to answer, Hawk picked up his plate and took it to the galley.

Alex followed him with her empty wineglass. "You seem to have an opinion on this subject. What kind of man should I say yes to?"

"That's easy." He set the dish down and picked up the wine bottle to refill her glass. "A Viking."

"Someone to lord over me." Her tone held a rough edge.

"Someone to protect you with their own life."

Surprise lit her eyes.

He took the glass from her fingertips and filled it halfway before handing it back.

She took it absently.

"Little Larry wasn't that guy," Hawk told her as he set the bottle down in a secure bottle holder.

She shook her head slowly, her lips parted. "No. Nowhere close."

The plane hit a patch of thin air and lunged slightly.

Hawk reached for her glass with one hand and for her with the other.

The length of her body pressed against his. The hip he held felt like porcelain that would break if he squeezed too hard, and yet the rest of her promised an entirely different experience with that same squeeze.

Several moments passed, and neither of them moved.

Eyes locked, breath . . . a little too fast.

Was that her body pressing even closer?

Damn . . .

Those eyes asked for what he knew he should avoid.

His lips parted.

As did hers.

Fuck.

A chime in the cabin from the cockpit sounded before Carson's voice poured ice over them.

They stepped back. Let air take up the space where their bodies had touched.

"Ms. Stone, Mr. Bronson, we're hitting some turbulence. Please keep your seat belts on."

Back at their seats, Hawk finished his wine, and Alex stared at the dark beyond the window.

Their almost kiss was forgotten.

Chapter Nineteen

"You look like shit."

Considering Hawk wore a tux like every other man at the reception, the insult pierced his jaded ego.

"You know how to make a man feel special, Stevie."

Chase and Piper's wedding ceremony had been filled with laughter and tears.

Nick officiated since apparently, he was the one who had signed the real license after the happy couple's legal marriage took place.

Max stood beside Chase and Alex beside Piper.

Piper was undoubtedly beautiful in a silk wedding gown and flowers in her hair as opposed to a veil.

Only Piper wasn't the one Hawk could focus on.

The maid of honor wore a similar style of gown, off the shoulder, pulled in at her waist and falling to the ground. Her golden gown matched the class she carried with her wherever she went.

She was the one that had invaded his sleep every night since the wine auction.

Before that, if he was honest.

And the "shit" look Stevie was referring to was due to those hours of lost sleep.

Memories in the form of alarming dreams woke him every morning. Some like they'd always been. He was staring down the barrel of a gun, knowing he wasn't going to escape the bullet. And terrified that the bullet would miss him and hit *her*.

It was the *her* that changed.

"You're not sleeping." Stevie's words were an accusation, not a question.

"I sleep." Hawk watched the wedding party as the photographer captured the memories of the day.

"You're having nightmares again, aren't you?"

Hawk pulled his attention off the Stones and directed it at Stevie.

"You wake up one time pulling a gun out, and you never live it down."

They'd been on an overnight assignment, and it was Stevie's watch. His past snapped him out of sleep, and Stevie was the one to have Hawk's gun pointed directly at her.

"Talking about—"

"I appreciate your concern. But I'm fine."

Hawk patted her on the shoulder and walked away.

The radio in his ear turned on. "I call bullshit," Stevie said for everyone to hear.

"What's bullshit?" Charlie asked from another end of the venue.

Hawk looked back at Stevie and shook his head.

She rolled her eyes and walked away.

⁓

"He's staring at you again," Nick whispered in Alex's ear.

They stood close to the cake table, participating in Nick's favorite pastime.

People watching.

But they weren't the only ones.

The hair on her neck had been on end all day, and when that familiar heat tingled up her spine, she'd turn her head to see Hawk close by, his eyes locked on her.

"It's his job," Alex reminded Nick.

"That gaze does not scream *paycheck*, it bakes in desire."

Alex sent Nick a disbelieving scowl. "Did you just say 'bakes in desire'?"

"I can't help it."

"Maybe if you stopped watching Regency era programming on Netflix, it would help."

Nick waved a hand in the air. "I finished watching it, now I'm reading the books. Women really had it hard back then. *Baking in desire* was a desired endgame."

"Being a rich widow was the endgame," Alex corrected him.

"Exactly . . . then they baked with whoever they wanted to bake with."

Alex laughed at the metaphor.

"Hawk is definitely baking for you."

Her neck tingled, the feel of his gaze brushed against her skin.

Alex turned just enough that she needed to glance over her shoulder to confirm what she already felt.

Hawk *was* staring.

Instead of looking away, which he'd been doing most of the day, his lips tilted up.

Nick gasped. "God, how do you get any work done with that going on all day?"

"I've seen him twice since the wine auction." They'd fallen into a pattern. The days Alex spent working from the estate, other members of the security team were close by. Hawk used that time at the office to ensure the new system was being installed to his liking. Then, on the days she came into the office, he was by her side.

Either outside the door of her office, inside on occasion, or across the room.

He was her shadow and impossible to ignore.

The moment in the airplane was never talked about.

In fact, they both acted as if it had never happened.

Only it did.

And Alex couldn't stop playing their conversation over and over in her head.

"What kind of man should I say yes to?"

"That's easy. A Viking."

"Someone to lord over me."

"Someone to protect you with their own life."

On an especially frustrating night when the words wouldn't shut up, Alex did a little online research about Viking men. And their women.

Apparently, the Viking men took their job as protectors of their wives and families to a very bloody end. Even though women were considered inferior to men, arguably a societal norm that was still practiced throughout the world, they were treated far better than in other cultures at that time.

If Vikings were still in existence, Alex could easily see Hawk standing among them. Shoulders back, eyes piercing . . . a sword strapped to his side. Cuts and scars on his skin as a reminder of battles won during the fights to keep his family safe.

Hawk raised an eyebrow at her from across the room, jolting Alex into realizing she'd been staring at him . . . for several minutes.

Nick cleared his throat and huffed one sharp "Ha!"

"Stop." She tilted her glass of champagne to her lips.

"I don't understand why you're not jumping on that," Nick said.

She glared at her friend. "Some of us think about the morning after, the next day."

Nick paused, his smile wicked.

Alex knew his next words were going to be scandalous.

"I'm sure he'd have all kinds of energy the morning after and the next—"

"Nicholas!"

Nick chuckled, glanced over her shoulder, and started to walk away. "I'll just meander over here and give you two a moment to discuss *lingering looks and lustful thoughts.*" His last words were a whisper.

But Alex heard them and, at the same time, felt the air around her zap.

"Did you need something, Ms. Stone?"

Hawk had started to use a formal title when she was at the office. Maybe to remind them both that almost kissing wasn't the wisest of choices.

In turn, she used his last name.

She cleared her throat and forced herself to face him.

Jeans on the man were something to behold.

But the tux? He hummed with James Bond vibes.

From the wire dangling from his ear to the weapon she knew he had at his side.

And she was staring again.

He'd asked her a question . . . what was it? "Uhm . . ."

"Did you need anything?"

"Ah . . . no."

He waited a breath. "You were staring."

Her gaze moved to his ear. "Can everyone hear me from that thing?"

"No. I have it silenced."

"Oh." Alex kicked herself. Since when was she at a loss for words?

The lights in the room dimmed, and the emcee invited Chase and Piper onto the dance floor.

Alex pivoted to watch her brother and sister-in-law as they held each other and the music started to play.

Hawk moved directly behind her. His warm breath floated against her skin, and his whispered words pressed against her ear. "They look happy."

Her neck tingled. "They are."

Hawk didn't move, not away, not closer. Although closer would be difficult without touching.

"Why were you staring, Alexandrea?"

Her name sounded like a caress. Parts of her body that hadn't tightened in a long time did so now. Her dress didn't afford her a bra, and she was sure that if anyone looked hard enough, they'd see how her body responded to Hawk's words.

What the hell should she say?

She swallowed, her mouth suddenly dry. "I was thinking about something you said," she told him honestly.

"Which was?"

Oh, God . . .

"Vikings."

"What about them?"

She turned her neck but didn't look him in the eye. That would be a fatal error. "I wondered if you descended from them."

He hummed with a soft laugh. "You pictured me as a Viking?"

Alex nodded but stayed silent.

Her skin jumped when Hawk placed his hand on the small of her back.

Such an innocent touch, but it made her eyes drift closed to simply capture the moment.

"I won't let anyone hurt you."

She let out a tiny gasp as he drew a circle on her back with his thumb.

The emcee invited the parents onto the dance floor, then the wedding party.

At the same time, Hawk's hand drifted away, leaving her cool and wanting.

"Go," he whispered, giving her a small nudge.

She wanted to grab his hand, pull him with her. Only that wouldn't look right, and questions would fly. Questions she wasn't sure she had the answers to.

Chapter Twenty

Hawk racked the barbell after his last rep and sat up on the bench he had been lying on.

He pulled a towel over his face. Sweat was a welcome relief.

Maybe if he pushed himself physically, sleep would outweigh his dreams, and he'd finally wake without adrenaline coursing through his veins.

"Look who made it in today."

The familiar voice had Hawk turning his head and splitting his lips into a smile. Standing, he thrust his hand out to greet his brother.

"When did you get home?"

Rhett pumped his hand and then pulled him in for a hug.

"Three days ago."

Hawk took a good look at him. "This is new," Hawk said, brushing a hand against his own face.

Rhett swiped at the beard covering his chin with a shrug. "You know how it is."

Yes, Hawk did.

A beard was a man's best disguise if unkempt and dirty. Toss in clothes to match the filth, an accent, or a second language, and you could be anyone.

"Mom hates it."

Hawk nodded. "Mom hates everything to do with the need for it."

Rhett was older than Hawk by fourteen months. They were close growing up. They had to be, with all the moving around they did. Hawk idolized his big brother and had no problem following him into his profession.

Only Hawk had gotten out, and Rhett still took long deployments deep in the South American jungles, pretending to be something he wasn't.

"She should be happy with one of us playing it safe."

"I don't think that's how it works, brother," Hawk said.

Rhett lifted his chin. "Where have you been? It's not like you to miss your gym time."

"I've been coming at different times. My client's schedule varies."

"Your client? As in one?"

Hawk nodded.

"Consistent?"

He knew where his brother was going with this. "It's a family business. She's the CEO."

"She's married?"

"No." Hawk realized he answered too quickly when Rhett lifted an eyebrow.

"Why does she need you?"

"Someone has threatened to put her in a grave. So far, the police have zero leads on who it could be."

Rhett nodded a few times. "I see your job hasn't changed so much."

Hawk thought of the private jet, the estate . . . the lack of humidity and men walking around with ARs on their backs. "The working conditions are better. Don't tell Mom."

"Who is watching out for your CEO now if you're here?"

"This isn't like Colombia or Guatemala. When she's home, the team is there. When she's out, I'm with her. And why all the questions? Looking for a job?"

"I've touched a nerve. You like this woman." It wasn't a question, and Rhett knew he was right before the words ever left his mouth.

"I know what you're thinking, and this isn't the same thing," Hawk told his brother. He lowered his voice. "Her father isn't involved in organized crime. He isn't even alive."

Rhett nodded. "All right. If you say it isn't the same thing, then it isn't the same thing."

"Good."

"Does she—"

"Are you here to work out, or should we go grab some tea?" Hawk interrupted.

Rhett threw his hands up in the air with a smile. "Got it."

Hawk retrieved his phone and car keys and moved to the next bench to start another set.

A missed call caught his attention.

He scrolled through, saw Charlie's name, then realized a text message came in right after the call.

Call!

Charlie was at the estate and wouldn't demand attention unless something was wrong.

Hawk turned away from his brother and put the phone to his ear.

Charlie answered on the first ring.

"What's going on?"

"She left."

Hawk went still. "Alex? What? Where did she go? Why didn't you stop her?"

"What, what? I don't know, and she didn't ask permission. One minute she was in the kitchen, and the next, she was driving out the gate."

"Everything okay?" Rhett asked.

Hawk shook his head. "I'll call you later," he told his brother before doubling his steps to his locker, grabbing his bag, and heading out the door. "Did she get a call? Did she say anything to you?" Hawk asked Charlie.

"She said something about work. I assume she meant the work she was doing from here."

Out in the parking lot, Hawk put his phone on speaker and scrolled through his phone to see Alex's location.

According to her GPS, she was on the freeway headed toward Stone Enterprises. "Damn it, Alex! Looks like she's on the way to the office." Hawk hit the button, unlocking his car before he reached it.

"I can head over."

"No. If someone is watching the house, they'll know you left. I'm on my way."

Morning traffic did what morning traffic did best . . . it sucked.

Forty-five minutes later, Hawk pulled up to the front of Stone Enterprises. Right behind Alex's Lexus.

Hawk strapped his gun holster to his side, ripped his weapon and ID badge from the glove compartment, and shot out of his car.

He pulled on a light jacket, but there was no mistaking the fact that he'd just left the gym and wasn't dressed for a day at the office as Alex's chaperone.

Hawk stormed past the front desk, straight through the security system, and to the elevators.

Those milling about the lobby gave him double looks.

The closer he came to the executive floor, the more unpleasant his demeanor became.

Every employee that slowed his ascent made his eye twitch.

Finally, the doors opened, and Hawk sailed by Kira at the reception desk and straight to Alex's office.

Hawk made eye contact with Dee and pointed to the closed door of Alex's office. "Is she in there?"

Dee blinked several times, opened her mouth, closed it . . . opened it again. "Yes."

Hawk took a step and reached for the door.

"She's in a meeting."

He didn't give a fuck.

He snatched open the door and pushed through like the force of a crashing wave.

At least five people stared at him from the sitting area of Alex's office. Whatever conversation they were having screeched to a halt.

Hawk met Alex's eyes in an instant. "Mr. Bronson, we are—"

"We need to talk." His breath heaved in his chest.

Alex stood and glanced briefly away. "If you'll excuse me, I'll only be a minute."

Hawk held the door open for her as she passed by.

"What . . ."

The moment the door closed, Hawk took hold of her elbow and led her to Chase's office, which he knew was vacant since the man was on his honeymoon.

Once alone, Alex pulled her arm free.

Hawk took several steps away before facing her. "*What* are you thinking?"

"What happened?" she asked.

"Why are you here? Why did you get in your car and sneak away from the security that you agreed was needed?"

Her shoulders slumped; her eyes narrowed. "You drove down here to ask me that?"

"Answer the questions, Alexandrea. Rushing to the hospital, the scene of an accident, these scenarios I can buy into, but here?"

The entire drive over, all Hawk could think was that Alex had been lured by whoever placed that bag under her car, and she was walking into some kind of a trap. Even though there was relief at the sight of her in what looked like a routine meeting and not a vacant office with no one able to locate her in the building, Hawk was pissed.

When she didn't answer right away, he added, "And why didn't you respond to my calls?"

"I . . . my . . ." She took a deep breath, then placed both hands on her hips and glared at him. "First, I didn't sneak. I left." Alex lifted two fingers in the air. "Second, my business sometimes requires unexpected and immediate meetings that cannot be put off or avoided. What you have so rudely pulled me away from is one of those meetings." She took a step closer. Waved another finger. "And third, I was on my phone the entire drive in and haven't had a moment to assure you or answer your call." She stopped directly in front of him, lips pressed in a firm line of annoyance.

That was rich.

Alexandrea was annoyed.

"You hired me to keep you safe." His words were a rough whisper.

She lifted her arms to the empty room. "I'm safe."

"And if this was a setup?" he yelled.

"And every person in that room was behind the Play-Doh bomb? Not likely, Hawk," she yelled back.

"You agreed to a bodyguard. The office protection, the house security."

She paused, tilted her head to the side. "I still do, but this couldn't be avoided. Besides, nothing has happened. Not so much as a peep from—"

Hawk reached out, grasped her arm. "From the person who likely knows your brother married this weekend and isn't in the office? The person who, if they are watching the estate, knew you left without me?" It would have been so easy to take her out on the drive down the Beverly Hills road or as she was exiting her car. On some level, Hawk knew those things could happen even with him by her side.

He squeezed his eyes shut with the sudden image of her falling back after the loud crack of a gunshot.

"Hawk?" Alex's voice had softened. Her fingers touched his hand as he grasped onto her arm.

He released her instantly, realizing he held her too tight. And then turned away and walked to the window.

Get a grip. No one shot her.

Still, the image lingered.

He heard her walk closer, and his tension started to ease when her hand touched his shoulder.

She's safe. She's alive.

"Hawk?" Alex stepped around him and looked into his eyes. The concern he felt for her rippled in her gaze at him. "Are you okay?"

He wasn't. Not really. And Hawk knew he was all kinds of fucked up with the feelings boiling under his skin.

Hawk lifted his palm to the side of her face. His fingertips brushed over the skin where the feared gunshot had struck in his mind.

The heat of their argument flashed in her eyes and morphed into something completely different. Passion, yes . . . but of a different kind.

Alex did not pull away from his hand, not even when he placed both palms on her face.

Her lips parted, and her breath mixed with his.

She was so damn beautiful. So damn alive.

"Hawk . . ." His name was a breath on her lips. Lips that tilted to his.

He didn't stop to rationalize or talk himself out of what came next.

He simply dove in.

Hawk pulled her forward and pressed his lips to hers.

She was still at first.

One second.

Two.

And then Alex pressed into him and kissed him back.

He coaxed her mouth open and tasted the sweet and tart of her tongue against his. He slid one hand to the back of her neck, the other to her waist, and felt her delicate fingers grasp his hip.

This was so much more than any dream that plagued him in his waking hours or lulled him to sleep at night.

Her touch, her taste . . . would hold on to him long after she was gone.

Hawk felt his body tighten in response, forcing him to remember where they were and how much he needed to end this moment.

No sooner had the thought entered his head than the lights in the room suddenly went dark.

He released her lips, his eyes widened.

Alex was looking at the closed door.

The darkness came with silence as the hum of the lights in the room was gone, the air vents no longer blew.

"Power outage?" Alex asked, looking at the ceiling.

The passion below his waist turned off almost as quickly as it had switched on. He reluctantly left her arms and walked to the door. Hawk tuned in to any voices or noise beyond the door but didn't hear anything.

"You have generators, right?" he asked.

"Yes, they normally kick on."

Hawk's spidey sense trickled up his neck.

He reached for the weapon at his side and released it from his holster.

"It's just a power outage," Alex told him.

"How often do they happen?" he asked as he reached for the door.

A sound in the room hummed, and the lights flickered before the emergency lights turned on. Not that they needed them with all the natural light coming into the room from the windows.

"We've had a few." Alex moved beside him.

"Stay behind me."

"I'm sure it's—"

He turned to her, his eyes were a warning.

Alex stopped talking and stood behind him.

Hawk eased the door open.

The noise from the people in the office was much the same as it had been when he'd stormed through only a handful of minutes before.

There were no sounds of alarm. No cries of concern.

Only the muttering of voices. One in particular asking if someone forgot to pay the electric bill.

Then laughter.

Hawk's shoulders relaxed as he poked his head outside and didn't see anything abnormal.

He holstered his weapon and opened the door farther.

Dee's desk was empty, and one of the men in Alex's office had stepped out into the hall.

Hawk turned to Alex right as the electricity in the building sprang back to life.

"Just a power outage," she said with a grin.

Maybe, but he'd still investigate and see if it was only in the building, or the block . . . or the city.

He blew out his first full breath he'd taken in an hour.

"I need to get back to my meeting," she told him.

Hawk studied her then, the dusty rose of her lips, which were a little swollen from their kiss, but whatever color she used on them was the kind that stained and didn't smear.

"I'll be right outside."

She looked him up and down. "Blending in?"

He lifted his hands and shrugged his shoulders. His gym clothes were about as acceptable as Alex showing up in a bikini. "Consequence of your actions." Truth was, he had a change of clothes in his car. Not a suit, but something more than shorts and a T-shirt.

He noticed the muscles of her neck work a swallow. "Try not to attract all the attention of the women in the office. I pay them to work."

For the first time in an hour, Hawk smiled.

Chapter Twenty-One

When Alex had left her office, Hawk wasn't the one standing by.

It was Stevie.

Alex was surprised to see the other woman, and from the looks on the lawyers' faces as they left Alex's office, they were, too.

There had been no escaping the next six hours of hell behind her desk. And in truth, she was somewhat relieved that Hawk wasn't the one driving her back to the estate at the end of the day.

Hawk had apparently driven her car back, returned, and left with his.

Maybe he needed to dissect what their kiss had meant as much as she did. And to do that, you needed time alone.

Or with a best friend.

Her text to Nick was code.

S.O.S. 6:00. Indian or Thai, you pick up. I'll have the wine.

Their college code was law. Whoever sent the message was hosting and couldn't be denied unless there were extreme circumstances.

Alex stared at her phone, waiting for Nick's reply. God, she hoped he wasn't busy.

Max and Sarah were in Phoenix, looking at retail space for the headquarters of the nonprofit Max was launching. A program to help orphaned kids in trouble with the law. A cause Max knew all too well since that had been his life.

Which meant the estate was empty, except for whoever was on tap for her security guard throughout the night.

A security guard that had yet to be Hawk during her sleeping hours.

How much rest would she manage if she knew Hawk was watching her sleep? Not that the security guards actually set eyes on her at night.

But now that she was one hundred percent sure of his attraction . . . *their attraction*, maybe he would be inclined to peek in on her when none of the other guards had.

Alex's phone buzzed in her hand.

Nick replied. 6:15. Indian. This had better be good.

Stevie hadn't said much from the driver's seat, or from her perch on the chair outside of Alex's office door all day.

"Thank you for stepping in for Hawk," Alex said.

"We're a team. Although I am surprised he asked."

"I wasn't expected to go in today."

Stevie's jaw was set, her eyes straight forward.

"I'm guessing you already knew that."

The other woman nodded. "Taking off the way you did was stupid. Could have gotten you killed."

The harshness of her tone stiffened Alex's spine. "That might be a bit extreme."

"You only think that because it's been a minute since the bomb threat. Several days of silence. Let me help you remember." Stevie reached for her phone, which was in a mount on her dash. Next thing Alex knew, she heard her own voice calling in a bomb threat.

"911, what's your emergency?"

"There's a bomb in the Stone Enterprises headquarters. Don't bother with security footage. I've taken care of that."

"There's a bomb?"

"More than one Stone belongs in the family plot."

"Where is the b—"

"Tick, tock. Tick, tock."

"Where—"

"Tick, tock. Tick, tock. Any death is on her hands. Evacuate the building. Let her know I'm watching."

Alex stared out the window, her jaw tightened.

"Do you need to hear that again?" Stevie wasn't playing around.

"No." And she didn't. Hearing the recording did exactly what Stevie wanted it to do.

It scared Alex.

"I won't be able to avoid the office forever," she said.

"Don't worry. Now that you've proven you're easily persuaded to leave the protection you hired for yourself, this caller will try something else."

"How do you know that?"

"It's what they do. They watch and wait for a weak spot, and then they strike. The next time you get a call that makes you consider leaving the estate, or work . . . or wherever alone, consider it to be a trap." Stevie turned onto the street leading to the estate, never once looking Alex's way.

Alex held her hands to keep them from shaking. "I was served papers today, for a lawsuit brought on by my previous employer. Our lawyers needed me—"

"Alive. Your lawyers need you alive." Stevie looked at Alex in that moment. "Nothing that happened in that office today couldn't have taken place an hour later."

The woman was right.

"It won't happen again."

Stevie stopped in front of the electric gate, lowered her window, and looked at the camera.

The gate opened.

"Hawk is very good at what he does. Let him do it."

Alex felt sufficiently scolded.

Rightfully so.

Even though Alex's job was important, rushing to the office wasn't worth the danger it could cause others by her actions.

By six fifteen, Stevie had handed Alex off to the guard on duty for the evening. There were now two of them. Neither one was Hawk.

Two, according to Stevie, because of the change of events and the fact that Alex was the only one home.

Wearing a lounging outfit that felt like cool wind on a hot day over her skin, Alex opened one of the bottles of wine she'd bought from the auction and let it breathe while she welcomed Nick in.

He pushed the bag of takeout into her arms as he walked through the front door. "I need to hear everything, but first . . . I need to change."

The smell of curry and spice made Alex's stomach rumble. In all the crazy of the day, she'd forgotten to eat.

A problem she planned on rectifying as soon as possible.

"Meet me in the family room."

Nick swung his overnight bag on his shoulder and marched to the closest guest room to change.

Alex set out wineglasses, plates, utensils, and napkins on a coffee table in the smaller family room.

Music played through the speakers, and the gas log fireplace had been turned on.

Nick's lounge suit was completely black, and his slippers were white and fuzzy.

They made Alex smile.

She shoved wine in his hand before he could ask the first question.

"Taste first."

"You're cruel, Stone." Nick put the glass to his lips and hummed when he pulled it away. "What is this magic in a bottle?"

"Right?" Alex took her second sip.

"Is this from the wine auction?"

"Yup."

"What did it cost?"

"More than you made today."

Nick rolled his eyes. "That wouldn't be difficult."

The man lied. He was paid well for his field of work.

He took another drink. "Start talking."

Alex sighed and moved to the table filled with boxes of food. She grabbed a pillow from the sofa and set it on the floor for her to sit on.

Nick mimicked her actions.

"I'm being sued."

Nick stopped mid-sit. "What? Who? Is it Melissa?"

"Not Melissa. Regent. They're saying I violated my nondisclosure with them."

"How is that even a thing? You inherited the company. You can't be sued for disclosing to yourself." He sat opposite her on the floor.

"It's not going to stop them from trying."

Nick reached for a container and removed the lid. "What did they say you disclosed?"

"Information on their bid for the Noel properties we need to dump."

"I don't understand how—"

"Hawk kissed me."

Nick dropped the spoon in his hand to the plate with a crash.

Stunned eyes stared at her.

The lawsuit was news. And it deserved some discussion.

But it had been a long-ass time since Alex's lips met anyone else's. And that needed much more airtime.

"Start. At. The. Beginning."

She did. From leaving the estate to Hawk barging into her office wearing gym shorts and a scowl. The true fear in his eyes, the kind Alex knew she'd remember for a while. And the moment she knew he was going to kiss her to after the power outage broke them apart.

Nick leaned on his elbows in rapt attention. "How was it?"

"Intense. It was the kind of kiss that lodges in your chest before it breaks free with fluttering waves."

"Butterflies," Nick said with a sigh.

"More than that. I swore I felt his hand trembling when he touched my cheek. And then he went all bodyguard on me, telling me to get behind him when he checked the hall during the power outage. As if someone was out there waiting for us."

"That's hot."

"I'm so shallow," she said, feeling the same way.

"Then what happened?" Nick asked.

"Nothing. I went back to my meeting, and when it was done, Stevie was sitting in the chair outside my office." Alex put the wine to her lips. They had yet to put the food on their plates.

"No calls? No texts?"

She shook her head.

Nick went back to the container that held chicken curry while Alex reached for the rice. "It's not like he was calling or texting before. Except to go over my schedule."

"He will."

Alex wasn't so sure. "He was scared. Something in the way he looked at me. I saw pain in his eyes."

"Maybe he thinks he can't have you. We both know that's not true," Nick teased.

"It was deeper than that."

He pulled his plate closer and picked up a fork. "Every Hollywood action film tells us that the bodyguard getting involved with the client makes them unable to do their job."

Alex paused. "You think?"

Nick shoved food in his mouth. "Maybe."

"I wonder if that's why Stevie was there and not him." Alex lifted her fork and stared at her plate. What if Hawk did pass on the personal bodyguard position to someone else? The thought had her swallowing hard.

"He won't be your bodyguard forever," Nick said. "Eventually, Mr. Play-Doh will be caught."

She tasted the curry and smiled. The hunger she'd pushed aside all day flooded in. "Stevie seemed to think we'd see something from Mr. Play-Doh sooner rather than later."

"*No bueno.*"

Alex didn't like any of it either. Waiting for the police to find something from what had already happened. Needing another act to find Mr. Play-Doh. Having to stay out of the office, working from home, and not having the ability to do so much as go and have a manicure without someone driving her. Even if that was Hawk. And maybe it was an even bigger suck because it was him. What was she going to do, take him to her annual gynecology visit?

She took another bite.

"I'm considering taking my family up on going out of town. Colorado, I think."

Nick grinned. "And taking Hawk?"

"Who knows if it would be him at this point. The lawyers will deal with the lawsuit. There won't be any need for me for quite a while. Chase will be back . . . he and Piper can handle whatever comes their way. I can clear my head. No one will know where I am. Play-Doh won't be a threat."

"Is that guaranteed?"

"How could he find out anything? You, my family, and Hawk's team would be the only people that knew where I was. Even the cleaning company that takes care of the cabin up there doesn't need to know it's me. They can just clean and stock the place with food before I get there and clean it all up when I leave. No need for them to see me at all."

"It's still winter in the Rockies."

"Barely."

"You don't have winter clothing."

Alex picked up her wineglass, smiled. "Good thing my best friend knows my size and my style."

Nick raised his glass alongside hers. "I know what we're doing the rest of the night."

Chapter Twenty-Two

Instead of going into the office the next day, Alex brought the office to her. Well, Dee.

The security staff rotated. Nick left by eight with the promise of returning with half a closet's worth of winter clothing by the evening.

As a personal shopper, Nick was the best. A skill Alex had tapped into many times since taking over the company. Shopping used to be a pleasure, but lately it proved to be a chore. And even more so when you couldn't leave the house without a babysitter.

Perhaps if Alex stopped calling the security team that, it would be easier. But it still felt as if her wings had been clipped.

Dee arrived at the estate at nine sharp.

It was obvious by the expression on her face that she'd never been there before.

In apparent awe, she looked at the ceiling and beyond Alex when they met in the foyer.

"This is . . . this is . . ." Nothing articulated beyond that.

"Yes, it is," Alex agreed. "I'm setting us up in the dining room for the day. Thank you again for coming here and not the office."

Dee took up pace behind Alex as she led the nervous woman through the rooms until they reached the dining room, which was actually the breakfast room. The formal dining room was almost never used.

"It's okay. I mean, it's not a problem. I'm . . . you're the boss."

Alex smiled and encouraged Dee to put her belongings down. She pointed out the closest bathroom and encouraged Dee to help herself to anything in the kitchen.

With her second cup of coffee in hand, Alex sat across from Dee and told her the plan.

"We need to shuffle my schedule. I'm going to take some time off, and I don't want anyone in the office knowing about it. It's why I asked you to come here."

Dee opened her laptop slowly. "Is there a reason?"

"For the time off?" Alex asked and then quickly answered. "I need it."

Dee shook her head. "For the secrecy. I supposed it doesn't matter, but—"

Alex tapped her finger on the table, wondering just how much to disclose. Dee was about as harmless as they came, and she didn't appear to socialize much with the office staff. Alex decided a half story was the best she could do. "The authorities haven't gotten any closer to the person behind the fake bomb and threat at the office. The timing of this, my vacation, might appear that I'm abandoning my post while I've asked everyone else to come in. Which isn't the truth. Chase will be back next week, and Piper plans on being available a couple hours a day. Remotely, at first. If no one knows I plan on being gone for a week and a half, we can avoid any talk of a double standard."

Dee nodded. "That makes sense, I guess."

Alex pulled her laptop computer in front of her. "Let's get you logged in to the house Wi-Fi and recognize the printer. We'll start by printing everything for the next three weeks."

Dee avoided Alex's gaze and started typing.

Movement from the other side of the room caught Alex's eye.

Hawk.

He wore a dress shirt, slacks, a coat draped over his arm, and a holster at his side. It was the second time in a week that she saw his gun. Had the man gotten larger since the day before? Or was Alex's opinion of him just greater?

His eyes drifted to Dee, then back to Alex.

"Good morning," she said.

"Morning."

Dee swiveled her head, looked at him, and stiffened.

Was it the sight of the man or the weapon?

Alex went with the latter.

"Do you have a minute?" he asked.

Alex slid out from the table.

She caught Dee's attention and pointed across the room. "Down that hall, second door on the right, there's an office where the printer is located. I'll be back."

"Yes, Ms. Stone."

Alex walked past Hawk and well into the living room, where they couldn't be overheard without seeing who was listening.

Hawk nodded behind him when they stopped. "What's she doing here?"

"It was either that or go into the office. I thought this was the better choice."

He peeked over his shoulder.

"She's harmless, Hawk. I'm having her clear my schedule."

"Oh?"

"I'm taking everyone up on their suggestions. I'm going on vacation as soon as Chase and Piper return." She took a breath. "If I don't leave, I'm likely to repeat what happened yesterday. And I realize that was the wrong thing for me to do. As Stevie reminded me, just because things have been quiet, that doesn't mean there isn't a threat."

A corner of his mouth turned up. "*Stevie* reminded you?"

It was Alex's turn to smile. "Somebody else did, too. But he gave me something else to think about."

She saw his Adam's apple bob in his throat. "About that."

Their eyes locked.

Alex stayed silent, her smile fell. She was not going to play her cards on what that kiss meant to her until she heard what it meant to him.

Shit, she had no idea what it meant.

"It was very unprofessional of me."

What did that mean?

"You regret it?" she asked.

"That's not what I said."

Alex crossed her arms over her chest and instantly scolded herself for the defensive body language. "Is this where you tell me it won't happen again?"

Hawk paused then.

Alex uncrossed her arms.

"I should."

That put a small grin on her lips. "Good," she said. "That was the most spontaneous moment I've had in over a year. Too much information, I'm certain."

Hawk brushed at the side of his face, his eyes roamed hers. "Alex, I—"

She placed a hand on his arm, felt a jolt of electricity with their connection. "Let's just leave this here for now. I already have enough to chew on while I'm trying to focus today. Any more, and I won't be able to function."

He placed a hand over the one she held to his arm. "Okay."

She smiled up at him and forced herself to step away or risk pushing into his arms and repeating their life-changing kiss. "Normally I'd have Dee arrange my travel accommodations. But since security is still needed . . ."

"I'll see it's taken care of."

"Chase and Piper will return on Monday. I want to leave on Tuesday, unless that doesn't work for you . . . or. That's presumptuous." She stopped herself. "*Whoever* is going to come with me."

Hawk lifted an eyebrow. "Do you want it to be someone else?"

It was her turn to throw his words back at him. "I didn't say that."

Their eyes locked.

He smiled and slowly said, "Where are *we* going?"

Her heart filled and heat rushed to her face. "Aspen. Ski masks and slopes. No one will recognize me. There's a service that will open the house up, bring everything we need in, and clean up when we leave. No need for anyone to know I'm there."

"You have a house in Aspen?" His question was more awe than inquiry.

"Aaron had a house in Aspen. I've never been there. I heard it was secluded and next to a stream."

"Cozy."

Alex shook her head. "Knowing my father, cozy won't be the theme. He didn't do anything small."

"Who can give me the information about the house?"

"Piper, but we're not interrupting them." Alex could dig through the family trust, but that would take hours to uncover. "My father's attorney. I'll forward you his contact information."

"Trusted?"

"Yes. If you tell him we need to be off the grid, he won't tell his own wife." Alex felt lighter just planning this. "And you already know Carson."

"I'll take care of everything, Ms. Stone," he smirked.

That made her laugh. "Thank you, Mr. Bronson."

She started to walk away.

"Unless something unexpected happens, I'll be away for the next two days. My brother is here from out of town. We haven't spent much time together."

For some reason the thought of Hawk taking time for his family warmed her heart. "I look forward to hearing about him. Should I call Stevie if I need to leave?"

"Yes."

Alex stepped to pass him.

Hawk placed a hand on her shoulder.

His dark eyes took her in. "You can always call me, Alexandrea." He lifted his fingers and stroked the side of her jaw.

She shivered.

Hawk dropped his hand, turned, and walked away.

∽

She was forgetting something.

Alex hadn't slept in two days, the reality of leaving had hit her twenty-four hours before Chase and Piper arrived home.

They'd stopped in Texas and picked up Hailey, and the estate was once again filled with all of them.

Ten days away would hopefully bring some clarity. Upon her return, there would be another board meeting, this one via Zoom on the off chance their wannabe bomber had a preference.

That was a thought for another time. Right now, Alex stood in the foyer, her bags were already in the car. And she knew, was absolutely positive, she was forgetting to tell Chase something. They'd gone over the schedule three times.

"It's going to come to me at thirty-two thousand feet," Alex said, shaking her head.

"And you'll text me. It's going to be fine, Alex."

"I'll go through my notes on the plane—"

"You absolutely will not!" Piper exclaimed. "Your vacation starts the minute you walk out that door."

Alex lifted the bag in her hand that held her laptop. "I'll have plenty of time for vacation. I'm sure my notes will—"

Piper reached for the computer bag. "This stays here."

"Piper." Alex tried to grab her bag back.

"Help me out here, Chase."

Chase put a hand in front of Piper as if blocking Alex from grabbing the bag back. "She's right, Alex. No work."

"But—"

"Did you need me to check in when we were gone?" he asked.

"No. But . . ."

"You don't trust me to take care of whatever comes up?"

That wasn't fighting fair. "I trust you."

"Then you won't need your computer," he said.

"What's all the yelling about?" Sarah asked as she walked down the stairs.

"Alex is trying to take her computer on vacation."

"I'm pretty sure that's against the law."

Piper laughed.

Alex felt sweat bead on her neck. "I want to be available."

Sarah grasped Alex by her shoulders, turned her toward the front door, and started walking her out. "The only thing you need to be available for is snowball fights and hot tubs in the snow."

Hawk and Max were at the top of the front steps when they made it outside.

"What's the matter?" Hawk asked the moment he saw her.

"I'm being ganged up on."

"We told her she can't work," Chase explained.

Hawk tilted his head back. "Ah, that would explain the sheer panic on your face."

"I'm not panicked."

For a moment, everyone was quiet, then they all laughed.

Sarah hugged her. "Have a great time."

Piper was next. "When you get back, everything will be running so smoothly, you'll plan another vacation by the end of spring."

Chase handed the laptop case to Piper and hugged Alex next. "We're in this together. Trust me."

I can do this. I can do this. "Okay." Her palms were literally sweating. How was it that everyone else was calm, and she was an inch away from losing her shit with worry?

Max was last. "Look on the bright side, you're not leaving everything in my hands. All those lazy fucks would be fired by the time you got back."

That made her grin.

"Don't let her work," Sarah told Hawk.

Hawk shook both her brothers' hands and assured them she'd be relaxed and refueled when she flew home.

Alex made it three steps down before she attempted one more time to plead for her computer. "What if there's a storm and we can't leave and the board meeting—"

Hawk's arm snaked around her waist and directed her attention to him.

"Alexandrea. Get in the car."

Her brows pulled together. "You're bossy."

His arm pulled her closer, his touch much more familiar than it had been before their kiss. "Do I need to pull out the Viking card, toss you over my shoulder, and show you just how bossy I can be?"

His words zapped the work worry away, feeling more like a promise than a punishment.

His fingers squeezed into her hip, his grin held a hint of wicked.

She put a little room between them. "I'm going. I'm going."

Alex marched to the car and climbed inside.

Chase held Piper's hand as they all stood on the steps, watching the car pull out of the driveway. "A hundred dollars says she is on the phone before they reach altitude."

No one took him up on his bet.

"She was so busy worrying about work, I bet she didn't check the weather conditions," Piper said.

"Is it bad?" Sarah asked.

"There's a big front coming in. Internet will not be a thing, and electricity will be sketchy."

"Hawk will keep her safe," Chase said. From what he just witnessed, he'd keep her warm, too.

"Two hundred says *they* join the mile-high club by the time they're back," Max said.

Piper laughed. "Glad I'm not the only one who noticed."

Sarah huffed. "I've been pushing that," she waved at the departing car, "since Hawk showed up."

Chase looked at Max and lifted a fist in the air.

Max met his fist bump while Piper and Sarah looked on.

Chapter Twenty-Three

Before they took off, she was texting Chase about a call he needed to take from someone in Sydney.

Hawk didn't even try and understand why the call was so important that it required an entire Wikipedia page of text before Alex finally put her phone down.

He stretched out and watched her struggle with whether she should call Chase and explain more or was clear enough with just a text.

"When was the last time you took a vacation?" he asked.

"October, year before last."

"Where did you go?"

"Nick and I went to Sedona. We saved to go to an all-inclusive resort spa."

"So, before Dad died."

Alex tossed her phone in her open purse and gave up on staring at the screen.

Mission accomplished, he thought.

"Yeah."

"Expensive?" he asked.

"The spa?"

He nodded.

"Very. But worth it. Daily spa time, organized hikes, yoga classes, organic food. We had a great time."

"And did you call in to work? When you were on this trip?"

Alex peered closer. "I didn't own the company."

"That wasn't the question."

She pulled her hair over her shoulder and played with the ends of it. In all the time Hawk had spent with Alex, he could only count on one hand the times she wore her hair down. It was either up in a ponytail, her work style, or up on her head . . . the cocktail party style.

He liked it down. He felt a part of her inner circle. Only the chosen saw her like this.

"Is this the way the week is going to be?"

"Depends on how many times you reach for that phone."

She growled, and he laughed.

"You're enjoying this entirely too much," she told him.

He leaned forward and rested his chin on tented fingertips. "I promised your brothers I'd keep you safe and bring you home relaxed. Unplug, Alex. It will all be waiting for you when you get back."

"I can't unplug. How will I know if there's an emergency?"

"Everyone of importance knows they can call me."

He saw the wheels spinning behind her eyes.

"Tell you what. Give me your phone."

Her eyes widened, horrified.

"You can check it once a day. Giving it to me will keep you honest."

The expression on her face was almost comical in her desperation to stay connected.

"Unless you're too addicted to the drama."

"I'm not addicted to drama."

"Prove it." Hawk reached his hand out, palm up.

"Fine!" She removed the phone from her purse, stared at it, then thrust it toward him.

That had been much easier than he thought it would be.

He made a point of powering the thing off.

Alex all but gulped before looking out the window.

Stepping off the plane and into the cool, crisp air of the Colorado Rockies brought an instant smile to Alex's face.

It wasn't that she relished the cold, but it was a welcome relief from what she called her "seventy-degree life."

No matter where she was, her world was seventy degrees. In the car on the way to work, the temperature was set somewhere between sixty-eight and seventy degrees. In the office . . . seventy degrees. Same with the house, the grocery store. And the constant outside temperature in Southern California, in the cities, didn't fall all that low, and even when it did dip to, say, fifty or forty-five, it wasn't long before she was back in that seventy degrees.

Bone-chilling thirty, or windchill minus two, was cold. It snapped you awake and forced you to pay attention.

Alex liked it.

Hawk had distracted her on the plane. Asking about her trips with Nick. Quizzing her on how she used to spend her weekends.

Relaying her life schedule brought to light that she was truly a workaholic. And with the fact that she'd reached for her phone more times than she could count since he put it away, Alex had to conclude that she was addicted.

Addiction was proof of not being in control.

That didn't sit well in her chest.

From the airport, Hawk drove a four-wheel-drive Land Rover that had been dropped off from the cabin. Another possession of her father's. Alex looked at the odometer. Less than three thousand miles. She wondered if her father drove any of his vehicles.

Even though Hawk assured her that the cabin had been stocked with food, they stopped at a grocery store anyway to pick up a few things that wouldn't hurt to have more of.

There was snow on the ground, but the roads were clear.

Aspen sat in a valley with the Rockies surrounding the city. A skiing and snowboarding destination, arguably for the rich and famous, meant that it was busy, but not socked with tourists who were priced out.

As they left the city and followed the GPS up into the hills to the Stone cabin, Alex noticed a street filled with shops and restaurants. A place she wanted to explore before the vacation was up.

The first turn off the main road meant more snow on the ground.

The second turn, and the pavement held patches of black ice.

The third, and that ice turned to snow tracked by tires. "I'm glad you're driving," she told Hawk.

"You haven't driven in the snow?" he asked.

"No."

"You should before we leave."

"I'm good," she said.

"For a woman that likes control, I'm shocked."

Was he laughing at her?

"When would I use this particular skill?"

"The next time you're up here."

He had her there.

"Maybe," she conceded.

The homes spread out, and the trees and snow thickened. Even though snow drifted on the edges of the road, the evergreens weren't burdened with tons of the white stuff on every limb. It was still beautiful. The sky was clear, and the sun did a great job of making the untouched snow glisten like a million diamonds had been tossed in just to add sparkle.

Their final turn was the most snow-covered of them all.

From what Alex could tell, only one, maybe two sets of tire tracks trekked in and out.

They crossed over a bridge with a frozen creek underneath. And then the "cabin" came into view.

Hawk slowed the car, and they both stared.

"Holy shit," Hawk exclaimed first.

Her thoughts exactly. "I told you he didn't do anything small."

They looked at each other and smiled.

From the drive, they could see the cabin was made with logs, or at least that was what the veneer suggested. Two-story and sprawling, with a garage on one side.

A giant porch with wooden columns and short fences wrapped around the front of the home.

Hawk pulled in front of the garage and pressed what seemed to be a garage door opener.

Nothing happened.

Not that it mattered, the keys to the Rover also had the keys to the front door.

They both jumped out of the car and walked to the snow-filled steps to the front door.

Hawk tried several keys into the lock before he found the one that worked.

Inside, the caretakers had turned on the heat. Not quite seventy degrees, but Alex would bet it was close.

Two giant coatracks framed the front door, as well as a cleverly designed boot tray.

The foyer had a two-story vaulted ceiling with massive timber beams that opened into a giant great room. The back of the room was nothing but windows. Cut up only by the material needed to keep the panes of glass in place.

Alex walked in with her jaw hanging open. The sectional sofa in the living room alone would sit ten. At one end of the room, a fireplace that could swallow a small child just asked for someone to strike a match. The stone carried all the way up the wall to the second story of the home. At the opposite end of the great room was a dining table for at least twelve and an open kitchen with a wood island that appeared to be cut from one massive tree.

Behind her, Hawk whistled. "This is something."

It was.

She smiled Hawk's way. "Should we find the garage so we can pull the car in to unload?"

"I like that plan."

Alex tossed her purse on a sofa table and shrugged out of her coat.

They walked through the living room and down a wide hall to where the garage needed to live. They found one guest room and then a laundry room. At the far end of the hall, a mudroom, complete with space for boots, skis, all the winter wear, and cubbies filled with towels, did justice to the size of the house. It was there they found the door to the garage.

Hawk flipped the switch, and the entire three-car garage lit up.

A two-door Jeep sat on one end, and the Rover appeared to have the majority of the space.

Hawk pressed the button and opened the garage door while Alex moved deeper and kept looking around. Beside the Jeep was a wall of cabinets. They were mostly empty inside, but they did have bags of some kind of gravel, or maybe it was salt. The kind that service workers put on pavement to keep the ice from forming . . . or making it melt. Alex wasn't sure exactly how that worked.

Hawk drove the Rover inside as Alex opened what she thought would be an exterior door.

It wasn't.

This was the toy room.

As soon as she heard the door to the car open, she called out, "You've got to see this."

Hawk walked to her side and gaped. "Holy shit."

There were two snowmobiles and two quads. Winter and summer fun were considered. One wall had snowboards of varying sizes and colors. A rack, three levels high, was filled with snow boots . . . all different sizes. Some still had the price tags on them. On the other end of that same wall were skis. A clothing rack had snow jackets and pants; most looked like they'd never been worn.

"It's like he bought up a store going out of business."

"Looking at this, you'd think my father liked to entertain."

"He didn't?" Hawk asked.

"To be fair, I don't really know. I've never been here before."

Another garage door opened to the other side of the property to pull out or put away the toys.

They backtracked through the house, this time bringing their luggage with them.

Hawk encouraged her to leave her bags behind while they figured out which rooms they were going to stay in.

A spacious staircase led them to the open second level.

An expansive game room, complete with billiards and a bar, a card table, and a foosball table, led into the hallway that housed the bedrooms.

At the farthest end, the primary bedroom might as well have been outside for all the windows brightening up the space. The king-size bed sat in the center of the room, a fireplace in front of it, and windows all around. Two sitting chairs faced the back of the house, with a view of the mountain beyond. The cream carpets over the dark hardwood floor were stunning, and the faux fur gray and white blanket on the bed begged to be curled up in.

"Do you want your bags in here?" Hawk asked.

She hesitated and moved to the chest of drawers. "I bet this was his room."

The furniture was empty.

"Think of it like an Airbnb. You'd never let the best bedroom go unused."

She peeked into the closet. It, too, was empty.

"Okay."

Hawk claimed the room beside hers. It also had a view of the mountain.

There were two more guest rooms on that level, one had two sets of bunk beds with queen mattresses on the bottom and a single on top.

"Looks like it's set up for kids," Hawk said.

Alex shook her head. "If he expected kids, there would be child-size skis and clothing. This was likely here when he bought the place, and he never switched it out. Anyone looking would think of him as considerate and welcoming." Alex looked Hawk in the eye. "His own children knew he wasn't that."

By the time they were done exploring the house, they'd found a cozy study, brightened by the snow outside the windows and warmed by another fireplace. This one smaller. Books filled a wall, and a desk sat to the side. A small home gym had a treadmill, some free weights, and a few exercise mats. To the side of that, a steam sauna and a door that led outside to a covered patio with a hot tub fit for ten. Outside the covered area, a firepit was surrounded by Adirondack chairs.

Once they'd explored the house, Alex said to Hawk, "I nominate you to schlep all our stuff upstairs, and I'll see what the caretakers think I can cook."

He paused. "You can't cook?"

"Can you?" she asked with a straight face.

He lifted one finger at a time. "French toast, scrambled eggs, and bacon. And I can grill."

Well, shit. "That's two more things than I can manage."

"Seriously?"

She smiled. "I'm a really good 'warmer upper.'"

"We didn't think this through." The man actually looked worried.

Alex grinned. "I can follow a recipe. I don't think we'll starve."

༄

As soon as the sun fell past the mountain, the temperature outside dropped.

Hawk deposited their bags and then brought in several armloads of firewood. Even though the center of the house proved warm enough, the windows sucked in the cold. He couldn't even imagine what it would cost to heat the massive space.

Not his circus and not his monkeys, Hawk reminded himself.

Bottom line, this was Alexandrea's, and she seemed just as clueless about what was there. According to her, neither of her brothers had ventured to any of Aaron Stone's extra homes.

It all seemed excessive for one man. Even one man with his one wife. Even split between the Stone children, it was over the top.

But it was damn nice.

No denying that.

Hawk took the liberty of piling up logs in the fireplace and springing flames to life.

All the way across the great room, Alex was busy putting something together for dinner.

He paused and took her in.

She wore a soft white oversize sweater with a pair of jeans. Her long straight hair was free of any binding and hung down her back. Alex sipped wine from a jewel-colored wineglass and hummed around the kitchen.

Hawk wasn't sure how it had happened, but she'd relaxed before their coats were even dry after coming inside.

"The fire is nice," she told him as he walked toward her.

"Made better by the snow outside."

"I couldn't agree more." She lifted her glass to him. "Wine?"

Hawk shrugged. "Sure."

Alex had already figured out the space and twisted around to get him a glass.

"Anything I can help with?"

"Tomorrow night for sure. Whoever stocked this place had a casserole ready with instructions."

"That's what I smell coming from the oven."

She handed him a glass of wine. "Chicken, rice, veggies, and some kind of crispy top. We'll get a couple meals out of it."

"Did you find any cookbooks?" He took a seat at the island and tasted the wine.

"No. And that's a problem. I'm going to have to find something online."

"Are you trying to get your phone back?" he teased.

Alex was busy cutting up vegetables for a salad. "Maybe." She popped a chunk of a carrot into her mouth.

"This is good." He lifted his wine in the air.

"I found Dad's stash. There's a wine fridge in the pantry."

"Expensive?"

Alex lifted her shoulders. "I wouldn't know. *Someone* took my phone, and I can't look it up."

"You're working every angle."

She finished with the salad and took a seat beside him. "I'm okay. I was afraid this place would feel stuffy or pretentious. Like him."

"It can't be stuffy with this many windows. As for pretentious . . . it feels like a model home. A designer one, but a home furnished to sell."

Alex looked around. "You're right. None of the art pieces, paintings, or sculptures that are everywhere in the Beverly Hills house."

"Your father's taste?"

"So it would seem," she said quietly.

"No family photos or vacation pictures either."

"You have to be invested in your kids to have pictures of them. And if he brought a mistress up here, he wouldn't want pictures of his wife all over the place." Alex delivered the words so coldly, Hawk winced.

"He sounds like a real charmer."

She rolled her eyes. "The thing that surprises me most . . . no office. Yeah, there's a writing desk in the library nook, but no office. It makes me wonder if he had ever been here."

"It was a *vacation* home."

Alex moaned. "Much as it pains me to admit this, the one trait I have from him is a work ethic. Or addiction. If he was ever here for more than a weekend, he worked. Guaranteed."

"Maybe Melissa used this place."

"She would have left a closet full of clothing." Alex paused. "Unless she came here after he died and cleared her space out."

"Wouldn't you have been told if that happened?" he asked.

"You'd think. But we were so distracted trying to find Max after our father's death, a lot of things, like Melissa salvaging what she could, would have gone unnoticed."

That made him wonder what else had gone unnoticed.

By the time they dug into their dinner, they were both on their second glass of wine.

"I've spent a whole lot of time talking about me," Alex said from across the dining table. "I haven't learned much about you."

"What do you want to know?" Hawk asked.

"Tell me about your family. You said you had a brother."

He nodded. "One. No sisters. Rhett and I were a handful from the get-go. I'm sure my parents decided that three of us would be too much to handle."

Alex smiled at that. "What kind of trouble did you guys get into?"

"The usual. Building something, tearing something up. Climbing up a tree just to fall out of it . . . then try it again with a cast."

Alex laughed.

"In high school, if Rhett cut class, I followed. If I got caught, he'd cover for me. The first punch I ever received was from my brother, the first one I delivered was to my brother."

Alex's eyes widened. "You beat each other up?"

He nodded. "If we fought at noon, we were shooting hoops by dinner. Drove my mother crazy."

"I can't imagine."

"We moved around a lot. Outside friendships were formed, but they didn't last any longer than a year or two." Hawk took a bite while Alex asked her next question. "We became each other's best friend."

"Why? Why did you move around?"

That was a big answer.

He swallowed and dug in again. "We were told it was because our father's job required it."

"*Told?*" Her brows lifted in question.

He nodded. "It started right as Rhett was going into middle school. We lived in the suburbs of Chicago. Our parents started fighting, so much that Rhett and I thought a divorce was coming. Instead we moved to a suburb of a suburb in Dallas. Then there was a shithole town outside of El Paso, then it was Nevada. Nevada didn't last long. We ended up on the West Coast and, eventually, close to our grandparents on our mother's side in Orange County."

"But this wasn't a job transfer," Alex stated.

"No. Dad was running . . . hiding. He worked for a textile company in accounting. He and a pissed-off colleague weren't happy with the profit margin the company was making while the people on the floor were barely making do."

"He stole from his employer." Alex put her fork down and picked up the wineglass.

"More like embezzlement," he said point-blank. "Mom made it sound like Dad was a modern-day Robin Hood." Hawk shook his head, took a bite, and talked around it. "Total bullshit. It may have started off that way, but in the end, he was skimming off the top and upped his own lifestyle. We went from having anything we wanted to practically living out of a suitcase."

"Holy crap." Alex had stopped eating to listen. "How did it end?"

"Rhett was in his senior year, I was in my junior year. Dad wanted to bounce again, and Mom put her foot down. She convinced him to turn himself in."

"He went to jail?" she gasped.

"Yup. And the crazy thing, he was out in eighteen months. Turns out the punishment for corporate embezzlement in Illinois is much more lenient than in places like Texas. An entire childhood of disruption, and he could have just gone to 'Daddy Camp,' and we could have led normal lives."

Alex began to laugh. "Daddy Camp?"

Hawk laughed along with her. "Wise words from my grandfather."

"And your mother stuck with him?"

Hawk shrugged. "What can I say, she loves the man. As she put it, she ignored the signs that we were living beyond our means. When he told her what was really going on, they fought but ultimately thought it was best to run. Then Rhett started showing interest in joining either the military or some type of law enforcement."

Alex used her glass to point at him. "That's why he turned himself in. Oh, the hypocrisy."

"Irony. Our grandfather put us through college, where we both earned degrees, and we ended up in the same field of law enforcement."

Alex pushed back in her chair. "Wow."

"You'd like my dad. He fucked up, no doubt about that. But he's a decent guy. Never missed a birthday or Christmas."

"Until he went to 'Daddy Camp'?"

"Hey, some camps have hiking and canoes. Dad's had yard time."

Alex started laughing so hard she had to put her wine down.

It felt good to laugh along with her. Hawk had come to terms with his father's crimes a long time ago. But seeing Alex's reaction was a welcome relief. "I half expected you to be overly judgmental about that story."

"Why?"

"You own a big company. I'm sure there have been cases like this somewhere on the books."

"I have no doubt. But in my case, it seems someone wants to hurt me, not rip me off."

Her comment splashed cold water on his face.

Alex slowly stopped laughing.

He leaned forward, reached for her hand that sat on the table. "I'm not going to let anyone get close enough to hurt you, Alex."

She took a deep breath, blew it out. "You should eat that while it's still warm. It might be the only good thing you get all week."

Hawk thought of how she responded when he kissed her and wondered how soon she'd let him repeat his efforts.

The smile that sat behind her eyes while they stared at each other promised that the time between thinking about touching her and actually pulling her close was going to be short-lived.

Hawk lifted the fork to his mouth and said, "We'll see about that."

Chapter Twenty-Four

Hawk insisted on cleaning the kitchen since Alex had made dinner.

Considering household chores were not on her list of favorite things, she didn't argue.

While he made busy in the kitchen, Alex returned to the reading nook and browsed through her options.

It had been over a year since she'd actually read a novel. Back when she could turn work off and enjoy life.

She couldn't help but wonder if those days would ever come back. Maybe if she could turn off Stone Enterprises while in Colorado, she could bring some of that switch home with her when she returned.

Two well-known novelist names stuck out to her, as did a few covers. After reading the descriptions of the books, she picked two and returned to the living room, where the fire welcomed her to curl up and snuggle in.

A large basket held several soft, furlike blankets.

Warm and tucked in, Alex opened the book and started at chapter one.

Hawk walked behind her and looked at the cover. "Crime fiction?"

She glanced over her shoulder. "Maybe it will give me some insight on your family dynamics."

"You're always thinking, Alex."

She turned back to the book.

"I'm going to shower."

"Okay." Only when he was walking up the stairs did she dare to watch him.

They'd spent the last twelve-plus hours alone, and he hadn't done more than touch her hand.

Not once did either of them mention their encounter since the day Alex decided to take time off.

That was made easier since Hawk had spent time with his family the days following their kiss. By the time he returned to his post at her side, Alex was in full "get shit done" mode. Tunnel vision took her to work in the morning, and her evenings were spent prepping everything Chase needed to take over when he returned.

But now it was time to full-on stop. Stop working. Stop worrying. And stop trying to predict what was going to happen between her and Hawk. For all she knew, he was up in his room right now, trying to figure out how to tell her that he'd thought twice about getting involved.

She couldn't blame him. Her life was complicated. She came with all kinds of strings. Most of which held up a company and demanded that she forget herself for the majority of the hours in her days.

And someone out there was trying to hurt her. Or maybe they just wanted to scare her. The only reason she saw Hawk as much as she did was because of his role of bodyguard. How could they even work outside of this exact situation? She worked sixty hours a week. How would they see each other between her schedule and his? She wouldn't need a babysitter forever.

Alex shook her head, dismissing her thoughts, and started on page one.

By the fifth page, she was yawning.

By the seventh, she'd snuggled deeper in the blanket.

By the ninth, her eyes were drifting closed.

When her eyes opened again, only the orange glow of embers smoldered in the fireplace. The lights in the room had been dimmed so low, she had to focus to see Hawk completely asleep in one of the chairs across from her.

He looked ten years younger sound asleep. The hard edges of his jaw and tense muscles eased, giving him the appearance of someone vulnerable.

Not an adjective Alex would have ever used to describe the man.

Yet there he was, his mouth slightly open, his head resting on the side of the chair.

Had he fallen asleep watching her? He could have just gone to bed.

Then Alex realized, no. He couldn't simply do that. Hawk was there for a purpose.

To keep her safe.

For a moment, she felt guilty for falling asleep on the sofa and keeping him up longer than either of them truly wanted to be.

Her watch told her it was after midnight.

Alex eased to her feet, trying to keep quiet and not wake Hawk up. The book she'd been reading fell from her lap when she stood.

The noise snapped in the otherwise quiet room. "*Shit!*"

Hawk's eyes sprang open.

"I'm sorry. I didn't mean to wake you."

He looked around the room before settling on her. He wiped a hand over his face and stood. "You were out. I didn't have the heart to wake you."

"I think I have some sleep to catch up on." She picked the book up off the floor and tossed the blanket to the side.

"You need it."

She yawned and ended with a soft moan. "I'll see you in the morning."

Hawk stepped closer, his eyes looked deep into hers.

He placed his palm on her cheek. For a minute, she thought he'd kiss her. He did, but those lips pressed to her forehead briefly. "Good night, Alexandrea."

As she walked up the stairs, Hawk stayed behind, turning off lights and checking the doors. She couldn't help but feel like this was the perfect start of her vacation. Even if she was going to bed alone.

◌

The sky had clouded over by the time Alex pulled her lazy ass out of bed.

It was the smell of bacon that pulled her to the kitchen, where Hawk was doing the honors of cooking breakfast.

It was nine thirty.

"Look who decided to wake up," Hawk teased.

"I slept like the dead," she announced. "How did you sleep?"

"It's quiet here" was his answer.

"Too much?"

Hawk shrugged.

Alex found the cupboard with coffee mugs and poured a cup of magic bean juice.

"What's on your agenda today?" he asked.

She leaned against the counter and brought the coffee to her lips. "I say we explore."

"Okay."

"Using the snowmobiles."

He cocked an eyebrow. "Have you ever driven one before?"

"No. How hard can it be?"

Hawk flipped a piece of French toast in the pan. "I guess we'll find out."

Two hours later, Alex stood on the all-terrain vehicle on skis, pulled the goggles from her face, and turned to where Hawk stood in the middle of the circle they'd been practicing on. "The movies make it look easy," she announced.

Hawk had tried it out first. And took to it like fish to water.

Alex, on the other hand, was having trouble with the timing of when to ease up on the gas to come to a complete stop.

"I think it will be easier for you with fresh snow."

She glanced at the sky. "I don't think we're going to have to wait long for that." The temperature was well below the freezing point, and the sky was turning gray.

But she wasn't overly cold. Driving the snowmobile took some serious effort that was keeping her warm. That and the multiple layers she wore to ward off the chill.

Hawk walked over to her, his helmet in his hand.

"How about this . . . I drive, you hang on. And tomorrow, if we get some fresh snow, you try again solo."

A slow, lazy smile spread on her lips. "Is this your way of getting me to wrap my body around yours?"

Her words surprised him.

Hawk looked her up and down openly. He stepped closer. "Remind me to pull a spark plug on one of these tomorrow."

Alex slid back on the seat and patted the space in front of her. "Saddle up, cowboy. I didn't come all the way out here to drive in circles."

A fresh wave of satisfaction washed over her when Hawk tossed a leg over the snowmobile and gripped the handlebars.

He powered the machine and looked over his shoulder.

Alex fixed the goggles over her head, and with Hawk's gaze connected with hers, he gave the machine some gas, they lunged forward, and Alex's body slid right up next to his.

She took the hint and wrapped her arms around his waist.

"This is better," she said.

Hawk put his helmet on, and his voice hummed in her ear.

"Hang on," he told her.

Alex had no idea that helmets for these kinds of toys came with Bluetooth speakers that made it possible to hear what others were saying.

Hawk started out slow as he entered the trees beyond the house. Most of the snow on the trees was gone, but the ground was still thick with a winter full of snow that never melted completely. And as much as watching the landscape was enjoyable, the feel of the man she held on to beat it all by a thousand percent.

He was solid, anchored. When he moved, she did. It was surprising to her how quickly she adapted to folding into him. Her thighs against his, her chest against his back.

It had been entirely too long since she'd been this close to anyone. Even with the dozen layers of clothing between them.

Hawk came to a stop on the edge of the trees and pointed out over a clearing. "That looks safe enough for some speed," he said.

"What are you waiting for, then?" she asked.

He grasped her arms and pulled her tighter and then found the throttle.

One second they were thinking about moving fast, the next they were digging up tracks in untouched snow with a sheer rush of adrenaline.

As one hour turned into two, Hawk's mastery of the snowmobile increased. And the more comfortable Alex was with holding on.

Tiny flakes started falling when they decided to head back to the house.

By the time they made it to the circle track they'd started in, those flakes had expanded in size and amount.

Alex was in heaven.

Living a life in Southern California meant that snow days simply weren't a thing. Yes, she'd seen snow fall. But not often, and almost never like this. In the mountains with no one else around. She knew there were neighbors, but their homes weren't close, and who knew if anyone was actually in them. For all Alex knew, the homes were vacation places for men like her father.

Vacant.

Hawk stopped by the machine he'd pulled out to use earlier. "Think you can manage bringing this around to the garage without me?"

"Driving it there isn't the problem. It's stopping."

He untangled from her and stood. "I have faith in you."

Alex didn't have anything to worry about. She stopped a good ten feet from the door and got off. She had no shame in having Hawk take it in the rest of the way.

She freed her head from the helmet and pulled the knit cap down over her ears.

The cold was getting to her, but the feel of snow dropping on her face felt too good to walk away from.

While Hawk parked the equipment, Alex walked around to the back of the house and watched as the branches of the evergreen pines slowly stacked snow up, one flake at a time.

And quiet.

Why was snow so quiet?

Alex reached down and picked up a handful and wondered just how many individual flakes made up what was in her gloved hands. Tens of thousands? A million?

The sound of Hawk's footsteps crunching in the snow behind her prompted the immediate manufacturing of a snowball.

If you didn't have a snowball fight, did snow even happen?

Surprise would give her the upper hand.

"What are you looking at?" he asked from several feet away.

"Nothing." Alex turned and pulled her arm back.

She noticed the second Hawk realized what she was about.

The first throw hit Hawk on his right shoulder. "This is how we're going to play?"

When he reached for the ground, Alex took off in a run, scooping snow as she went.

A snowball whizzed by, missing by inches. "Ha!"

She fired another round. It didn't get anywhere close.

And before she could make more ammunition, Hawk hit his mark on her chest. "Game on!" she shouted.

Laughing, Alex found shelter behind a chair and started rounding balls.

She made four before she realized the world was too quiet.

"Hawk?"

He didn't reply.

She snuck a peek and didn't see him.

Alex stood to get a better look, and a snowball smashed into her back.

"How the?" She didn't even aim, she just threw the snow in Hawk's direction.

He was laughing and walking toward her, both hands full. "Know where your opponent is at all times," he suggested.

She backed up. "You wouldn't hit an unarmed woman, would you?"

He pulled an arm back.

Alex turned, laughing, and ran.

Hawk made chase, his snowballs launched, and all Alex had the time to do was bend to the ground to pick up an armful of snow and toss it on him as fast as she could.

He dodged and weaved as if he were on a football field. Both of them running around each other, snow flying.

She felt snow falling down the inside of her jacket and hanging from her hair. And in the split second she stopped and realized that cold, Hawk pounced and rolled them both on the ground.

Alex couldn't stop laughing. She used her body weight to roll on top of Hawk. Her legs straddled his waist.

"This is more like it," he said, his voice a low, playful growl.

"Like this?"

"Yeah."

Alex wiggled her hips against his.

Hawk gripped her thighs.

And then Alex smashed two hands filled with snow on his face.

Feeling quite pleased with herself, Alex shifted her weight to stand up.

Hawk wouldn't have it.

Those muscled, capable arms wrapped around her waist, and the next thing she knew, she was on her back with both of her arms stretched above her head, where she couldn't repeat the snow-in-the-face move.

They were both breathing heavy, with smiles so big, Alex's face hurt.

"Now what are you going to do?" Hawk asked.

What was she going to do?

Stare at his smile.

Enjoy the sparkle behind his eyes and the way his gaze drew her in.

With her chest still heaving, her smile slowly fell. She bit her lip and saw Hawk's gaze fall to her teeth.

Alex swallowed and moistened her lips with her tongue.

"Fuck," Hawk whispered before his lips crashed down on hers.

Cold lips quickly warmed with the sheer intensity of their joining.

The weight of him pressing her against the snow-covered ground was a sensation she could drown in and never regret.

She opened her mouth to his, soaked in the taste of him.

Hawk kissed her so hard and so long, she started to forget where they were.

His hands released hers and moved to her head.

She felt the thickness of his gloves and the cool splash of snow that pressed into her face simply because of where they were.

All thoughts of snowballs and playing in the snow were gone, and a whole lot more filled Alex's mind on what they should do next.

Hawk's kiss eased just enough for Alex to choke out, "Inside."

He nodded and was off her in two seconds, his hand grasping hers to help her off the ground.

On her feet, she lifted on her toes and locked her lips to his.

Hawk hummed over her and grasped her hips.

She hopped up and wrapped her legs around his hips before he walked them to the back door of the house.

Hawk struggled to hold her and open the door. Lord knew Alex wasn't making it easy on the poor guy. She nipped at his lip, sucked in his tongue.

They made it inside, the back door crashing as it shut.

Hawk walked her straight past the mudroom and deposited her on the top of the dryer in the laundry room.

Their lips stayed pressed together, her legs spread with him settled oh so comfortably between them. And they both started tugging at their clothing. Gloves flew, boots were kicked off.

Hawk shed his coat and tossed it to the side. When Alex went to do the same, Hawk caught the back of her head, grasped her hair, and pulled it just enough to bare her throat. His lips grazed where her pulse danced and shot a wave of awareness between her thighs. "Yes," she whispered.

She wanted this man, this feeling. Each time their lips met was like a declaration. A branding. *This is mine. I'm claiming it, and no one else can have it.* That's what Hawk's touch was telling her.

Alex was here for it.

All of it.

She tugged at his snow pants.

Hawk struggled to get them off. Down to their regular clothing, Hawk claimed her mouth again. This time when she wrapped her legs around his hips, he was much more capable of maneuvering around the house. But he didn't take them far.

He kicked at the ground-floor guest room until the door banged against the wall.

Alex laughed under his kiss and fell with him on the bed.

Hawk stopped then, their eyes opened. "You're so goddamn beautiful, Alexandrea. I want to hear your cries in my ear when I make you come."

His words alone made parts of her body pucker and spasm. "Yes, please," she said with a smile.

A leg slipped between hers and pushed hard against her core.

Her eyes rolled back, along with her head.

"Just like that," he muttered, his lips pressed to her ear.

She pulled his shirt over his head, and her hands finally met with his flesh.

Corded muscles of his shoulders and back. All the promises his clothing tried to hide but couldn't were now out for her to touch and taste.

She raked her nails over his back and felt him shudder.

That was control.

Control she never wanted to give up.

Their lips met again, hot, wanting.

The feel of Hawk's palm sliding under her shirt felt like fire and ice. Still chilled from outside, but so hot deep under her flesh.

He paused, hips hovering over hers. "Condom?" he asked.

She shook her head. "IUD."

"You sure?"

"Shut up and kiss me."

The man took directions well.

He rolled them over, pulled off her shirt. Palms cupped her breasts through her bra. Hawk lifted his head, buried his face, and licked.

This was passion, this was what poets wrote about. Alex wondered, briefly, if the intensity of this moment, this man, was because it had been so long since she'd experienced anything like this. Or was it him? He was so damn intent on touching all of her. Rolling her on her back, then on top of him.

She reached for his pants, brushed her hand against his straining cock under the fabric.

Hawk moaned and stilled.

She brushed down the length of him and back up, loving the way he shuddered.

When she moved to pull his pants down, his hand caught hers. "Not yet," he whispered.

And before she could protest, he rolled her onto her stomach. Strong hands started at her waist and painted her back. His lips brushed her shoulder, then the other one.

He lifted her hips and tugged her pants down.

When she tried to move, he held her down with one hand on the small of her back. "Let me," he said.

With only the bed under her, her body stretched out and nearly naked for him to do whatever he pleased with, the vulnerability of her position was filled with excitement.

Hawk dropped her pants to the floor.

Out of the corner of her eye, she saw him stand long enough to shake the rest of his clothing free. Then he was back on her. Quick fingers unclasped her bra, he kissed the space where the strap had been. Trailing his hands down her back, he reached her hips and played with the strap of her panties.

She closed her eyes, waiting for him to touch more, anything.

Alex arched into his hands and gasped when he spread her legs. The feel of his lips on the small of her back made her close her eyes. The next sensation was Hawk running his hand down her bottom before reaching between her legs. Fingers pushed past her underwear and slid over her sex.

Alex moaned and rode up on his hand. Her body responded, asking for more with a jolt.

Hawk sprawled out beside her, his fingers moving in lazy circles.

Every inch of his body molded to hers, his sex pulsed on her back and promised to fill her . . . soon.

"So damn beautiful," he whispered in her ear.

Only she was having a hard time concentrating on his words. She was wet and open, and Hawk was . . . close, she was so close.

He pressed his cheek against hers.

Alex craned her neck and kissed him. Only she couldn't hold on.

"Let me hear it, Alex. Let me hear you cry out."

Fingers swirled and played, in, around. And then she was over. Over the crest, over the wave, and her cry filled the room in her release.

"Yes, just like that."

Her body started to go lax, but Hawk wouldn't have it. He rolled her on her back and claimed her lips. Her panties hit the floor, and the length of him found her.

Their eyes met, their kiss hovered, and Hawk pressed himself home. Her back arched, and pleasure started to build once again.

This Viking of a man pressed her back into the bed, filling every part of her. His name on her lips, his hands everywhere on her body. Gentle and then not, playfully controlling with the promise of ecstasy on the other side.

Alex surrendered.

Trusting everything Hawk wanted of her.

Their bodies rose and fell together. He told her—showed her—how beautiful she was to him. Until whispering became too much and all that was left was to find the peak together and hope they would softly land on the other side.

Chapter Twenty-Five

For a woman who craved control, she surrendered in Hawk's arms.

That excited and scared the hell out of him.

Wearing only bathrobes, they relaxed in the kitchen, picking at some cold cuts and fruit, calling it lunch.

While they had been discovering each other, the falling snow had started coming down hard. Well over an inch and a half was covering all the places it had melted off before.

Alex sat on the counter, her bare feet dangling, her robe showing just a hint of her right breast . . . and popping blueberries into her mouth. "Did you check the weather forecast, by any chance?"

"No. Did you?"

"You have my phone."

Hawk tilted his head to one side. "A phone you haven't asked for," he said.

Unashamed, she looked him up and back down. "I've been distracted."

"Oh, is that all it takes?"

Another berry hovered over her mouth. "Don't shortchange yourself."

The woman was good for his ego.

Hawk had his phone charging in the living room and left to find it.

The wind outside had kicked up, and snow was frosting the sides of the windows.

He opened his phone and clicked into a weather app.

The satellite view came in, showing the snowfall outside.

Then he scrolled down the page and stopped walking halfway to the kitchen. "Oh, damn."

Alex hopped off the countertop and walked to him. "What is it?"

He read the report and handed the phone to Alex.

She blinked a few times and looked at the phone again. "Am I reading this right?"

Hawk looked out the window and up. He didn't see a generator when they'd done the tour the day before. He needed to get dressed and take another look.

"Four to six feet of snow?" Alex sounded just as shocked as he was. "Is that normal?"

"The best way to gauge normal is to see how the locals are responding." He picked up the TV remote and turned it on. A midday news broadcast told them all they needed to know.

"The real issue with this storm is the one-two punch, although those in the higher elevations may not notice a break between storms. Expect at least two feet to fall overnight and into tomorrow. By the evening we should see a short break, but by noon Friday, expect three to four feet."

The coverage shifted to the grocery stores, where a reporter was talking to locals about what they were stocking up on to ride out the storm.

There was enough empty space between the shelves to concern Hawk.

Not that he worried they'd go hungry.

The caretakers must have known the forecast. There was enough food in the pantry and refrigerator to carry them for three weeks instead of one and a half.

"We have a wind event with this weather system, so expect power outages and delays in clearing the roads."

Hawk switched off the TV and turned to Alex. "I'm going to check the gas situation and see if there is a generator somewhere."

Alex looked out the window. "This place is going to get cold if the power goes out."

He reached for her, pulled her close. "I'll keep you warm."

That had her smiling. "And when we need to sleep?"

"There's plenty of firewood." He kissed her briefly and let her go. "I'll look for a generator. See if you can find any candles, lanterns, flashlights."

"What about cooking?"

"Worst comes to worst, we can cook over the fire. But my guess is there is a tank for the gas, and that will still work."

"In that case," Alex said, "I need my phone."

"Work doesn't need you."

She patted his shoulder. "Not work. I need to write down some recipes while I have the chance."

He kissed her, wanted to linger. "I'll get it. It's probably best to keep it charged."

"Somebody was a Boy Scout."

"Naw. But I am familiar with living off the grid." He patted her butt. "Time for a scavenger hunt."

The generator was found in a closet in the back of the garage. It still had the zip ties and tape, as if it had been pulled out of the box and stored.

Two five-gallon containers with fuel lived nearby. Not to mention the fuel for the snowmobiles that was stored in the toy garage.

It wouldn't run the house, but it would keep a coffeepot going, plus a few lights and the plug-in portable heater Hawk found next to a stash of camping supplies.

For a man who didn't spend much time there, Aaron Stone had thought of everything one could need when living in the mountains.

Or maybe the credit Hawk was giving belonged to someone else. Like the caretakers.

Yeah, that would be more likely.

Hawk moved the generator to the open patio that was off the kitchen. There was enough overhead coverage to keep the thing from being buried in snow, yet it was open enough to not asphyxiate them anytime they opened the door. Hawk brought every possible device he believed they would need should the power go out.

From what he'd seen on the forecast, the power going out was a given.

Once all the extension cords, the portable heater, lights, and even a hot plate were ready to go, Hawk started the many trips back and forth to the shed where the firewood was stored.

He imagined the walk from the back door to the shed in six feet of snow. Already, he was trekking in a few inches that had piled up on what was already there. But six feet. That was eye level for him. Hell, Alex would have to jump to see over the snow if the skies dumped that much.

Maybe he was being naive, but he was looking forward to being trapped in a mini-mansion with Alex.

He'd crossed the line with their first kiss. He might have been able to get back from that . . . but now that he knew how she tasted, how she felt . . . the way she looked at him and sounded . . .

Hawk shook his head and filled his arms with more firewood.

He had no doubt he'd kick himself later for caring for someone he was supposed to be guarding. *Caring.* Not the right word.

Not the right emotion.

Only he didn't trust himself to dissect his feelings right now.

Their chemistry and connection were off the charts, and he'd have to be a saint to deny her, or him, what they were experiencing.

No.

He'd enjoy this. Enjoy her.

And worry about tomorrow next week sometime.

He smiled into that thought, dumped the armload of wood on the back porch, and went back for more.

∽

Alex found an entire cupboard filled with emergency supplies. Boxes of candles in all shapes and sizes. Several scented ones, mainly the smell of cinnamon and baking spices.

She found flashlights and batteries and even a radio. The kind that was used before cell phones.

That seemed extreme.

But who knew?

Once all the necessities had been located, Alex concentrated on the food they had . . . and how to cook it.

After taking screenshots of a dozen ideas, Alex concentrated on what they should try that night.

Hawk had to know that cooking would be a group effort. If it was left up to her, she'd eat salads, fruit, bread, and anything out of a can. Judging from the size of Hawk, that wouldn't work for him.

The man was an unexpected surprise.

Never in a million years would she have predicted him.

Since she'd inherited her father's estate, the only men that approached her were either twenty-plus years her senior or men like Lawrence, looking for someone to pay their bills.

Outside of her social circle, men simply didn't walk up.

Hawk swooped in. From day one.

His whispers of Vikings and suggested touches amplified their sexual encounter. There was something liberating about letting someone else sit in the driver's seat. A truth she wouldn't say aloud and would probably deny if asked.

Alex heard the door to the patio open and diverted her thoughts.

Analyzing what was going on between them was for another day.

Alex wanted to live in the now.

And from the size of the snowflakes falling from the sky, she'd have a good week to do just that.

Falling asleep in Hawk's arms had been heaven, waking up without him by her side felt lonely.

Which was beyond stupid.

Alex had slept alone virtually her whole life.

Outside of long weekends with past boyfriends, and most of those from her college days, Alex had slept alone. Not even a cat or a dog curled up beside her.

She turned to look at the bedside clock. 7:13 stared back at her.

Which meant they still had power.

Though after looking out the window, she didn't know how.

There had to be at least two feet of fresh powder, with trickles of more floating to the surface.

An easy smile lifted her spirit.

It was spectacular. The branches of evergreen trees were completely white, drooping with the weight like a wet blanket over a pet.

Alex crossed to the window and opened it a crack.

Cold air rushed in, but so did the scent of the fresh winter air.

And quiet. No birdsong, no rustling of leaves or trees. Just the peace and quiet that could only happen high in the mountains with slow-setting snow.

The high winds the weathermen had forecasted didn't manifest overnight. Maybe they had that wrong. God knew the meteorologists in Southern California only seemed to get it right about half the time.

Bundled in a bathrobe, Alex made her way downstairs.

The scent of coffee drew her to the empty kitchen. After filling a cup, she went on the search for Hawk.

She found him in the gym.

Music from a portable speaker played as Hawk lay with his back on the bench, his hands holding two large weights that he was pressing into the air.

He wasn't wearing a shirt.

He hadn't noticed her walk in, so she watched in silence at the ease with which his muscles rippled.

Alex had started to believe that six-pack abs were something Hollywood airbrushed in for the sake of the egos on the screen. That they didn't truly exist in the wild. At least not to the scale of Hawk's.

She licked her lips in appreciation.

The barbells hovered in the air. "Are you just going to stare?"

He had seen her.

"Yes, I am."

Another rep was squeezed in the air.

"I thought you'd sleep for another hour," he said.

Alex set her coffee on a nearby cabinet and walked over to him.

"And I thought you'd be next to me when I rolled over this morning."

"I'm an early riser." He watched her walk around the bench.

Unable to stop herself, Alex loosened the belt of her robe and tossed a leg over him.

She was wearing a nightgown. One she'd tossed in her bag at the last minute in hopes of a moment like this one. Otherwise, she'd be in no more than a T-shirt.

Instead, the black silk spaghetti strap nightgown did a great job of enhancing her natural assets.

The kind Hawk had enjoyed the night before.

She should probably give the man a chance to rest but . . . Alex had some making up to do.

Undesired celibacy had a way of making one think of sex way too much.

Hawk groaned, those weights still in his fists.

His eyes, however, were boring into hers.

"Are you comfortable?" he asked, teasing.

Alex wiggled her hips until she felt the rapidly growing length of him press between the folds of her sex. Even through their limited clothing, she felt his warmth. "That's better."

She traced a finger over his torso, outlining the muscles on display. Hawk hadn't moved.

"You can continue with your workout. Don't let me stop you."

Those weights hit the floor, and Hawk's hands rested on her exposed thighs. "You're fulfilling a lifelong fantasy."

"I am?" She flicked one of his nipples and gave it a little pinch. "Which one is that?"

His hands traveled up as hers traveled down.

"A beautiful woman walks in, catches me in a vulnerable position, and takes advantage of me." He pushed his hips up, bringing his pulsating heat into a much more pleasurable position.

"You don't look vulnerable."

His eyes rolled back when she rolled her hips against his. "Take advantage of me anyway?"

Alex shrugged her robe off and did exactly that.

⌒

"It's beautiful up here. You and Chase need to make the trip. Max and Sarah, too. It's ridiculous that it sits vacant."

Alex convinced herself that one check in was perfectly acceptable on her third day at the cabin. She'd told Piper about the house, the toys . . . the two feet of snow with the promise of more.

"You sound relaxed," Piper told her.

"I am. I needed this."

"Everyone but you knew that."

Alex took a deep breath and asked what she really wanted to know. "How is everything at the office?"

"Well, dammit," Piper cussed.

"What?"

"I lost the bet."

"What bet?" Alex asked.

"The one between Chase, Max, me, and Sarah. Chase said you'd ask about the office right after you said hello. Max said it would be somewhere between thirty seconds to a minute, and I gave you three whole minutes."

Alex couldn't help but laugh. "And Sarah?"

"She thought you'd wait until right before you hung up."

"Ahh, I knew I liked Sarah best." Alex curled her legs under her and stared out at the view. There were too many clouds in the sky to see the mountains behind the house, but the winter wonderland was stunning without them.

Piper laughed. "The office is fine. Chase hasn't burned the place down, and nobody has been fired."

"Not even Floyd?"

"Sadly."

"Have we heard any more from Regent's law—"

"Nope. Don't even finish that question. You are on vacation, the only thing that needs to be considered is if you're going to have a cocktail or a glass of wine. Snowboarding or shopping. None of us are going to give you one answer to any work questions."

Alex grumbled, and Piper laughed.

"Fine."

That just made Piper laugh harder.

Resigned to talk about other things, Alex asked something she'd wondered since they'd first arrived. "How much time did my father spend up here?"

"Not a lot. A handful of long weekends. Three, maybe four over the last few years he was alive."

"And Melissa?"

"No. She hated the cold. I assumed he found someone else there to occupy his time."

"That's gross. Not surprising, but gross."

"I don't know for sure. He never asked me to send flowers to anyone in Colorado."

Aaron Stone had made a habit of asking his assistant to send "It was wonderful to meet you" flowers, along with "I miss you" flowers to his wife. Often at the same time.

"Did he work up here?"

"Your dad always worked."

"But there isn't an office. No printer, no computer. The desk looked like something you'd sit your kids down in to do their homework."

"That's strange. He could have brought his laptop with him. I don't remember."

"I can't even find a cabinet with any homeowner files. You know, like manuals for the appliances or warranties for the ATVs."

"Maybe those are here."

"That doesn't even make sense."

"You said it's a big house. Maybe you just haven't found them yet," Piper said.

Alex shook her head. "The good thing is, there is nothing of him here to remind me of who slept here. Not as much as a forgotten sock."

"Maybe the caretakers went in and got rid of it all."

"Someone would have said something if that was the case. If you get a chance, can you ask Stuart? Not that it really matters, I guess. But it would be nice to know if there were instructions to empty the place out." Stuart was her father's estate attorney and executor of his trust. The man that had known Aaron Stone better than any of them.

"That's an easy phone call."

"Thanks."

Piper let out a sigh. "Now that we have all that out of the way . . . how is Hawk?"

Alex sunk deeper in her chair with a sigh. "Unexpected."

Piper all but purred on the other end of the phone. "This, I need to know more about."

The front door opened and the man in question walked in, along with a gust of cold air.

"That's going to have to wait," Alex said.

"He's there, isn't he?"

"Yes." Alex smiled at Hawk.

He looked between the phone and her eyes. "I leave you alone for thirty minutes and you're on the phone."

She huffed unapologetically. "You shouldn't leave me alone."

Piper was laughing. "I will take the sound of that and let my imagination run wild," she said in Alex's ear.

"Give my niece a kiss," Alex said, avoiding Piper's imagination.

"You guys be safe. I heard the storm is pretty big."

Hawk took his coat off, hung it up to dry.

"I'll text and let you know we're okay . . . so long as the phone police gives me the opportunity."

The phone police was shaking his head.

"Don't give us an extra thought. I'm sure Hawk will take care of you."

Hawk walked directly to her.

Alex let her eyes feast. "I'm sure he will."

Chapter Twenty-Six

When the wind started rattling the windows, Hawk knew the weathermen had it right. It was only a matter of time before the power would fail.

But he'd done all that could be done. Even taking the time to shovel the flakes that had fallen the night before from the driveway. In addition, he salted the space in hopes of making it a little easier to get out if they needed to.

It was likely a wasted effort, but the workout was worth it.

To be fair, both of his workouts had been worth it.

Alex had found a thousand-piece puzzle and had dumped it out on the coffee table in the living room.

He was surprised to see her humming to herself and bouncing around either on her knees or sitting cross-legged as she separated the pieces by color and shape.

The oversize sweaters she had taken to wearing were just as inviting and soft as the woman in them. Her hair hadn't been up since they entered the state. He liked it.

Here she was just Alexandrea. Not Ms. Stone. Hawk knew he was witnessing a side of her that few knew existed.

With her suggestion, he'd found a novel and had started to read while Alex put the edges of the puzzle together.

He managed two pages before Alex started chatting. "Did you and your brother ever put together puzzles?"

"When we were kids." Hawk looked back down at his book.

"On our family vacations, and by *family*, I mean Chase, me, and our mom . . . we would find a local store wherever we were and buy the largest puzzle we could find that showcased the area. I think it was our mom's way of getting us off our cell phones." The whole time Alex spoke, she didn't look up once.

"Clever."

She was quiet for a moment.

Hawk read one line.

"We had to finish it before the trip was over. Bad weather, no problem. If one of us got sick, a puzzle was our medicine. If we got in a fight, by the evening, we were huddled over one of these, trying to stay mad but couldn't."

He put the book down and took up space across from Alex.

She looked up, smiled, and then explained her strategy.

Of course, she had a strategy.

Alex had a plan for everything.

They'd gotten the entire perimeter put together when the power flickered twice and then immediately went out.

"I guess that answers that question," Alex said.

"The way it looks outside, I'm surprised we made it this long." Hawk stood, stretched his arms over his head. "I'm going to close all the doors to the rooms we're not using. Try and keep some of the heat in."

Alex arched her back. "I could use a break."

They had about an hour before the sun went down, which they used to ready the house and then put some food together.

A task that proved to them both that a cooking class might be in order when they returned home.

Despite burning the rice, they managed to cook a meal with the gas range that they could eat.

Hours later, spent after partaking in what was by far the best pastime Hawk had ever experienced, Alex's cheek rested on his bare

shoulder. The fireplace in the primary bedroom was more than suffi-
cient to keep the room warm.

They stared at the flames and learned a little more about each other.

When Alexandrea's fingertips brushed over the scar on his hip, he
knew the question was coming.

"How did you get this?"

Hawk had lied about the wound so many times that the answer
hovered on his lips.

He considered telling her his practiced lines but found himself
telling the truth instead. "I was on the wrong end of a gun."

Her hand stilled, and she lifted her cheek enough to look at him.
"You were shot?"

"Humm" was his answer.

"How, why?"

The concern in her eyes touched him.

He guided her head back to his chest and stared at the fire. "I was
in Guatemala. I had infiltrated the compound of an arms dealer. It was
a long-term assignment. The cartel men I fell in with were the distrib-
utors. We wanted the top guy."

He went silent. That day replayed like a looping video in his head.

"What happened?" she asked in a whisper.

"They caught on to me. They put a gun in my hand and told me
to shoot one of the grunts they used as slave labor. To prove I could be
trusted."

Alex's hand stilled.

"I was fucked. I either murdered someone in cold blood or risked
being killed myself."

"Oh, God."

"The kid was seventeen. They'd caught him taking the equivalent
of fifty bucks. For food for his family. He was dead whether I did it
or not."

"What did you do?" There was a tremor in Alex's voice.

Hawk stroked her hair.

"I didn't kill him. I told them to take the fifty bucks out of my pay and let the kid go."

"Please tell me they—"

"Like I said. He was dead either way. They dragged his body out one door and me out another. The gun they'd put in my hand wasn't even loaded. They knew I was a mole. The only reason they kept me alive was to learn who else was dirty." The memory of the hole they'd put him in, the smell of death, the darkness . . .

Hawk would spare Alex those details.

"I maintained my lie. Told them they had it wrong. After a week with no rescue attempt, they pulled me out of my cell."

"Your boss left you there to rot?"

"My boss didn't know I was compromised. If there had been another agent in the camp, I didn't know them. Once they let me out, I knew I had a small window before they'd test my loyalty again."

Gabriella slipped into his room. Tears ran down her face as she threw herself at him. "I tried to get to you. I begged my father to let you go."

"Shh," he whispered in her ear. Taking a lover on an assignment hadn't been planned. Only Gabriella was used to getting what she wanted. She damn near asked her father, the man in charge, to give Hawk to her as a birthday gift.

"Make her happy. If you don't, I'll have to kill you." Santiago patted Hawk on the shoulder before walking away.

Hawk knew the only reason he was thrown in a hole and not shot on the spot was because of her.

Any other man, and they would have been dragged out with the seventeen-year-old kid.

Hawk held her, thankful he no longer smelled like the sewer he'd rotted in for a week. "I'm okay," he told her.

She pulled away, looked at him. "Are they feeding you?" She grasped his hands and looked him over. "They didn't cut you, did they?"

She was looking for missing fingers or ears.

"I'm whole, Gabriella."

Her forehead hit his chest in relief.

"It's all going to be fine now. Things will go back to normal. I told them you weren't a spy. I, of all people, would know if you were."

Twisted morality ached in his head.

He couldn't let guilt stop him now. "They won't go back to normal. We both know that."

She grasped his shirt. "They will."

"Your father won't be happy until I kill children or rape women. Is that the kind of man you want me to be?"

Conflict swam in her eyes. "I want you alive."

Then the answer was yes.

Why was he surprised? She loved her father, and his crimes were barbaric.

Hawk held her face in his hands. "And you can live with that?"

She blinked, then nodded.

She kissed him then and didn't let go until she fell asleep.

The problem was, he'd fallen asleep, too.

And when he woke, it was to the bedroom door banging against the wall from being kicked open.

Hawk rolled naked off the bed and reached for his gun.

A gun that hadn't been returned to him since he'd been released.

Santiago's second in command, Emilio, held a gun to Gabriella's head.

It wouldn't dawn on Hawk until much later that Gabriella had been fully clothed.

"You were shot while trying to escape?"

Alexandrea's question pulled him out of the memory. A memory he kept to himself.

"Yeah."

She lifted herself just enough to press her lips to the scar. "I'm sorry that happened to you."

"You have nothing to be sorry for."

Her lips moved to his soft, sweet . . .

Then she settled once again in the crook of his arm.

Her breathing settled, and her frame started to go lax. "I'm glad you made it out alive," she whispered.

Hawk stroked her arm and stared into the fire.

Made it out alive so he could sleep with an assignment once again.

You would think he'd learn.

Alex is different, his heart declared.

How so? his head argued.

∽

The weatherman got it right.

When the storm had been reduced to a dusting of flurries, five feet and some change had fallen from the sky.

They were on day three of no power.

Hawk had used Mother Nature's icebox and filled a chest with food, which he left on the back porch to stay cold.

Even though the porch was covered, that didn't stop the snow from piling up inside.

Never in all her years had Alex personally seen the amount of snow that was on display as the storm fluttered out.

The snowdrifts along the house were even more impressive. Seven, even eight feet where the wind had blown snow and piled it up.

Alex and Hawk both bundled up and decided to put some effort into clearing a path from the house to the shed, where more firewood was stored. In addition to that, Hawk insisted on shoveling snow from the driveway.

With a lot of effort, they managed to open the garage door manually. And then proceeded to laugh at the enormity of snow staring back at them.

Alex positioned herself behind Hawk and attempted to push him into the wall of snow, only to have him turn around, pick her up, and toss her in.

"You'll pay for that."

"You promise?" he asked, staring down at her.

She reached her arm out for him to help her to her feet. Her attempt at pulling him with her was laughable.

Once they pushed through the snowdrift, they could see the outline of the driveway where Hawk had shoveled the first two feet between storms.

Even though clearing the snow was hard work, Alex found herself enjoying the physical labor. Tossing snow in Hawk's direction had its advantages, too.

The path to the shed was harder, the snow deeper. The real challenge was where to put the misplaced snow. Tossing it over five feet was laughable.

Somewhere in the final three or four feet of distance to clear, Alex offered Hawk her encouragement before backtracking into the warmth of the house and a hot shower. Something they still had, thanks to the gas-powered hot water heater.

Warm and once again dry, she went in search of another book while there was still light coming in from outside.

She pulled two books and then saw a title from the author she'd just read on the highest shelf. Using the chair at the writing desk, she climbed up to retrieve it.

And the shelf moved.

Alex sprang back, peered closer, then gave the shelf a push.

A hidden door opened and revealed what Alex knew the house was missing from the day they walked in.

An office.

She stepped off the chair, pushed the door, and walked inside.

Alex was instantly reminded of a similar door Chase had found in their father's walk-in closet behind a shelf filled with shoes. Only inside that room lived a safe.

Immediately on her right was the desk and a computer. Built-in filing cabinets, a printer. And on the opposite side of the room . . .

A safe.

Taller than her.

Wider than her.

"What the fuck, Dad."

꒰꒱

Hawk descended the stairs, his hair still wet from his much-needed shower.

"Hey, Hawk?" Alex called from somewhere beyond the kitchen. "There's something I need you to see."

He followed her voice to the study. "Did you find a cookbook?" he asked, teasing.

"Better than that."

He walked around the corner and stopped.

The wall of books was displaced, and Alex stood on the other side.

"A secret room?"

Alex sat behind a desk with what looked like the contents of said desk spread out over it.

She pointed to the opposite side of the room.

A massive safe filled up a major section of the windowless wall.

"How did we not see this?"

"It's a theme."

Hawk looked at the door and saw a magnet up at the top. The electronic kind that needed a code or a fingerprint to open.

Unless the power went out and the battery backup went dead.

His eyes searched the wall the hidden door lived in and saw a power box above it. "What do you mean *a theme?*"

Alex kept digging through the drawers in the desk as she spoke. "There's a hidden room at the estate. With a safe inside."

"Rich people have safes," Hawk mused aloud.

"If this safe has in it what the other safe has, there is more to it than just a place to hide a few precious belongings and documents."

"What's that?" *Drugs? Weapons?*

"It's hard to explain. I'd rather show you."

Alex was looking at random pieces of paper and tossing them aside.

"What are you looking for?"

"The code. Chase and Alex found the code for that safe in Dad's desk. My guess is, he needed to keep it consistent, or he'd forget it himself."

"Wouldn't he just memorize it?"

"According to Piper, memorization wasn't his strong point."

Hawk walked over to the safe and took a good look. It was the kind that would survive a fire. Which made sense up here in the woods.

"Ha!"

Alex waved a piece of paper in her hand. "This has to be it."

She rounded the desk and approached the keypad.

The numbers beeped as she entered the code.

On the last one, a loud click filled the room.

Hawk stood to her side as she eased the heavy door open.

Alex smiled, and Hawk's jaw hit the floor. "Holy fuck."

"Yup. Just what I thought."

The safe was stuffed full.

He reached in and pulled out a fistful of currency. Euros, each with bands on them saying *10,000*. Then there were American dollars, Chinese yuan, Russian rubles, Arabic dirhams. And more that Hawk couldn't identify.

Beyond the money were coin containers.

He lifted one and opened the top.

"Gold coins."

"Yup." Alex wasn't surprised.

A .45 caliber Smith & Wesson handgun sat on one shelf, several filled magazines to its side.

And a shotgun. Both of which Hawk did not touch.

Alex reached for the gun.

Hawk stopped her.

"You don't know what that gun has been used for."

Alex snickered. "My father wasn't capable of—"

"Using a weapon against someone? Then why does he have it?"

"Safety," Alex said.

"Maybe. Maybe not. You said the other safe looks the same?"

"Pretty much."

"Even guns?"

She pointed at the handgun. "If not the same, similar. One handgun, one shotgun."

This had *illegal* written all over it.

"Your dad was up to something. There is no legitimate reason for a man as wealthy as your father to have this much cash in this many currencies." The whole thing put an ugly feeling in the pit of his stomach.

"He was so driven by money, Chase and I thought that maybe he just needed physical evidence of his wealth to . . . I don't know, stare at?"

Hawk laughed, pulled Alex close enough to kiss her head, and let her go. "I love that your thoughts stopped there."

"You're laughing at me," she said.

He shook his head. "Your innocence is refreshing. This," he pointed at the contents of the safe, "says racketeering, money laundering, bribery, drugs . . ." Prostitution, human trafficking, and yes . . . illegal firearms. But Hawk left that out.

"I can't imagine it."

"How well did you know your father?"

"I didn't."

Hawk met her gaze. "Start imagining it. It might give us a clue as to who planted the Play-Doh bomb. The person who threatened you."

Alex took a step back. "I never even considered that."

Hawk knelt down to the bottom of the safe, where stacks of documents and folders were piled.

"Are there documents in the other safe?"

"Yes. It's how we learned where to look for Max. A clue was hidden in the receipts of artwork certificates."

Hawk opened a file and saw what looked like a deed to a property. Maybe the one they were in. He pulled out folders and stacked them. "If it's okay with you, I'd like to take the guns in, have them dusted for prints and run through ballistics."

"You mean to see if they were used in a crime?"

"Yes."

"You really believe he was into something illegal."

Hawk picked up the folders and stood. "The cartel that put a hole in me, the walls of their home were literally filled with cash. The kind that can't be traced. The only way you spend this money is wading through the mud."

Alex blew out a breath. "And to think I came in here looking for a suspense novel."

He handed her a stack of papers. "Why read fiction when you have this?"

৩

Hawk tapped the fake EU passport against his knee. The picture inside was Aaron Stone, with a fake name and nationality.

He stopped counting when the cash equaled one million. From the looks of the stacks, there was likely another million in euros and a few hundred thousand in miscellaneous currency.

Then there was the gold coin. A couple hundred grand, easy.

"Your dad didn't have this to look at," Hawk announced. "This was an escape plan."

Alex sat on the floor by the fire, thumbing through the documents while Hawk was estimating the monetary value of what was in the safe.

"Escape from what?"

"In order to determine that, we need to know how he skimmed this money."

Alex put the papers in her hand down and gave him her full attention. "I've spent a lot of time looking over the books in the last five years of Stone Enterprises. I didn't see anything."

"You wouldn't. If done right, it would take a forensic accountant to find these kinds of missing numbers."

"He could have just written himself owner distribution draws."

"Possibly. He'd have to do it in small sums, and you'd likely be able to trace that. Large sums are a red flag."

"Over time, though . . ." Alex suggested. "Wait."

Hawk looked up.

"We did find cash draws from an account that Dad set up to pay off Max's mother."

"With this kind of money?" Hawk asked.

"No."

He put the passport down and picked up a file from the stack. "Obtaining money from other countries you do business in isn't difficult, but the Russians don't like their money leaving their country. He worked hard to get it out." What Hawk left out was the danger factor. If you were caught taking more than ten thousand out of Russia, you'd likely be detained for a very long time.

"Why bother, then?"

"Bribes?" Hawk asked, more to himself than a question that Alex needed to answer.

"Well, we know he was capable. Ultimately, he bribed Max's mother to stay silent about him."

Hawk sighed. "The money is dirty. The question is, How dirty? If this was his escape plan, along with whatever is in the other safe, then he was worried about losing his company. Or not being able to access its funds."

"How could that happen?"

"The government hates tax evasion. If an investigation took place, they could seize control of Stone Enterprises and everything Aaron Stone. Not one credit card would work. Without this," Hawk pointed at the money, "he couldn't put gas in his car."

"Even if he was innocent?"

"Guilty until proven otherwise," Hawk told her. "Regardless of what you might think."

Alex stared at him with worry in her eyes. "The crimes stay with the company, not the person . . . right?"

Hawk knew where she was going with her question. If Stone Enterprises was accused of tax evasion, everything the Stone children inherited could be at risk.

"I'm not an expert on fraud investigations. I know some people and can poke around. But before we do any of that, we try and determine what happened and who was involved. Why did your dad need this? Was he using this money to bribe others? Where did the money come from? Did he expect an investigation? Your father didn't need to skim off the top of his already profitable company. If the company was struggling, then maybe," Hawk mused.

"He was expanding too quickly. He took advantage of fire sales after the pandemic and leveraged the profitable parts of the company to fund the purchases of the others."

"Any risk of going bankrupt?"

Alex shook her head. "More like risking a takeover. Although he had the majority shares." She sighed. "He was obsessed with money. It didn't faze us when we found the first safe. Truth is, we've been too busy to give it much thought."

It didn't make sense. "Then we're back at *why*. And how many more of these safes are out there?"

She rubbed her temples. "It hurts my head."

"Yeah, and we're supposed to be here for R&R, not mind bending over the sins of the father."

"We can't just leave this here," Alex said.

Hawk waved a stack of euros in the air. "It's a damn good thing you have a private plane, then. This would never pass TSA."

Chapter Twenty-Seven

The power flickered back to life the day before they were scheduled to return home.

The caretakers had notified Hawk that they'd arranged for a private plow to clear a path to the main road. Which afforded them an opportunity to see the actual town of Aspen and eat a meal that they didn't cook. Neither one of them was sad to leave the cooking behind for their last dinner in Colorado.

They purchased three large suitcases and packed the entirety of the contents of the safe into them. Having a private plane was never more appreciated. No questions . . . no inspections.

Alex was convinced that something huge was going on behind the scenes, and she and her brothers were going to be caught in the crossfire sooner rather than later.

With the fire in the bedroom keeping them warm on their last night, Alex and Hawk sat up against the headboard, talking like they had nearly every evening.

"Are you ready to go back?" Hawk asked.

"I am. How does that look, though? Do I keep hiding out at a home office and let this Play-Doh wannabe bomber keep me hiding?"

"There are a lot more security measures in place. My guess is whoever was behind that won't be able to do the same thing twice."

Alex found a comfortable place at Hawk's side with his arm around her back. "Good. I don't like weakness. I don't like showing it, I don't like seeing it."

"You're one of the strongest people I know," Hawk said.

His hand stroked hers in silence.

"There is something we need to discuss before we leave tomorrow," Hawk began.

As the hours had drawn closer to their departure, Alex could see Hawk struggling with something.

She couldn't stop the feeling of darkness coming over her. "Why do I feel I'm not going to like this."

He took a deep breath. "We need to keep this part of our relationship as close to the chest as possible."

That was better than "This was fun, but it needs to end."

"Define 'close to the chest,'" she said.

"Public. At the office, on the street."

Alex pushed off his chest and disengaged their hands. Dread stuck in her throat. "You're embarrassed?"

Hawk choked on a laugh. "Are you kidding me?"

"Then why?" She stared directly into his eyes.

"Your safety."

"What could be safer than my personal bodyguard being in my bed?" Her voice rose, and she scooted a couple of inches away to get a stronger look at him.

"I didn't say I wasn't going to be in your bed, we just can't tell the world that's where I am."

"You need to spell this out for me. What is the problem with—"

"I know from experience that the bad guys exploit weakness. If the person that threatened you is watching, they can use my feelings for you against us. Use whatever you're feeling against you. Protecting you became more difficult the moment we kissed. A more honorable man wouldn't have allowed this to happen." He pointed a finger between the two of them.

"You're dripping in honor."

From the expression on Hawk's face, he didn't believe her.

He took her hands in his. "If they know about us, and they plan on striking again, they will do it when I'm not there. They will wait until I'm not at your side."

"We don't know that."

"You can fight me on many things. I like the challenge. But please take my lead on this. Don't fight me on this. Trust I know what I'm talking about."

The irony of having someone in your life and needing to hide them. It's as if she were truly living her father's life. Secret lovers, clandestine rendezvous. An affair.

"My family will know. I can keep a professional poker face, but I can't lie to my family."

Hawk drew her hands to his lips, kissed her knuckles. "I can work with that."

"And Nick. Honestly, he'll smell you on me."

That made Hawk smile.

"You're always telling me how unaware I am of what's going on around me. You clearly have a skill at reading people. Do you have any tips to share?"

"Seriously?"

She sighed. "The day will come when my personal armed security won't be standing next to me."

"Getting rid of me already?" he teased.

Alex rolled over on her stomach and propped her chin on her hands. "Enlighten me, wise one."

Hawk nodded a few times. "Okay. Let's talk about body language. You already understand, and demonstrate on the daily, how to make people in the room listen. How to tell them you're in charge without saying that you're in charge. What I don't see from you is reading others' body language. Body language says a lot more than the words coming out of someone's mouth. Look beyond what they are saying. How far apart are the words that are coming out of someone's mouth from how they are acting? When I'm talking with someone I believe is guilty of anything, I watch their movement more than I listen to them. What are their eyes doing? How is their posture? Do they stutter on any word? If someone else is in the room, are they looking at them?"

"A disconnect?"

"Exactly. A lot of people think they're good actors." He shook his head. "They're not. Is there warmth in the eyes of the man who says he loves his wife?"

Hawk ran a hand down the side of Alex's face, his eyes soaked her in, his lips parted.

"Or does the man look away?"

Hawk didn't.

"Listen to your gut and look for visual cues to reinforce your feeling. Shuffling feet, fidgeting . . . did they answer a question too fast? Ask questions quickly, see if you can catch that person in a lie. You'd be surprised how rapidly a lie will slip out. It's hard to keep a lie straight when you don't give someone time to think."

"Be the offense."

"Exactly. If the person you are talking to is hiding something, don't show everything in your hand. Make them think you know something that they think you don't know. Be in charge. We both know you like that."

Alex reached out and placed her hand on his chest. "I like it when you take charge."

"I noticed."

Her fingertips danced over the muscles of his chest and slowly moved lower.

"I know a few things about body language." She pulled herself up on an elbow and watched her fingers peel back the sheet covering Hawk's hips.

His breath caught.

Alex smiled.

"Are you going to teach me something?"

Her hooded gaze found his.

The rise and fall of his chest increased. He shifted his eyes to his cock that twitched under the sheet.

Alex hummed. "I think you already know about this."

Her hand dipped lower.

Hawk caught the back of her head, and his thumb grazed her lips.

She twisted, caught his thumb, and sucked on it hard.

His hand tightened, and a soft growl released in the back of his throat.

"How about a refresher course?"

The sheet fell down past his hips.

Alex settled in and slid her tongue up the length of him. "I like that idea."

Their body language tutorial ended in a way that neither one of them would ever forget.

An hour later, watching the flames turn to embers, Alex felt the even flow of breath coming from Hawk in his sleep. He'd made love to her, slowly and completely. And for the first time since they'd shared a bed, he fell asleep before she did. In fact, she'd not once seen him actually sleeping except in the chair on their first night at the cabin. He was always out of bed when she woke, leaving her feeling alone.

A deep insecurity festered, and it was pushed deeper by knowing that Hawk wouldn't acknowledge her in public once they returned home.

His reasons sounded legitimate. But what if there was more to it? What if this was only . . . this. Wonderful but brief?

Alex felt an ache in the back of her throat and swallowed it down.

He was her Viking.

He had given her hope for a future that might not be spent alone. He didn't want anything from her other than her. Intimacy, laughter . . . sharing ideas. Playing in the snow. Fighting over jigsaw puzzle pieces and cooking really awful meals together. He wasn't there because of her wealth. Emasculating him wasn't something she thought she could possibly do. Only maybe that was where she was wrong. Perhaps the opinion of others did bother him.

Alex tried not to think about the statistics of her ever achieving a truly compatible partner. No one was more versed on how unlikely it was for Alexandrea Stone to find loving happiness. The higher a woman's IQ, the higher the bank account, their position in business, the less likely a man could overcome all those facts and stick around.

She squeezed her eyes closed and tried to rid her mind of her dark thoughts.

Doubting their relationship into failure was a real possibility.

The truth was, she was well acquainted with sensing a man pulling away.

If that happened, she'd end things before allowing him to hurt her.

She felt a tear fall from her eye, despite how hard she tried to hold it back. She wanted him to be her Viking. She wanted the love that was blooming in her chest to be given a chance to grow.

Her eyes drifted closed, and she forced her thoughts to more pleasant images.

∽

Emilio pressed the barrel of his gun into Alexandrea's temple.

Fear gripped Hawk so hard and fast he couldn't catch his breath. Not Alex.

He promised to protect her.

Emilio yelled at Hawk in Spanish. Every word he understood. "Digame! Dime el nombre de tu espía, o la mataré." *Tell me. Tell me the name of your spy, or I will kill her.*

"Help me, Hawk."
Emilio's eyes hardened.
Hawk yelled.
The gun exploded.
Alex slid to the floor.

Hawk rolled off the bed, hit the floor, and was standing with his gun in front of him before his eyes came into focus.

Alex stood there, hands in the air. "It's me. Hawk, it's me!"

"Jesus, fuck." He lowered his weapon and dropped it on the bed.

His hands shaking.

He'd fallen asleep.

He'd fucking fallen asleep.

Hawk heard Alex's breathing over his own. "Oh, God. What was . . . oh, God."

He walked around the bed and gathered her in his arms.

"I'm sorry. Fuck, Alexandrea. I'm so sorry."

Her body shook so hard her teeth rattled. "You were thrashing around. Speaking in Spanish. I tried to wake you."

Hawk crushed her head to his chest.

She wasn't dead.

Her body wasn't lifeless on the floor of a Guatemalan jungle.

Only he was the one that held a gun on her.

All week Hawk managed to watch her fall asleep and then sneak out of the room. He caught his sleep on the sofa in the living room. Ready to plead insomnia and his desire to not wake her.

An excuse he used twice. Though most nights, Alex slept like the dead.

He pulled away and looked her in the eye. "I'm sorry."

"You scared me."

"I'd never hurt you." How could he promise that?

She nodded and let him hold her.

⌒℧

At an altitude of twenty-six thousand feet, Alex broke the silence that had plagued both of them since they'd left the cabin.

Hawk had left her to sleep alone after his nightmare. Sleep that didn't come until dawn had started to break.

From the look on Hawk's face, he hadn't slept either.

His apology followed what felt like self-loathing.

Alex had no doubt that the nightmare had caused his reaction. Not that her memory would let her forget the blankness in his eyes before he realized where he was and what he was doing.

Then it dawned on her . . .

"This has happened before," she said without preamble. "Your nightmare."

Hawk glanced at her and didn't deny it.

"It's why I never once woke up with you by my side."

"Alex, I—"

"Did you even sleep in my bed?"

He looked away.

She shook her head. "I thought it was me. That maybe sleeping beside me was too intimate."

"It's not you. It's not that."

She leaned forward. "Why didn't you tell me?"

"I didn't want to scare you."

She huffed a forced laugh. "Too late."

He turned back to the window. "We all have our baggage. This is mine."

"Your baggage is deadly if you sleep next to a gun," she argued.

"It won't happen again."

She fell back in her chair. "Because you won't sleep with a gun? Or you won't sleep next to me?"

He didn't answer.

"What . . . that's it? You won't give me the chance to help you with this?"

"It's not your cross to bear."

"You protecting me isn't your cross either, yet here you are."

"That's different," he replied.

"How?"

He didn't answer.

She paused. "Because I pay you?"

Her words looked like a physical blow across his face. "It has never been about the pay."

"Then how is it different, Hawk?"

He refused to answer.

Emotion swelled in her chest. "I thought maybe we had something good going here."

"Alex."

She lifted a hand in the air and undid her seat belt. "Save it."

Alex moved to the back of the plane and put the only distance she could between them.

The bedroom on the plane was the perfect place to get through the time left of the flight.

Chapter Twenty-Eight

Alex went from carefree and lax back to corporate CEO like she flipped a switch. Worse, she resembled the boss with her family in a way Hawk hadn't yet seen.

At some point on the plane, she'd informed her family they were on their way home and that an emergency meeting was needed.

Stiff politeness replaced warm smiles and laughter.

Hawk knew he'd done that.

He pulled his fucking gun on her. The woman he was protecting, the woman he wanted safe above all others.

Yet he was the threat.

All Hawk could do was stand back and watch while Alex greeted her family. Her quick recap of their time away was reduced to "It was nice to get away. The snow was unbelievable."

Two sentences he wouldn't use when describing some of the best days of his life.

Chase and Max shook his hand, thanking him for watching out for her.

He couldn't tell them "You're welcome" or "No problem." Not when his protection of Alex was no longer an obligation.

From the moment he'd seen her in the parking lot being hassled by Bakshai's man, Hawk was dedicated to the task of keeping her safe.

Once they were settled in the massive living room, Alex unzipped one suitcase at a time until everything was sitting there, looking like a pot of gold at the end of the rainbow. "We found this in a safe in a hidden office."

"It looks exactly like what we have upstairs," Max said.

"Why?" Chase asked rhetorically. "Why did Dad have this?"

"Hawk has a theory," Alex said, looking directly at him for the first time in hours.

Everyone turned to him.

"There are only a few reasons why your father would have this kind of liquid cash. He needed it as an escape plan. Or needed it to give to someone else without it being traced. Because your father was worth billions, the escape plan is laughable. Though he might have had need of it if Stone Enterprises was seized and all of his accounts were frozen. A few million might tide him over for a time."

"Seize? As in the government?" Chase asked.

Hawk nodded. "This alone says racketeering, corporate espionage, skimming off the top, you name it. Your father didn't quite fit the profile of drug runner or mob boss."

"And he didn't need to skim from his own company," Piper said. "He was quick to write an owner distribution check whenever he wanted."

That was useful information, Hawk thought. "Large sums of money that were cashed into this and stuffed away? How long did you work for him?" he asked Piper.

"A little over five years."

"Is this five years' worth of owner distribution draws?"

"It's hard to say. Considering there is just as much upstairs, I'd say no. Not in the time I worked with him."

Hawk reached into one of the bags and pulled out a passport. "Your father's face, a different name. We need to see if this name is associated with a bank account somewhere in the world. And would it work for long? Men like your father can't disappear. Not easily."

"Unless they fake their own death," Sarah said quietly.

Chase huffed. "Unfortunately, that isn't the case. I saw his body. He's dead."

Hawk hadn't considered that. Nice to have the theory cleared up quickly.

"What are all these files?" Max asked.

"They're confidential information memorandums. We call them CIMs." Alex said. "Basically, this is what a marketing department provides to potential buyers of a business."

"Are they a part of Stone Enterprises?" Chase asked.

"No. None of these are hotels. They could be a part of a business Dad owned outside of Stone Enterprises. Or were . . . or wanted to be. I honestly don't remember all of them, and most have a management company doing the day-to-day work. Leaving Dad with nothing more than waiting for a paycheck."

Piper picked up a random file and started looking through it.

"The best course of action is to get a list of these companies and compare them to anything linked to your father. How deep did you dig into the other safe?" Hawk asked.

"Not far. Those documents were more about property. Actual homes, art, things that cost more money than they are worth," Chase said.

"Alexandrea said something about safety deposit boxes," Hawk said.

"Money and gold. No documents."

Hawk started to pace. "How many homes did your dad own?"

"There is another place in Italy. The one Melissa thought was a gift to her," Alex said.

"There is an apartment in Manhattan and another in London," Piper stated.

"Jesus," Max said. "How many roofs does one person need?"

"The real question is if there is more where this came from in those locations," Hawk pointed out.

The answer in Hawk's head was yes. Aaron Stone spread out his hush fund . . . or whatever it was he used this money for.

"It's sketchy shit," Sarah said.

"It's not illegal to have a safe filled with money if the money can be accounted for. The passports we can overlook for now. But if you find evidence of fraud, tax evasion, any of the scary scenarios you read about in *The Sunday Times*, we need to gather as much information as possible before anybody outside of this room knows about it." Hawk made eye contact with everyone one at a time.

"The real threat of the FBI coming in and seizing the company while they undertake an investigation is a serious reality we all need to consider," Alex stated.

Alex turned to Max and Sarah. "How do you both feel about a trip to Italy via London?"

Sarah pushed her glasses higher on her nose with a grin. "If we must. I'm sure we can take one for the team," she teased.

Alex nodded. "After Texas, then."

Chase turned to Piper. "I can hop over to New York and be home the same day."

She nodded. "I'll get to work putting together a database with the companies in these files with everything I can learn about them. See if there is a common link beyond the CIMs being in the same safe."

Hawk was impressed by how they all assigned appropriate tasks to get to the bottom of this.

"I'll use my contacts to run the names used in the passports and ballistics on the weapons," Hawk said.

"What do we do with all this?" Piper asked.

"Document everything you find, where you found it. Video yourselves counting the money with date stamps in confidential files. I'm talking locked down, encrypted shit. If and when the government needs to get involved, you want your asses covered. Right now, it is reasonable to believe that your dad liked to look at money, and he had the ability to write those owner distribution checks and cash them instead of putting them in a bank." Hawk took a breath. "And ask yourselves who else could have known about these safes. Melissa? Someone else on the top floor? A friend? Ask yourselves *why*."

"What about *how*?" Sarah asked.

"I'm more interested in why . . . What was your father afraid of?" Hawk asked.

"Nothing," Alex muttered.

"No. This is fear. I can smell it," Hawk insisted.

Alex looked at him again. Her smile less than welcoming . . . almost tired.

She stood. "I'm going to shower, change . . . and start counting."

Hawk watched her retreat with a heavy heart.

"I'll show you the other safe," Chase told Hawk.

༄

Chase and Max stood in the driveway once again, watching Hawk drive away.

"What the hell happened in Colorado?" Max asked.

"I don't know. Piper thought for sure Alex and Hawk were getting along."

"They barely looked at each other."

"Maybe they had a fight," Chase said. "I'll see if I can pull Alex aside and ask."

Max nodded a few times.

"What do you think about all this money laundering business?"

Chase ran a hand through his hair. "I think our dad had a lot of people in his life that tolerated him. If the government seized Stone Enterprises, he would have lost it. The company meant everything to him. More than us, his wives . . . anyone . . . anything. If he did something illegal to get all that cash, something serious went down to compromise the business."

"The government shuts shit down and asks questions later," Max said with a sigh.

"We'll get to the bottom of it," Chase said.

They turned back toward the house.

"I'm going to ask Sarah to marry me," Max said from nowhere.

Chase paused and then opened his arm and pulled his brother in. "That's awesome. We love Sarah."

"Piper has figured out what kind of ring she likes. I just need to know where to go and get it."

Chase narrowed his eyes. "Piper didn't say a thing to me."

"I asked her to be on the down-low." Max stood tall. "Any suggestions for a jeweler?"

"Piper loves her ring."

"Great. The sooner, the better. I want to pay for it while I still have money."

Chase shook his head. "I don't think we have to worry."

Max raised an eyebrow. "If you grew up the way I did, you'd know that as fast as it can be given, it can be taken away."

"I hope you're wrong, brother."

They started walking again. "Any idea when you want to propose?" Chase asked.

Max smiled. "Italy seems like a place where a woman would like to be proposed to."

Chase patted Max on the back. "I'm happy for you."

"Me too."

❦

The rest of the week following her vacation, Alex spent much of her workday at the estate. The rotation of security included everyone but Hawk.

He sent her a text every morning telling her who was going to be there.

Alex's reply was just as warm and fuzzy as his message.

It wasn't.

And it hurt. More than she wanted it to.

The Tuesday preceding the wedding in Texas, Alex couldn't hold off on going into the office any longer.

Three days at the office.

That was all Alex had to endure at work, with Hawk standing like a damn statue in the corner of every room she entered. Or flanking doors when she needed him outside.

Truth was, she needed him way outside. As in outside the building.

The ride in had been painful.

Alex had opened one of the files from the safes and pretended to be deep in thought about what she was reading the whole drive in.

She couldn't recall a word of the CIM if her life depended on it. The entire time she sat in the passenger seat, she tried to disregard the scent of the man driving. Closed her eyes against the memory of his hands stroking her hair as they watched the fire while the snow fell outside. Of the feel of him moving inside her . . .

"Alexandrea . . ."

"You probably shouldn't call me that at the office." She didn't mean to sound so cold, but her words were delivered in ice.

"We need to talk."

She twisted in her seat. "You had last week . . . the weekend. Why do this now?" She glanced at the clock on the dashboard. "Twenty minutes before I have to work, and you can't afford to be distracted with emotion. Or maybe you won't have an emotional response."

"That's not true."

"Then pump the brakes, Hawk. I need to work. So do you."

He didn't argue . . . which, if she were being honest, upset her. She wanted to know what was going on in his head. But he didn't care to know what was going on in hers enough to push the issue. Hawk drove the rest of the way in uncomfortable silence.

A headline of a tabloid shortly after her father had died described Alex as having the perfect resting bitch face. Most of the time when she walked through the Stone building, she attempted a partial smile to avoid that description.

But no matter how hard she tried, the smile didn't come.

Alex tucked the file in the top drawer of her desk when Dee walked in with her computer and a cup of coffee.

"Is he going to stand out there all day?" Dee asked.

"Yes."

"For how long?"

Alex clicked into her schedule. "I don't know."

"Is he your bodyguard?"

She dropped her hands on top of her desk. "I would think that's obvious."

Dee snapped her head up, looked directly at her, then back down to her laptop. "I'm sorry. I shouldn't have asked."

Alex internally slapped herself. "No, I'm sorry. I didn't mean to jump at you. When I'm here, Hawk is here. It won't be forever."

"Okay."

When her eleven-thirty meeting with Floyd began, Hawk attempted to follow her VP into her office.

"It's okay," Alex said to Hawk. Hoping he understood that meant he didn't need to be in the room.

Hawk pinched his brow together, said nothing, and stared at the man everyone in her family didn't trust.

Alex witnessed the internal struggle he was having with her request . . . a request that was more demand than anything.

Hawk was a distraction. Watching him standing guard reminded her of his cold stare when he'd woken from his nightmare. Then the cold that followed when he refused to talk to her about his obvious trauma response.

Worse, watching him put an ache in her chest she didn't want to name.

When she agreed to keep their private life private, she never thought it would be this easy to act like they meant nothing to each other.

If anything, there was hostility bubbling between them as the day rolled on.

"I'm right outside," Hawk said loud enough for Floyd to hear.

Alex placated him with a smile and lifted a hand to the door, requesting that he close it as he left.

"I feel like we have the Secret Service around when he's here," Floyd said.

"That's about right."

Floyd took a seat on the sofa. "Is there something I should know about?"

Alex sat in one of the chairs and crossed her legs as she sat back. She weighed her response. "Someone personally threatened me." Alex kept the bomb threat out of it. "Chase and Max insisted on a bodyguard."

"Really?" Floyd looked surprised.

"Not something very many men have had to worry about."

He paused. "I'm sorry to hear that. Any, ah . . . idea who it could be?"

"We're narrowing down our search," she lied.

"Was it personal? Or do you think the threat was something business related?"

Floyd's question felt off. "We don't know. Every possibility is being investigated."

"The police are involved, then."

"If someone threatened Ann's safety, wouldn't you call the authorities?" Alex asked.

"Yes, yes. Of course."

"Let's get to work," Alex said, changing the subject.

Floyd caught her up on their top issues. They spoke briefly about the Regent lawsuit. Somewhere in that part of the conversation, Floyd suggested that her father hadn't considered how Regent would handle an employee of theirs becoming direct competition overnight. "But breaching a nondisclosure? It will be thrown out before we can think about settlement negotiations."

"Our lawyers agree. Let's hope it goes that way. We don't need more problems."

Floyd nodded a few times.

"Is there anything else?" Alex asked. "Anything come up while I was away that Chase didn't handle?"

"No."

"Good." She stood. "We'll be leaving early on Friday for our mother's wedding. By Monday, it will be business as usual."

"I thought you were all staying out until Tuesday."

"I've had enough time off," she said.

Floyd stood and hesitated. "I spoke with Nasser Bakshai."

She paused, the hair on Alex's neck stood up.

"Another cocktail hour?"

"Not that. He told me that his father was disappointed that you didn't attend his event in Dubai. He was under the impression you were going."

Something that Hawk had said to her when they were talking about the people he spied on during his time in South America echoed in her head. *Body language says a lot more than the words coming out of someone's mouth. Look beyond what they are saying.*

"His impression was wrong," Alex said.

Floyd shuffled his feet.

Nerves?

Anxiety?

"He's an important man, Alex. He might even be able to help with whoever threatened you."

"How exactly can he do that?" Alex asked.

"He has an international reach that local authorities may not have access to."

"You mean Nasser's father has that reach?"

Floyd cleared his throat. "Yes."

Alex folded her hands in her lap with ease she didn't feel. "I have a feeling Ashraf's 'friendship' comes with strings."

"I don't know about that."

Was Floyd trying to convince her or him? Because he was doing a shit job of convincing her of anything other than the Bakshais making Floyd squirm.

"Why is this important to you?" she asked.

"It's not."

His response was too fast.

"I feel as your VP that it's my responsibility to point out the associates that you want to keep on your good side."

"It's hard to keep a lie straight when you don't give someone time to think."

"How is he an associate? We don't do business with him."

"He's valuable."

"How so?"

"He just is. Your father kept the Bakshais close."

"For what reason?" she fired back.

"They're an influential family," Floyd offered.

Alex paused to give Floyd a moment to catch his breath.

"So are we."

Floyd blinked twice . . . three times.

"I won't run to the snapping fingers of anyone. Not anymore. Especially to men like Bakshai."

"What is that supposed to mean?" Floyd asked.

She stepped closer. "To men that don't have the balls to come directly to me and ask why I chose not to attend an event they hosted. Instead of asking my vice president to voice their disappointment for them."

"It was a passing comment in conversation," Floyd defended.

"You went to Dubai, then?"

"No."

"Then what need did you have to be speaking with Bakshai?"

"I-I've known them for many years," Floyd said.

"It's personal, then?"

"Well—"

"Golf course conversation?" she asked. Giving Floyd something to anchor his answer to.

He took the bait.

"Exactly." Floyd lit up and looked away.

You're lying.

"We were playing a round, and Nasser brought this up."

You're still lying.

"At the country club? I think I saw something about it on the expense report," Alex said.

Floyd nodded. "Yes. I know you don't golf, but there are still a lot of things that can be learned by hitting small balls into smaller holes."

Alex smiled in an effort to put him at ease. "I completely understand. An office expense well worth it."

"Families as rich as them don't golf at the local course."

"I wouldn't expect them to. Still, I have no intention of joining the Bakshais now or in the future."

Floyd's face fell.

"You can tell them that . . . or not. It makes no difference to me."

"Can I ask why?" Floyd asked.

"Don't show everything in your hand. Make them think you know something that they think you don't know."

She lowered her voice. "I think you know."

Floyd went white.

Ghost white.

Chapter Twenty-Nine

Hawk pulled out of the parking lot and into traffic.

The day had gone by at such a painfully slow pace, Hawk thought the clock was turning backward.

Watching Alex and not seeing her smile, not one hint of what they shared.

It cut like no knife ever had.

"I had an interesting conversation with Floyd today," Alex said from the passenger seat.

"Oh?"

"He said that Ashraf Bakshai was *disappointed* that I didn't go to his little party in Dubai."

The mention of the man's name had Hawk gripping the steering wheel hard. "What party in Dubai?"

"I told you about the invitation."

"I would have remembered that detail."

Alex looked straight forward. "If I didn't, I meant to. Anyway, when Bakshai came to the office, he invited me to Dubai."

Hawk could only imagine what would have been waiting for her if she had gone. The guy was a sleaze.

"Floyd said the son told him about Daddy's hurt ego. The whole conversation felt off."

"You think?" Hawk asked sarcastically.

"I did what you suggested."

Hawk looked over. "What was that?"

"I watched Floyd's body language. Asked questions so fast, he didn't have time to think of his answers. Most of which I'm sure were lies. I told Floyd that I had no intention of taking Ashraf up on any invitations. Floyd was adamant that I try and keep in good standing with the man."

"Why?"

"Exactly what I asked. 'Why is this important to you?' He went on about how my father kept in contact with him. They're influential people, yadda, yadda. I blew Floyd off. I told him I had no desire to deal with people who had to go through my VP to voice their feelings about my lack of appearance. Floyd looked like he wanted to throw up."

"Did these people call him?"

"I think so. Floyd told me he was playing golf with Nasser. On a corporate country club membership. Which I can easily check to see if Floyd was lying. I'd bet a hundred bucks he wasn't anywhere near a golf course last week."

Hawk tapped his fingers on the steering wheel, not happy with where this was going.

"I told Floyd that I had no intention of seeing the Bakshais again. And then suggested Floyd tell them that . . . or not, it was up to him."

Hawk couldn't help but think Alex was poking a sleeping bear.

Alex twisted in her seat and looked directly at him.

"Then Floyd asked why."

Hawk glanced at her. "What did you say?"

"I said, 'I think you know.'" Alex grinned.

"Fuck."

"And Floyd looked like he'd seen a ghost. All the color washed out of his face."

"God dammit, Alex. I should have been in that room."

"He wouldn't have brought any of this up if you were." She turned back to staring out the windshield.

"These are dangerous people. Ashraf wants to get you alone."

"I see that."

"Don't let him."

Alex turned her head his way. "Of course not."

"What does Floyd think you know?" Hawk asked.

"I have no idea. But there is something."

Hawk wanted to be mad at her for talking about these people without him there to witness it.

Then there was the other part of him. The part that put a smile on his face.

"Floyd is scared of these people," Hawk said. "Why? And was your father afraid, too?"

"It's hard to picture, but maybe. Piper might be able to shed light on that."

Hawk smiled. "Well played, Alex. You caught him in a lie you can prove. Determined that Floyd is afraid of this guy and determined there is some kind of secret being kept."

"Do you think this has anything to do with the money? The bomb threat? The fake passports?"

Hawk pulled onto the freeway. "The fact we have so many choices of what Bakshai could be behind is disturbing."

"I can't help but think everything is linked," Alex said.

"Feels that way."

They were quiet for a few moments.

"Everyone in the office is asking about you. I told Dee that I've been threatened, and that's why you're there. I didn't mention the Play-Doh bomb connection."

"The bomb threat is far enough back that the office staff probably won't put two and two together. Eventually, my presence will go unnoticed."

"Like the Secret Service?"

For a moment, Alex's playful tone made Hawk forget about their discourse. "Without the sunglasses," he said with a smirk.

"Well, we know more today than we did yesterday," she said with a small smile.

"And have five more questions."

Alex released a long-suffering sigh as she rubbed her temples.

"Headache?"

She lowered her hands to her lap. "I'm fine."

Two words that were the kiss of death.

∽

Chase stood beside Jack Morrison, his now stepbrother, with a drink in his hand and a smile on his face.

Together, they looked over the hundreds of guests filling the reception. Chase held a whiskey. Jack had a beer.

"My dad is talking about retiring," Jack told him. "Said he's done what needed to be done and that it's my turn."

Chase glanced over. "How do you feel about that?"

"The truth?"

"Yeah."

"Overwhelmed. I know the business. Know he'll be there for questions. But to be *the* boss?" Jack shook his head. "Makes me completely responsible for a whole lot of people."

Chase brought the liquor to his lips. "People on the outside think it's all jets and mansions. It's not."

"No."

"You're more equipped to take over the company than we were. Your employees are lucky," he said.

"You and Alex have adapted."

Chase didn't want to bring business into the wedding, but since Jack had opened the door, he might as well walk through it.

Chase nodded away from the crowd. "There's something I should tell you."

Once they were far enough away from being overheard, Chase gave Jack the short version of their concerns. "In addition to the contents of the safes, this Ashraf Bakshai guy is borderline stalking Alex. And Floyd seems to have a stake in Alex and Bakshai becoming chummy."

"If it's business, why Alex? Why not talk to you?"

Chase shook his head. "I think we both know the answer to that question. Alex was one of the only women at his 'executives and their mistresses' party. Men like Bakshai are used to women falling in line." Just saying those words put acid in the back of Chase's throat.

"Women and your VP Floyd Gatlin."

"Alex set Floyd straight. Should Bakshai not take kindly to that, our guess is we haven't heard the last of him."

"I can do some digging."

Chase smiled. "I hate to ask."

Jack just stared. "We're family. You have a problem? I have a problem."

"I'd appreciate it. Hawk is searching through his police and investigator angle."

"Good, good. About Hawk . . . he and Alex?" Jack left his question open-ended.

"You saw that?"

"Saw it? I felt it. It's like when I've done something to upset Jessie and she tries to ignore me," Jack said. "And that kind of tension is only tolerated when two people are passionate about other things."

"Trust me. We're all aware. Something happened in Colorado that neither of them are talking about."

Jack patted Chase on the back. "That's the funny thing about love. You can't stay mad forever."

Chase turned back toward the guests that mingled several yards away.

Hawk stood on one side of the room.

Alex on the other.

Was this love? Certainly attraction.

Anything short of love on either of their parts, and Hawk would likely have pushed off his bodyguard duty to a colleague, and Alex would have fired him. Instead they continued to tolerate each other.

"Interesting perspective," Chase mused.

Chapter Thirty

Sleep wasn't her friend.

It seemed the insomnia fairy was parked over Alex's bed and couldn't be shooed off, even with a can of Raid.

It didn't help that Alex spent her days checking the CEO boxes and her nights cross-referencing the names in the CIM files with the Stone Enterprises database. Considering all but three of the CIMs weren't companies they owned, most of her research was coming up empty.

She and Hawk still hadn't cleared the air. Every time there was time, it was the wrong time. That was keeping her up as well.

Alex drank the last of her cold coffee and stared into the cup. The caffeine wasn't working. It was barely lunchtime, and she was tempted to lie down on her office sofa and take a nap.

Only that was where Hawk sat reading an article on the oil industry and the companies the Bakshais dealt with.

A knock on her office door shot Alex's dreams of a nap out of her head.

"Come in," she called out.

Dee walked in with her purse slung over her arm. Her gaze shifted from Alex to Hawk and back again. "Uhm. I'm going to . . . lunch."

Alex glanced at the clock. It was five past noon. "Thank you." Not that Dee needed to announce her walking away from her desk. But it seemed the woman felt obligated to reveal her every move of the day.

"I, uhm . . . I mean, can I . . ."

Alex smiled in hopes of helping the woman relax.

"I have to pick up my son from school. The nurse called. I might be a little later coming back from lunch. I mean . . . can I come back late from—"

"Dee. It's fine. Take the rest of the day. Sick children need their moms."

Dee's shoulders sunk in relief. "Are you sure?"

Alex stood and grasped her cup to refill it. "Positive. Let the office manager know if you need tomorrow off so we can get a sub."

"Thank you, Ms. Stone." Dee glanced at the cup in Alex's hand. "Do you want me to get you more coffee before I go?"

Alex held the cup to her chest. "I'm capable. Thank you."

Dee nodded, once again glanced at Hawk, and shuffled out the door.

"Every time I think Dee is growing comfortable in Piper's shoes, something shifts, and she is once again afraid of her own shadow."

"Nervous people are hard to be around," Hawk said. He placed the papers on the table. "How about we get something more substantial in you than coffee."

"I'm really not—"

"Alex!"

She placed the cup on the table. "Fine. There's a deli around the corner. We can walk there." Maybe that would wake her up.

Hawk looked down. "In those shoes?"

"I was born in heels."

Hawk smiled, and for a moment, she was transported back to Colorado, where their smiles were heartfelt and often.

Alex retrieved her purse and cell phone and started for the door.

Before they got to the elevator, her phone rang.

Mrs. Steiner's name displayed on the screen.

She smiled and instantly missed seeing the older woman across the hall.

Alex put the phone to her ear. "Hello, Mrs. Steiner."

"Hello, sweetie. How are you? Are you ever coming home?"

Alex and Hawk waited by the elevator, along with a few others. "Eventually. How are you? Do you need anything?"

One of the faces from Accounting glanced at her and smiled.

"I could use a trip to Walmart. I'm almost out of tissues, and they have the cheapest ones that don't make my nose want to fall off my face."

Yeah, Alex missed the lady.

Sending Mrs. Steiner tissue was never the answer. Her need to go to the discount superstore had more to do with getting out than what she was getting when she was out.

"Can you be ready at five thirty today?"

"You don't have to jump, Alexandrea. I can wait."

Alex smiled. "It's not a problem. I'll take you out for dinner."

Mrs. Steiner drew out her words. "Well . . . if you're sure."

"I'm positive."

"Taco Mike's?"

"Tacos sound perfect."

The elevator door opened, and Alex used its arrival to end the call.

⁓

It felt like forever since Alex had been in her own space.

She missed it. She loved her family, but having alone time was impossible.

Alex knocked on Mrs. Steiner's door first, letting the older woman know she was there.

After a few minutes in her apartment and a quick change of clothes to something more Walmart compatible, Alex and Hawk stood in the center of Mrs. Steiner's apartment, waiting for her to gather her purse, phone . . . shoes.

It was Walmart and a taco shack, and Mrs. Steiner was dressing for dinner at the Ritz.

She would probably like high tea at the Ritz.

Alex made a mental note to schedule one in the not-too-distant future.

"I won't be but a minute," Mrs. Steiner called from the bedroom.

"Take your time."

"Can your boyfriend change the burned-out light in the kitchen? I have extra bulbs in the pantry."

Alex glanced at Hawk and let the "boyfriend" comment go.

"Happy to, Mrs. Steiner," Hawk called out to her.

"And my smoke detector started making noise last week. Why do those things always happen in the middle of the night?"

She and Hawk both looked up at the ceiling.

Said detector was hanging from a wire.

"I hit it with a broom. I might have broken it."

Both Alex and Hawk laughed.

"It looks dead to me," Hawk said quietly.

"At least she didn't try and change the battery by herself. I took her stepladder away last year to force her to ask me for help."

"Smart thinking."

Hawk pulled a chair from the dining table over to assess the smoke detector damage.

"When was the last time you opened a window in here? It's stuffy."

Alex opened one in the kitchen, hoping to get rid of the smell.

"I don't like the cold," Mrs. Steiner said.

Alex checked the kitchen garbage. It was empty.

With nothing to do but wait, she took the opportunity to look through the stacked-up mail on the coffee table.

Alex shuffled through bills and junk mail before setting them aside.

A package with a large white label had her name on it.

"Every person's home over the age of seventy-five has an odor you can't identify," Hawk said from the top of the chair.

Alex revisited the kitchen, found a pair of scissors in Mrs. Steiner's junk drawer, and returned to the living room to open her package.

"Yep, it's dead," Hawk said.

"We'll pick her up a new one and install it after we get back. Unless you don't have time."

Hawk hadn't yet complained about his long hours. Aside from a few days after they'd returned from Colorado, Hawk hadn't passed on his babysitting baton once. Alex gave him the opportunity to do so often.

"One of these days, you're going to stop saying that."

"One of these days, you're going to take me up on it. You can't be my shadow forever."

Hawk looked at her from the chair he stood on. "You're not a job for me, Alexandrea."

She didn't want to analyze what she was to him. Or what he was to her.

Not right then.

Alex cut into the package and folded back the cardboard.

The smell hit her first, and then Alex got a good look at what was inside.

And gasped. "Oh, good God."

Hawk was off the chair and by her side in one leap.

Alex placed a shaking hand over her mouth to keep it from screaming.

Inside was an old stuffed teddy bear. Someone had pulled the button eyes off and replaced them with sewn-in *X*s. Hanging from one arm of the toy was what looked like a tiny, *dead*, newborn animal.

As much as Alex wanted to tear her eyes away, she couldn't.

A note was pinned to the chest.

Sins of the Father.
Sins of the Daughter.
Tick Tock.
Tick Tock.

Dried drops of blood covered the inside of the box.

Hawk placed a hand on her knee.

She sucked in a deep breath and wanted to choke.

"You okay?"

She swallowed. *No,* she thought and nodded her head yes.

Mrs. Steiner emerged from her bedroom. "I'm ready."

Chapter Thirty-One

Media vans mixed with police cars outside Alex's complex.

According to Mrs. Steiner, the box had arrived the day before.

Upon inspection, the box hadn't been mailed. There was no postage and no return address.

A return address would have been too easy.

But that did mean someone had personally dropped it off.

The recording from the camera over the mailboxes had been recovered and was being analyzed.

Fitzpatrick had a team dusting for prints from the front door, to the parking garage, to the mailboxes themselves.

Alex helped Mrs. Steiner pack up several of her things. There was no way she was going to let the older woman stay there after this.

Stevie approached Hawk in the hallway.

"I just heard from my contact. None of the guns you found were registered. So far, no matches on unsolved crimes."

Hawk ran a hand over his jaw. "Innocent men don't have unregistered weapons."

Stevie shrugged. "You know how the database is. Things get missed."

True. As much as the government wanted to pledge that every weapon legitimately purchased through the proper channels was recorded in the "database," as with any computer, files got corrupted.

"Did Stone have *any* registered weapons?"

"One. A .40 Glock."

"We haven't found one of those."

Alex walked into the hall, looked one way, then the other.

Seeing Hawk, she walked over. "They said we can go. Mrs. Steiner is getting tired."

"Give me a minute," he said, his voice soft.

She walked back into the apartment.

"She's taking all this really well," Stevie said.

"Seems the more that happens, the higher that shield goes up." The fact that Alex could even be in the same room with him after he'd leveled a gun in her face was remarkable.

"You really care about her."

Hawk pulled his attention away from the door Alex had slipped behind. "She deserves someone who isn't damaged."

"Fuck that. Everyone around you sees how you look at each other."

"Still flawed."

Stevie paused. "You don't trust yourself."

Her words were too close to the truth. "I need to get her home."

Stevie grabbed his arm to keep him from walking away. "You know, Hawk, sometimes the fastest way to get past the fire is walking directly through it. It's gonna hurt, but it's worth it on the other side."

He blinked several times. "I gotta go."

The sound of Stevie clicking her tongue followed him down the hall.

∽

Mrs. Steiner didn't linger on the contents of the box in her possession. She'd shown concern for Alex and insisted that she didn't need to go with her to the estate, but she ultimately gave in.

Now she was in heaven.

She said the estate was "better than the fanciest hotel I have ever stayed in."

But the biggest joy . . .

Hailey.

She latched onto Alex's niece, and instant love took over.

Kit hugged Mrs. Steiner's side with a watchful eye but eased into her presence rather quickly. The dog knew which people to trust better than any human around. Alex was convinced of it.

When Piper put Hailey down for bed, Mrs. Steiner finally retired to her room. "I haven't had this much excitement since I marched on Washington during the Vietnam War."

In the end, Alex was pleased with her decision to bring Mrs. Steiner to the estate until it was truly safe to go home.

After showering off the taste of the day, Alex joined Chase, Piper, and Hawk in the kitchen.

"How are you doing?" Piper asked when Alex relaxed into a chair.

Chase poured her a glass of wine, which she accepted with a tired smile.

"I'm okay," Alex said. Except for the never-ending headache and constant fatigue. Both of which could be attributed to the context of her daily life.

"You need to move out of that building," Chase said.

Alex didn't bother fighting him. "I know."

Chase stared at her with disbelieving eyes.

"I'll call a moving service. Put my things in storage until I find a better situation." She lifted the wineglass to her lips and put it back down before drinking any of it.

"That was too easy," Chase said.

Alex looked up, saw everyone watching her. "What?"

Piper patted Alex's hand.

"Max called," Chase began. "He didn't find a lot in London. A small amount of British pounds and euros, along with a nearly empty flat and a few of Dad's things. The caretakers said that no one has been there since last year."

"Before Dad died?" she asked.

"Yeah. Italy wasn't the same story. Max found a safe in the back of a wine cellar."

"And?" she asked.

"He thinks someone got to it. There wasn't any money, nothing of obvious value. He found a shotgun, ammunition, and more documents," Chase said.

"Was there evidence of a break-in?" Hawk asked.

"Not according to Max. The top five shelves of the safe were completely empty."

"Like someone cleaned it out," Hawk observed.

"That's how it sounded. He did find one piece of information that I wasn't expecting."

Alex looked at her brother and made a rolling motion with her hand. "Which is?"

"Another passport. This one from the United Arab Emirates. With Floyd's name and Dad's face."

"What?"

"It had one stamp coming into the US with a visa from San Francisco."

"No exiting stamp?" Alex asked.

"Those aren't issued. All that would be required is a return plane ticket or a ticket showing the passport holder was moving on in their travel," Hawk explained. "What was the date of the stamp of entry?"

"Six years ago."

"The same time Dad started collecting these CIMs," Alex said.

"Does your dad have any personal property in the UAE?" Hawk asked.

"No," Alex said. "We do have hotels in Dubai and Abu Dhabi."

"Any idea when Dad last visited there?" Chase asked Piper.

"He was constantly out of the office. The one that could answer that the quickest is Carson. The flight records are more accurate than a hotel reservation. Obviously, the company hotels accommodate everyone on the list, but there is no guarantee that the room isn't filed under 'Company Comp.'"

Alex rubbed her forehead. "If we are working with the assumption that the safe in Italy was packed the way the other two safes were, then who knew about it? Who took the money?"

"Aaron could have cleared it out," Hawk suggested.

"If he did, wouldn't he have taken everything from it? The safe was in the back of a cellar?" Alex asked.

"Yes."

"Not as hidden as the others," she said. "No secret rooms?"

Chase shook his head.

Alex remembered the look of anger on Melissa's face at the reading of the will. "Didn't Melissa believe that the Italy property was a gift to her and therefore belonged to her?" she asked Chase.

"Yeah." Chase's eyes started to spark.

Alex glanced at Piper. "And didn't you say that Melissa was all about Italy while Dad spent his off time in Colorado?"

"Yes," Piper said.

A light bulb went off in Alex's aching head. "We've been wondering where Melissa came up with the money to buy Yarros's shares of Stone Enterprises."

Surprise stared back at Alex from her brother.

"You think she stole it," Hawk said.

"Do you have a better idea? We know she snuck into this house after she had been locked out."

Piper cringed. "I remember that day."

Melissa had cornered Piper and nearly had her ass handed to her by Kit for her efforts.

"Maybe she knew all about these safes. We know she stole a few of Dad's watches."

"What's so great about a watch?" Hawk asked.

"Watches worth a small fortune," Piper answered.

"Did you file charges?"

Alex rolled her eyes. "Why bother? We didn't want them, and we didn't really care that she took them. At that point, we were still reeling from inheriting everything." Alex paused. "Let's assume she flew to Italy and walked away with two . . . three million. That combined with the value of the watches, plus what was in her prenuptial—"

"How much was that?" Hawk asked.

"Five million. That still doesn't quite make up for what Yarros would want for our stock."

"But it might be enough for him to slide in and buy Starfield hotels. Who knows what kind of arrangement Melissa and Yarros have," Chase said.

"I think we need to have a chat with our step-mommy." Just saying that made Alex cringe.

"I'll contact Carson in the morning and have him confirm who was in the air at the time of this time stamp in the fake passport," Piper said.

"Have him pull everything six months before and six months after," Hawk said. "Something happened in that time frame. We need to find out what."

Alex leaned forward on her elbows and sighed like she was a woman twice her age. "I think it's time to mend fences with Melissa."

"What?" Chase's question was as sharp as the look coming from Piper.

"Hear me out. What motivates her?"

"Money."

Alex pointed at Piper. "Exactly. She married Dad for his . . ."

"Money," Chase finished.

Alex nodded. "She didn't care that everyone watching thought she was a gold digger. She wore that like a badge of honor, just as Dad wore her as the trophy wife she was. She didn't need loyalty. Hell, Dad's infidelity probably took her off the sexual hook more often than not. Melissa probably introduced Dad to his mistresses."

Chase and Piper nodded but stayed silent.

"What does every gold digger long for? Marry a rich old man with one foot on a banana peel and the other in the grave. Only Dad wasn't that old or that frail. But he was a workaholic, and from the looks of everything we're finding, he was living a double life."

"One that required fake passports and a whole lot of cash," Hawk finished.

Alex appreciated how Hawk's thoughts ran right alongside hers. "That equals stress. Stress and a bad lifestyle are easily linked to an early grave."

"So is dealing with people that are in that double life," Hawk said.

"If an accidental gunshot wound was the cause of his death, then I'd agree. But since a heart attack is what took him out, we need to work with that." Alex played with the stem of her wineglass. "Dad dies and Melissa pops some bubbly and dances naked in the house, only to learn that Dad completely shafted her in his death."

No one disagreed.

"Chase and I laid bets on how fast she'd be hooked up with another sugar daddy. Hell, she'd lived a billionaire life. Five million probably made her feel like she was in the soup line at the homeless shelter. But that isn't what Melissa did. She managed to buy out Yarros and earned a seat on our board. Which I'd have to admire if I was on the outside looking in. If she'd been in a loving relationship with Dad, she might have been given shares in the company that would at least maintain some of her lifestyle."

"Only Dad didn't know how to love," Chase said.

"Hence the shafting. If she relieved the Italy safe of its monetary value but left the passport and the documents, she either had her eye only on the shiny objects in the safe and didn't bother looking at what was in the documents. Or . . . purposely left the documents because they were useless to her."

"She wouldn't know a CIM if it bit her in the face," Piper stated.

"Agreed. She sits in our board meetings acting like she understands what we're talking about, but she's clueless."

"Melissa only walks in that room to make you both uncomfortable," Piper suggested.

"Mission accomplished. She doesn't want control of Stone Enterprises. She wants the money. I say we give her an olive branch."

"Elaborate," Chase said.

"We give her back something she thought was owed, and maybe she feels comfortable enough to ask for something else. We tell her we know about the safe in Italy and have considered that she might be the one who took the money in it . . . but hell, how can we blame her? As far as we're concerned, she deserved it."

"To serve what purpose?"

"To see how she responds when we suggest the money in it was gained from illegal activity. Is she shocked? Complacent? Did she have any clue about what Dad was up to?"

Hawk stared at Alex with a smile on his face.

As much as she wanted to ignore that look of pride in his eyes, she couldn't.

"And if she denies the stealing from the safe?" Piper asked.

"You don't press it," Hawk said. "You're not looking for a confession."

"We're looking for so much more."

~⊚~

Hawk followed Alex when she pleaded exhaustion and her desire to go to sleep.

Thankfully, she didn't deny him. He had to come to some kind of agreement with her.

They walked through the door to her room, and Hawk closed it behind him.

She crossed the room and stood by the window, looking out at the darkness beyond.

"I can't keep doing this," Hawk admitted.

She didn't turn, didn't look at him. When she spoke, it was soft and pained. "I understand."

Hawk hesitated. "You do?"

"I think we can both agree that I need more protection now than ever. I'm sure the other members of your team are quite capable of keeping me safe."

Hawk froze. "No, Alexandrea."

She turned, looked at him.

The sadness in her eyes punched him in the stomach.

He strode toward her and took her hands in his. "I can't keep this distance. I've been walking through the days since Colorado, trying to figure out how to fix us."

For a minute she said nothing.

"You can't fix anything without letting me in. Let me in, Hawk." Her eyes shifted back and forth between his.

"It's not that simple," he said.

"Then there is nothing to fix." Alex tugged at her hands, but he didn't let go.

He took a breath and told her what he could. "Yes, I've had bad dreams . . . hell, nightmares. Yes, they are linked to my past. But now is not the time to work it out, Alex."

"There is never a perfect time to work through trauma."

He let go of one of her hands and brought his to her cheek. "You already have a threat to your well-being. You don't need to add me to the mix. Do you know how many times I have damned myself for what happened in Colorado?"

"You didn't mean to."

"That sounds like an abused woman making excuses for her abuser." His hand fell to her shoulder.

"Abuser? Is that what you think you are? It was a dream."

"I pulled my gun on you. I could have—"

She gripped his arm. "You didn't. If you truly want to fix us, you need to let that guilt go. Tell me what happened."

"Haven't you had enough for one day?"

Alex let her arm fall. "Unless you're going to reveal some unforgivable premeditated crime, I want to know. I need you to trust me. We can't have a relationship if there isn't trust."

It was Hawk's turn to let her go and look out the window into the darkness.

Alex stood next to him . . . silent.

"It was Guatemala."

"When you were shot?" Alex asked quietly.

He nodded. There was no way to come clean about Gabriella without sounding like a manipulative ass.

"Her name was Gabriella. She was the cartel boss's daughter. We had a . . . I don't know what to call it. It wasn't a relationship in the way you think about relationships."

"You were lovers?" Alex asked.

"Yes. She wasn't married. Her father didn't care who his daughter slept with, and our relationship put me in a greater position to get my job done so I could get out of there."

"You used her."

Hawk leveled his eyes with Alex's. "I would love to tell you that I didn't. But the truth is, we used each other. I wouldn't have gone there if she was some innocent bystander. I don't believe in sexual collateral damage."

A strangled smile rested on Alex's face as she sat on the edge of her bed.

Hawk continued.

"If it wasn't for Gabriella, I wouldn't have lived for five minutes after they put a bullet in the head of the kid that took fifty bucks. I was released from the cell a week after they put me in. They threw me in my room, told me to clean up . . . fed me. Part of me thought I was being given my last supper. Another part thought maybe they believed me. I had maintained my innocence and they believed me. Twenty-four hours after I was released from the cell, Gabriella came to me. She said

she pleaded with her father. Told him I wasn't a spy. I told her that I'd
be tested again. That her father wouldn't be happy until I murdered or
raped someone. She encouraged me to do what her dad wanted. To be
that kind of man. To earn her father's trust so we could continue being
together."

"That's sick."

"I agree. But to buy myself time, I told her I would do it. She stayed
with me that night. I knew I had a short window of time to get out of
there. I'd planned my escape, only I fell asleep." If only he had kept his
eyes open.

"Shouts at the door of my room had me rolling out of bed and
reaching for my gun. Only my weapon hadn't been returned to me."

"Your nightmare," Alex whispered.

Hawk nodded.

"Emilio, Gabriella's father's second in command, held her at
gunpoint."

"What?" Alex said.

"He came in the room, kicked the door shut. Told me to start
talking or he'd waste Gabriella and put the gun in my hand."

Hawk felt awful at the look of horror on Alex's face.

"It took my head a minute to catch up with what was happening.
There was a silencer on the gun Emilio held. Which made me believe
he was working alone. Santiago would kill him if he threatened his
daughter. Only Emilio had a thing for Gabriella and never liked the
fact that she and I got together. Using her to get me to talk started to
make sense."

Alex sat quietly and listened.

"I maintained my innocence. Told him to put the gun down.
Gabriella was crying, begging that I do something. Tell Emilio what
he wanted to hear."

Hawk blew out a breath.

"Then I realized that I was naked, and she was dressed. We'd fallen asleep together. Gabriella wasn't telling me to save her, she was telling me to give Emilio what he wanted."

Alex's jaw dropped. "She set you up."

Hawk nodded.

"I knew then that Emilio wasn't going to hurt her. He was making demands. I told him I'd cooperate. I found my pants, my shoes. I said I'd talk to Santiago directly. I got closer. Gabriella looked relieved."

Hawk rubbed a hand to the back of his neck. "I went for the gun. Emilio was dead before he hit the floor."

Alex filled her lungs and let it out slowly. "And Gabriella?"

"She'd retreated to the other side of the room. She had a gun. Only she wasn't a killer. I knew that. She watched as I grabbed a bag I had filled before she'd come to my room and jumped out the window. I didn't head straight to the jungle."

"Why?"

"I needed Santiago and his men to focus on something more important than me. The cartel loved their liquor. The higher the octane, the better. I'm amazed at how quickly things can catch fire in the middle of the rainforest."

"You went for the weapons," Alex assumed.

Hawk shook his head. "I set the house on fire. The walls were filled with cash. With everyone trying to put the fire out, they wouldn't go after me."

"Then how did you get shot?"

Hawk shook his head with a harsh smile and even harsher laugh.

"I underestimated Gabriella."

"Oh my God," Alex said.

"She shot me as I was jumping on a motorcycle. And then watched me leave."

"She didn't want to kill you."

"I don't know. She almost succeeded. The gunshot was survivable. The infection, by the time I was treated, nearly took me out. The movies always paint delirium as this traumatic experience someone goes through until a fever breaks. What they get wrong is how much it lasts after the doctors are gone and only a physical scar remains."

"And now you relive that night."

"Yes."

"Will these people come after you?" Alex asked.

"Those that are still alive think I'm dead."

"What do you mean? Did the fire kill them?"

Hawk shook his head. "The man Santiago reported to wasn't happy about his loss from the fire. When they found out that an American agent had infiltrated, they weren't happy. The cartel did what they do. They wipe the slate clean and start over. Santiago was part of that collateral damage."

"And Gabriella?"

Hawk rubbed his fingers together. He could practically feel her blood on his hands. "She was never going to live a normal life. The family she was born into wasn't something she could ever divorce. If we hadn't been lovers, she may not have suffered her fate—"

"She tried to kill you," Alex said in his defense.

"And yet I'm alive, and she is not."

Alex walked over and reached for him. "She wanted you to be a murderer for her. How many times did she look away and ignore, or participate in . . . someone else's death? You said so yourself, she was never going to live a normal life when her family was part of the cartel. You are not responsible, Hawk."

He knew that on some level.

"As much as I hate how this has hurt you, how it haunts you in your dreams, I would worry more if you were completely unfazed. It shows you're human and you care."

"I didn't want any of this to touch you."

"I see that clearly now. Knowing where you're coming from explains your desire to keep us secret. Why there was any hesitation to be together in the first place. But I'm not her. And other than the fact that she and I both had asshole fathers, I think that's where the similarities end."

Hawk placed his hand on her neck. "You are nothing alike."

"I wish I could guarantee that you'll never see someone with a gun to my head."

"Fuck, Alex. Don't say that!"

She squeezed his arm. "If you ever did. You'll know it's not because I'm betraying you."

Hawk folded his arms around her and buried his head in her hair. "Don't ever say that again. Don't put that picture in my head."

"That isn't your nightmare?"

He wanted to deny her.

"I can't sleep beside you, Alex. Not right now."

She drew back to look at him. "I figured that out. I don't think I could sleep if there was a loaded gun by our bed."

"And I can't protect you if there isn't one. You need my protection more than my snores."

She huffed out a short laugh.

Hawk placed a finger under her chin and forced her to look at him. "I want to work through this. For you. For us. It just can't be today."

"Even Vikings bleed, Hawk. We might not be able to fix it today. But we started the healing."

"Is that how you see me?"

"You put that thought in my head, and it's never left. Eventually I'm going to ask for the intimacy that comes with sleeping with you in my arms. But I am willing to wait until it's safe for both of us."

"You're incredible, you know that?"

Alex lifted her chin. "I need you to show me," she whispered. "It's been entirely too long."

Hawk started to lower his lips to hers.

Alex stopped him with one finger to his mouth. "I have a condition."

"Always negotiating," he teased.

"I'm not pretending we aren't a thing. Not here. Not at the office tomorrow."

He straightened his shoulders. "You're not going to the office tomorrow."

Her hand fell. "I *am* going to the office tomorrow. I'm going to tell the press that I have some kind of a stalker and let the press do what they do best."

"Which is?"

"Ask all the questions. Who? Why? What do they have to gain? Maybe the press hits a nerve. Maybe the stalker gets nervous and backs off. All the eyes turning outward is the best form of situational awareness. Don't you agree?"

Hawk couldn't deny her strategy.

"You win," he told her.

She stepped closer, lifted her lips to his. "Now . . . where were we?"

Her kiss was sweeter than any honey on the planet.

And when they fell into bed and Hawk reacquainted himself with the taste of her skin and her moans in his ears, he knew he wasn't going back.

If he needed to return to the jungle to work through his trauma, he'd do it.

For her.

Chapter Thirty-Two

Alex, Hawk, and Chase stood outside Stone Enterprises with the press pointing cameras their way.

She gave them the information Fitzpatrick had approved and answered their questions. Alex even went so far as to chastise her stalker for terrorizing an eighty-five-year-old woman. It was almost like kicking a box filled with puppies.

She stretched the truth and suggested the authorities were narrowing down their search, and she was confident that they'd be caught soon.

When the three of them stepped out of the media lights and were in the elevator, Hawk grasped her hand and laced her fingers with his. "You poked the bear."

"Good. I hate playing defense."

Chase glanced at her, looked at her hand in Hawk's, and turned to smile at the closed elevator door.

All day her phone rang. Board members expressing their concern. Old colleagues from Regent. Friends of the family . . . aka Aaron Stone's golf buddies. And several new members of their life from Texas.

Jessie, Jack Morrison's wife, asked if there was anything she could do.

Katie, Alex's new stepsister, offered her marksmanship skills if they were needed.

And Alex's mom and Gaylord checked in from their honeymoon. "Who do I need to bring down?" Gaylord had asked.

"As soon as we know, you'll know."

It took some reassurance that she was safe and for them to continue to celebrate their marriage.

It felt good.

All of it. The support and genuine concern.

The best part was the man typing away on the computer, trying to connect the dots.

They'd made love like they were dying of thirst in the desert. They'd held each other briefly after, before Alex kicked Hawk out of her bed with a tease and a tickle.

And she'd finally slept.

The world wasn't tilting as hard as it had the day before. Even with the new threat . . . or a reoccurrence of the old. Hawk was the rock she wanted to hook her anchor to.

He'd opened up to her, which was huge.

On the way to work, Alex had asked him to tell her when something happened that triggered a nightmare or a memory. Then they could talk about it, make it less. And once they were safe to truly deal with the trauma, he promised to get in touch with the help that had been given to him when he'd left his federal job.

But that wasn't today.

Alex went back to work in silence until Dee pushed through an unexpected call from Melissa.

Alex put her on speaker for Hawk to hear.

"Alex."

"Hello, Melissa."

"I've seen the news," she said.

Alex used silence as a tool.

"I suppose I can expect another visit from the police," Melissa said.

Alex watched Hawk as she spoke. "I can't control who the authorities talk to. And you and I haven't exactly been on good terms."

"I wouldn't—"

"If it makes you feel any better, I don't think you would either. I mean, what could you possibly gain from hurting me?" Alex asked.

Melissa jumped at Alex's words. "Nothing. But the papers are saying awful, hateful things about me."

Hawk scribbled on a piece of paper and slid it across the desk.

Olive branch.

"Maybe if we met in public. Lunch or coffee, and the press saw us getting along, those awful things would go away."

Melissa was quiet. "You'd, ah . . . you would do that?"

Alex released an exasperated sigh. "You're on the board, Melissa. We both have something to lose if the market value of Stone Enterprises goes down because of what the press is spitting out."

"Why do I feel like there is a catch?" Melissa asked.

"Because you're smart," Alex said.

Hawk grinned ear to ear.

"If we find out you are my stalker, I will deliver you to jail in your own car."

There was a pause.

"When can we meet?"

Alex fist-bumped Hawk.

She set up a meeting for later that day.

⟡

As expected, the press parked themselves on the street, with cameras focused on them.

Melissa, wearing a skintight dress, took a seat opposite Alex and pasted on a fake smile. Her designer bag was tossed on the chair beside her, a Ralph Lauren stiletto tapped against the air after she crossed her legs and sat back.

"We need to be seen, not heard," Alex told her. "And the press has lip readers. Although we both know they will make up what they want to."

Melissa cheated her chair so that her back was to the window.

Alex approved with a nod.

"So, what should we talk about?" Melissa asked.

"As it turns out, there are a couple of things. And before you get defensive or think I'm trying to set you up, you need to know *I don't care.*"

Melissa hesitated. "You don't care about what?"

Alex lowered her voice. "We know about the safe in Italy."

Melissa blinked . . . twice. She sat up taller. "What safe?"

Instead of clarifying, Alex repeated herself. "We don't care. We don't care about what was in the safe. We don't care about the watches."

"I have no idea—"

Alex lifted her fingertips from the table. "If I were you, I'd say the same thing. Don't say anything for a minute and hear me out. Chase and I . . . we didn't expect anything when Dad died. How could we? Dad didn't care about us."

Melissa stayed silent, a practiced smile on her lips.

"The only thing Dad cared about was money. Can we both agree on that?"

Melissa's nod was minuscule.

But it was the affirmative Alex needed.

"And Stone Enterprises was his way to get that money. He would protect it at all cost. Not you, me . . . Chase. And certainly not Max. Agreed?"

Another nod.

Alex leaned forward. "It wasn't so much as what was taken from that safe, but what was left in it. And why there was a need for that safe in the first place."

There was just enough confusion on Melissa's face to suggest she didn't know what Alex was talking about.

"I don't know anything about a safe."

"Fine. For argument's sake, let's pretend that you didn't. Who did? Who else knew about that safe . . . and the other ones?"

Melissa's chin went up.

Her expression unchanged.

"Right now, the authorities are digging through every possible motive and person who could gain anything by hurting . . . or killing me. We haven't directed them to the safe because we think they will focus on you and miss the real stalker."

"Why would they focus on me?" Melissa asked.

"You thought the Italy house was a gift to you, right?"

"That's what your father said."

"And you spent a lot of time there? And you went there after Dad's death."

"I was told I could retrieve my personal belongings." Melissa uncrossed her legs and sat forward.

Alex smiled at Melissa's confession of being at the house.

"Which means the police will accuse you of taking what was in the safe. Unless there was someone else that knew it was there." Alex folded her hands in front of her and waited.

Silence stretched for what felt like an eternity.

Melissa glanced over her shoulder and smiled at the flashing lights of the photographers from the sidewalk.

"Paul spent time there," Melissa admitted after she turned back to face Alex.

"Yarros?" Alex wasn't expecting his name.

A small nod.

"Can you say he positively knew about the safe?"

Melissa didn't answer.

"If he was asked, would he say you told him about it, or he told you?" Alex shook her head when Melissa didn't answer. "Never mind. Don't answer that."

A picture started to come to life in Alex's head. Maybe Melissa didn't know about the safe until Paul told her. He suggests she takes what's in it to give to him for his shares. Now Yarros has Melissa in his fist. Since she committed a felony, stealing that large of a sum.

"Do you think Paul knew about what else was in that safe?"

"What else was in this supposed safe?" Melissa asked.

Alex had to hand it to Melissa. She wasn't saying anything self-incriminating.

"Something you wouldn't want anything to do with, Melissa. Dad was doing something he shouldn't have been. That's how the contents of the safe got in there in the first place. And whatever that was, it looks like someone wants to hurt me for it." Alex reached across the table, placed a hand on Melissa's arm. "If Paul asked you to do what I think he did, for the purpose of selling you his shares, I wouldn't put it past him to use that as blackmail in the future. I honestly think you're being used as a pawn here. But what the person holding the chess pieces isn't anticipating is that we have no intention of pinning any blame on you."

Melissa narrowed her brow. Her smile all but a memory. "Why?"

Alex noticed Hawk move from where he stood by the door. His gaze had never left their table.

"Money means nothing if I'm dead."

Melissa pulled in a sharp breath.

Alex reached into her purse and removed a bulky envelope.

"What is this?"

Alex thought about how it would look from the paparazzi's view.

She opened the envelope and pulled out two car keys. "The Aston should have been yours. Dad was a dick to take it away."

Melissa's hand shook as she reached for the keys.

"The pink slip is signed. Bill of sale is one dollar," Alex said.

"I, ah . . ."

"I know. We don't know how else to show you that we truly don't care about what was taken. If we can't narrow any leads down, we're going to have to tell the investigators about the safe, what was in it. And we think that's going to put a lot of things in jeopardy. If there is any question of foul play that is linked to the company, none of us will have anything." Alex sat back as a thought flashed in her head.

Except Paul. He sold his shares to Melissa and isn't invested anymore.

For a woman who had always had some smart retort to anything Alex had ever said, Melissa was eerily quiet.

Alex smiled at Hawk.

"The car is parked in front of the office."

Alex reached for her purse and scooted her chair back.

"Are you expecting a *thank you* for what was mine to start with?" The words were harsh, but Melissa's delivery held humor.

"It wouldn't suck," Alex replied.

There was no *thank you*.

Alex laughed and stood. "You know where I am if something comes to mind that you think I should know."

Melissa stared at the car keys.

Alex placed a hand on Melissa's shoulder. "It still makes me want to hurl when I picture you sleeping with my dad."

Melissa coughed on a laugh, and Alex walked out the door.

Chapter Thirty-Three

Some families gather around a television and watch whatever the latest number-one miniseries is until someone cries uncle after six back-to-back episodes, and everyone drags their asses to bed.

Not the Stone family.

Wearing yoga pants and T-shirts, Alex and Piper had every file from all three safes scattered all over the great room.

Two days after Alex's conversation with Melissa, Max and Sarah had returned home with the not-so-surprising news of their engagement.

And sadly, the way the news was being celebrated was by following the bouncing ball Aaron had left behind.

Sarah's background in journalism made her the perfect fit for researching the current state of the companies that were named in the CIM files.

Hawk had found a giant scratch pad and had lined out their list of suspects. From the teddy bear, Play-Doh bomber, to Melissa, Yarros, and Floyd. He even put a faceless question mark over a silhouette picture to indicate there may be a player they weren't aware of.

Chase and Max were actively counting, and making accounts for, the money from the safes.

And Alex felt that they were a breath away from a breakthrough.

She fisted the original CIMs of Stone Holdings, which was purchased six years ago, and explained how the company came to be to Sarah.

"The CIMs in the safe for FassCo, the food distribution company that Dad bought and changed the name to Stone Holdings, show one location on the chopping block."

"Kansas City," Max said from where he sat counting money. "I told you about it, Sarah."

"We have a management company running the business," Alex said.

"Running it into the ground," Max pointed out.

"Except they are doing well in the Indiana and Georgia centers."

"Tell that to the employees in Missouri that are losing their jobs," Max said.

"Being the boss means making hard decisions."

Max nodded in agreement.

"Whose name is this?" Sarah turned a paper from the CIM report around. "P. Lexington?"

Alex shrugged.

"Max?"

"No idea. That isn't a name I heard of when I was there."

"I think I've seen that name before." Piper leaned across the coffee table and started to dig. "Here it is."

"Which company is that?"

"A-Star Rentals."

"The luxury rental cars?" Hawk asked.

"One and the same," Alex told him.

"Stone Enterprises owns that?"

"Technically it's a separate company. Just like Stone Holdings. If the company goes down, it doesn't take Stone Enterprises with it." Alex typed into her laptop and pulled up the short details of A-Star Rentals. "The company was purchased five years ago," Alex announced.

"Who manages it?" Hawk asked.

Piper and Alex responded at the same time. "Via Corp."

Hawk moved to Alex's side. "Are there any car rental sites that are losing money?"

"If I remember right, there were two locations that were closed down two . . . maybe three years ago," Piper told them.

"I found a Philip Lexington, CPA, in the employee roster at Via Corp," Sarah told them.

Alex did a search through the CEO email in hopes of finding some communication between her father and this man. "No emails from him."

Piper pushed to her feet. "We should be checking Aaron's home computer. If something dirty was going on, it probably wouldn't be linked from 'I Am the Boss at Fraud dot com.'"

Alex followed Piper into her father's office and pulled a chair beside the desk.

Piper logged in and started poking around.

"I doubt Dad left anything self-incriminating on his personal computer," Alex said.

Piper ran searches in Aaron's email.

Nothing.

Then in his documents.

"Lexington.Gatlin.doc" stood out like a dog in a cat shelter.

Alex and Piper stayed silent as the document was opened, and they both scanned what it said.

Alex slowly started to smile. "Is this our smoking gun?"

Piper hit the print button. "Your dad certainly wants it to look that way."

Back in the living room, Alex handed the documents over to Hawk.

"Dad kept copies of emails back and forth from Floyd Gatlin and Philip Lexington. Emails that suggest Floyd was working with Lexington to skim off the top of corporate profits from portions of the companies in question. Stone Holdings, Kansas City. A-Star Rentals, Miami and Houston."

"That would show where the money in the safes came from," Chase said. "My guess is that cash was used to bribe the employees to cook the CIMs or to make the sales go through."

"With everything indicating Floyd was behind it all." Alex rubbed her temple.

"I have one big problem with that," Hawk said as he pointed to the piles of cash. "Your dad had the money."

"He also had a passport with Floyd's name and his face," Chase said.

Piper walked back into the room with more papers. "I found more," she said.

Alex took the documents.

"Gatlin and Sparrow. Gatlin and Mason Beef Company. Gatlin and Ricco Farms. We don't own any of these," Alex said.

Piper reached for the documents she'd been looking at before they went on the email quest. "They are from companies Gatlin was 'encouraging,' with monetary compensation, to cook the CIM reports so the businesses were sold at a much lower rate than market value."

"But if we didn't buy those companies, who was he bribing them for?" Alex asked.

"Good question. Sparrow, Mason Beef, and Ricco Farms were all sold to different companies."

"Dad was setting Floyd up for the fall if he was caught," Chase concluded.

Hawk nodded.

"Do you think Floyd knew about any of this?" Sarah asked.

"Maybe. It would explain his hunger to get into the CEO chair by any means possible. He'd be able to use the position to cover things up. Move the evidence pointing at him toward someone else," Chase said.

"If he knew about the setup, he has to be on our list of suspects in regard to the threats toward Alex." Hawk glanced at Alex.

Alex sighed. "Floyd has been nothing but nerves since we took over the company."

Hawk walked over to his flip notes. "If your father was setting Floyd up, there's going to be a money trail directly to him. Or . . . a safe with money in it that only Floyd could have access to. And since we have a passport from UAE, I'd bet a hundred bucks we find a Floyd Gatlin bank account there."

Max, who had been observing the conversation without commentary, added his two very observant cents in.

"We still don't know why. Why did Aaron drum up this elaborate scheme to skim off the top of his own company? Or bribe other companies to sell to anyone else? And why stop with Stone Holdings or A-Star Rentals?"

Everyone looked at each other.

No one had an answer.

"These are people's lives he was fucking with," Max spat out. "Families who depended on their jobs to feed their kids. It's one thing if a business fails regardless of the efforts to keep it afloat. It's another to purposely screw it over and put people out of work."

Alex glanced at Chase. "We told you Dad was an asshole."

Hawk lifted a pen and circled names on his giant paper. "After the conversation with Melissa, we have reason to believe that Yarros knew about the Italy safe, and maybe even these incriminating documents inside. He dumps his shares on the unsuspecting stepmother and goes off to run his own business. Melissa . . . did she know your dad was skimming funds? Did she know anything about Aaron setting Floyd up?" Hawk circled Floyd's name. "Our bundle of nerves knows more than he is letting on. Maybe he knew Aaron was setting him up. Men like him break under the right pressure."

Alex narrowed her gaze. "What kind of pressure?"

"The kind Fitzpatrick can provide. And if they're not successful . . ."

Alex shook her head. "We're not the bad guys. We're not stooping to their level."

Hawk put the pen down and moved in front of her.

With both hands on her shoulders, he looked directly in her eyes. "Someone out there has threatened you. Frightened you and taken away the freedom of moving around without worry of assault or worse. If I have to have a 'persuasive conversation' with a not-so-innocent person to find out who that is . . ." Hawk shrugged.

"I'm with Hawk on this one," Max added.

Alex looked at Chase.

"I punched your prom date," Chase reminded her.

She grinned. "It was homecoming."

∽

Alex woke to a text from Melissa.

All it said was **He knew before I did.**

No details, but all the confirmation they needed as to what happened to the money and what it had been used for. If Yarros knew about the money, he might have known about the blackmail and skimming. Just because there weren't any guns pointing at Starfield hotels, that didn't mean they weren't there. Alex had to remind herself that while she and the family were playing junior FBI agents, they were way out of their league in truly investigating everything.

Maybe Starfield had a much greater potential for profitability than the CIMs suggested, and Yarros knew it. Which was why he used Melissa to take the money in the safe to pay for his shares in Stone Enterprises.

It all made sense in Alex's head.

She'd lay bets that Yarros knew her father was up to something that jeopardized the company, which was why he wanted out and was willing to sell his shares to Melissa at a reduced rate.

The pieces were falling into place.

Alex, Hawk, and Chase arrived at the office together and left together the entire week.

The tabloids were rerunning the "Stone Heirs" stories and encouraging Hollywood to make a miniseries.

As ridiculous as that sounded, Alex welcomed the media questions and poking around.

Nothing new had happened in the days following the sick gift.

Everyone in the family agreed to give Fitzpatrick time to investigate what they had to work with to see if Floyd or Yarros broke under the questioning.

They all knew that time was getting short on how long they could keep the fraudulent business practices of their father to themselves.

There was a very real possibility that the feds or CIA would come in and stop operations to investigate.

But there was nothing more they could do about that. International searches for bank accounts weren't as simple as a Google search.

Alex was at her desk.

Hawk had taken up the familiar position on her office sofa.

"Do you want the good news or the bad news?" Hawk asked after he disconnected the call from Fitzpatrick.

That wasn't a good sign.

"Bad first."

"The lobby video at the apartment complex was hacked. Nothing but snow on the recording for several hours in the middle of the day."

"Dammit."

"The good news is we aren't completely reliant on the lobby cameras. They are pulling together as much as they can from home security cameras. The ones businesses use in the corner stores. They think we will have something in a day or two."

"I hope they see a face."

"If not that, maybe a license plate of someone getting out of a car with a box."

"That would be great," Alex said.

"They have already started questioning the individual board members. Trying to determine what the 'Sins of the Father' comment meant."

Hawk saying those words out loud left a bad taste in her mouth.

"What kind of sick person sends a dead kitten to get their point across?"

"Sociopaths," Hawk said, deadpan.

She shook her head. "I don't see that personality in any of the people we know are connected one way or another."

"Don't underestimate anyone, Alex."

She instantly thought about Gabriella. "I'll try not to."

Hawk winked at her from across the room.

A loud knock sounded on her office door, followed by it being opened without an invitation.

Hawk was on his feet, his hand on his gun, before the light from the hall filtered in.

Floyd filled the doorway. "We need to talk."

Dee was behind him. "I told him you were busy."

Floyd looked at Hawk and then the gun. "What the . . ."

"Barging in my office is a health hazard, Floyd. Or did you miss the press conference the other day?"

"Put that away," Floyd demanded.

"I kind of like it where it is." Hawk moved to stand in front of Alex but tilted the barrel of the gun to the floor.

"I can have a conversation with my colleague without the threat of violence." Floyd glared at Hawk.

"That starts with common courtesy, like knocking on a door and waiting to be invited in."

Alex moved closer to Hawk and placed a hand on his back. "It's okay."

Hawk clicked the safety back in place and holstered his weapon.

"We need to talk. In private."

"Not happening." Hawk glared.

"I'm with Hawk on this one. Whatever you need to talk about can be said in front of him."

Floyd's nose flared.

Alex looked at an anxious Dee beyond the door. "Thank you, Dee. Hold my calls."

"Yes, ma'am."

Alex returned to her desk and sat.

Hawk took up a space at her side.

Floyd had no choice but to sit across from her.

"Why are the authorities at my home talking to my wife?"

"They are?" Alex asked.

"Don't play dumb."

"I know nothing about that, Floyd. I was told they were going to talk to you."

He looked from Hawk to her.

"I told them I had nothing to do with the threats against you."

Alex shook her head. "For someone who has nothing to do with anything, you sure are jumpy."

That seemed to calm him down.

Or at least make him take a quick look in the mirror.

"They are questioning if I was at home on Sunday between twelve and four."

"So?"

"I wasn't home."

Alex sat forward. "The police are looking for the person who dropped off my little 'gift,' Floyd."

Floyd ran a hand through his hair. "It wasn't me."

Alex looked at Hawk. "Help me out here."

"If it wasn't you, tell them where you were." Hawk crossed his arms over his chest.

"Why do they suspect me anyway? What do I gain if you weren't in your father's chair?"

"You tell me?" she asked.

She and Hawk exchanged glances with an unspoken . . . *let him tell his story and see what he knows.*

"Chase would fill it, or your father's other son."

"You mean my other *brother*," Alex corrected.

"Either way. It won't be me. We all know that." Floyd's voice rose an octave. His words were rushed together.

"Did you tell the police you were at home on Sunday?" Hawk asked.

"Yes."

"And you weren't?"

"No."

Hawk shrugged. "Then if I were you, I'd either get a lawyer or start talking to the police."

Floyd's eyes couldn't open any wider. "I don't need a fucking lawyer. I didn't do anything," Floyd yelled.

There was another knock at the door.

"Alex?" Chase said from the other side.

"Come in."

Floyd tossed his arms in the air. "Great."

"What's going on? I heard you from my office." Chase closed the door behind him.

"Floyd was just telling us that he had nothing to do with my teddy bear but can't tell the police where he was when the package showed up on my doorstep," Alex summarized. "Did I get that right?"

Floyd snapped his gaze from one of them to another and back to Alex.

Three sets of eyes stared back in silence.

"Fuck."

"The police are going to be very interested in this conversation, Floyd," Chase said.

"I'm not the best husband, all right? But I love my wife."

Alex closed her eyes and pinched the bridge of her nose. It wasn't a secret that Floyd had the same appetite for women that Aaron Stone had. "Do you think anyone in this room is going to cover for you and your mistress? I almost feel sorry for you, Floyd."

"I don't," Chase said as he came to lean on Alex's desk to stare at Floyd. "I recall you threatening my wife in an effort to keep your infidelity from Ann."

"I didn't—"

"Save it. There are way too many questions about your loyalty to this company. Your name keeps coming up in all the wrong places."

"What are you saying? I've given this company everything."

"You've pushed the line one to many times." Chase held eye contact with Floyd, his jaw was a firm line. "You've spoken in opposition of us since we took over. You give Alex about as much respect as you do your wife. Which should be a compliment . . . but isn't."

"And now you come in here asking us to cover for you? For all we know, you sent that package," Alex said.

"I didn't—"

Chase took hold of the edges of the desk and spoke slowly and clearly. "You have twenty-four hours to put in your letter of resignation, or we'll be forced to fire you."

Floyd came out of his chair. "You can't do this."

"We just did," Alex backed up her brother.

"I didn't fucking threaten you!" He leaned forward.

Chase stood in front of him.

Floyd lifted his hands and stood back. "I'll tell the police where I was."

"That's a good idea," Alex said.

Floyd smiled.

No one else in the room said a thing.

"It's not a reason to fire me."

Chase started to talk.

Alex stopped him. "We have some interesting documents Dad left us, Floyd. And you don't seem the least bit surprised by that information."

Floyd stiffened.

"Saving your marriage might be the least of your concerns. Once the documents are in the right hands, you won't have the ability to speak with any of us without a lawyer," Alex told him.

Floyd ran both hands through his hair as he stepped away from them and turned in a circle.

"I didn't do anything."

"Some of the accounts have come up short," Chase told him.

He swiveled toward Chase and lifted a finger in his face. "That was your father, not me."

"It's hard to question a dead guy," Chase said.

"You wouldn't be so flippant if you understood exactly who you're dealing with." Floyd's anger started to shift into fear. "If you fire me, they're going to . . ."

"Going to what?" Hawk asked. "Who are *they*?"

Floyd started to pace. "Fuck, fuck, fuck!"

Hawk moved to stand in front of the door. "Start talking, Floyd. Or you leave me no choice but to hold you here until the police come and take you into custody."

"These people reach into prisons."

That had Alex swallowing hard.

Hawk didn't seem fazed. "That sounds like a *you* problem."

Floyd walked to the other side of the room and hit the wall with his fist. "Fuck."

Alex's heart was racing. The fear rolling off Floyd was palpable.

Floyd turned and looked between them. "Bakshai."

Alex froze.

"What about him?" Hawk asked.

"He throws his little parties to learn executive secrets so he can blackmail influential men like your father."

"Our dad didn't care who knew that he was sleeping around. It wasn't an industry secret," Alex said.

"Your dad . . . he . . ." Floyd sucked in a breath. "He woke up next to a dead mistress after an entire room of people witnessed him arguing with her . . ."

Alex's jaw dropped.

Hawk recovered first. "You're suggesting Aaron Stone murdered someone."

Floyd shook his head. "I'm saying Bakshai was blackmailing Aaron to keep the dead mistress from being found. Your dad denied killing her."

"Why did he tell you?" Hawk asked.

"I was with him at the party. He called me in a panic. By the time I made it to his room, Bakshai was there, saying he'd take care of it."

"And you kept the secret, which made you an accomplice," Hawk concluded.

"I told Aaron he was set up. That we should have come home and gone straight to the police."

"Where did this happen?"

"Dubai."

"Let me guess, this was six years ago?" Chase asked.

Floyd paused. "Yes. How did you know?"

"Lucky guess," Chase said.

"What did Bakshai want in return?" Hawk asked.

"I'm not really sure."

"Oh, come on. You want us to believe that?" Hawk walked back beside Alex.

"Your dad didn't tell me, directly. I think he was bribing people to make it easier for Bakshai to obtain more American land for his oil company. Aaron went on a binge of buying businesses that weren't going to turn a profit. When those businesses eventually failed, we dumped them."

"You mean sold them to Bakshai," Chase suggested.

Floyd shook his head. "No. Not directly."

"Why wouldn't Bakshai just buy the failing companies himself?"

"He needed to be twice removed from any illegal activity or risk his American soil holdings being seized," Floyd told them reluctantly.

Alex screwed up her face and looked at him. "You just said you *thought* Dad was bribing people, now you seem to know exactly what was going down."

"I didn't . . . I don't," Floyd stammered.

"What happened after Aaron died?" Hawk asked.

"I thought it was over."

"That was naive. You're alive and still work here. Did Bakshai start pressuring you?"

Floyd's throat worked a swallow. "Bakshai insisted that Alex and I come to his gathering when he was in LA. I told him I couldn't do that."

"But you did . . . why?" Hawk's sharp eyes matched the tic in his jaw.

"Fuck!" Floyd ran both hands through his hair. "Bakshai reminded me that the dead woman could just as easily have been killed by me to protect my boss." Floyd sucked in a rattling breath. "I didn't have a choice."

Chase's entire body shifted. "Why did Bakshai want Alex there?" His words were slow and cold.

"I-I don't know."

"If our father didn't murder the woman that was used to blackmail him . . . did Bakshai?"

Floyd's eyes twitched to each of them. "Bakshai wouldn't have done it himself."

"But his goons would." Hawk's voice was so low, Alex could hardly hear him.

"I wasn't going to be an accomplice again. Wasn't going to be set up for something I didn't do."

Chase came off the desk and pushed right into Floyd's face. "But you had no problem throwing Alex at that man." Chase shoved Floyd back until he hit the wall.

Alex stood and rushed in to stop Chase from punching him.

Hawk got to Chase faster than she did and pushed him aside.

But not to stop Floyd from being punched. Just to stop Chase from being the one that threw it.

Floyd's head snapped back with the impact of Hawk's fist hitting his jaw.

Hawk had his forearm against Floyd's chest as he pinned him to the wall. His right hand at his side to access his gun.

Floyd looked like he didn't know what was going on while blood swelled on his lip.

Alex stepped forward, but Chase held her back.

"Those sleazeballs tried to get Alex alone." Hawk pulled Floyd away from the wall just to shove him back. "She could be dead right now, you fucking coward."

"I didn't—"

"And then you tried to send her to Dubai, knowing who this man was."

Hearing the venom in Hawk's words and, more importantly, the real danger she'd been put in, she no longer wanted to stop anyone from hurting Floyd.

Hawk tossed Floyd from him like a bag of garbage.

Floyd landed on his knees and didn't bother standing back up.

Alex started to shake.

Hawk turned then and gathered her in his arms.

"It's okay," he whispered.

She buried her head in his shoulder.

"This is way beyond what we thought. Call Fitzpatrick," Hawk said to Chase.

Chapter Thirty-Four

Alex stood in front of the board at an emergency meeting.

Flanked on both sides of her were Chase and Max. Beside them, Piper and Sarah. In addition to the board were the entirety of the executive staff and their executive assistants. And every corporate lawyer Stone Enterprises employed.

Hawk stood beside two Federal Bureau of Investigation agents.

On the opposite end of the room, Gaylord and Jack Morrison sat with their team of lawyers.

Considering the sheer number of bodies in the room, it was shocking how the sound of the cold air being forced through the vents could be heard.

It was as if no one wanted to break the spell.

The board members simply looked from one person to another and then back at her.

Alex took a fortifying breath, smiled at her brothers, and began.

"Thank you for coming to this emergency meeting. The last one didn't go so well."

A few smiles lifted on faces.

"I wish this was under more pleasant circumstances. Before we get too far into it, I'd like to introduce you to Special Agent Baker and Special Agent Kenna."

Baker and Kenna looked around the room and nodded but stayed silent.

"Chase, Max, and I expect everyone's full and complete cooperation while the FBI runs their investigation."

"What investigation?" Mrs. Monroe asked.

Alex smiled at the friendliest face on the board. "We have reason to believe that Aaron Stone was responsible for embezzling money out of Stone Enterprises and our sister companies."

Expressions of disbelief muttered around the room.

"Floyd Gatlin was removed from his position for misconduct. He is actively being investigated. If Mr. Gatlin contacts any of you, we'd highly suggest that you request counsel during your conversations with him."

"He stole money from the company?" Julia asked.

"We're not clear on that yet, Julia. You'll be asked to turn over every book, document, computer, hard drive . . . everything. One of our lawyers will be with you at all times. Just as Piper is not responsible for what our father did when he was alive, you are not responsible for any wrongdoings Floyd has done."

Julia placed her hand over Piper's.

"Another name you need to consider before accepting his calls is Paul Yarros," Alex told them.

Melissa looked across the table and met Alex's eyes.

"He is being investigated. He appears to have had knowledge that a possible corporate fraud case was pending. Melissa, like the rest of us, is cooperating fully. The minute this investigation goes public, our stocks will fall. Do not do anything foolish. Our lawyers will represent who and what is in the best interests of this company."

Alex made a point of sweeping her gaze around the room. "If anyone in this room was a part of our father's illegal activities, you will be found."

"Alex, is this related to the threats against you?" Mrs. Monroe asked.

Hawk offered a smile of encouragement.

"The parties that we know were involved with our father's activities are very dangerous. We believe they are behind the threats and will be actively looking for proof. That part of the investigation is not public yet. In the meantime, there will still be heavy security here at Stone Enterprises." Alex took a seat and rested her hands on the table. "This is going to hurt. The crimes of our father is a price that Chase, Max, and I will have to pay. Not in the legal sense, but financial. The sister companies involved appear to be mostly exclusive to our father's investments. Mostly, but not all. Our father encouraged this board to agree to the purchase of several nonprofitable companies for what looks like the sole purpose of skimming money from them. Once this investigation is complete, these companies will be financially compensated and sold or closed. The compensations will be the responsibility of the guilty parties."

"But your father is dead."

"His estate is not. We have been advised to expect the possibility of the estate's assets being seized. If this happens, we won't be able to touch our funds for an undisclosed amount of time. This puts the company at large at risk and is the reason the Morrisons are with us today. Gaylord and Jack have graciously offered us their counsel and financial backing, if needed, to get us through this time."

Gaylord winked at her from his seat.

Alex glanced at Max, then Chase. "Anything you want to add?"

"Yeah," Chase said.

She sat back and set her hands in her lap.

"Alex has worked harder for this company than anyone in this room over the last year. She's had to make unpopular decisions. All in an effort to make everyone in this room feel comfortable with the transition from our father's leadership to ours. And now, from the grave, our father is haunting us once again. The bomb threat this building received was targeted at Alex."

The sound of disbelief rippled through the room.

"The latest threat, and what the media hasn't gotten ahold of yet, was a child's toy holding a dead infant kitten and a note suggesting Alex pay for the sins of her father."

"Holy crap," Julia said.

Alex wanted to stop Chase from bringing all this up with the board but wasn't going to undermine him in front of others.

"I know that the FBI's investigation will not find anything to implicate this family. Therefore, I expect nothing but unwavering loyalty to Alex from the people in this room moving forward."

"Well said, son," Gaylord voiced from his chair. "Might I add my own word of caution." He sat forward and looked around the room. "The moment Vivian and I married, the three Stone children became my family. Yes, that includes Max. It also includes the families they brought with them. Their enemies are my enemies. Cooperate with the investigators. Come clean before you're found out. I don't take kindly to the abuse of women. And that little filly," Gaylord said, pointing to Alex, "she's had way more abuse than anyone in this room. Don't add to it."

Alex felt tears thicken behind her eyes.

Max cleared his throat. "I've already done time in jail. I have no problem going back for my sister."

Alex took gulps of air with an open mouth to keep from openly crying in front of the board.

Hawk moved to her side and placed a hand on her shoulder.

He didn't need to add his threats. His presence was warning enough.

Alex glanced at the men in her life and placed a hand on her chest for the love she felt for all of them. "Thank you," she managed. "I'll leave the rest of this meeting to the FBI agents and our lawyers."

～

Federal agents were a constant presence on the executive floor.

A comfort and a curse.

Hawk wasn't stuck to Alex's hip, which gave him the opportunity to meet the executive staff and try to build a rapport. To get a feel for who knew Aaron Stone on a personal level.

Another comfort of the FBI's presence was the real-time results of their investigation.

Video footage from a parking lot camera caught a person holding a box and walking toward Alex's complex. Their face was obscured by a dark, oversize hoodie. The hands, however, were not.

Caucasian of slight build. No obvious mannerisms that distinguished them as male or female.

The suspect walked past the parking lot camera holding the box and, shortly after, passed by again without it.

They couldn't positively identify a vehicle the suspect exited or entered. To complicate things more, there were two bus stops nearby. The recordings from the buses that made stops in that location leading up to the suspect dropping off the package were currently being evaluated.

The running theory was Bakshai hired someone to carry out the threats.

Between the information Jack obtained on how Ashraf Bakshai operated and the data collected by the feds, if the Bakshais didn't discover dirt on the people they wanted to control, they created it. If that didn't work, they offered "protection" from perceived threats. All of which pointed to the Bakshais planting the Play-Doh bomb and sending the teddy bear.

The emails between Ashraf and Floyd used strong language without admitting any wrongdoing. Correspondence between Ashraf and Floyd from before the Bakshai event had been found, indeed demanding Floyd and Alex's presence. In the email, Ashraf suggested the "other children" remain absent. Another record of a phone call took place after Ashraf had made a visit to the office, and again after the flower delivery. The final email was post–sick teddy bear and before Floyd's meltdown.

A line that stuck out in the email was what the feds were paying the most attention to: "Avoiding my phone calls is not in the best interest of Stone Enterprises. Aaron Stone's secrets, once revealed, will damage everyone."

Even though Floyd had confessed his role in the arrangement between Aaron and Ashraf to Alex, Chase, and Hawk, he wasn't talking to the feds.

The man had obtained a lawyer and, according to the federal agents, was only days away from a formal charge.

Everything Aaron Stone had set up in the paper trail pointed at Floyd. At the same time, the vast amount of currency pointed fingers at him. Which had the feds scratching their heads. Either Aaron had intentions of putting the money in Floyd's possession and died before he could do it, or Aaron believed the feds would never find the hidden safes. Or—and this was what Hawk believed had taken place—Aaron needed cash to bribe those that Bakshai told him to bribe. No one leaves a paper trail when illegal actions are involved, if they can avoid it. Aaron Stone had enough money to keep wire transfers and bank accounts away from that activity. At any time, if Aaron believed he was going down in a fall, he'd make sure that money wasn't anywhere near him when the authorities were brought in.

Two days into their investigation, a bank account in Abu Dhabi was located under Floyd Gatlin's name. To Hawk, finding that account was all the evidence he needed to understand Aaron Stone's motives. There was enough physical evidence pointing at Floyd for a "reasonable doubt" verdict to set Aaron free, should it have come to that.

Aaron Stone might have been an asshole, but he wasn't stupid.

Hawk and Alex were currently packing Alex's belongings in her apartment. Surrounded by cardboard boxes and Bubble Wrap, they decompressed from the first week of the investigation.

"It appears that your father had everything figured out. The only factor he didn't consider . . . was dying." Hawk stacked a wrapped plate into the box with the kitchen items.

"I can't imagine he'd have cared what happened to Stone Enterprises after his death. It wasn't as if he cared what his legacy would go down as."

"I couldn't disagree more. He had Floyd set up to take the entire fall if this crashed around him while he was alive. And yet he kept incriminating evidence pointing at himself if things were discovered after his death. Maybe he actually considered what would happen to Stone Enterprises, and you and Chase, if there wasn't a finger pointing back at him."

Alex stood there, staring across the room . . . frozen. "Aaron only cared about himself."

Hawk took the wrapped plate from her hand and placed it in the box.

"Then why did he mandate you find your half brother before selling anything off? Why tell you about Max at all?"

"To . . . I don't know, protect the estate from Max learning about him and coming after the estate at a later date?"

Hawk smiled. "That would still suggest he cared."

She blinked away her doubts. "I can't see it."

"And what if the reason he didn't bring you and Chase into the business was because of the blackmail from Ashraf?"

That was where Alex could argue against her father doing anything for unselfish reasons. "That only accounts for the last five to six years of his life."

"Still, if he wanted to make amends, it would have come at a price for both of you."

Alex stifled a yawn. "If you knew the man, you'd understand how off you are."

"And yet he still left you and your brothers everything."

She reached for another plate. "Including a full-blown corporate fraud investigation to navigate. A case that could easily freeze up every part of that inheritance."

Hawk took the plate from her. "Which brings us full circle as to why he held on to the evidence to incriminate himself."

Alex offered a placating smile. "I appreciate you trying to find anything to suggest our father was actually trying to do right by Chase,

Max, and me. But the sad truth is, the man was a horrible father. I spent my whole life trying to prove myself to him. To earn his love and respect. Even in his death, I've worked myself sick to do more, be better, stronger, and for what? Running his company better than he did will never be noticed by him. It has taken all of this time for me to realize it's over. I'm never going to find a hidden letter from him saying how much he loved me and wanted the best for me . . . us. It's over. He's gone. I don't have to prove myself to him, the staff at Stone Enterprises, the board. I have a family that loves me. He simply wasn't a part of it."

Hawk took one of her hands in his and squeezed. "You're something . . . you know that?"

"The only good thing about any of this is meeting you," she said.

⁓

A spa day out with Nick wouldn't have been the same with Hawk playing bodyguard.

And until the feds could get a solid lead on whoever dropped off the package, and use that person to determine who hired them, Alex still needed protection.

Therefore, the spa day was brought to them.

The bedroom in the pool guest house was transformed into a spa, including massage tables and room for pedicures and manicures.

"How are you holding up, really? Don't lie to me," Nick said. "You know I'll call bullshit."

Alex had her hair saturated with something silky and yummy that needed to marinate for a good half hour. Meanwhile, the technician was taking care of the mess she called feet.

Nick was face down on a table with a masseuse working out the kinks.

"I'm exhausted. I look at my computer and can't focus. I'm not eating like I should. If I had a cough or fever, I'd think I was sick."

"You sure that's not Hawk keeping you up late?"

"He keeps me up, but not late. Two sentences into pillow talk, and I'm out."

"That sounds like my dates," Nick said.

"Men aren't the only ones that pass out after sex."

His muffled chuckle made her smile.

"You've been complaining about this tired thing for a while. Have you considered seeing a doctor?"

"Our company is being investigated for fraud. My fatigue is justified."

Nick turned his head and looked at her. "Not that I like to think about these things, but . . . when was the last time you had a period?"

Alex closed her eyes and leaned her head back. "Two years ago."

"What?"

"IUD, remember? I haven't had anything for two years."

"What if it failed?"

Alex opened one eye and stared at her bestie. "I'm not pregnant, Nick."

"Are you having sex?"

She closed her eyes, thought of Hawk's weight on her as his lips said magical things in her ear. "The best ever," she replied.

Nick put his face back into the donut hole of the massage table. "If you start throwing up, take a test. I don't want to be plying you with alcohol only to learn I'm polluting my niece or nephew."

"You would be such a bad influence." She reached for the stem of her mimosa.

"I'm the best kind of bad influence, and you know it."

Yes, yes, he was.

Alex sipped her champagne with a splash of orange juice and felt a slight recoil in her stomach.

Come to think of it, she hadn't enjoyed the taste of wine in the past few weeks.

After she'd returned from Colorado.

She shook her head.

Nick's power of suggestion was screwing with her.

❧

The next morning, Alex and Piper stood in the bathroom waiting for the ten minutes that the pregnancy test said you needed to wait.

"Thanks for picking this up," Alex said for the fifth time.

She'd gone from not being able to stay awake to being up all night worrying.

Alex had cornered Piper and told her what she needed.

"I don't know if I should be excited for you or worried?"

Alex shook her head and rubbed her hands together. "I haven't felt like myself in weeks."

Piper gave a lopsided grin. "That lasted for six months for me."

She wasn't ready for a child.

And how would she break it to Hawk? She'd guaranteed him that this couldn't happen.

"This isn't the right time."

Piper placed a hand on her shoulder. "You'll be okay, regardless."

The timer on Piper's phone went off.

Alex reached for her sister-in-law's hand and picked up the test from the package it sat on.

A long sigh escaped her lips.

"Negative," Piper said.

A strange ache settled in Alex's chest. "Good. Yeah, see. I knew I wasn't."

Piper furrowed her brow.

Alex let Piper's hand go and tossed the test into the trash. Then turned on the water to wash her hands.

"You okay?" Piper asked.

"Of course. Why wouldn't I be?" Alex didn't give her time to answer. "I'll call my doctor tomorrow."

"It's all right if you're disappointed."

"No. No. I'm not. It isn't the right time."

"It is the right man, though."

Alex turned off the faucet, reached for a towel. For the first time in her life, Alex truly considered if Hawk was the right man.

The man you did plan to have children with.

The Viking to always be there and watch over you.

To love and grow old with.

"It's hard to let my mind go there," Alex finally said. "I'm afraid that if I say the things I feel, the bubble will burst, and he'll be gone."

"That isn't going to happen. Hawk isn't your father. He isn't going to abandon you."

Alex screwed up her face with the thought. Was that really her fear?

"Just because you convinced yourself that you'd never meet the right man, that doesn't mean it couldn't happen," Sarah continued. "The only real question you need to ask yourself is . . . do you love him?"

Alex swallowed the lump in her throat and stared at her hands on the sink. "I'm afraid to."

Piper leaned against the counter and ducked her head to get into Alex's line of sight. "But do you?"

Alex nodded . . . slowly.

Piper took Alex's hands in hers and squeezed. "Then enjoy. Let yourself love him. And see where that leads. There is no rush for anything."

Alex glanced at the garbage can. "That's a good thing."

Piper squeezed her fingers before letting go. "Your hands are warm. Are you sure you don't have a fever?"

Fanning herself with those warm hands, Alex said, "It's stress."

Chapter Thirty-Five

Hawk drove down the streets of Beverly Hills on the familiar path to Stone Enterprises.

Alex had been unusually quiet most of the weekend. With the exception of the day she spent with Nick doing the spa thing, he'd been around.

Truth was, he hadn't seen the inside of his apartment in weeks.

He didn't miss it.

Not that he thought the Stone Estate was where he needed to be, but he didn't see himself in a one-bedroom space with people living above and below him.

Helping Alex pack up her place drove him to consider what his next moves were when it came to the two of them. While they had been together at the hip out of necessity, Hawk wasn't sure he wanted it any other way going forward.

Maybe not every moment of every day. That seemed to be the space they'd been in since they met. But living together.

They had started to sleep in the same bed. Alex insisted that they try to make it through the night.

Hawk placed a biometric safe holding his weapon beside their bed. A step he felt was needed to make sure he was fully awake before reaching for a gun.

But something had happened after he'd opened up about Guatemala. Yes, he still had nightmares, but they didn't feel as real, and he'd only once found himself on the floor after his memories woke him.

The first week into their new arrangement, Hawk would open his eyes to Alex softly saying his name and asking him to wake up when his nightmares came. She assured him she was safe and that everything was okay. They would hold each other, and Hawk would answer the questions Alex had about his dreams. The more he talked, the less his dreams consumed him.

The mornings after the nights when the dreams didn't come were the best he'd had in his life. Hawk would watch as Alex's eyelids fluttered open. Her body would stretch and fold over his until they were both awake.

Hawk wanted that every day . . . with her.

They'd been so focused on the series of events surrounding Alex's life that they really hadn't had time to explore a life with just the two of them.

Well, with the exception of Colorado.

The memory of their snowball fight surfaced and put a huge smile on his face.

They needed more days like that.

And more nights like the peaceful ones they'd had in the snow. Where he could stroke her skin and tell her how beautiful she was and how she made him feel.

Hawk felt his pants tighten.

He shifted in his seat and scolded the lower half of his body to behave.

With her hair pulled back in the slick ponytail she donned for her work persona, Alex stared out the window, lost in thought.

Gripping the steering wheel, Hawk gathered the nerve to ask her a question he might not want the answer to.

"Alex?"

"Hawk?"

They both said each other's name at the same time.

Smiling, he said, "You go first."

"No. You go ahead."

He pulled to a stop at a red light and looked across the car. "What do you think about moving in with me?"

Surprise shifted behind her eyes. Along with it, a smile slid over her lips.

"You know . . . when all the crazy settles down and you can go back to a more normal day-to-day life?"

She bit her lower lip and tried to hide her smile.

Relief rolled down Hawk's spine. Her eyes alone said she loved the idea.

"Good," he said. "I'm glad we have that settled. Now, what did you want to say?"

"Excuse me. I don't think I said yes yet."

Yet.

The light turned green. Hawk inched forward in the morning traffic. "What are your conditions?" he asked, teasing.

She laughed and stayed quiet.

"Well?"

"I don't know yet."

Hawk actually snorted.

He reached for her hand and folded it in his.

"Are you going to smile like that all day?" she asked.

He nodded several times. "Pretty much."

"I'll have conditions."

"I have no doubt." He brought her fingers to his lips and kissed them before letting go. "What were you going to say?"

"I took a pregnancy test this weekend," she said, not missing a beat.

The air rushed out of his lungs, and his foot punched down on the brakes too hard.

Alex let out a tiny noise. "Sorry. I shouldn't have just blurted that out while you were driving."

Pregnancy?

A baby?

He needed air.

"It was negative," she said in a rush.

A worried smile looked back at him. "No baby?"

"No. I'm not. But I thought maybe I was. I didn't think I should keep that to myself."

Hawk reached for her again.

Damn.

With his eyes back on the road, Hawk's heart rate started to return to normal. "Sweetie. I say this with all the love in the world."

"Yes?"

He turned the corner with one hand on the wheel. "Your situational awareness skills need CPR."

Alex moaned. "You're right. That was—"

"Dangerous." He kissed her hand again and went back to driving. LA traffic was a two-handed job. "The next time you tell me you think you're pregnant, please make sure I'm sitting down and not behind the wheel of a car, where I can get us both killed."

"I can do that."

His brain cells returned in slow motion. "Why did you think you were pregnant?"

"I haven't felt right for a few weeks. Tired, borderline nauseous, when I'm not at the office my brain is in a fog. I've convinced myself that it's stress, and it may be . . . but I needed to rule out the most obvious possible cause before I cry wolf to a doctor."

"You've been under a lot of pressure. But I'd feel better if you saw someone."

Alex smiled and looked in her lap and got quiet.

Hawk took a deep breath. "Were you disappointed?"

"What?"

"That the test was negative?"

"No. Of course not." Her words were rushed, and Alex turned to look out the window when she said them.

Hawk would have a whole lot of trouble with a daughter as beautiful as Alex. The boys would show up in droves.

The image of chastity belts and towers too tall to climb filled his head.

And the negotiations?

Holy hell. They'd have to have a son just to balance it out.

"Are you?" Alex broke his thoughts with her question.

He smiled and shook his head. "Would it freak you out if I said yes?"

"What?"

Hawk blew out a breath. "Yeah. I am. That's crazy, right?"

"Uhm . . ."

"I've never given it a lot of thought. Other than to try and avoid it. But . . . you're different. I literally just imagined what our daughter would look like and how I'd have to sit at the door with a shotgun to keep the boys away. And how you would both spend hours negotiating if she was too young to date. And how a son would have to balance the estrogen and keep an eye on our daughter when she was at school . . . so yes, Alex. I'm disappointed but at the same time looking forward to that life."

Alex was staring at him with moisture in her eyes.

"Are you good with that?" Hawk asked her. "That I'm thinking like that about us?"

Her quiet was starting to worry him.

"I wasn't expecting that answer," she finally said.

"That makes two of us."

Alex reached for his hand.

And the world felt right.

❧

Dee fidgeted behind her laptop during their morning meeting, her eyes kept looking at the door.

"Are you okay?"

"Yes, but . . . it's strange with them here. I'm afraid to delete an email or put something in the shredder pile."

"I can understand that. It won't be forever. If you're concerned about deleting or shredding things, ask them."

"And they ask a lot of personal questions."

Alex sat back, finished the rest of her second cup of coffee. Caffeine was a habit she might need to curb if and when she and Hawk had those babies he'd so vividly seen on the ride in.

"That will get worse before it gets better, I'm afraid. I do wish there was a way around that."

Dee nodded and returned to their work at hand.

The entire day was filled with phone calls and Zoom meetings, all in an effort to ease the concerns of the management in the many regions where their hotels lived.

She and Chase had divided the work and were basically living on coffee and willpower.

Before Dee left the office, Alex handed her the phone number of her doctor. "I need you to make an appointment for me with my doctor. I wouldn't ask, but with my schedule as crazy as it is, you'd know best when I can squeeze it in."

Dee blinked a few times. "Okay. What do you want me to tell them is wrong?"

"Just a checkup. But one I'd like to not wait a month to have."

Dee spotted the empty coffee cup, picked it up. "More?"

"Please, and keep them coming."

"Of course, Ms. Stone."

◦

Hawk leaned against the counter in the executive break room lounge with Piper and Julia.

"I'm surprised they haven't reminded me who I had sex with on prom night," Julia complained.

The FBI agents were conducting background checks on and interviewing everyone who had direct daily contact with Floyd. As well as those in close proximity to Aaron before his death.

Which meant Piper was in the office to answer questions.

"I didn't go to prom," Hawk chimed in.

"I didn't either, but I had a date, and we did have sex," Julia admitted.

The three of them laughed.

"The people on this floor that will have it the hardest will be Arthur and his team. The accountants are expected to find discrepancies," Piper suggested.

"Not when the CEO is approving the reports," Hawk said.

Both of the women nodded in agreement.

"Maybe they'll find an account that Robert is hiding from me and I can go after more child support."

"Keep living the fantasy, Julia. I'll be here when you get back to Earth."

∾

The time on her computer said eleven thirty. Alex had yawned no less than five times on her last call and purposely cut the conversation short.

Her office couch was inviting her to take a break.

The kind with her feet up and her head on a pillow.

She squinted her eyes to see the names on her schedule for the remainder of the day. Too many names.

Alex buzzed Dee and asked her to come in.

"Yes, Ms. Stone?"

"I thought I had an eleven thirty."

"They canceled while you were on your last call. Something about a computer glitch."

Alex slumped in her chair. "Thank God. I can't keep my eyes open."

Dee stood there staring. "The coffee isn't working?"

"No. It's stale anyway."

"I have an energy packet in my purse. They help me on days after my son has kept me up late. They work really well."

Alex wasn't one for energy shots. Not since college. But something had to help. "You wouldn't mind?" Alex asked.

Dee slowly smiled.

"I insist."

Alex kicked off her shoes and sat down on the couch. Her next call was after lunch. Even a half an hour would help. Maybe by then, the energy drink would kick in.

Dee returned with a Ziploc bag.

"You poor thing." She found a glass and a bottle of water and mixed the energy drink.

She returned to Alex's side and handed her the glass. "It's a little bitter."

Alex didn't care.

She swallowed it in one pull and reached for the bottle of water to chase the bitter down.

"That should help."

Alex kicked her feet up on the sofa and let her eyes close. "Hold my calls until one."

"Not a problem . . . Alexandrea."

∽

Hawk made his way to Alex's office, hoping he could convince her to go to the deli down the street for lunch.

It was five past twelve, and Dee was still at her desk.

"Is she on a call?" he asked, pointing to the closed office door.

"No. She's, ah, resting. She asked that I not let anyone disturb her until after lunch."

"This has been rough on her."

Dee stared at him. Said nothing.

"I'll just poke my head in."

Dee rushed to her feet. "Don't wake her. Her afternoon is full."

"It's okay, Dee. I won't."

Like the nervous secretary Dee was, she walked behind him when he quietly opened the door and looked in.

Alex was knocked out. With a small blanket tossed over her.

He backed out of the office and closed the door as quietly as he could.

Dee jumped back and rubbed her hands on her pants. "I'm going to eat lunch at my desk so no one disturbs her."

"I appreciate that," Hawk said. "She could use the nap."

Hawk made his way back to the employee lounge, whispering, "That chick is strange."

⁓

The room spun like a children's toy on drugs.

There was exhausted, and then there was this.

Alex's tongue felt larger than her mouth. Her lips tingled with the feeling like a limb that was waking up from a cramped position with new spikes of electricity. Only they hurt.

This wasn't normal.

Or maybe she was dreaming?

No. She was in her office.

Dee had given her something to help her stay awake.

Then why did Alex have the memory of her assistant sitting on the edge of the coffee table in the room, smiling?

"That's it. Go to sleep. Go to sleep. Tick. Tock. Tick. Tock."

Alex rolled to her side, tried to get her legs to work, and fell to the floor for her efforts.

Hawk!

⁓

Piper and Chase left the building for lunch and promised to return with food for Hawk and Alex when she woke up.

The employee lounge was relatively empty.

Probably because Agents Baker and Kenna were at a table, eating, and the employees were scared to death of them.

Except Julia, who was reading a book and eating a sandwich.

Hawk took a seat opposite Julia and captured her attention. "Piper says you know all the gossip on the employees here."

Julia looked over the pages of her book. "I wouldn't say all."

"What do you know about Dee? She's afraid of her own shadow."

Julia glanced at the open door and lowered her voice. "I don't really know. To tell the truth, I barely noticed her when Piper was around. She just sat in the background and did her work."

"Does she socialize with anyone?"

Julia shook her head. "We've invited her to happy hour. But eventually gave up."

Hawk glanced at the FBI agents he knew were listening. "Did you find anything on her? Abusive husband or something?"

Baker and Kenna looked at each other.

"Trauma often causes people to go into their own shell, where it's safe," Baker said.

"What kind of trauma?"

Baker shrugged. "The husband drove himself and their son off a cliff."

Julia's hand holding her book fell to her lap. "What?"

"Suicide. Apparently, the factory the husband worked in closed down. They were struggling financially. The husband checked out."

Hawk couldn't imagine doing that to his family, a wife. "Why kill the son?"

"Who knows? One day she had a husband and a kid, the next day, nothing. That's bound to shut you down socially."

"I'll have to give her more slack . . ." Only something wasn't right.

"Her new husband and child must have helped," Julia suggested.

"What are you talking about?" Baker asked.

Hawk nodded. "Yeah, she needed to pick up a sick kid from school a couple of weeks ago."

Julia smiled. "He's always catching something. The only time off she takes is to care for her kid."

Kenna dropped the phone he was scrolling onto the table. "There isn't a new husband and kid. Dee lives in a studio apartment by herself."

"Then why would she tell everyone she's married and has a son?"

Hawk's heart started to pound in his chest.

He looked directly at Baker and Kenna. "This factory that closed down . . . did it belong to Stone Enterprises?"

"Ahh, fuck!"

Hawk was out of his seat and running down the hall before Julia asked, "What?"

Baker and Kenna ran from behind.

༄

Nothing worked.

She opened her mouth to yell, but only a squeak came out.

It was as if an electrical charge had eliminated her ability to use any muscle properly.

Dee had given her something.

And every moment that passed threatened to take her deeper into oblivion.

"Someone." The word came out as a whisper.

Her eyes closed, and she fought to open them.

She lay on the floor where she'd fallen from the sofa when she attempted to stand.

It took what felt like the strength of ten men to scoot her body back six inches. Getting to her desk looked like crossing the Grand Canyon on foot.

And the door . . .

Was Dee on the other side? Was Dee telling everyone she was sleeping, just ticking off the minutes until the drug in her system shut her eyes for good?

Alex had no idea why Dee would do this.

Tick.

Tock.

The stuffed animal, the Play-Doh bomb . . . why?

Thinking about that hurt her head.

Alex managed another six inches.

The table to the side of the sofa held a glass lamp. She reached for the cord and pulled.

The lamp swayed to one side.

Alex tugged on the cord again. This time, the lamp fell.

The splintering of glass sounded like a bomb in Alex's ears.

She heard the door to her office open and close.

Thank God. "Help."

Shouts from the hall had Alex falling back to the floor in relief.

Hawk's voice.

Her Viking was coming.

Alex's eyes opened to see Dee standing over her, a gun in her hand. "Why can't you just die?"

The door to the office shook with the force of someone's body being thrown against it.

Dee reached down, grabbed Alex's arm, and slid her across the room, farther away from the door.

"Get up," Dee screamed in Alex's face.

"I can't."

Dee pushed the barrel of the gun into Alex's temple.

"Stand up!"

Alex struggled with her limbs until she managed to get on her knees.

The door to the office flew open and bounced against the wall with a thundering clap.

Hawk was there, gun in his hand, pointing at the both of them.

Alex locked eyes with Hawk.

His nightmare.

She was living his nightmare.

∽

Alex was alive.

Her eyes glossy, her head rolling back and then snapping back to attention.

"I'll shoot her. One more step and she's dead."

"Put the gun down, Dee."

"We don't want to hurt you."

While the agents spoke directly to Dee, Hawk focused on Alex. "We'll get you out of here, hon. Stay with us, okay," he said.

"We want to help," Baker said, his words calm and steady. "Put the gun down and let Alex go."

"Don't fall asleep, honey. Eyes open."

Alex responded. Her chin came up, those eyes . . . her beautiful, vibrant eyes dulled with drugs.

"It's her fault," Dee cried, yanking Alex back.

A familiar punch to the stomach hit Hawk hard.

The frail office staff member held the woman he loved like a broken doll. The gun in her hand acted as a kickstand to Alex's limp head.

He'd done it again.

Hawk had underestimated what was the weakest link in the office.

Only Dee wasn't whimpering now. She wasn't shyly looking away or averting her eyes so that others couldn't see into her.

"Put the gun down, Dee."

"She did this. She killed them." Dee tugged on Alex's body each time she said *she*.

"No, Dee. Alex didn't close the factory," Kenna said.

Dee blinked. Stepped back.

Alex was struggling to keep weight on her legs.

Even if Dee didn't use the gun, Hawk felt Alex slipping away.

"What did you give her?" Hawk yelled.

Dee didn't answer, she smiled with pure evil behind those dilated eyes. And then started to laugh. Slow and loud.

"Hurting her won't bring your family back, Dee. Let us help you."

"You don't want to help me. You throw people away. She ends lives with a flick of her pen." Dee used the gun as an extension of her hand by waving it in the air.

Hawk noticed Baker moving slightly to the right as Kenna did the same to the left.

"Alex is trying to keep factories open, Dee. That's why we're here. To give jobs back," Baker told her.

Dee shook her head. "No. As soon as you leave, she'll do it again. They all do it. Her father did it. Now her."

"Did you drug Aaron, Dee?"

Dee smiled. "Didn't get a chance."

Alex's head rolled back.

Dee struggled with the weight of her.

"Wake up, Alex! Don't you dare go to sleep." Hawk's breath came in short waves.

"She needs help, Dee. You don't want her to die," Kenna said.

Dee rested her face against the top of Alex's head. "Yes, I do."

Hawk saw red.

Alex was too close. If any of them attempted a shot, it could be their bullets that took her out.

Panic threatened to take control.

He took a step forward.

The gun came away from Alex's temple, and Dee waved it in his direction. "Don't move."

Hawk froze.

Alex opened her eyes wide and clenched her stomach.

The sound of sirens screamed in the distance.

Dee looked to the window. The gun moved in the direction of Dee's gaze.

Alex doubled forward and started to vomit.

And a bullet ripped through the silence in the air.

"No!" Hawk screamed and rushed to Alex's side.

Blood splattered everywhere. And for a brief moment, Hawk wasn't sure if it was Dee or Alex that had been shot.

His ears vibrated with the effect of the gunshot, and he felt more than he heard Alex's body shake as she continued to purge.

Hawk held her so that the contents of her stomach fell to the floor and not the blood-splattered suit she wore.

When she stopped, Hawk lifted her in his arms and removed her from the lifeless woman behind her, as Baker and Kenna moved around Dee, assuring there wasn't any lingering threat.

"We need an ambulance!" Hawk yelled when he reached the hall.

He sat down with her in his arms. Her body limp, barely conscious. "Stay with me, Alex."

"Hawk?"

His ears still rang.

"It's me. I'm here. I love you, Alex. Don't you leave me."

"Love."

He could barely hear what she said. Hawk rocked her in his arms. "Stay with me."

Baker ran out of the room, took one look at the two of them, and started barking commands.

Chapter Thirty-Six

It took over a week in the ICU to stabilize Alex enough to be moved to a room where she saw more than doctors and nurses and brief glimpses of Hawk and her family.

Dee had given her enough of a tranquilizer to kill her if she hadn't been found in time. Already, her kidneys were starting to shut down.

The toxicology screening shocked everyone. Dee had been slowly poisoning Alex with arsenic.

Tasteless, odorless, and added to her daily coffee.

There was a bag of it found in Dee's purse, and even more at her home.

The woman's torment of Alex and constant shifting of tactics—bomb threats, bloody teddy bears, and then poison—ensured that no one in the family, or the team guarding Alex, could predict her next move.

All because of a woman's misplaced grief over the loss of her family.

The moment Alex was placed in a normal hospital room, a reclining chair was put at one end of the room, and Hawk never left.

Through the seemingly endless rounds of dialysis needed to bring her kidneys back to health, he stood by holding her hand.

When the nightmares woke her, he was there.

And when enough of the tubes and monitors were removed, he'd climb in beside her and hold her until she fell asleep.

During the days, the rotating door of visitors made the room into a florist's shop.

Her mother forced Chase and Max to take Hawk home to shower and rest. But he never stayed away very long.

When Alex had energy, they talked endlessly about their lives, childhood . . . the dreams they had and still wanted to achieve.

As much as Hawk had tried to keep Alex from seeing the aftermath of Dee's assault, it wasn't a vision she'd ever forget. Death in the woman's stare, blood everywhere.

The night before her discharge from the hospital, her family sat around her room, talking about everything and nothing at the same time.

"How is the investigation going?" Alex asked for the first time.

Nick stood up with a whoop and placed the palm of his hand facing up in the air. "Pay up, suckers. I won!"

One by one, her family pulled wallets and purses out, and hundred-dollar bills filled her best friend's palm.

Alex looked at Hawk.

"Don't look at me. I wasn't in on their bet."

Nick counted his winnings. "The bet was how soon before you ask about the office and the investigation."

"I was the first to lose," Chase said.

Piper nudged her husband. "He didn't think you'd make it out of the ICU."

"I gave you three days after the ICU," Piper said.

"Max said a week, and I thought you'd wait until you got home," Sarah said while Max shrugged.

Alex glanced at her mother and Gaylord.

Vivian shook her head with her hands in the air.

"Well?"

Chase sat forward, his arms on his knees. "They should be wrapping things up in the next month or so. We'll have a monetary number soon on what the company is owed by Dad's estate."

"And a substantial retainer will be held in reserve for pending civil suits," Piper added.

"Nothing you need to worry about, little filly," Gaylord said. "You have one job."

"Get better," Vivian said.

Alex looked around the room. "What about . . . the office. My . . . office?"

Hawk placed a hand on her leg. "It's all taken care of."

"You know how my staff was only using half of the third floor?" Chase asked.

"Yeah."

"We moved all the executives down there," Max told her. "I've had a lot of fun helping the demo team beat the shit out of those walls."

Alex found a laugh. How many times as a kid had she wanted to take a baseball bat to her father's precious office to get the man's attention?

"Your remodel plans are underway. You won't recognize the place when we move back in," Chase told her.

"Floyd?"

"He won't go without an accessory charge. Though no one is convinced it will stick. There is too much evidence suggesting Aaron was setting Floyd up for a fall," Hawk explained. "The Bakshais denied any involvement. And without a body or even the identity of the woman Floyd claims was murdered, the feds can't pin anything on them."

"What about the companies associated with the CIMs? The bribes that put those properties in Bakshai's hands?"

Hawk lifted his shoulders to his ears. "If the feds have anything solid on that, they're not sharing."

"You've worked with the government, what do you think will happen?" Max asked.

"I think the accusations against Bakshai are the tip of a very big iceberg. If Floyd's testimony is true, Aaron wasn't the only one stuck in a vicious cycle of doing the man's bidding. And since the companies associated with the CIMs don't all point in the same direction, my guess is Bakshai is also a pawn."

"More like a rook," Gaylord said. "Aaron was the pawn. And anyone like him."

"If Bakshai is ever eliminated from the chessboard, we'll know the threat is deeper. Deep enough that your father didn't know who the real boss was and couldn't point a finger if he wanted to. I don't think the world has heard the last of the Bakshais. But they won't be bothering you," Hawk assured Alex.

"How can you be so sure?" Chase asked.

Alex wanted that answer, too.

"Because you hold nothing incriminating. Nothing to testify if the man was charged with a crime. All you have is what Aaron put in a safe that was turned over to the feds. And only an idiot would violate the FBI's strong suggestion that he keep his distance. Bakshai is many things, but he is not an idiot," Hawk said. "In my experience, whoever is pulling Bakshai's strings would see the man dead if he did something to shed light on their operation. Trust me, he won't so much as send a Christmas card."

Hawk's affirmation was helpful to hear.

Alex put a hand over her mouth to hide her yawn.

Her mother patted Alex's hand. "That's our cue to leave."

The room echoed with the sound of her family gathering their belongings.

"You sure you don't want to come back to the estate?" Max asked.

Alex looked at Hawk, shook her head. "I have my own babysitter."

Max kissed her cheek and shook Hawk's hand.

Sarah slipped around Max. "Nick has agreed to help with the wedding planning. Let me know when you're up for us crashing your place and stealing your expertise."

"Give the meal planning to someone else," Hawk suggested.

"Hey!" Alex chided playfully.

"Cooking was never her strong point," Vivian whispered to Sarah.

No More Yesterdays

"I'm being ganged up on here. Gaylord, help me out."

He tilted his hat and winked. "I'll hire a chef. Problem solved."

Chase kissed her next.

"I'll be back in the office—"

"When the doctors say and when everyone in this room agrees," Chase said.

"Those are two vastly different things."

Piper placed a hand on Alex's leg. "We have you covered. No one deserves time off more than you."

She knew everything was running without her. Which put a calm in her that hadn't been there before. Not even in Colorado. Stone Enterprises had survived the storm with the captain passed out in a stateroom. Which meant the crew members were doing their jobs.

Gaylord pinched her cheek. "I'll bring your mother back next week, unless you need us sooner."

Alex captured his hand, looked him in the eye. "Thanks . . . Dad."

Gaylord froze.

Vivian sucked in a breath.

"Is it okay if I call you that? We didn't really ever have one, and you've been more of a father for me than Aaron ever was."

Gaylord was never at a loss for words. Yet he stood there staring at her with moisture building behind his eyes.

The room grew silent.

"It would be an honor to be your daddy."

Alex felt emotion clog in her throat.

Gaylord took his hat off, leaned down, and folded her in his arms. There was nothing like the big Texan's hug.

She heard him sniffle before letting her go. "Soon as you're up for it, you're coming to Texas to pick out your horse."

Alex wiped at her own tears. "Oh?"

"We'll find the feistiest mare you can handle."

"If you insist, Dad."

365

Gaylord put a hand to his chest and his Stetson back on his head. He reached a hand to Hawk. "I'm counting on you to keep her safe, son."

"That's my plan."

Nick was the last to say good night.

And he did it in the way only Nick could. He glanced over his shoulder to the open door of the room. "Do you know if our nephrologist is single?"

"Nick!"

"What? He's employed, definitely a team player . . . I didn't see a ring. You're always telling me to pick better men."

Alex shook her head. "I always tell you to pick *one* man."

He rolled his eyes. "Oh well. My mother would approve of a doctor."

Alex giggled.

Nick brushed a kiss on both sides of her face. "I'll call you tomorrow. And make sure I'm available to take you to your follow-up appointments."

"Get out of here." She pushed him away with a smile.

Hawk placed a hand on her leg and stood. "I'll be right back."

He walked with her family out of the room, and she found herself alone.

Alone with the flowers.

And to think, on Valentine's Day, the sight of flowers had annoyed her.

Even Dee had flowers on her desk.

The memory of the mousy woman took center stage in Alex's vision. Dee taking down the schedule, calling her Ms. Stone and hiding her eyes, bringing her coffee.

Alex's breath caught, and heart rate started to soar.

"*Tick. Tock.*"

The gunshot.

The blood.

Alex closed her eyes and tried to get ahold of her breath.

"Sweetie?"

Without opening her eyes, she reached for him.

Hawk was there in an instant.

"Deep breaths. You got this. You're here, you're alive. I'm with you."

She swallowed.

"Come on. Deep breath, one, two, three, four, five. Exhale, one, two, three, four, five, six."

Her eyes fluttered open.

Hawk stared directly into her soul. He repeated his counting, and she forced herself to follow his directions.

Alex was back in the hospital room.

Hawk lowered the rail on the bed and lay down beside her. His hand stroked her arm, her head resting on his shoulder. "I'm right here," he whispered.

"I'm okay."

"What was it this time?" he softly asked.

What was it this time that set her off?

Even though her body had healed, her head was still a giant work in progress.

A coffee cup.

The shy nurse.

The way one of her doctors had called her Ms. Stone after she told him not to.

A phone ringing.

The most random shit set her pulse racing and had her gasping for air.

"The flowers," she told him.

He waited.

"She sent herself flowers from her husband on Valentine's Day."

"I'll send you chocolate," Hawk said, kissing the top of her head. "I love you," he whispered.

She closed her eyes and soaked in his words.

Words he hadn't stopped saying from the moment she opened her eyes in the ICU.

Life had proved too fragile to wait even a moment without sharing how she felt. And she loved Hawk, with every fiber of her soul.

"I love you, too."

Epilogue

"This one has a better view," Alex said.

"The other one had security gates."

"We can put security gates on this one."

"The other one put more distance between us and the neighbors."

"This is sitting on three acres!"

Alex and Hawk stood outside of the Malibu home overlooking the infinity pool that gave way to the Pacific Ocean below. The bright blue water danced in the sunlight and instantly put Alex at ease.

The ocean had been her comfort place since that awful day.

So, when the time finally came for her and Hawk to pick out a new home, they both chose an ocean-view home.

"If this is the one you like." Hawk put his arm around her shoulders.

She placed one around his waist. "No, you're right about the neighbors."

"This has plenty of room."

Alex pulled away just enough to give him an evil eye. "You liked this one more the whole time."

He shrugged. "What can I tell you? I like arguing with my fiancée."

Alex started pushing him toward the pool.

Hawk locked his feet in place and grasped her around her waist to avoid getting wet. "I go, you go."

She wrapped her arms around his neck and stopped struggling.

Once Alex was ready to return to the office, Hawk had booked a trip for them in Sedona.

Instead of taking the plane, they'd packed the car, stopped at a convenience store to stock up on road-trip-appropriate food, and hit the trail.

As Hawk had told her afterward, if you could road-trip together without a major fight, you were meant to be.

They spent time hiking and wine tasting . . . sitting in a hot tub and soaking up the brilliance that was the red rocks of Sedona, Arizona.

As their last adventure before heading home, Hawk booked a hot air balloon excursion.

The ride included a photographer and their pilot.

As they climbed up in the wide open, quiet sky . . . with only the sound of the gas escaping into the massive balloon to keep it in the air, Hawk went down on one knee.

She stood there speechless and staring with her mouth open in a perfect O. And Hawk said things Alex would never forget.

"I didn't see you coming. I never saw myself as husband material. And then you showed up . . . sweet at first and then kicking and screaming. Pushing every time I pulled and pulling every time I pushed. I cannot give you the things you can give yourself. I don't have an airplane to take you to far-off places. Or a mansion to hide you away from the evil in this world. But I do have me. My love . . . my dedication and commitment to making you the happiest woman in the world. I'll hold you when you're sad, stand beside you when you're strong, and carry you when you're weak. But most important . . . I will love you, Alexandrea. The way you deserve to be loved, from this day to my last . . . if you'll let me. Let me be your forever Viking. Marry me, Alex. Please tell me you'll marry me."

He opened the box he had in his hand, and a beautiful oval diamond sat on a delicate leaf design of rose gold.

And it was perfect.

By now, the tears were flowing, and her head bobbed on her shoulders like a toy. "Yes, yes, yes."

The rest of the balloon ride was a blur.

But Alex knew this . . . she would never again look to the sky, see a hot air balloon, and not think of that day . . . and her Viking.

And now that same man teasing her for the sake of teasing, and she couldn't be happier.

"I think we found our house," she said, smiling.

"I do, too."

Alex lifted on her tiptoes and pressed her lips to his.

He held the back of her head and prolonged their kiss until mouths opened and tongues were involved.

When he pulled away, she bit her lower lip and dug her fingertips into his chest. "We'll finish that later."

"Yes, we will." Hawk turned to the view once again.

Alex lifted her hand. "Give me your phone. Let's take a picture to send to the family."

Hawk did as she asked, and Alex turned the camera around to take a selfie.

She moved Hawk to the right . . . then the left, until the pool and ocean were behind them.

She snapped a couple of pictures.

"One more."

They smiled into the lens.

And before Hawk could say oops, Alex pressed her hand into his chest and shoved.

Hawk hit the pool with a "Whoop."

He came up laughing.

Alex doubled over at the look of him, fully clothed, treading water in a pool they didn't yet own. "You know, honey. You have zero situational awareness." She snapped her fingers in the air. "Gotta be on your toes around me."

He swam to the edge.

She focused his camera and captured the moment.

"I'll get you for that."

"Bring it, big boy."

He swiped at her leg.

She easily jumped out of his way.

The splash of water wasn't avoidable, and the front of her quickly looked a whole lot like him.

Hawk pulled himself out of the pool and looked at his feet.

One shoe was missing.

Alex couldn't stop laughing.

He lowered his head and started stalking her way.

She backed up slowly. "You'll ruin your phone."

"I'll buy another one."

She turned to run, he gave chase and caught her in a few feet. He half carried her back to the pool.

"Don't, don't. Uncle."

"You want me to show mercy?"

"I'll make it worth your while," she negotiated, still giggling so much that her stomach hurt.

Hawk stopped. "Fine. I won't throw you in."

She sighed.

And Hawk threw his arms around her and soaked her to the bone with his wet clothes.

She was struggling to get away, both of them laughing like kids on a playground, when the real estate agent stepped out of the house and cleared her throat.

The look of shock put Alex and Hawk back into hysterics.

"We'll take this one," Hawk announced.

The agent shook her head and walked back inside. "I'll write up the offer."

Hawk turned Alex around and held her from behind.

Every inch of her was wet.

"We're going to have the best life," he announced.

"We already do."

⌒9

The day the FBI put their investigation to rest and the restrictions on Aaron Stone's estate were lifted, two things happened.

First, the Beverly Hills estate was put on the market.

Their time in the mansion together as a family was something they'd all cherish. Regardless of the circumstances that put them there, Alex, Chase, and Max bonded like siblings should in that time. And even though the ghost of Aaron Stone no longer haunted them in that space, none of them wanted to keep it.

And the second thing that happened was the unexpected trip to visit their dad.

Wineglasses in hand, they stood in silence.

Hawk stood at Alex's side, Chase by Piper's, and Max by Sarah's.

Hailey slept in the stroller with Kit standing guard.

And Aaron Stone's grave sat in complete concrete stillness. There was no evidence of anyone visiting. No dead flowers to pull away, no memento of memories and love set atop.

Just the man's name with the dates of his existence in this world. No loving this or dedicated that.

The Stone children all had something they wanted to say.

Chase started. His eyes on the grave, his fingers cradled in Piper's. "I sat through your funeral listening to the drivel pouring from the mouths of the people who knew you. Or thought they knew you. Only none of them did. They didn't know the lengths to which your selfishness reached. Or the depth of disregard for the people you brought into this world. None of your wives mourned you. And now none of your employees look back at your leadership as anything but a veil to hide your sins. I have this amazing woman and beautiful daughter, and I'm happy that they don't have to endure your hate and selfishness. I have two things I'm thankful for that came from you."

Alex squeezed Hawk's hand.

"That you died when you did, giving me the urgency to find Piper . . . and telling us about Max."

Chase looked up.

Max nodded his gratitude.

"He's pretty fucking amazing."

Max took a breath.

Blew it out.

It was Max's turn. "Chase has enough hate for both of us. I am thankful. But not for your money and certainly not your name. You gave me something money can't buy. You gave me a family in your death. And that's all that truly matters. Too bad you never saw that. I, too, am happy you died when you did. Chase, Alex, and I can live the majority of our lives knowing each other. Instead of waiting until you were eighty and we'd only have a handful of years left."

Sarah took hold of Max's arm and buried her head into it.

Hawk looked at Alex and offered a nod of support.

"All I ever wanted from you was love. But the only thing you loved was you. Power, money . . . you. I can't help but feel that leaving us your world was not the benefit it appeared to be, but a curse. You gave us everything, and at the same time, you knew we could lose it all because of your actions. Your circle of friends and enemies put targets on our backs. My back. All those years, I pined for your attention, and when I got it, it nearly killed me. But you did love your company. And secretly knew that Chase and I would search out Max because we're decent people. It's true that none of us would be here without you. We wouldn't have our partners at our sides. And that, Aaron Stone, is the only reason we're here today. The only *thank you* you'll receive from us."

Alex lifted her glass. "To Aaron Stone. A terrible father, disgusting human, narcissistic, egocentric, womanizing piece of dirt that did one thing right." Alex stopped looking at the tombstone and glanced between her brothers, her sisters-in-law, and Hawk. "He brought us together. It's time to look to our future and put our yesterdays behind us."

Chase lifted his glass. "I can drink to that."

"So can I," Max said.

They turned away from their father's grave without a backward glance.

For Alex, her heart was clear. The hate and disappointment of the father who couldn't love didn't fill the space it once had.

Hawk kept an arm over her shoulder, kissed her head. "I love you."

"I love you," she whispered back.

"How much was this bottle?" Sarah asked, sipping the wine as they walked away.

Alex looked in the glass and shrugged. "Twenty bucks."

Piper started to giggle.

Chase joined . . . and before they knew it, the cemetery was filled with laughter.

Acknowledgments

Thank you to my team at Montlake: Maria Gomez, you are always so supportive of my work. Lindsey Faber, your attention to detail is always spot on. Thanks for helping me get this book into top shape. And all the copy and line editors, beta readers, marketing team, and let's not forget everyone at Audible . . . thank you.

Jane Dystel, my agent extraordinaire and friend. You mean the world to me.

To my readers: Can you believe this is my forty-fifth published work? It's you, dear readers, who have given me the ability to write the books to keep you entertained. While I may have the talent to do the work, without readers, I'd be forced to make my living doing something completely different. Which makes me eternally grateful for you. I'm happy to call many of you friends, and I look forward to meeting the rest of you at future events and book signings.

Here is to forty-five more!

Happy Reading,
Catherine

About the Author

Photo © Catherine Bybee

New York Times, Wall Street Journal, and *USA Today* bestselling author Catherine Bybee has written over forty books that have collectively sold more than eleven million copies. Her titles have been translated into more than twenty languages. Raised in Washington State, Bybee moved to Southern California in the hope of becoming a movie star. After growing bored with waiting tables, she returned to school and became a registered nurse, spending most of her career in urban emergency rooms. She now writes full time and has penned the popular Not Quite, Weekday Brides, Most Likely To, and First Wives series.